MARTYR!

MARTYR!

Kaveh Akbar

Alfred A. Knopf
New York 2024

THIS IS A BORZOI BOOK
PUBLISHED BY ALFRED A. KNOPF

Copyright © 2024 by Kaveh Akbar

All rights reserved. Published in the United States by Alfred A. Knopf,
a division of Penguin Random House LLC, New York, and distributed
in Canada by Penguin Random House Canada Limited, Toronto.

www.aaknopf.com

Knopf, Borzoi Books, and the colophon are registered trademarks of
Penguin Random House LLC.

Library of Congress Cataloging-in-Publication Data
Names: Akbar, Kaveh, author.
Title: Martyr! / Kaveh Akbar.
Description: First edition. | New York : Alfred A. Knopf, 2024. |
"This is a Borzoi book"
Identifiers: LCCN 2023008466 (print) | LCCN 2023008467 (ebook) |
ISBN 9780593537619 (hardcover) | ISBN 9780593537626 (ebook) |
ISBN 9780593802359 (open market)
Subjects: LCGFT: Novels.
Classification: LCC PS3601.K37 M37 2024 (print) |
LCC PS3601.K37 (ebook) | DDC 813/.6—dc23/eng/20230306
LC record available at https://lccn.loc.gov/2023008466
LC ebook record available at https://lccn.loc.gov/2023008467

Jacket image based on an Iranian miniature. Chris Heller/Alamy
Jacket design by Linda Huang

Printed in the United States of America
Published January 23, 2024
Reprinted One Time
Third Printing, February 2024

for the martyrs, who live

MARTYR!

☀

My God, I just remembered that we die.

—*Clarice Lispector*

CYRUS SHAMS

——— ✦ ———

MAYBE IT WAS THAT CYRUS HAD DONE THE WRONG DRUGS IN THE right order, or the right drugs in the wrong order, but when God finally spoke back to him after twenty-seven years of silence, what Cyrus wanted more than anything else was a do-over. Clarification. Lying on his mattress that smelled like piss and Febreze, in his bedroom that smelled like piss and Febreze, Cyrus stared up at the room's single light bulb, willing it to blink again, willing God to confirm that the bulb's flicker had been a divine action and not just the old apartment's trashy wiring.

"Flash it on and off," Cyrus had been thinking, not for the first time in his life. "Just a little wink and I'll sell all my shit and buy a camel. I'll start over." All his shit at that moment amounted to a pile of soiled laundry and a stack of books borrowed from various libraries and never returned, poetry and biographies, *To the Lighthouse, My Uncle Napoleon*. Never mind all that, though: Cyrus meant it. Why should the Prophet Muhammad get a whole visit from an archangel? Why should Saul get to see the literal light of heaven on the road to Damascus? Of course it would be easy to establish bedrock faith after such clear-cut revelation. How was it fair to celebrate those guys for faith that wasn't faith at all, that was just obedience to what they plainly observed to be true? And what sense did it make to punish the rest of humanity who had never been privy to such explicit revelation? To make everyone else lurch from crisis to crisis, desperately alone?

But then it happened for Cyrus too, right there in that ratty

Indiana bedroom. He asked God to reveal Himself, Herself, Themself, Itself, whatever. He asked with all the earnestness at his disposal, which was troves. If every relationship was a series of advances and retreats, Cyrus was almost never the retreat-er, sharing everything important about himself at a word, a smile, with a shrug as if to say, "Those're just facts. Why should I be ashamed?"

He'd lain there on the bare mattress on the hardwood floor letting his cigarette ash on his bare stomach like some sulky prince, thinking, "Turn the lights on and off lord and I'll buy a donkey, I promise I'll buy a camel and ride him to Medina, to Gethsemane, wherever, just flash the lights and I'll figure it out, I promise." He was thinking this and then it—*something*—happened. The light bulb flickered, or maybe it got brighter, like a camera's flash going off across the street, just a fraction of a fraction of a second like that, and then it was back to normal, just a regular yellow bulb.

Cyrus tried to recount the drugs he'd done that day. The standard bouquet of booze, weed, cigarettes, Klonopin, Adderall, Neurontin variously throughout the day. He had a couple Percocets left but he'd been saving them for later that evening. None of what he'd taken was exotic, nothing that would make him out and out hallucinate. He felt pretty sober in fact, relative to his baseline.

He wondered if it had maybe been the sheer weight of his wanting, or his watching, that strained his eyes till they saw what they'd wanted to see. He wondered if maybe that was how God worked now in the new world. Tired of interventionist pyrotechnics like burning bushes and locust plagues, maybe God now worked through the tired eyes of drunk Iranians in the American Midwest, through CVS handles of bourbon and little pink pills with G 31 written on their side. Cyrus took a pull from the giant plastic Old Crow bottle. The whiskey did, for him, what a bedside table did for normal people—it was always at the head of his mattress, holding what was essential to him in place. It lifted him daily from the same sleep it eventually set him into.

Lying there reflecting on the possible miracle he'd just experienced, Cyrus asked God to do it again. Confirmation, like typing your password in twice to a web browser. Surely if the all-knowing creator of the universe had wanted to reveal themselves to Cyrus, there'd be no ambiguity. Cyrus stared at the ceiling light, which in the fog of his cigarette smoke looked like a watery moon, and waited for it to happen again. But it didn't. Whatever sliver of a flicker he had or hadn't perceived didn't come back. And so, lying there in the stuffy haze of relative sobriety—itself a kind of high—amidst the underwear and cans and dried piss and empty orange pill bottles and half-read books held open against the hardwood, breaking their spines to face away—Cyrus had a decision to make.

ONE

MONDAY

——— ✦ ———

KEADY UNIVERSITY, 6 FEB 2017

"I WOULD DIE FOR *YOU*," CYRUS SAID ALONE TO HIS REFLECTION IN the little hospital mirror. He wasn't sure he meant it, but it felt good to say. For weeks, he had been playing at dying. Not in the Plath "I have done it again, one year in every ten" way. Cyrus was working as a medical actor at the Keady University Hospital. Twenty dollars an hour, fifteen hours a week, Cyrus pretended to be "of those who perish." He liked how the Quran put it that way, not "until you die" but "until you are of those who perish." Like an arrival into a new community, one that had been eagerly waiting for you. Cyrus would step into the fourth-floor hospital office and a secretary would hand him a notecard with a fake patient's name and identity on it beside a little cartoon face on the 0–10 pain scale where 0 was a smiling "No hurt at all" face, 4 was a straight-faced "Hurts a little more," and 10 was a sobbing "Hurts worst" face, a gruesome cartoon with an upside-down U for a mouth. Cyrus felt he'd found his calling.

Some days he was the one dying. Others, he was their family. That night Cyrus would be Sally Gutierrez, mother of three, and the face would be a 6, "Hurts even more." That's all the information he had before an anxious medical student in an ill-fitting white coat shuffled in and told Cyrus/Sally his daughter had been in a car accident, that the team had done all they could do but couldn't save her. Cyrus dialed his reaction up to a 6, just on the cusp of tears. He asked the medical student if he could see his daughter. He cursed, at one point screamed a little. When Cyrus left that evening, he grabbed a chocolate granola bar from the little wicker basket on the secretary's table.

The med students were often overeager to console him, like daytime talk-show hosts. Or they'd be repelled by the artifice of the situation and barely engage. They'd offer platitudes from a list they'd been made to memorize, tried to refer Cyrus to the hospital's counseling services. Eventually they would leave the exam room, and Cyrus would be left to evaluate their compassion by filling out a photocopied score sheet. A little camera on a tripod recorded each exchange for review.

Sometimes the medical student would ask Cyrus if he wanted to donate his beloved's organs. This was one of the conversations the school was training them for. The students' job was to persuade him. Cyrus was Buck Stapleton, assistant coach of the varsity football team, devout Catholic. Staid, a 2 on the pain scale: "Hurts a little bit." The little cartoon face still smiling even, though barely. His wife was in a coma, her brain showed no signs of activity. "She can still help people," the student said, awkwardly placing his hand on Cyrus's shoulder. "She can still save people's lives."

For Cyrus, the different characters were half the fun. He was Daisy VanBogaert, a diabetic accountant whose below-knee amputation had come too late. For her, they'd asked him to wear a hospital gown. He was a German immigrant, Franz Links, engineer, with terminal emphysema. He was Jenna Washington, and his Alzheimer's was accelerating unexpectedly quickly. An 8. "Hurts a whole lot."

The doctor who interviewed Cyrus for the job, an older white woman with severe lips and leaden eyes, told him she liked hiring people like him. When he raised an eyebrow, she quickly explained:

"Non-actors, I mean. Actors tend to get a little"—she spun her hands in tight circles—"*Marlon Brando* about it. They can't help making it about themselves."

Cyrus had tried to get his roommate Zee in on the gig, but Zee'd blown off the interview. Zbigniew Ramadan Novak, Polish-Egyptian—Zee for short. He said he'd slept through his alarm, but Cyrus suspected he was freaked out. Zee's discomfort with the job kept coming up. A month later, as Cyrus was leaving for the hospital, Zee watched him getting ready and shook his head.

"What?" asked Cyrus.

Nothing.

"*What?*" Cyrus asked again, more pointedly.

Zee made a little face, then said, "It just doesn't seem healthy, Cyrus."

"What doesn't?" Cyrus asked.

Zee made the face again.

"The hospital gig?"

Zee nodded, then said: "I mean, your brain doesn't know the difference between acting and living. After all the shit you've been through? It can't be like . . . *good* for you. In your brain stem."

"Twenty dollars an hour is pretty good for me," Cyrus said, grinning, "*in my brain stem.*"

That money felt like a lot. Cyrus thought about how, when he'd been drinking, he'd sell his plasma for that much, twenty dollars a trip, his dehydrated hangover blood taking hours to sludge out like milkshake through a thin straw. Cyrus would watch people arrive, get hooked up, and leave the facility in the time it took him to give a single draw.

"And I'm sure eventually it'll be good for my writing too," Cyrus added. "What's that thing about *living* the poems I'm not writing yet?"

Cyrus was a good poet when he wrote, but he rarely actually wrote. Before getting sober, Cyrus didn't write so much as he drank about writing, describing booze as essential to his process, "nearly sacramental"—he really said it like that—in the way it "opened his mind to the hidden voice" beneath the mundane "argle-bargle of the every-day." Of course, when he drank, he rarely did anything else but drink. "First you take a drink, then the drink takes a drink, then the drink takes you!" Cyrus would announce proudly to a room, to a bar, forgetting from whom he'd lifted the line.

In sobriety, he endured long periods of writer's block, or more accurately, writer's ambivalence. Writer's antipathy. What made it almost worse was how much Zee encouraged Cyrus whenever he *did* write something; Zee'd fawn over his roommate's new drafts, praising every line break and slant rhyme, stopping just short of hanging them up on the apartment refrigerator.

"'Living the poems you're not writing?'" Zee scoffed. "C'mon, you're better than that."

"I'm really not," Cyrus said, sharply, before stepping out the apartment door.

WHEN CYRUS PULLED INTO THE HOSPITAL PARKING LOT, HE WAS still pissed off. Everything didn't have to be as complex as Zee constantly made it, Cyrus thought. Sometimes, life was just what happened. What accumulated. That was one of the vague axioms from his drinking days to which Cyrus still clung, even in sobriety. It wasn't fair that just because he was sober, everyone expected him to exhaustively interrogate his every decision. This job or that job, this life or that. Not drinking was Herculean enough on its own. He should've been afforded more grace, not less. The long scar on his left foot—from an accident years before—pounded with pain.

Cyrus signed into the hospital and walked through the halls, past two nursing mothers sitting side by side in a waiting room, past a line of empty gurneys with messy bedding, and into the elevator. When he got to the fourth-floor office, the receptionist had him sign in again and gave him his card for the afternoon. Sandra Kaufmann. High school math teacher. Educated, no children. Widowed. Six on the pain scale. Cyrus sat in the waiting room, glancing at the camera, the "Understanding Skin Cancer" chart on the wall with gruesome pictures of Atypical Moles, Precancerous Growths. The ABCs of melanoma: Asymmetry, Borders, Color Change, Diameter, and Evolution. Cyrus imagined Sandra's hair crimson red, the color of the "Diameter" mole on the poster.

After a minute, a young medical student walked into the room alone, looked at Cyrus, then at the camera. She was a little younger than him, wore her auburn hair behind her head in a neat bun. Her impeccable posture gave her a boarding-school air, New England royalty. Cyrus reflexively hated her. That Yankee patrician veneer. He imagined she got perfect SATs, went to an Ivy League school, only to be disappointed by Keady as her medical school placement instead of Yale or Columbia. He imagined her having joyless, clinical sex with the chiseled son of her father's business partner, imagined them at a fancy candlelit restaurant dourly picking at a shared veal piccata, both ignoring the table bread. Unaccountable contempt covered him, pitiless. Cyrus hated how noisily she opened the door, sullying the stillness he'd been enjoying. She looked at the camera again, then introduced herself:

"Hello, Miss Kaufmann. My name is Dr. Monfort."

"Mrs. Kaufmann," Cyrus corrected.

The medical student glanced quickly at the camera.

"Erm, excuse me?"

"Mr. Kaufmann may be dead, but I am still his wife," said Cyrus, pointing to a pretend wedding ring on his left hand.

"I, I'm sorry, ma'am. I was just—"

"It's no problem, dear."

Dr. Monfort set down her clipboard and leaned her hand against the sink she'd been standing near, as if resetting. Then, she spoke:

"Mrs. Kaufmann, I'm afraid the scans have revealed a large mass in your brain. Several large masses, clumped together. Unfortunately, they're attached to sensitive tissue controlling breathing and cardio-pulmonary function, and we can't safely operate without risking severe damage to those systems. Chemotherapy and radiation may be options, but due to the location and maturation of the masses, these treatments would likely be palliative. Our oncologist will be able to tell you more."

"Palliative?" Cyrus asked. The students were supposed to avoid jargon and euphemism. Not "going to a better place." Saying the word "dying" as often as possible was recommended, as it eliminated confusion, helped hasten the patient through denial.

"Uhm, yes. For pain relief. To make you comfortable while you get your affairs in order."

Get your affairs in order. She was doing terribly. Cyrus hated her.

"I'm sorry, Doctor—what was it? Milton? Are you telling me I'm *dying?*" Cyrus half-smiled as he said the one word she'd yet to speak out loud. She winced, and Cyrus relished her wincing.

"Ah, yes, Miss Kaufmann, ah, I'm so sorry." Her voice sounded the way wild rabbits look, just on the cusp of tearing off out of sight.

"*Mrs.* Kaufmann."

"Oh right, of course, I'm so sorry." She checked her clipboard. "It's just, my paper here says 'Miss Kaufmann.'"

"Doctor, are you trying to tell me I don't know my own name?"

The medical student glanced desperately back at the camera.

A YEAR AND A HALF AGO IN EARLY RECOVERY, CYRUS TOLD HIS AA sponsor Gabe that he believed himself to be a fundamentally bad person. Selfish, self-seeking. Cruel, even. A drunk horse thief who stops drinking is just a sober horse thief, Cyrus'd said, feeling proud to have thought it. He'd use versions of that line later in two different poems.

"But you're not a bad person trying to get good. You're a sick person trying to get well," Gabe responded.

Cyrus sat with the thought. Gabe went on,

"There's no difference to the outside world between a good guy and a bad guy behaving like a good guy. In fact, I think God loves that second guy a little more."

"Good-person drag," Cyrus thought out loud. That's what they called it after that.

"OF COURSE NOT, MRS. KAUFMANN, I'M ABSOLUTELY NOT TRYING to argue," the medical student stammered. "The paper must have misprinted your name. I'm so sorry. Is there anyone you'd like us to call?"

"Who would I have you call?" Cyrus asked. "My principal? I'm all alone."

Dr. Monfort looked clammy. The red light on the camera was blinking on and off, like a firefly mocking their proceedings.

"We have some great counselors here at Keady," she said. "Nationally ranked—"

"Have you ever had a patient who wanted to die?" Cyrus interrupted.

The medical student stared at him, saying nothing, pure disdain radiating from her person, barely bridled fury. Cyrus thought she might actually hit him.

"Or maybe not wanted to die," Cyrus continued, "but who just wanted their suffering to end?"

"Well, *like I said,* we offer a wide range of palliative options," she hissed, staring at Cyrus, Cyrus-Cyrus, beneath Mrs. Kaufmann, willing him toward compliance.

He ignored her.

"The last time I thought I wanted to die, I got a fifth of Everclear, ninety-five percent alcohol, and sat in my bathtub drinking it from the bottle, pouring out a bit on my head. One pull for me, one for my hair. The aim was to finish the bottle that way and then light myself on fire. Theatrical, no?"

Dr. Monfort said nothing. Cyrus went on,

"But when I'd finished maybe just a quarter of the bottle, I realized suddenly I didn't want to burn everyone else in the apartment complex."

This was true. That little flicker of lucidity, light, like sun glinting off a snake in the grass. It happened a few months before Cyrus had gotten sober, and it wasn't until he was already good and drunk that he even remembered the existence of other people, and the fact that fire spreads, that if he lit himself on fire in a first-floor apartment bathtub, everyone else's apartments would likely catch fire too. Booze worked that way sometimes, clarifying—briefly—what his mind couldn't. It was like sitting in the optometrist's office, booze flashing its different lenses in front of your face and sometimes, for a second, it'd be the right prescription, the one that allowed you to catch a glimpse of the world as it was, beyond your grief, beyond your doom. That was the clarity alcohol, and nothing else, gave. Seeing life as everyone else did, as a place that could accommodate you. But of course a second later it'd zoom past clarity through a flurry of increasingly opaque lenses until all you were able to see would be the dark of your own skull.

"Can you believe that?" Cyrus went on. "I needed to be drunk to even consider that a fire that consumed me in a bathtub wouldn't just go out on its own."

"Mrs. Kaufmann . . . ," the medical student said. She was wringing her hands, one of the "physical distress behaviors" Cyrus was supposed to note in his evaluation.

"I remember actually sitting there in the bathtub, doing the calculus of it. Like, do I even care if I take other people with me? These strangers. I had to work out whether or not they mattered to me. How fucked up is that?"

"Mrs. Kaufmann, if you are struggling with thoughts of suicide, we have resources . . ."

"Oh c'mon, just talk to me. You want to be a doctor? I'm sitting in front of you, talking. I ended up walking myself outside the apartment complex, wet with the alcohol, though not too wet, it evaporated quickly I think, I remember being surprised at how wet I wasn't. There was a little grassy patch between our building and the one next to us, a picnic bench with one of those built-in charcoal grills. I remember thinking that was funny, lighting myself on fire next to a grill. I brought out the Everclear and the lighter, I remember—this is bizarre—it was a Chicago Bears lighter. I have no idea where it came from. And I sat there at the bench feeling, despite the Everclear in and on me, I remember sitting there feeling, not happy exactly but simple, maybe? Like a jellyfish just floating along. Someone said alcohol reduces the 'fatal intensity' of living. Maybe it was that."

Outside the clouds had grown fat and dark with rain, the whole sky a wounded animal in some last frantic rage. The hospital room had a tiny little window high on the wall, probably placed there so people from the street couldn't look in. The medical student didn't move.

"Do you have this organ here?" Cyrus asked her, pointing at the base of his throat. "A doom organ that just pulses all the time? Pulses dread, every day, obstinately? Like it thinks there's a panther behind the curtain ready to maul you, but there's no panther and it turns out there's no curtain either? That's what I wanted to stop."

"What did you do?" the medical student asked, finally. Something in her seemed to have relaxed a little, conceded to the moment's current.

"I went back inside my apartment." Cyrus shrugged. "I wanted to stop hurting. Being burned alive felt suddenly like it'd hurt a lot."

Dr. Monfort smiled, gave a tiny nod. Cyrus continued:

"I took a shower and passed out. I remained. But so did the dread. I thought getting sober would help, that came later. Recovery. And it did, in its way. Certainly it made me less a burden to the people around me, created less dread in them. But it's still in me, that doom organ." He pointed again at his neck. "It's in my throat, throbbing all day every day. And recovery, friends, art—that shit just numbs it for a second. What's that word you used?"

"Palliative?"

"Right, palliative, yeah. All that stuff is palliative. It stills the suffering, but it doesn't send it away."

The medical student paused for a moment, then took a seat on the chair across from Cyrus. She was tinted with black-blue rays from the window as if marked by some celestial spotlight. She said, very deliberately, "You know, *Mrs. Kaufmann*, it's entirely possible, common even, to have psychological co-morbidities. It sounds like you've been getting help for addiction issues, which is great. But you may also have another diagnosis alongside it that's going untreated, an anxiety disorder or major depression or something else. It could be useful for you to seek help for those as well." She smiled a little, then added, "It's not too late, even with the tumors." It was her way of inviting Cyrus back into the performance, and he obliged. He felt suddenly flush with embarrassment.

Cyrus behaved agreeably through the rest of the act. When they finished a few minutes later and the medical student left the exam room, he wrote her a quick but glowing report before rushing out of the hospital in a flurry of shame.

TWO

From: Rear Admiral William M. Fogarty, USN

To: Commander in Chief, U.S. Central Command

Subj: FORMAL INVESTIGATION INTO THE CIRCUMSTANCES SURROUNDING THE DOWNING OF A COMMERCIAL AIRLINER BY THE USS VINCENNES (CG. 49) ON 3 JULY 1988 (U)

IV. OPINIONS

A. GENERAL

1. The USS VINCENNES did not purposely shoot down an Iranian commercial airliner.

THAT EVENING, CYRUS DROVE HIMSELF TO AN AA MEETING AT THE Camp5 Center, Keady's local recovery clubhouse. It was a converted Craftsman home, gabled roof, rickety wooden frame painted dingy lavender. A fixture of crusty old-timers chain-smoked perpetually in the parking lot while embarrassed kids with court cards avoided eye contact as they shuffled in and out on the hours.

Cyrus walked through the fog of cigarette and vape smoke into the front entrance and up the stairs to the little window where Angus B., a no-nonsense old-timer, worked during daytime hours, selling cups of coffee and cookies for fifty cents, egg salad sandwiches for two dollars, all money going toward Camp5's monthly rent. Cyrus got a cup of coffee and went downstairs to the dim basement. Six long plastic folding tables were spread out across a dark open room, each table surrounded by uncomfortable wooden campus-surplus chairs.

His sponsor was there. Gabe B., Gabriel Bardo. He was in his late fifties, thirty-three years sober. He'd grown up in Orange County, wove in and out of the television world, and now taught playwriting at the local community college. Gabe looked like an oak tree in a denim jacket, his face all jaw, big white mustache, big hands perpetually cracked from working on this or that project. He was already sitting at the far table in the room when Cyrus walked in, so he wordlessly settled into the empty chair beside him.

Cyrus had trouble paying attention in the meeting. The topic was "life on life's terms," which was so broad as to be functionally meaningless. A middle-aged white man celebrated thirty days for the fourth time in a year. Everyone clapped. An old-timer rhapsodized about his own magnanimity in a recent business dispute, saying, "If you're coasting, it means you're going downhill." Everyone nodded. His shirt read "I don't run, I RELOAD" in big white letters. An aquiline young woman talked about doing coke in the bathroom of her daughter's preschool open house. Everyone laughed. Gabe shared about his son—Shane, after the western—struggling in school, skipping classes, generally being a teenager. Talking about his recently blowing up at Shane over leaving the kitchen in chaos, Gabe said, "For me, the difference between heaven and hell is not giving a shit about the mess."

The room mooed in approval. A few more people shared. Cyrus hadn't planned on saying anything, was mostly there out of habit or inertia, but toward the end of the meeting something restless in him stirred and he spoke:

"Hi, I'm Cyrus, addict-alcoholic." A couple heads turned over to him, but mostly the folks knew who he was, what he looked like.

"I snapped at this woman at work today. I didn't know her at all and I was shitty for no reason. And you know? It felt good. It felt so good, putting her on her heels like that. Being in control. We're always talking in here about surrendering, surrendering. 'Relieve me of the bondage of self, that I may better do *thy* will.' Giving up control. But it's those moments of rushing the cockpit where I actually feel anything anymore, where I remember who I am. Rushing the cockpit? Bad metaphor." Cyrus smiled, took a deep breath. "There are no big decisions in my life. Mostly I just sit around listening to my brain saying the same shit over and over: 'Wouldn't you rather be masturbating?' 'Wouldn't you rather be *overwhelmed*?' And the answer is always, always yes, yes. I turn my headphones up till it hurts, act like a dick to a random woman just doing her job. Because it feels different than nothing. Which is all sobriety is. Nothing. Nothing in every direction. It used to be I'd only feel something if it was the most extreme ecstasy or the most incapacitating white-light pain. Drugs and booze sandpapered away everything else. But now everything is in this textureless middle."

A weaselly younger guy, Joe A., made a big show of turning around to look at the wall clock. Cyrus went on:

"When I was little and my dad was the right kind of drunk, he'd insist I pray before bed. 'Just talk to God, talk to your mother. Tell them how you feel.' They were the same thing, talking to God and talking to my dead mom. And so I did, I'd tell God I was fucking miserable, I'd beg my mom to make me feel less sad. Even at seven, ten years old. I'd offer these trades, I'd say, 'You can take twenty years off the end of my life if you stop making the ones I have so miserable.' I don't even know what I was so sad about. I had friends. I wasn't hungry. But the rot just sat in my gut. God? My mom? They were just words. That's the thing. The woman at work today, she was saying these *words* to me, all these words. And they were so empty; I hated her for it. This program too. Just words. I mean, I used to piss the bed all the time and try to kill myself. And I don't piss the bed anymore, at least. So there's something here, right? Objectively. But I resist it. I feel sad all the time. Angry. If I'm being rigorously honest, I still think most of you are fucking idiots. If we met outside these rooms, you'd probably try to deport me—"

"Outside issue!" barked Big Susan, a tiny but gruff old-timer who, despite her nickname, actually stood under five feet. "Non-AA-related!" Her voice made everyone in the room sit up a little straighter.

"See, that's what I mean," Cyrus said, holding up his hands at Big Susan. "Recovery is made of words, and words have all these rules. How can anything so limited touch something as big as whatever the fuck a 'Higher Power' is? How can it get rid of the big ball of rot inside me? It feels like this giant sponge sucking away anything in the world that's supposed to feel good. What words can touch that?" Exasperated, Cyrus snorted at himself. "I don't know. I don't know. I'm sorry."

He slumped down in his chair, exhaled. The room was quiet for a second, two seconds—an eternity for this group—and then Mike P., a former crack addict turned coffee-shop owner, started sharing about what a good day it was to be sober, the sun and clouds and trees. Gabe looked down at Cyrus for a fraction of a second with a kind of nod and pursing of his lips that meant something like "Well, that was interesting."

AFTER THE MEETING GABE ASKED CYRUS IF HE WANTED TO GO TO Secret Stash, Mike P.'s coffee shop downtown, and Cyrus knew it wasn't actually a question. They drove separately, Gabe in his blue Volvo, Cyrus in his old Chevy Cavalier. Gabe got to the café first, and when Cyrus walked in Gabe had just finishing ordering— a double espresso for himself, black Americano for Cyrus. The two men waited wordlessly for their drinks, then found a little circular two-top in the back. The walls were lined with some high school artist showcase, their section featuring charcoal sketches of teenagers making grotesque faces inside hand-drawn Instagram frames.

"So," Gabe said, finally, "a God made of words, huh?" He ripped open a brown cane sugar packet and poured it into his espresso, swirling it around. The coffee shop was playing that loud Arcade Fire song that played at hockey games.

"I don't know, man," Cyrus said. "I'm just sad. Aren't I supposed to talk about that?"

"Sure," said Gabe, "sure." He leaned over the table, staring at Cyrus. "You've got a little red in your eye."

"What?"

"A blood vessel or something?" Gabe pointed to the corner of his own right eye to indicate where to look. Cyrus pulled out his phone camera, used it to see himself. A little red Pangea in the white of his eye bleeding into his iris.

"Oh, shit."

"You okay?" Gabe asked.

"Yeah, I don't know. I probably slept funny or something."

"Or something, sure. Okay: God made of words, you're sad. Keep going." He took a sip of his espresso, which left a little moon of foam at the edge of his white mustache.

"That's it, really. The big pathological sad. Whether I'm actually thinking about it or not. It's like a giant bowling ball on the bed, everything kind of rolls into it."

"Maybe you don't believe God wants you to be happy? God, your mother, poetry, whatever. What makes you so special that everyone else deserves that *except* you?"

"What does that even mean? 'God, your mother, poetry, whatever.' I have no idea what you or Big Susan or Mike or any of those people mean when they talk about 'higher power.' Most of those guys probably mean an old bearded dude in the clouds who gets mad when I suck a dick, who sends all Muslims to hell. What use is that higher power to me?" Cyrus paused. "I've been reading all these ancient mystics. I think if I could find some Persian higher power, something in Islam . . ."

"Oh that's fucking bullshit." Gabe rolled his eyes theatrically. The open mouths of the charcoal teenagers snarled horrifically down. "You're the most American kid I know. *You* taught Shane how to play Madden, how to torrent Marvel movies. You buy fucking *vinyl records*. We're having this conversation in Indiana, not Tehran."

Gabe was the only person in Cyrus's life, white or not, who spoke to him this way. There was something in it, a kind of old man punk "fuck-it"-ness Cyrus had long admired, even if it meant Gabe sometimes danced well past the third rail of political correctness. Still, however abstractly he envied Gabe's ability to speak unencumbered by the rhetorical hygienics du jour, in this specific instance, still harried from the episode with Dr. Monfort, Cyrus quickly grew flush with righteous fury.

TWO YEARS AGO WHEN CYRUS WAS DOING HIS FIFTH STEP— cataloguing to Gabe all his deepest most tucked-away secrets—and casually mentioned having slept with men, Cyrus expected shock, at least one of Gabe's "well, that's something" looks. Instead, Gabe informed Cyrus that he'd slept with hundreds of men himself.

"Southern California in the seventies," he'd shrugged, like it was a given.

"I expected you to be more surprised," Cyrus admitted. "My being straight passing or whatever."

"Oh sweetheart," Gabe chuckled, "you think you're straight passing?"

GABE LOOKED LIKE, AND REVERED, JOHN WAYNE. HIS FACE ALL chin and jaw, cavernous dark eyes like weeping poppies. He built sets from scratch with his playwriting students, scavenging old pallets from around Keady's campus sprawl and loading them into his Volvo. He was a single parent to Shane after his wife, whom he'd met in AA, relapsed and disappeared from Indiana without a trace. Cyrus had come to expect certain constitutional surprises from his sponsor, sizing him up to be one kind of man—starchy, conservative—only for him to illuminate again and again the wide gulf between the image on his dust jacket and the story inside.

Cyrus elected to say nothing to Gabe's Indiana-not-Tehran crack, just crossed his arms and jutted out his lower lip in a vaguely combative stance. Gabe continued:

"I've read your poems, Cyrus. I get that you're Persian. Born there, raised here. I know that's a part of you. But you've probably spent more time looking at your phone today, just today, than you've spent cutting open pomegranates in your entire life. Cumulatively. Right? But how many fucking pomegranates are in your poems? Versus how many iPhones? Do you see what I mean?"

Cyrus wanted to kick him in the face. For being racist. For being a little right.

"I'm not trying to be an asshole," Gabe said, his voice softening. "But it's a schtick. It's a schtick and it's holding back your recovery. And your art. Nobody else is going to say it to you as plain as I am. Nobody can. I'm fine with you being pissed at me. That shitty face you're making. I can deal with that. What I can't deal with is you going back out and drinking over this. Hurting yourself."

A skinny guy next to them was wearing giant headphones, typing furiously into his laptop, like a movie hacker trying to crack into the Pentagon. Out of the coffee-shop speakers, some breathy ballad Cyrus didn't recognize.

"Is there an action item in this monologue?" Cyrus snarled, finally. Gabe leaned in.

"Do you know what the first rule of playwriting is?"

Cyrus shook his head, barely. Even allowing Gabe's questions felt like a concession.

"You never send a character onstage without knowing what they want."

Cyrus frowned. "I know what I want," he said.

"Do you?" Gabe was hunched over, his big palms flat on the round table making it look like a wooden dinner plate.

"I want to matter," Cyrus whispered.

"You and everyone else. Deeper."

"I want to make great art. Art people think matters."

"Good. Keep going."

"Isn't that enough?" Cyrus was exasperated.

"Cyrus, everyone and their mailman believes they're an unacknowledged genius artist. What do you, specifically, want from your unprecedented, never-to-be-repeated existence? What makes you actually different from everyone else?" Gabe picked his teeth with his pinky nail. He was missing an incisor, which made him look a little boyish.

Cyrus paused, then said, finally:

"I want to die. I think I always have."

"Hm." Gabe squinted. "We'll revisit that. Keep going."

"Jesus, I don't know. My mom died for nothing. A rounding error. She had to share her death with three hundred other people. My dad died anonymous after spending decades cleaning chicken shit on some corporate farm. I want my life—my death—to matter more than that."

"You want to be a martyr?" Gabe asked, raising his eyebrows.

"I guess. Yeah, actually. Something like that."

"Cyrus," Gabe said, smiling, "you can't even wash your own dirty clothes." He nodded down at Cyrus's T-shirt, wrinkled and specked with coffee stains near the collar. "You think you're going to be able to strap a bomb to your chest and walk into a café?" His voice didn't change at all when he said "bomb," but it made Cyrus wince.

"Do you even realize how racist that is?" Cyrus whispered, anger rising in his throat like a snake crawling out of its hole—bilious, licking the air.

"Am I wrong?" Gabe asked, earnestly.

"I don't mean that kind of martyr," Cyrus declared. "Though—"

"Yes?" Gabe asked. The bit of espresso foam on his mustache looked ridiculous.

"Can you imagine having that kind of faith?" Cyrus asked. "To be that *certain* of something you've never seen? I'm not that certain of anything. I'm not that certain of *gravity.*"

"That certainty is what put worms in their brains, Cyrus. The only people who speak in certainties are zealots and tyrants."

"Sure, sure. But there's no tiny secret part of you that envies that clarity? That conviction?"

"I'm not uncomfortable sitting in uncertainty. I'm not groping desperately to resolve it. I got four DUIs in a month because I was certain I was in control. That's what certainty did to me. It put me in jail for eighteen months. Have you read the third step lately?"

Cyrus rolled his eyes. The third step was the one where you turn it all over, your entire life, to God or poetry or your grandma or whateverthefuck.

"Have you been listening to me at all?" Cyrus asked. "I don't even know what my higher power is."

"That didn't stop you from getting on your knees with me a year ago and asking it to remove your suffering."

"Asking *what*?" Cyrus asked. "What were we even talking to?"

"Who cares?" Gabe answered. "To not-your-own-massive-fucking-ego. That's the only part that matters."

"Do you ever listen to yourself?" Cyrus asked. The snake was reared up now, rattling its tail. "How sanctimonious you get trying to control other people's lives? Maybe because your own life is so fucked up. Maybe because your kid's a screw-up and your wife picked booze over you. Maybe that's why you're trying to commandeer my life to make yourself feel better about yours. Calling me fake Persian? Calling me a dilettante?"

"I don't think I called you a dilettante," Gabe said calmly.

"You know what Borges said about fathers and mirrors? They're abominations. They both double the number of men."

"I'm certain, actually," said Gabe, "that I never used the word 'dilettante.'"

"You're not even listening to me!" Cyrus was getting loud. The hacker guy looked over at their table.

"Yes yes," Gabe replied, his voice still level. "You're upset with me and quoting Borges in order to cudgel me with your great intellect. Very impressive."

"Fuck you," Cyrus said, standing up. "I don't need this. I don't need you lecturing me and I don't need this bullshit cult of bullshit."

Cyrus grabbed his untouched coffee, stepping away from the table. Gabe didn't move. Nick Cave's voice was coming out of the speakers: "hernia, Guernica, furniture." Cyrus stormed to his car and drove away from Secret Stash—from Gabe—flooded with a narcotic blend of righteous indignation and self-pity. His foot throbbed. In the rearview mirror he caught a glimpse of himself; the red spot had swallowed up the whole right side of his right eye, colors melting into each other like a painting by Rothko.

Cyrus was furious at himself for not having said something more cutting when he stood up than "bullshit cult of bullshit." He drove home thinking of better alternatives: limp-dicked Republican church, coven of racist crones. It was soothing, to stop time and rework memory, imagining through the thesaurus multiverse. Vapid temple of words. Scumbag Caesars vivisecting God. He thought about all the poets he'd read whose rapturous ecstasy overwhelmed even language's ability to transcribe it. Cyrus realized he couldn't remember the last time he'd felt even a glimmer of incandescent, effortless good. That would be his last AA meeting, he decided. And his last time talking to Gabe.

THREE

FOR AS LONG AS HE COULD REMEMBER, CYRUS HAD THOUGHT IT unimaginably strange, the body's need to recharge nightly. The way sleep happened not as a fact like swallowing or using the bathroom, but as a faith. People pretended to be asleep, trusting eventually their pretending would morph into the real thing. It was a lie you practiced nightly—or, if not a lie, at least a performance. And while performance did not necessarily void sincerity, it certainly changed it. The speech you practiced in front of the mirror was always different than the one you ended up giving.

Nothing else worked this way, insisting upon pretending. You didn't sit in front of a plate of rice, pantomiming swallowing in order to take the tiny grains into your stomach. Sleep alone demanded that embarrassing recital.

As if to incentivize the whole ordeal, the body offered you dreams. In exchange for a third of your living, you were offered sprawling feasts, exotic adventures, beautiful lovers, wings. Or at least the promise of them, made only slightly less intoxicating by the curious threat of nightmare. How sometimes, at random, your mind would decide to reduce you to a whimper, or a gasp, in the night.

These terms were non-negotiable, and if you didn't agree you went mad, or you got sick, or you died. Cyrus had read about it over and over. After just twenty-four hours without sleep, you lost coordination and short-term memory. After forty-eight hours, your blood sugar spiraled, your heart began to beat irregularly.

It was hard for Cyrus not to see waking as the enemy. The way it corroded your power to exist—to live and think with acuity—until you finally submitted. Being awake was a kind of poison, and dream was the only antidote. What if everyone was more conscious of this? How would it charge, make more urgent, their living? "I have been poisoned, I have only sixteen hours until I succumb."

Since Cyrus was very young, he'd been a terrible sleeper. As an infant, he slept so little his father, Ali, thought he might have a disability. Cyrus would stare out from his crib with sleepy, unmistakably angry old eyes, as if to ask, "Do I really have to do this?"

Ali would rock his son back and forth, rub finger circles in his scalp, sing to him, take him on late-night drives, but still Cyrus held on to his waking with desperate ferocity, a tiny horse trying to climb out of a muddy lake, only to sink further and further in. When his infant body could hold out no longer, Cyrus would finally fall asleep, and then always wearing a perplexed, annoyed look on his face that seemed to ask, "Who thought of this?"

CYRUS'S SLEEPING ONLY GOT WORSE AS HE GREW OLDER. AS A BOY he began experiencing sleep terrors. Without warning or provocation he would rise in the night screaming, crying, sometimes battering himself violently. Cyrus's sleep panics came to rule Ali, became the god to whom he prayed, pleaded, offered tribute.

Ali would go to his son during these fits, trying to shake him awake, but if Cyrus did wake it would be into a state of petrifying fright, with no sense of where he was or what had sparked his fear. His father would rock him and beg as he had begged countless times before, "Koroosh baba, please. Just sleep. Cyrus baba. Sleep."

But Cyrus would keep screaming or crying or thrashing, sometimes for hours, before falling back into a tense rest, like a tongue in a mouth between bites.

Often Cyrus would wet himself and Ali would have to change his clothes and his sheets before returning to bed for a few hours. It would mean an extra trip to the laundromat, an extra load to wash and dry, an extra hour, an extra $2.50.

If Ali had ever spoken to anyone about this time, he would have said it felt like a profoundly unfair arrangement—the universe that took his wife from him should have at least given him an easy child. A fair-tempered good-sleeping child. It was injury to injury, Ali felt, a finger rooting around an open wound.

Ali's wife, Roya, died just a few months after Cyrus was born. The circumstances were unspeakable. She had been flying to Dubai to spend a week with her brother Arash, who had been unwell since serving in the Iranian army against Iraq. Arash was visiting Dubai for a few months and Roya had impulsively decided to go join him, to shop, to eat, to rest. She'd been exhausted since the pregnancy and birth, distant from Ali and from her own son. This trip, Ali hoped, would help her reset, help to restore her warmth. It would be Roya's first time ever on a plane, and her first time leaving Tehran since Cyrus's birth. She was jittery with nerves. She had left the house wanting to look good, wearing her favorite outfit: a slim white trench coat and smart wool slacks, despite the July heat. She packed gifts for her brother, the new Black Cats tape and some Persian nougat candy.

Shortly after takeoff, Roya's plane was destroyed by a U.S. Navy boat. Just shot out of the sky. Like a goose.

A U.S. Navy warship, the USS *Vincennes*, fired two surface-to-air missiles. One hit the plane and instantaneously turned it, and the 290 passengers on board, into dust. The reports really said that, Iran Air Flight 655 had been "turned into dust." Maybe that was supposed to make the families feel better, it being so instantaneous. Made from dust, returned to dust. It was clean in a way, if you didn't think about it too much.

There were sixty-six children killed on board Iran Air Flight 655. It would have been sixty-seven. But Roya had told Ali that their son was too young to fly, that she had earned a break from childcare after the long pregnancy. Otherwise. Otherwise.

· · ·

ALI HAD BEEN THE ONE WHO WANTED A CHILD. HIS WIFE WAS LESS sure. Roya's mother had been doting, endlessly affectionate. She'd design crafts and activities for her children. She'd cook three full meals a day plus snacks and cookies. She filled the house with books and art and music. She was the kind of natural, instinctive mother who made mothers around her feel inadequate.

Roya knew she would never be able to be the sort of mother her own mother had been, the kind who quivered with love like a wet branch. Even as an adult, Roya could hardly be bothered to feed or bathe herself.

Roya's mother had spoiled her children the way grandparents spoiled their grandchildren. Roya thought she'd spoil a child the way rain spoiled a drive. Still, Ali insisted he'd do the lion's share of the parenting.

"I am not a typical man," he'd say. "The late nights, the diapers. Teeth coming in! Ridiculous little teeth!" He'd grab Roya's hand when he said things like that. "I feel so excited about all of it."

Roya would shake her head.

"That's just because you don't understand."

Eventually, though, Roya assented. Cyrus was born March 13, 1988, a week before Nowruz, the Persian new year. All around Iran, people were imagining themselves moving through the future with slimmer bodies, better jobs. Families set out beautiful displays of sprouts, sumac, coins, garlic, and dried fruit to usher in the new year. Fat goldfish made lazy circles in little bowls.

THE BIRTH HAPPENED FAST. ROYA HAD BEEN LYING IN HER HOSPI-tal bed. The nurses kept asking her if she was uncomfortable, if she was in pain, but she really wasn't. Not comfortable, of course, but not in agony either. She thought maybe this was a bad sign. After a few hours, she started to feel more pressure and reached her hand down, only to feel the baby's hair. She shouted for a nurse. Fifteen minutes later, her child was in the world. The birth wasn't like she'd heard. Her doctor wasn't even in the room when it happened.

The baby had come out without wailing or tears, and Roya didn't cry either, just played with his tiny impossible digits. She thought he looked like a fruit. She joked they should name him "Bademjan," the Persian word for eggplant.

"We can make eggplant stew. He will be best friends with a tomato."

Ali stood at her side weeping enough for all three of them, saying "Alhamdulillah" over and over. He wasn't particularly religious, but what else does one say when one's son is born?

"He has eyes! Alhamdulillah. He has hair! Alhamdulillah."

The baby had been so decorous, so solemn about the whole ordeal. He kept flashing his eyes around to study the new lights, the new faces.

"Alhamdulillah. Like a little king," Ali said.

They named him Cyrus.

IN THE WEEKS FOLLOWING ROYA'S DEATH, ALI WAS LEFT TO DO THE lion's share of the parenting, and the rest of it too. He wanted to get out of Tehran. He wanted to get away from Roya's friends and family, who pestered him endlessly with unannounced visits and condolences and stews. He was sick of covered dishes from old women: ghormeh sabzi, chicken koobideh. He was sick of people's pity.

He hated having to convince people he was both sufficiently immobilized by despair and also doing okay enough to take care of himself and his son. People would try to help him by cursing the United States and he hated that too. What did they know? The United States had shot his wife out of the sky, not theirs.

Ali had been the one to make the phone call to Roya's brother Arash, who was waiting in his rented Dubai apartment for his sister to arrive. Arash wailed and howled—deep, bestial howls that even over the phone and across the room caused Cyrus to stir. Not crying but howling, as a wounded animal, crazed with rage and confusion, howls. Arash was already unwell since his service in the war, but Roya's death tore into him like an arrow. For months, Arash did not speak, and then when he did he made little sense. Ali almost appreciated this in his brother-in-law. It was honest, at least. More honest than stock condolences, frozen chelo kabob left on his doorstep.

Ali's anger—a moon. It grew so vast it scared him, so deep it felt like terror. On the news he saw the vice president of the United States say: "I don't care what the facts are. I'm not an apologize for America kind of guy."

That Ali's family, his friends, could put words around their anger meant it was a different thing entirely from what he was feeling. Ali's anger felt ravenous, almost supernatural, like a dead dog hungry for its own bones.

Sometimes he wanted to get away from Cyrus. He'd sit in another room, smoking in the dark—he'd started smoking again—and when his son stirred Ali would wait as long as he could before sighing, going in to grudgingly care for him, to see dead Roya's living brown eyes staring up at him from the crib. Ali stopped eating or answering the phone. His rage hardened into a plaque around his heart. He felt it, felt himself hardening too, and leaned in. He began buying jugs of homemade wine from a neighbor, applied for a visa. He studied himself in the mirror, thought his teeth looked sharper.

Ali fed Cyrus cold baby formula, resented the powder. He wanted to be able to make milk with his own body. Roya had bought several weeks' worth before she left, but that had long since run out. It wasn't fair, him having to buy this alien formula made of who knew what. It was probably the formula keeping Cyrus awake at night. The formula company probably did that on purpose, put caffeine in the powder so the baby would wake up and you'd have to feed them more and more formula. That was how the world worked. Mercenary. Nothing to be done about it.

One day, Ali saw a flyer from a big U.S. chicken company advertising farm jobs in Indiana, America. No English required. "Get cash your first day," it said. A new beginning away from everyone's thin performances of rage, grief, pity—that became, in an instant, all he wanted in the world. A chicken hadn't shot his wife out of the sky. Ali took the flyer down, folding it into his pocket.

A month later, they moved together, the widower and his sleepless king. Ali had sold everything in Iran or given it away—his TV and furniture, his military pistol and Roya's wedding dress, a pearl brooch and two Pahlavi gold coins. They brought to their Fort Wayne apartment only what they could fit in a single trunk—bowls, clothes, birth certificates. Ali's military boots, which he figured he could use on the farm. A couple of crumpled doodles Roya made while nursing Cyrus—a windowpane at night, a giraffe. A small wedding photo: Ali and Roya sitting together under a white cloth lifted above them by a cast of relatives, Arash holding a corner, smiling warmly down at his sister. With all these, the trunk was barely half full. Ali did not cry when the plane took off from Tehran, but wept a little, silently, as it landed in Detroit.

Cyrus hardly slept on the flight, but when he did there were no terrors. He cooed a little. He seemed fascinated by what was happening, the vibration from the engines, the endless vistas of blue. The Shams men began their lives in America awake, unnaturally alert, like two windows with the blinds torn off.

FOUR

BANDAR ABBAS, IRAN

———— ✴ ————

SUNDAY, 3 JULY 1988

SHE'D NEVER BEEN ON A PLANE BEFORE THAT DAY, HAD NEVER HAD occasion to fly. It wasn't that they couldn't afford it—her husband's job was decent, and though they weren't rich, they were surviving better than many. She'd seen it: old matriarchs rolling up the rugs on top of which they'd raised their children, their own and often their brothers' and cousins' as well. They'd drag the carpets, one heavy roll under each armpit, into the market, selling them for next to nothing.

It was like that everywhere in Tehran. Men were raising chickens in their bathrooms, in their closets—these houses you could smell from a block away. Meat had gotten so expensive. Every Sunday an old man from Tajrish would drive into the city with his son and sell baby chicks out of his truck bed. There was always a long line to buy. Dozens of men and boys would wait there all morning for the chance to fill their pillowcases with writhing baby birds. Those who returned home with pillowcases still empty would be scolded by their wives, slapped by their fathers. Some tried throwing rocks at pigeons, sparrows, not wanting to arrive home completely empty-handed.

At night, desperate young women walked the sidewalks along Reza Shah Street—now called Revolution Street—hoping the men who approached would be solicitous, clean, wealthy, and not of the secret police. Mostly they were right, but sometimes they weren't. Once, walking with her husband back home, the woman had seen a girl, just a teenager, being pushed into an idling white van. The girl was screaming, "Why?! I am peaceful! I am peaceful!"

The men said nothing, only pushed her in and drove off. Remembering this gave the woman chills. She stirred in her seat and her feet kicked an empty bottle of mineral water, left behind on the plane by some previous passenger. For some reason, this settled her. Proof that, in the past, the plane had indeed gone up and come down. She'd never been on an airplane before that day, but her first flight early in the a.m., from Tehran to Bandar Abbas, was mercifully dull. Half-empty, and nobody sat near her. The flight attendants served tea, sesame bread with butter and sour cherry jam. She took none, then tried to remember if she'd eaten anything before leaving home that morning. The morning felt like a week ago, a month, a second. This flight, she'd be sure to eat whatever was served.

When she'd stepped onto this plane, her second of the day, second of her life, going from Bandar Abbas to Dubai, she found it was nearly full. Strange, because the gate had been relatively sparse. A couple had been trying to hush their two crying boys, infants, whose wailing gave her an eclipsing sense of relief, then guilt.

Quietly she'd moved to the back and tried to sit down in a seat next to a portly middle-aged man with a severe mustache and yellow-tinted glasses. He glared at her wordlessly with a mix of contempt and menace. An attendant quickly scampered over to check her ticket: "27D, not 25D, dear," and showed her to her correct seat, a window next to an older Arab woman wearing a black chador who smiled absentmindedly before returning to her book.

As the airplane safety procedures played over the intercom, she stared out the window, trying to think about nothing, watching the little men hurry about the tarmac. Even with the plane on the ground, they looked so small. Ridiculous. She patted her coat pocket for her passport: still there. The passport, the face inside, was precious. She hunched over herself a little, as if to protect it.

The plane began rolling, the men on the tarmac fading away. The woman, eager to vent her anxious energy, opened the Iran Air flight magazine tucked into the seat in front of her. Flipping through, she scanned an article titled "Kashan Rugs: Most Famous in the World." Another, "Travel to Shush, the Center of Ancient

Civilization." In that one, a full-page photograph of a winged stone sphinx. "From the Palace of Dariush," said the caption underneath, "Older than the Roman Colosseum!" Some solace in history, perhaps, knowing other civilizations had also destroyed themselves. In fact, the record seemed to suggest such destruction was inevitable, the endpoint of every people.

Around Iran, statues of the shahs had been torn down and replaced with statues of the ayatollahs. Scowling men. In Qom, future mullahs studied those faces, practiced their own glowers in bathroom mirrors. "More Holy Men Than Any Other Culture," the local posters bragged.

In Isfahan, the old capital, soldiers showed up unannounced at the doors of old women, saying, "Congratulations, your sons have been martyred."

The mothers would have to hold back their tears, wringing their lips into the eerie not-quite-smiles they'd spend the rest of their lives perfecting. They were the lucky ones. Inside Tehran's Revolution Square, the sons of other mothers hung from cranes.

ONCE THE PLANE WAS IN THE AIR, SHE FINALLY FOUND HERSELF relaxing. At least for a time, she was leaving that horror behind. Horror, which lived on the ground. In the past. In the air, in the present where she was, it was calm. Still. The plane chimed peacefully. The Arab woman next to her had folded her book across her lap and was now drowsing lazily, head tilted toward the aisle.

She tried not to think about the people she was leaving. She'd earned that. More than earned it. She refused the hot knot of guilt rising up in her throat. *You will not be needed,* she said to it in her mind, swallowing. So much could still go wrong, of course, but for the first time in as long as she could remember, she could inhale fully, feel the air filling the bottom of her lungs. Even this, breathing, felt freighted, suddenly more meaningful, the way money means more to the poor than the rich.

"Emkanat." That was the word. Possibilities. She couldn't recall when she'd said it last. Staring out the window, she tried to remember. She'd awoken so early that morning in Tehran, it was like her brain was still turning on. The sun, blistering pink around its edges. Clouds beneath her like a thin cloth drawn over cooling milk. Beneath that, ocean. Blues and blues and blues. In the distance, two tiny floating pebbles of white. Were they moving? Getting nearer?

Her husband, her family, her friends—everyone she knew in Iran was cynical, believing that to hope was ignorant, even murderously naïve. But tomorrow would be better than today. For the first time in ages, she really believed that.

FIVE

WASHINGTON, July 3—A United States Navy warship in the Persian Gulf shot down an Iranian passenger plane today that the Navy said it mistook for a jet fighter, and Iran said all 290 people on board were killed.

"Action Is Defended,"
The New York Times, July 4, 1988

CYRUS AND ALI SHAMS

———— ✴ ————

INDIANA, USA

MERCIFULLY FOR ALI IF NOT FOR CYRUS, AS THE BOY GREW THROUGH childhood and into adolescence, his sleep terror became less frequent, eventually disappearing entirely only to be replaced entirely by potent insomnia.

To Cyrus, even as a boy, this felt worse since he was conscious for its effects. Every night he would lie awake, endlessly reprocessing the day's events, discovering in these rehashings slights and conversational missteps that hadn't in the moment occurred to him to worry about. He'd work to try to convince himself these affronts were imagined, then his brain would offer its rebuttal: they were real, and each person he'd maligned would remember it forever—the friend whose new sneakers Cyrus hadn't noticed, the teacher whose hello he'd accidentally ignored. The cycle repeated endlessly.

Sometimes, Cyrus worried about getting deported, being sent back to an Iran he couldn't recall. Or worse. He didn't understand his father's visa status but knew it was precarious. There was always paperwork. Ali had cautioned Cyrus to answer people's "where are you from" queries with "I don't remember," insisting upon his own ignorance, however nonsensical, until they gave up. According to Ali, the alternative—announcing his Iranianness—was to invite violence, harm. Cyrus's father was always vague about this part, and that vagueness kept Cyrus awake too.

Cyrus's brainstorms often continued all the way until his father woke at 4:30 to go to the nearby industrial chicken farm, arriving at 5:30 six days a week to feed the birds and take necessary measurements—how much feed and water consumed, how much waste produced—before the rest of the laborers showed up to collect eggs. For his willingness to come in an hour earlier than his coworkers, Ali made an extra $1.25 an hour, which added up, he'd tell Cyrus frequently.

One month Ali bought a Big Mouth Billy Bass with the "extra money." It was a cheap mounted rubber fish that would move its lips to a digitized version of Bobby McFerrin's "Don't Worry, Be Happy." It was a ridiculous extravagance, one the two Shams men loved with a chilling lack of irony. Ali would play it and Cyrus would drop whatever he was doing to join his father in the apartment's single bedroom, laughing at the ur-robot flopping and rasping along. When years later Ali died and Cyrus came home from college to organize his father's things, a few boxes of clothes and dishes to Goodwill—not much, really—the singing fish was one of the few of his father's relics he'd kept.

It was just the two Shams men in America. It was just the two Shams men anywhere. Once a year on Nowruz, Ali would call his dead wife's brother, Arash, and they would talk to him a bit, only about superficial things—Cyrus's successes in school (never his stumbles), what they'd been eating, Iranian football.

On occasion, Ali would try to explain to Cyrus what happened to Arash during the war.

"The fighting with Iraq made your uncle sick," Ali told his son.

Ali explained that Uncle Arash had been tasked with the strangest job in the Persian army. At night, after the human wave attacks and the mustard gas left countless dozens or hundreds of Iranians dying on the battlefield, it was Arash's job to quietly and secretly put on a long black cloak, get atop a horse, and ride around the battlefield of fallen men with a flashlight under his face. He was meant to look like an angel. He was meant to inspire the dying men to die with dignity, conviction. To keep them from suicide. The delirious dying men would see Arash on his mount, in his illuminated hood, and believe they were being visited by Gabriel himself, or the twelfth imam returning for them.

"Your uncle was an angel," Ali told his son. "Literally. He helped a lot of people."

For hundreds of dying Iranian men, Arash on horseback was the last thing they saw. Which meant Arash watched hundreds of men die. Cyrus had a hard time wrapping his head around it, and if he was being honest, so did Ali.

Seeing so much death left Arash permanently sick. PTSD, it might be called elsewhere. As it was, Arash lived alone on government assistance in the foothills of the Alborz mountains. He could care for himself, cook and clean, but he couldn't hold a job, would often go days without sleeping. After his sister's death Arash flew back to Iran and withdrew even further into his own neuroses. He began seeing ghouls out the windows, demons, angels, Iraqi soldiers. He'd flinch at gunfire nobody else could hear. Ali told Cyrus that Arash still sometimes wore his black robes from the war, spoke to the Angel Gabriel as if they were sitting together at a table.

The Shams men called Arash once a year just after Cyrus's birthday to wish him happy Nowruz, and Cyrus's uncle was always glad to hear from him. But of course there was the inescapable, unmistakable timbre of grief in his voice, even in Farsi, even over the phone across the world—Arash's parents, then his sister, and now his brother-in-law and nephew had all left him to be feasted on by his ghosts.

IN AMERICA, ALI DRANK GIN AT NIGHT TO HELP HIM FALL ASLEEP.

"A man's body isn't meant to sleep while the sun is still out," he'd tell Cyrus, pulling a plastic gin bottle from the freezer. He'd sit and watch basketball during winter, or whatever was on the free movie channels otherwise—gauzy thrillers and police dramas—and drink gin mixed with orange juice until the final score or movie credits rolled. Then he'd go to his room and sleep like a mountain.

While his father slept easily, Cyrus struggled. Some nights he'd just give up, rising to read or draw or eat a snack. This was risky, since their apartment was so small. It was difficult to move without disturbing Ali's sleep—once, Cyrus knocked a bowl of grapes onto the floor and his father woke in a confused rage, emerging from his bedroom to half-consciously slap Cyrus's face and rip his library paperback of Simpsons comics in half down the spine. This kind of violence was rare in the Shams household, but the spectre of it dominated Cyrus's consciousness.

When he returned the destroyed book, Cyrus told the librarian that his little brother had accidentally ripped it and that he was really sorry. She laughed and didn't charge him anything, but for years after that every time he saw her she would ask how his little brother was doing, recommend this or that kid's book to take home for him.

"This one has plastic pages, it should be safe from him!" she'd laugh. Sometimes out of embarrassment he'd check out whatever book she recommended.

Since that night with the grape bowl, Cyrus mostly just stayed in his bed, often worrying about the previous day or the next, sometimes trying to sleep, mostly just trying to not think.

He'd seen a movie once on TNT where Sandra Bullock's character talked about meditation as a process of simply focusing on the feeling of air passing over her top lip as she breathed. Sometimes he'd try that. It made the air feel colder, like water going up his nose.

Other times he'd bargain with God, promising to finally read the Quran or not touch himself in the shower in exchange for a single night of deep sleep. He made these pleas desperately, urgently, but they seldom worked, and neither made any serious attempt to honor their agreement.

At some point, in order to break the endless circles of corrosive thinking, Cyrus began writing little dialogues in his head. It was like a philosophical exercise, except instead of great thinkers from antiquity, Cyrus would script conversations between his personal heroes and beloveds: he would imagine his father speaking to Michael

Jordan, his crush at school would speak to Madonna, Batman might speak with Emily Dickinson.

Usually this was just a fun game, a way to play at writing in his head and keep his mind occupied enough to stave off anxiety for five minutes at a time. Sometimes though, maybe one night in three, his brain would begin playing along.

Cyrus would start consciously imagining a conversation, scripting it and conjuring what Cindy Crawford might be saying to Inspector Gadget, fashioning banter and incisive quips, and then slowly he'd begin to fade into light sleep. His unconscious would start writing more and more of the conversation until finally, under the best conditions, he'd be fully dreaming the interaction—his characters would talk to each other for his benefit, a movie he'd cast and staged himself.

It became a way of visiting the titans of his psychic life, a Faustian trade-off with his insomnia. It was the only way he could spend time with Marie Curie, Allen Iverson, Kurt Cobain. It was the only time he got to hear his mother's voice.

WHEN HE LEFT FOR COLLEGE TO STUDY LITERATURE AT KEADY University, a state school in Indiana that gave him good financial aid, Cyrus began drinking immediately. He arrived a week early for freshman orientation and people on his floor were talking about going to a party at a guy's older brother's apartment. Cyrus said he would go with them to hang out but he wouldn't drink. He wanted to be among these new people but had no interest in making himself sleepy and mean like his father got with gin. Cyrus got drunk for the first time that evening. By the end of the night he was laughing, stealing beer cans out of strangers' hands. He accidentally tore down a shower curtain, which made everyone laugh, including Cyrus.

Growing up, Cyrus didn't know anything about drinking other than it was something only low people did. That's what his father called them, "low people." Usually, Ali told Cyrus, they died from it.

"If they don't end up in jail first."

What his own father did every night with the gin was different. Ali explained this again and again. His drinking was controlled, pharmaceutical. How else could he fall asleep early enough to wake up at 4:30 and go to a chicken farm? Ali needed it. Low people drank because they wanted to, because they lacked imagination or drive. And they suffered for it.

Once, when he was in first grade, Cyrus went on a school field trip to Chuck E. Cheese. His whole class got to go for reading a certain number of books during the year. It was a big deal, there was an area on the blackboard where his teacher counted down to the day: "24 days till Chuck E. Cheese!" "21 days till Chuck E. Cheese!"

When the day finally arrived, they took a bus and everyone got to eat pizza and drink soda. The waitress passed around Cokes and root beers in paper cups. Cyrus had no idea what root beer was and couldn't believe they were giving it to little kids. He asked for a cup of Coke, but when he took a sip, it didn't taste like Coke. It tasted like medicine. Like what he imagined alcohol tasted like. It was beer, *root* beer. The school gave everyone five dollars' worth of game tokens, but Cyrus just hid in the bathroom and cried in a stall until it was time to go back to the school.

When the bus dropped him off at home that night his father was watching an episode of *The Waltons* in which a character was dying of alcoholism. There was a scene where the character, painted in yellow stage makeup, was drunk and jaundiced and curled up in a closet like a question mark. Cyrus asked his father, "Does everyone who drinks beer die? Even if they only drink a little bit?"

Ali looked up from the TV.

"Yes," he replied, matter-of-factly.

Cyrus spent the rest of the week preparing to die. He mentioned nothing to Ali—he was still at the age when the fear of getting in trouble with his father dwarfed all others, even the fear of death. He watched Ali brush his teeth, clip his toenails, thinking: "This is the last time I'll ever see him brush his teeth. This is the last time I'll ever see him clip his nails."

Within a month of leaving for his dorm at Keady University,

Cyrus was drinking nightly, experimenting with weed and benzo-diazepines and, once that month, very drunk, heroin. He started having sex, smoking cigarettes. It was like being born—there were so many feelings he'd never felt. He'd wasted years with meditation and chamomile. There were all these seasons nobody even mentioned. New wets, new warm soft heats. He wanted to live in them all.

CYRUS'S FATHER, ALI, DIED FROM A SUDDEN STROKE AT THE START of Cyrus's sophomore year in college. It was quick, and while Cyrus was, on hearing the news, pulverized, it quickly became clear to him that his father had been living only to ensure his son's safe passage into adulthood. Ali had rarely expressed deep joy about anything—occasionally he'd shout at the end of close basketball games and then, almost as if ashamed of himself, he'd shut up completely, more grave even than he'd been before. Mostly, Ali's granite features seemed to operate only out of resignation to necessity, obligation. Once Ali had delivered Cyrus into college, into his own autonomy, perhaps it seemed to him, consciously or unconsciously, that his long and difficult journey on earth could be finished. Death had long overtaken Ali's mind; now, it had simply overtaken his body.

The men at the chicken farm where Ali worked for nineteen years put together a little memorial, gave Cyrus a posterboard with "ALI SHAMS" spelled out in big dollar-store party letters. They (or, more likely, their wives) had decorated it with farm photographs taken of Cyrus's father over the years, mounted on squares of colorful cardboard: Ali in farm scrubs holding a chicken under the wings, Ali frowning in the break room over a cup of coffee. Cyrus took the posterboard with him back to his dorm room, but it depressed him in a way he couldn't name. One afternoon he threw it in the residence hall's giant dumpster.

With Ali dead, Cyrus was alone in the world. He'd never known his grandparents, and save his uncle Arash, he had no family left. Maybe this should have made him feel lonely or scared but really it didn't make him feel much of anything. It had already been just

Cyrus and his father for so long, and Cyrus rarely called home at the end, so the subtle shift to complete parentlessness didn't actually make him appreciably lonelier than he already had been. This was hard to admit, and made Cyrus feel like a bad person.

Mostly what Cyrus felt was empty. A crushing hollowness, which governed him. He should have died on the plane with his mother, but he'd been left home. With his father now dead, Cyrus had no parents left to worry over him. What was left of his life had no intrinsic meaning, he knew, since such meaning could only be shaped in relation to other people.

Cyrus managed what grief he did have, or milked it really, leaned into it, by drinking more, using more. Cyrus wrote plaintive emails to his professors alerting them his father had died, and they in turn excused him from classes and passed him charitably. Sometimes they'd recommend the school's counseling services, which Cyrus would pretend he'd never heard of, though he had already manipulated those services into a robust loadout of narcotic prescriptions— Xanax, Adderall, Ambien, Neurontin, Flexeril—each name like an alien flower.

Cyrus created a miniature economy out of these drugs, trading them for street drugs like weed or cocaine or MDMA or heroin. Often, he'd then trade *those* for booze. The drugs were exciting new lovers, each with fresh ways to touch him, new ways to turn him on. They came and went and came and came. But Cyrus's true love, his bedrock, his soulmate, was alcohol. Alcohol was faithful, omnipresent, predictable. Alcohol didn't demand monogamy like opiates or meth. Alcohol demanded only that you came back home to it at the end of the night.

Cyrus and alcohol settled into a kind of easy domestic bliss. The university offered him a grief leave, so he took it—two whole semesters deferred, then a term with only one course, tapering slowly back up to full-time. It would take a few extra years to graduate this way, but Cyrus didn't care. Keady seemed as good a place as any to live. Whatever pretensions and high purpose he'd once held for his future gave way to the delicious primacy of the present. Cyrus wanted what everyone wanted, he figured—to feel good all the time. It seemed rational: Why would anyone choose feeling shitty when feeling good was an option? He cycled mindlessly between lovers, friends, bosses, counselors, professors, each with their own loadout of minor and major crises. Cyrus felt safe amidst them all, knowing that if anyone got too heavy, too warm-blooded, he could simply drink to jettison up above them until they disappeared. It was infuriating that nobody had told him about this, he thought. Life's invincibility cheat code.

Cyrus slept easily these years after his father's death. He would passively drink or dose himself into it without trying. Sometimes this brought back the night terrors from his childhood. He'd rise in bed and start speaking gibberish: "Wobbler warbler wraith" or "okay the roots clapping," or "nurse here is where I am burning!"

In the mornings Cyrus would have no recollection of anything— neither his oracular soliloquies nor the bizarre unremembered dreams that provoked them.

Other times the narcotics feeding on Cyrus's sleep took over their vessel entirely, like an office fire feeding itself on oxygen by bursting through a window. He'd walk to the fridge—eyes open and empty like pills you could crush and snort—and chug another beer. People would talk to him and he'd grunt as he made his way back to sleep, always dreamless and teetering on the verge of something darker, endless.

His drunkenness sometimes moved like this, unaccompanied. Eager to keep itself alive.

Often Cyrus would piss himself as a result of these unconscious drinks. He'd wake up, feel the coldness—always the coldness first, coldness being so much of wet—and clean his mess with the exasperated resolve of someone digging their car out of ice. It was the unpleasant but necessary cost of being able to move through the world.

When Cyrus got sober after years of living this way, years after his father passed away, he found his ability to fall asleep naturally had completely atrophied from disuse; his sober insomnia even worse than it had been in his adolescence. Melatonin, meditation, chamomile, Benadryl—nothing could touch his sleeplessness. It was as if his body was obstinately trying to reclaim the waking it had lost while Cyrus was drinking.

The only thing that helped at all, sometimes, was returning to the dream dialogue game from his childhood. He hadn't had cause to play it for the years of heavy narcotic sleep, and at first when he tried, it felt hokey, contrived. But it was, at least, something to do with his restless mind.

Sometimes, he'd strike upon a turn of phrase or an idea that he'd jot down to explore further in his writing. And sometimes, miracle of miracles, the script started to write itself. Sleep would take over and Cyrus would once more find himself listening in on a conversation between heroes, beloveds.

This was how he started speaking with Scheherazade, Spider-Man, Rimbaud. How he reunited with his father. It's how he started talking with his mother again, after years of dreamless silence.

LISA SIMPSON AND ROYA SHAMS

———— ✳ ————

LISA EYED CYRUS'S MOTHER.

"I didn't expect to see *you* here," Lisa said, saying "you" with the particular vein of incredulity only her voice, among all human voices, could produce.

"Have we met before?" asked Roya.

They were in a white room. Its blankness overwhelmed; against it, Roya's blue lipstick and Lisa's yellow skin pulsed like neon.

"I'm Cyrus's friend. My name is Lisa Simpson."

Roya's eyes got big.

"You know Cyrus? How is he doing? I haven't seen him in years."

"I know! He's talked to me about you. You're not watching from where you are?" Lisa studied Roya's face, which barely moved when she spoke. Maybe it didn't move at all, not even her lips.

"Cyrus must be, what, how old now?" Cyrus's mother used the American "Cyrus" instead of the Persian "Koroosh," but pronounced "Cyrus" the Iranian way, "sigh-e-*ROOSE*"—adding an extra half-syllable in the middle, snapping the r like taffy.

Lisa was getting anxious: "You really can't see him?"

Roya winced. The room began to come into clarity around her, a great hall with high ceilings and windows blocked with long scarlet drapes. A long table, some sort of dark wood. There had been a fancy meal; scattered across the table were melon rinds and lamb bones and half-filled glasses of wine. Something that had once been a roast duck, stuffed with pistachios. There was a fireplace and in it some logs blazed silently, casting shadows of Roya and Lisa many times their actual size.

"It doesn't work like that," Roya said. "It's not flying around, smiling happily down from a cloud."

Two chairs appeared and they both sat down, facing the flames. Lisa was flat, two-dimensional, and when she turned to face Roya's chair there was a fraction of a second where she disappeared completely.

"So you can't see anything on earth?" Lisa's voice relayed some mixture of impatience and disbelief.

"Have you ever heard of the butterfly effect?" asked Roya.

"We read that story in Miss Hoover's class," said Lisa, a little too eagerly. "Ray Bradbury."

"Right. When people think about traveling to the past, they do it with this wild sense of self-importance. Like, 'gosh, I better not step on that flower or my grandfather will never be born.' But in the present we mow our lawns and poison ants and skip parties and miss birthdays all the time. We never think about the effects of that stuff." Roya was working herself up. "Nobody thinks of now as the future past."

On the food table, in between silverware and plates, grass had begun growing. Its growth was visible to the naked eye, getting longer each second. It was patchy grass, not healthy looking, but still it grew and grew quickly until the food remnants and table settings were completely lost in it.

"It's the same way with the future," said Roya. "We plant a tree imagining our kids will play under it one day, or we go to some shitty business meeting because it might be the one where our boss singles us out for a promotion. Every tiny decision becomes mired with importance, and we're immobilized."

Lisa stared. This hadn't been her experience. Wild, grand things did happen to her, quickly, as a result of her actions. It was almost eerie. She couldn't go for a walk or visit a petting zoo without sparking a madcap escapade.

"I don't know," Lisa said. "I don't know."

Roya continued:

"We have difficulty seeing our present selves in history the same way we view our past and future selves. That's all I'm getting at."

The table full of grass had become Lisa's bed, the great hall morphing into Lisa's bedroom. Out the window it was storming, the lightning occasionally illuminating a craggy oak near the glass.

"Sure, that makes sense," said Lisa. She and Roya were sitting next to each other on the bed. Lisa's feet dangled a foot off the floor. "But what does that have to do with Cyrus?"

Roya said, "Well, we fly through our days. We move from one decision to the next, only we're not even aware they're decisions. We treat our minds like crowns, these magnificent crowns on our magnificent autonomies. But our minds aren't crowns. They're clocks. It's why we invest everything in our stories. Stories are the excrement of time. Someone said that."

"Adélia Prado," said Lisa.

"Adélia Prado, right," Roya answered. "How did you know that?" Roya asked.

Lisa blinked. The silence hung between them like a bell.

"I flew once," Lisa said, finally. "I was getting braces, and they put a gas mask over my face. Suddenly I was flying over a giant field, this giant field of flowers and eyeballs and hands."

"That sounds terrifying." Roya was sipping tea now, and getting larger. Against the bed, Lisa's dress looked like a red handkerchief.

"It actually wasn't too bad," Lisa said. "I think I was so excited to be flying I didn't feel any fear."

Roya laughed.

"What?" Lisa asked. Roya stared at her, waiting. Lisa shrunk even smaller, now a drop of yellow paint against a drop of red.

"Oh my gooosh," Lisa said, dragging out the *o* like someone who had just solved a difficult math problem. "I'm so sorry about . . . I forgot about . . ."

"It's fine." Roya chuckled. "I wasn't afraid either. One second I was flying, the next I was dust."

Lisa's face got very flat, almost blurry.

"Turned into dust," she muttered under her breath.

"Turned into dust," Roya replied.

They both sat quietly for a minute. The light was warm and blue, despite the storm outside.

"What did you want to be when you were my age?" asked Lisa, now the size of a teddy bear.

"How old are you?"

"I think I'm eight. Maybe sometimes I'm seven."

The rain was beginning to come in through the windowpane. The glass had gone mushy, bad.

"When I was that age, I had this idea about being an oceanographer florist."

"Hah! What's that?" Lisa was leaning into Roya, like a sunflower bending into the sun.

"We had an uncle who sold flowers," said Roya. "He rented a field where he grew them and every morning he would cut bundles and put them in his bike basket and ride them into the market to sell."

Lisa nodded along, and Roya took a sip from a silver teacup.

"One day I saw pictures of a coral reef in a book from the Tehran library, and I decided I would be the first florist who cut and arranged coral into beautiful bouquets. Taking my uncle's idea and improving it."

"Aw, that's very sweet," Lisa said. "But coral is alive!"

"So were flowers, I figured. So was yeast. I didn't really understand coral. I just wanted to swim in it, to put my fingers through it."

"Soon there won't be any left," said Lisa.

"What's that?" asked Roya.

"Coral. It's all dying."

They both paused.

"How do we move through all this beauty without destroying it?" asked Roya.

Lisa looked up at her. Now when Lisa moved her head her features were lagging a second behind the rest of her face, so her eyes and mouth sort of dragged through the air for a moment before settling into position.

"Stop that," Lisa said.

"Stop what?" asked Roya.

"Stop trying to make everything mean something," Lisa said. "Trying to flatten everything to a symbol or a point. The coral is dying because of microbeads in body wash and because of Monsanto and because there's no reason for anyone powerful enough to do anything about it to do anything about it."

Roya stared down at the little girl, who was now the size of a little girl. Yellow skin, white pearls, red dress. The bedroom was filling with water. A saxophone floated out from under the bed and Lisa picked it up. She started playing a song that seemed to be about the immeasurable mercy of animals, though it had no words.

SIX

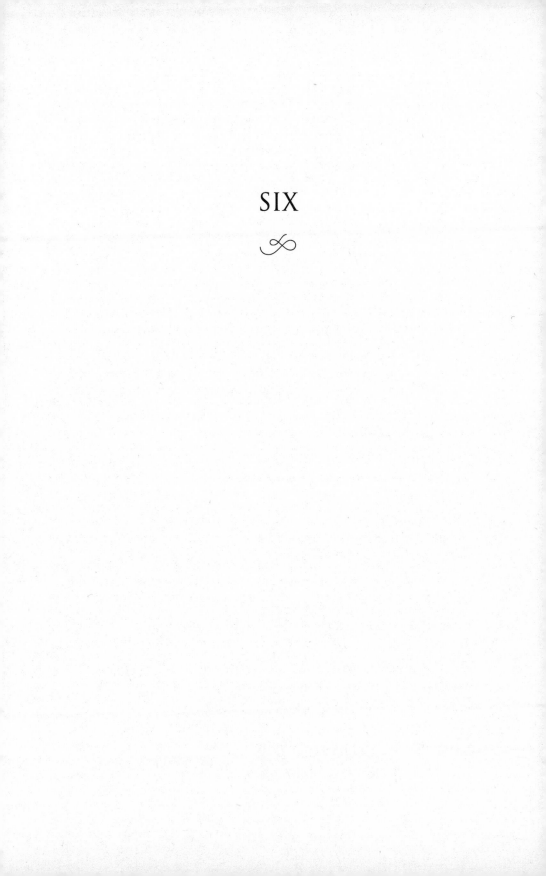

ROYA AND ARASH SHIRAZI

— ✴ —

TEHRAN, 1973

SEVERAL NIGHTS THE PAST MONTH ROYA HAD WOKEN UP COVERED in urine. She was ten years old, too old to still be wetting the bed. Her older brother Arash, nearly twelve, shoulders already getting broad, would pinch his nose at her over breakfast, even after she'd washed and changed out of her wet clothes, saying, "Oof, Roya, you smell like a dead cow."

"Dirt on your head," she'd hiss back.

Roya had stopped drinking water with dinner, gulping down her spoonfuls of dry rice and potato kotlets and only pretending to take sips from the water glass her mother set before her, then dumping it into the sink after dinner. She'd use the bathroom right before bed, staying on the toilet long after she'd finished to ensure she'd expelled every last drop. Her tongue would be so dry it'd scrape hard against the roof of her mouth. Still, she would wake up soaked, reeking.

Her parents largely ignored the issue. Her father, Kamran, would silently shave, brush his boots, and leave for work on the Tehran power grid without saying goodbye. Her mother, Parvin, would ball the sheets and clothes into the basket to take to the laundromat, eyeing Roya with frustration and pity.

When you are ten, shame stitches itself into you like a monogram, broadcasting to the world what holds you, what rules your soul. In school Roya could smell the dank must even though she'd soaped it away and changed into fresh clothes. The scent wasn't so much on her as it was of her, compositional. It clung inside her nose like a kind of rot. She was certain everyone else could smell it.

Later in her life Roya would fantasize about getting a nose job. She was at times obsessed, devastated by her own nose's sweeping bigness. A lover, a British academic, once described her as "Hellenic." She may as well have said "beaky." As Roya aged and grew more and more into her face, she tried to see it as a kind of Persepolian nobleness. A crown worn on the face. This only half worked.

In school, Aghaye Ghorbani would ask her class to solve for x and they would. He told them to list favorite words and phrases and classmates said "mahtab," "firuz," "duset daram." He was trying to make a point about how the most beautiful words ended in vowel sounds, but his students' examples weren't supporting his thesis. Roya studied the faces of her classmates, trying to figure out which ones could smell her stink. Every glance, every furrowed brow, seemed to Roya to be directly at, because of, her.

"Roya?"

She hadn't been paying attention.

"Sorry. What was the question?"

A few classmates snickered.

"Your favorite word, khanoom?"

She panicked.

"Bini?" she offered, saying the Persian word for nose.

The class laughed openly at this, but Aghaye Ghorbani nodded.

"Good! The nose itself is not beautiful, but listen to the word. *Bi-niii*," he said, drawing out the final syllable. "These sounds are undeniably beautiful."

Two girls in the front of the room looked back at Roya, then at each other, and laughed. Roya slid down into her chair, her embarrassment like a stone on her chest, sinking her into the earth.

That night she picked at her food as her family talked around her. Her brother and father spoke about a football match in which a favorite player had been ejected on a dubious red card. Her mother talked about using baking soda to cut the tartness of the pomegranate molasses she'd used in the fessenjan they were eating.

"You can use less sugar that way, Roya jaan" she said to her daughter, who nodded as if taking notes in a future cookbook. Her mother loved her dearly, and loved sharing domestic tricks with her, as if giving Roya a leg up in a future exactly like her own, full of baking soda and pomegranate molasses. Roya, only ten, already knew she wouldn't have a future like her mother's. She didn't know what kind of future she wanted for herself, but when she tried to imagine it, there were no dining tables, no kitchens either. Mostly there was open space, freedom and passion, heat obscuring everything like a candle flame smocking its wick.

That night before bed she sat on the toilet so long her father knocked on the door to make sure she was okay. Roya hadn't drunk water save a few sips at breakfast and her throat felt raw, brittle. When she curled into bed, she prayed to God that she would wake up dry, that he would spare her parents the disappointment of another wet morning.

"Can you please control yourself tonight?" Arash asked from his side of their shared bedroom. "It stinks enough in here already."

Roya said nothing in response, knowing any rebuke would only encourage more cruelty. And she knew he was right, too. They wanted the same thing.

That night, as Roya and Arash slept restlessly in their bedroom, their parents whispered in the next room about the things parents whisper about: Kamran had received notice that his power company would be shut down. He had heard about a textile distributor who was hiring electrical workers in Qom, two hours away from their home in Tehran. Parvin didn't want him to take it, didn't want him to live away from their family. But they both understood there were few alternatives, the economy growing worse and worse for folks like them. They knew people who had already turned to unspeakable crimes—against others and against themselves—to make ends meet. Parvin had a cousin to whom she was forbidden to speak because of how she'd been paying her rent. Each week, it seemed, there was another story.

Outside, it was atypically chilly for Tehran. Foxes slinked around the dark hunting for partridges. Parks of ironwood and eelgrass sucked potassium from city soil. Roya was dreaming of flowers, great yellow and red flowers growing from everywhere, out the walls of buildings and from the eyes of goats. When she woke, it was to a hiss, like a balloon deflating. She felt a pressure around her, a folding into space. She didn't move but opened her eyes a little in the dark. Standing over her in her bed was Arash. Her brother's pants were unzipped; he was urinating directly onto her.

SEVEN

From: Rear Admiral William M. Fogarty, USN

To: Commander in Chief, U.S. Central Command

Subj: FORMAL INVESTIGATION INTO THE CIRCUMSTANCES SURROUNDING THE DOWNING OF A COMMERCIAL AIR-LINER BY THE USS VINCENNES (CG. 49) ON 3 JULY 1988 (U)

(t) The sound of missiles going off was recorded on IADNet.

TUESDAY

———— ❖ ————

Cyrus Shams, Zee Novak, and Sad James

KEADY UNIVERSITY, 7 FEB 2017

SITTING ON THE NAPLES CAFÉ PATIO DURING THE OPEN MIC'S intermission, Cyrus had been telling Zee and their friend Sad James about his fight with Gabe, about his sponsor's obnoxious white gall and how it'd all cemented this new idea for a writing project—maybe even a book—about martyrdom.

"So like a whole collection of poems just about people who died?" Sad James asked as he pulled from his back pocket a little red plastic pouch of Bugler tobacco.

"Like that Jim Carroll song," added Zee.

"I'm not sure exactly yet," said Cyrus. "That's what I'm trying to figure out. I'm writing, it's taking shape as I go. I don't even know that it'll be just poems."

There were two campus coffee shops at Keady. One, Bluebarn, featured single-sourced beans, baristas with self-serious framed certificates advertising their training at "Espresso Academy," and beautiful mid-century modern furniture. Every time Cyrus had been there, the baristas were almost off-puttingly friendly, Stepfordian. He'd felt tempted to ask for his coffee with just a splash of misanthropy, please. Or at least sullen ambivalence. Their eagerness felt offensive, too much to bear.

The other cafe—called Naples though it was owned by a Palestinian-Turkish couple—featured Costco coffee beans, a single rusty and unreliable espresso machine, and uncomfortable campus-surplus tables and chairs. The two coffee shops were on the same block, and Naples wasn't even particularly cheaper than Bluebarn, but out of some oblique sense of cultural loyalty or class antipathy, this had become the spot favored by the local young countercultural-ists. It's where one might find fold-and-staple punk zines with names like *Rat!* and *SPUNK GXRLS* left on chairs, where undergraduate DSA chapter meetings continued late into the night while teenage Marx-ists laughed loudly through sugary lattes and shabby beards.

The Naples Tuesday night open mic had become a mainstay of Cyrus and Zee's friendship. It was a small affair, not much to distin-guish it from the myriad other open mics happening elsewhere in the country—except this was *their* open mic, *their* organic commu-nity of beautiful weirdos—old hippies singing Pete Seeger, trans kids rapping about liberation, passionate spoken-word performances by nurses and teenagers and teachers and cooks. As with any campus open mic, there was the occasional frat dude coming to play sets of smirky acoustic rap covers and overearnest breakup narratives. But even they were welcome, and mostly it felt like a safe little oasis of amongness in the relative desert of their Indiana college town, a healthy way to spend the time they were no longer using to get drunk or high.

Naturally, Naples didn't have its own sound equipment, so Zee would usually show up fifteen minutes early with his beat-up Yamaha PA to set up for Sad James, who hosted every week. Sad James was called this to distinguish him from DJ James, a guy who cycled nightly through the campus bars. DJ James was not a particularly interesting artist, but he was well-known enough in the campus community to warrant Sad James's nominative prefix, which began as a joke but somehow stuck, and to which Sad James had grown accustomed with good humor, even occasionally doing small shows under the name. Sad James was a quiet white guy, long blond hair framing his lightly stubbled face, who played intensely solemn electronic songs, punctuated by sparse circuit-bent blips and bloops, and over time at Keady, he had become one of Zee and Cyrus's most resilient and trusted friends.

On this night, Cyrus had read a poem early, an older experimental piece from a series where he'd been assigning words to each digit 0–9, then using an Excel document to generate a lyric out of those words as the digits appeared in the Fibonacci sequence: "lips sweat teeth lips spread teeth lips drip deep deep sweat skin," etc. It was bad, but he loved reading them out loud, the rhythms and repetitions and weird little riffs that emerged. Sad James did an older piece where the lyrics "burning with the human stain / she dries up, dust in the rain" were repeated and modulated over molten beeps from an old circuit-bent Game Boy. Zee—a drummer in his free time who idolized J Dilla and John Bonham and Max Roach and Zach Hill in equal measure—hadn't brought anything of his own to perform that evening, but did have a little bongo to help accompany any acoustic acts who wanted it.

On the patio listening to Cyrus talk about his new project, Zee said, "I could see it being a bunch of different poems in the voices of all your different historical martyr obsessions?" Then to Sad James, Zee added, "Cyrus has been plastering our apartment with these big black-and-white printouts of all their terrifying faces. Bobby Sands in our kitchen, Joan of Arc in our hallway."

Sad James made his eyes get big.

"I just like having them present," Cyrus said, slumping into his chair. He didn't add that he'd been reading about them in the library, his mystic martyrs, that he'd taped a great grid of their grayscale printed faces above his bed, half believing it would work like those tapes that promised to teach you Spanish while you slept, that somehow their lived wisdoms would pass into him as he dreamt. Among the Tank Man, Bobby Sands, Falconetti as Joan of Arc, Cyrus had a picture of his parents' wedding day. His mother, seated in a sleeved white dress, smiling tightly at the camera while his father, in a tacky gray tux, sat grinning next to her holding her hand. Above their heads, a group of attendees held an ornate white sheet. It was the only picture of his mother he had. Next to his mother, his father beamed, bright in a way that made it seem he was radiating the light himself.

Zee went on: "So you could write a poem where Joan of Arc is like, 'Wow, this fire is so hot' or whatever. And then a poem where Hussain is like, 'Wow, sucks that I wouldn't kneel.' You know what I mean?"

Cyrus laughed.

"I tried some of that! But see, that's where it gets corny. What could I possibly say about the martyrdom of Hussain or Joan of Arc or whoever that hasn't already been said? Or that's worth saying?"

Sad James asked who Hussain was and Zee quickly explained the trial in the desert, Hussain's refusing to kneel and being killed for it.

"You know, Hussain's head is supposedly still buried in Cairo?" Zee said, smiling. "Cairo, which is in which country again?"

Cyrus rolled his eyes at his friend, who was, as Cyrus liked to remind him when he got too greatest-ancient-civilization-on-earth about things, only *half* Egyptian.

"Damn," Sad James said. "I would've just kneeled and crossed my fingers behind my back. Who am I trying to impress? Later I could call take-backsies. I'd just say I tripped and landed on my knees or something."

The three friends laughed. Justine, an open mic regular whose *Blonde on Blonde*–era pea-coat-and-harmonica-rack Bob Dylan act was a mainstay of the open mic, came outside to ask Zee for a cigarette. He obliged her with an American Spirit Yellow, which she lit around the corner as she began speaking into her cell phone.

In moments like these Cyrus still sometimes felt like asking to bum one too—he'd been a pack-and-a-half-a-day smoker before he got sober, and continued his habit even after he'd kicked everything else. "Quit things in the order they're killing you," Gabe told him once. After a year clean he turned his attention to cigarettes, which he finally managed to kick completely by tapering: from one and a half packs a day to a pack to half a pack to five cigarettes and so on until he was just smoking a single cigarette every few days and then, none at all. He could probably get away with bumming the occasional cigarette now and again, but in his mind he was saving that for something momentous: his final moments lying in the grass dying from a gunshot wound, or walking in slow motion away from a burning building.

"So what are you thinking then? A novel? Or like . . . a poetic martyr field guide?" asked Zee.

"I'm really not sure yet. But my whole life I've thought about my mom on that flight, how meaningless her death was. Truly literally like, meaningless. Without meaning. The difference between 290 dead and 289. It's actuarial. Not even tragic, you know? So was she a martyr? There has to be a definition of the word that can accommodate her. That's what I'm after."

Sad James and Zee nodded supportively along. They both knew Cyrus well enough to not be flustered by his directness. But Cyrus was, for his part, more than a little surprised by the words as they came out his mouth, how they gave shape to something that had long been formless within him. It was like the language in the air that night was a mold he was pouring around his curiosity. Flour thrown on a ghost.

"Her death is tragic on the human level," Sad James countered. "That difference was tragic to you, to your dad, to your families."

"Sure, sure, but that level of tragedy wasn't legible to the U.S. or to Iran. It's not legible to empire. Meaningless at the level of empire is what I mean by meaningless. Like my uncle. He's not even dead, but the Iran-Iraq War fucked him up so bad he doesn't even leave his house anymore. He thinks he still sees ghosts and soldiers and shit. And he didn't enlist in the Iranian army because he wanted free college or health insurance or whatever people do here. In Iran there's no choice. If you're a man, you're drafted. If I went back today, I wouldn't be allowed to leave until I did my military service."

On the air, the smell of tobacco mixed with Chinese takeout from the spot across the street, spilled beer from the bar next door. In the void between the city's two miniature skylines—each made up of apartment complexes and university buildings and banks and student housing—a few stars floated around like the last Cheerios in a bowl of black milk. Cyrus was working himself up:

"The version of my uncle he might have been was killed in the war, and for no reason at all. Him personally losing his mind didn't lose or win the war. It's meaningless. That's what fucks me up. My dad drops me off at college and then dies like, barely a year later. I'm not saying all this to say 'poor me' or even 'poor us.' But none of those deaths meant anything. I don't think it's crazy to want mine to. Or to study people whose deaths mattered, you know? People who at least tried to make their deaths mean something."

"It's not crazy," Zee said. "I get it. Or I mean, I don't get it, I don't have your experience. But I understand why you want to write this." He paused.

Sad James asked, "Do you think you'll put this stuff in the book? Your mom, dad, uncle? Or treat it more like reporting? Like research?"

"Great question," said Cyrus, shrugging his shoulders. "All I know is I'm fascinated. Like in Iran, there are these schools for the children of men killed in the war, who they call 'martyrs.' Those martyr schools are the good schools, the fancy schools, you try to get your kids into them. Kids with healthy parents grow up jealous of orphans, because the children of martyrs get automatic college admission, all this special treatment. I've heard of children of martyrs trying to hide it, like they're ashamed of all the privilege. Like trust fund kids, except instead of trust funds they have dead parents. It's nuts."

Sad James shook his head in disbelief, taking it in. Zee was now lighting a cigarette of his own. He started smoking early, with great affect, the sort of teenage smoker who ashes the cigarette when it doesn't need to be ashed and takes long extravagant inhales. Though he'd figured it out a bit over the years, there was still something thespian about the way he smoked, like watching Elizabeth Taylor smoke onscreen. His slow-burning American Spirit papers heightened this effect.

Sad James offered, "It reminds me of that art exhibit in New York, I think at MoMA, with that artist who's dying in the museum? Something like that? Did you guys see this?"

"Dying in the museum?" Zee asked.

"Yeah, there was a thing going around Twitter. You probably saw it."

Cyrus and Zee looked at each other and shrugged. Cyrus had missed the social media train completely, a small point of pride for him now, though his friends still filled him in on all the daily outrages, goofy memes, famous people volleying passive-aggressive bon mots at each other. Sad James pulled out his phone, clicked around for a moment. His cigarette was burning unevenly between his right pointer and middle fingers.

"Ah, here it is. It's at the Brooklyn Museum, not MoMA."

He handed the phone over to Cyrus, and Zee bent over Cyrus's chair to look. Open was a tweet of a flyer with 2.2k likes and 465 retweets. On the left side of the flyer was a woman's face, a face dusted with the cosmic jaggedness so often found on the dying. She didn't seem too terribly old in the picture, maybe fifty, though it was hard to tell with the very sick, and her bald head emphasized how tightly her sallow skin was pulled over her skull. Even in the tiny cell phone pic, her eyes looked like deep dry wells—you could almost hear the dryness echoing. On the right side of the flyer, in giant letters: DEATH-SPEAK, a curious construction that could be read either as a command or a modified noun. Beneath it:

"Internationally renowned visual artist Orkideh presents her final installation, DEATH-SPEAK. Visitors will be invited to speak with the artist during the final weeks and days of her life, which she will spend onsite at the museum. No appointments necessary. Opening Jan 2nd."

"Whoa," said Cyrus, handing the phone to Zee.

"It seems kind of exactly like what you're talking about, right, Cyrus?" said Sad James.

"I think so, yeah. Wow. I mean, I don't know. I think she's even Iranian."

"What?" said Zee, reading the phone. Then, catching up with the conversation, "Wait, how do you know that?"

When Cyrus was a boy, his father Ali would drive him on

once-yearly trips to Chicago to visit a Persian restaurant called Ali's Sofreh ("You didn't know I had a restaurant?" Ali Shams would joke with his son). It was, as far as they knew, the only Persian anything within a reasonable driving radius of Fort Wayne. These trips were a tremendous indulgence for Ali Shams, who viewed even cheap fast food as an extravagance. For Cyrus, they were the source of incredible anticipation—he would fantasize for days in advance about what he'd read on the drive, about what he'd order at the restaurant. Even years after his father died, in some Pavlovian trace, thinking about anything Chicago—the Sears Tower, Navy Pier, Scottie Pippen—still made Cyrus hungry.

Once, during a trip to Ali's Sofreh when Cyrus was eight, Ali had begun quietly pointing to each server, each restaurant worker.

"Persian," he whispered to Cyrus about a woman pouring water. "Arab," he said about a moppy-haired kid bussing a dirty table. "Persian," he said about the balding man sitting alone at a table with papers and a calculator. "White," he said about a curly-haired woman talking on the phone behind the bar. Cyrus couldn't understand how his father could know these things. To him, each of the people Ali'd pointed to looked vaguely like himself—dark-skinned, dark-haired.

"I thought everyone here was like us," Cyrus said to his father.

"Of course! That's what they want," Ali explained. "They want you to think everyone here is Iranian. It makes the restaurant seem *authentic*."

Their waitress came to check on the table and Ali asked her for the bill. When she left to retrieve it, he looked at his son.

"What do you think?" he asked.

Cyrus paused for a moment.

"Arab?"

Cyrus's father shook his head and laughed. The waitress returned with the bill and Ali studied the bill for a moment, then handed her a plastic card.

"Persian," he whispered to his son.

Cyrus was mystified. Incredulous, he asked, "How do you know?!"

Smiling, Ali said, "It's easy. We're just *uglier*."

In anyone else's mouth this might have seemed self-deprecating, cruel even. For a second Cyrus had wondered whether Ali got the English confused, meant it the other way around, that everyone else was uglier than Iranians. But something in his father's smirk suggested to Cyrus that he knew exactly what he was saying. There was a kind of pride in Ali's face when he said it, that Iranians were uglier. There was a satisfaction that took Cyrus years to unpack.

That day on the patio of the coffee shop looking at the picture of the dying artist on his friend's telephone, Cyrus had seen exactly what his father was able to see. What Ali had called "ugliness." Not scornfully. This artist—Orkideh—had undoubtedly been beautiful, was still beautiful even—her high cheekbones and great wide eyes were undeniably striking. But ugliness, the Iranian ugliness Ali had meant, was earned. Cyrus's father, who listened almost exclusively to the Rolling Stones even before coming to America, who called the Beatles "a band for girls." Who owned exactly three pairs of pants: two for work, one for the house. Cyrus's father, whose arms were perpetually crisscrossed with old and new farm scars, torn raw by the idiot terror of frightened birds. Cyrus's handsome ugly dead father.

It had taken Cyrus a decade, more, to really be able to identify what Ali had meant by "ugly." The hardness of a smile line, softness in the folds under an eye. But here on the face of this dying artist, that ugliness was everywhere apparent.

Instead of trying to explain all this to his friends, though, Cyrus said simply, "I'm pretty sure 'orkideh' is Farsi for 'orchid.'"

"Wow," said Zee.

"Whoa, yeah, wow," added Sad James. "You should write to her about your project. I wonder if there's a way to email her." He tapped at his phone for a minute. Justine opened and closed the Naples door behind them, pouring a random prerecorded acoustic ballad out into the patio air.

"You were right!" Sad James reported, poking at his phone. "It says she grew up in Iran and left 'sometime after the revolution.' Says she's got a terminal cancer diagnosis and is refusing radiation. She's living and sleeping and eating fully in the museum, accepting no treatment or drugs except pain management. Says she will talk to museum guests for four hours a day until she can't."

"Honestly, you should go to the exhibit and meet her," said Zee.

Cyrus snorted. The idea of simply jetting across the country as if driving to the store seemed to him a luxury reserved for Richard Branson, Bill Gates. "Sure, I'll just fly to New York to catch an art exhibit. Then I'll fly to Madrid to catch a bullfight. I'll fly to the Orient to trade spice."

Sad James laughed, but Zee persisted.

"Seriously, Cyrus, why not? You're starting on this whole big project around 'alternative martyrdom' or whatever, and then there just happens to be a dying Iranian woman saying 'come talk to me about death'? I'm not a clouds-parting-burning-bush sort of guy. But if anything has ever seemed like a sign, this seems like a sign."

Cyrus shook his head:

"What world are you living in where you think I'm available to just up and fly to New York on a whim?" he said.

"I mean . . . ," said Sad James, cocking his head.

Zee leaned over the table, said, "Dude, you're just treading water here. You have been for years. You work that bizarre job pretending to die or whatever, not even full-time. You graduated years ago, you don't have a partner. You just mope around not writing, feeling sorry for yourself. You're the definition of available."

"Jesus," Cyrus said.

"*Flexible.*" Sad James corrected, trying to soften Zee's language. "You're currently *open* to the *vicissitudes* of fate."

"You want to be a writer," Zee went on. "*This* is what writers do. They follow the story. It's an inflection point. You can keep being the sad sober guy in Indiana who talks about being a writer, or you can go be one."

Cyrus studied Zee's face, which had grown suddenly flinty, dry. His roommate's tawny skin seemed pulled extra tight, almost quivering against the hard flesh underneath. Cyrus couldn't deny that he'd been treading water, that he was approaching his thirties with no meaningful achievements to his name save his sobriety, save a useless English degree he'd cheated and manipulated his way to get.

"I guess I do still have my mom's bounty," Cyrus offered, finally.

He called the money the U.S. had paid his father for his mother's death her "bounty." Even though the U.S. never fully claimed responsibility for shooting her plane out of the sky, in 1996 they eventually gave the families of each victim a check: $300,000 for wage-earning men, $150,000 for women and children (the majority of the dead). Cyrus's father had never touched this money, instead leaving it in an account to give to Cyrus on his college graduation. Cyrus had used some of it to pay off his college debt, a bit more to pay off various credit cards he'd run up. After that, he'd felt gross using what money was left for anything so banal as simply living. Using blood money, even for good, felt bad. Inescapably. Still, the idea of visiting the artist was growing on him. Sad James and Zee winced a little when he said "bounty."

"Okay, I guess I *could* go out for a weekend. It is within the realm of possibility. But I have no idea what I'd say to her."

"Just ask her why she's doing what she's doing," Zee said. "It sounds like it's what you're talking about, like she wants her dying to mean something."

"Honestly, she might just be in a ton of medical debt," added Sad James. "One last gig so her family doesn't inherit a billion dollars of doctor bills."

"Christ. It's so fucked up that that could actually be the reason," said Cyrus.

Sad James nodded, then shook his head. Zee ashed his cigarette dramatically, then said, "Listen, if you end up going to New York, I'll go with you. We can split the cost of a shitty hotel. I'll get someone to cover my shifts for a weekend. We could go *this* weekend. Why wait? It'd actually be rad to get to bop around the city for a minute while you work on your book stuff."

"Shit, man. I'll be with you two in spirit," said Sad James. He worked a merciless corporate billing gig that only grudgingly gave him even the weekends off. "I really think you two should do it, though."

Inside, the open mic attendees were beginning to stir, staring out through the Naples windows at the friends' table, wondering when they'd finish smoking and come back inside to resume the evening. Cyrus was not in the habit of spending lavishly, or spending much at all. Between what he made working at the hospital and answering phones a few nights a week at Jade Café, he made enough to eat and pay rent. But this artist, what she was doing, seemed pretty extraordinary. An opportunity. Eerie, even.

In Cyrus's active addiction it had taken dread and doom bringing him to his knees, or euphoric physical ecstasy elevating him half-literally out of his body—to break through his dense numb fugue. In sobriety, he still sometimes erroneously expected this of the universe—a stark shock of embodied rapture, the angel dropping from the sky to smack him with clarity's two-by-four. Cyrus was beginning to realize that the world didn't actually work this way, that sometimes epiphany was as subtle as a friend showing you something they saw on Twitter.

"This weekend?" Cyrus asked hesitantly.

"She's dying, Cyrus," said Zee. "I don't think you can wait."

Cyrus chewed on his bottom lip.

"Fuck. I think I'm gonna do it," he said, feeling suddenly thrilled.

EIGHT

ZEE NOVAK

———— ✳ ————

EARLY SPRING, THAT'S WHEN I FIRST THOUGHT I MIGHT LOVE HIM. That time of year when, in Indiana, each afternoon the sun came out to melt the previous night's snow. Curious buds poked their heads through the topsoil into the suspicious heat, only to be rebuked at night by sudden frosts. I was waiting tables at Green Nile, slinging weed here and there to friends. Cyrus was still answering phones at Jade Café, hanging out at the library, at Lucky's Bar.

We'd been living together for a year, not long after we'd both graduated, me a semester before him even though he'd started school before me, spending our time dating whoever was in front of us, drinking a lot. This was a year before Cyrus got sober, before Gabe and AA, before I osmotically stopped drinking in solidarity, to make things easier for Cyrus. Making things easier for Cyrus, I realized only much later, had begun to take up a lot of my energy.

Once a week, Cyrus and I would go to this guy Jude's house off the highway. Cyrus found Jude's post on Craigslist saying he needed some yardwork done, that he could offer fresh groceries in exchange. Intrigued, especially at the possibility "fresh groceries" might be a euphemism for something more exciting, we got in touch. It turned out "fresh groceries" literally meant fresh groceries. Every Saturday we'd get a little high and go over to Jude's house ostensibly to do yard work, but really to let Jude sit in his underwear in a rickety lawn chair drinking a beer and watching us pretend to do yard work.

He never touched himself, never touched us either. He'd just lay there in nothing but dingy tighty-whities and sandals, watching us. The work was beside the point. Once the lawn was mowed and the hedges trimmed, he'd just have us pull nails from stacks of old boards, dig and fill big holes in the yard. It was the watching-us-work that did it for him, whatever *it* was. And in return, after our weekly hour, he'd take us to his kitchen where he had shelves and shelves of grocery items— rice, lima beans, peaches in syrup, mostly scratched, dented, expired—and let us load up a few paper shopping bags.

He said, one of the few times he said anything more than which pile of logs to move, which two-by-fours to paint, that he was a wholesale grocery distributor for a few of the local supermarkets. That he sometimes managed to bring "stuff like this" home. Cyrus called our Saturday visits to Jude "grocery shopping."

"Like volunteering in a co-op," he'd said once on our way to Jude's house.

"Except sexier," I added.

"Oh my god," said Cyrus. "Yeah. Are we doing sex work? Is this sex work? Are we selling our bodies?"

"Angela Davis would say we're all selling our bodies," I said, smiling. "That the only difference between a coal miner and a prostitute is our retrograde puritan values about sex. And misogyny."

Cyrus rolled his eyes, asked, "And what would Zee Novak say?"

I laughed: "Zee Novak says free groceries are free groceries."

So every Saturday we went, worked under Jude's creepy but ultimately unthreatening watch. He was a shrimpy guy, not too much older than us but already balding, wispy blond hair over a perpetual wince, the sort of crestfallen man who looked like he'd been getting short-shrifted for a lifetime and had given up complaining about it. All sinew and pale white, it seemed like this hour of watching us work in the sun might be the only time all week he spent outdoors.

This particular Saturday we arrived a little later than we normally did. Cyrus had traded some of his scrips for a fentanyl patch and spent the previous evening like a chemist, dissolving the patch in alcohol, then evaporating the alcohol over an old glass chessboard.

"Sixty-four tidy doses!" he beamed, holding up the chessboard once his tincture finished drying. He took such pride in being "good at drugs." I could take them or leave them; my mom was always fucked up on some combination of prescriptions and ayurvedic snake oil, benzos, and traditional Egyptian remedies based on the Book of Thoth.

"You know they could diagnose and treat diabetes?" she'd say of our ancient Egyptian ancestors.

"So can we," I'd think but not say.

Still, Cyrus's enthusiasms were infectious, so we each licked two chessboard fentanyl squares and drove over to Jude's. The feeling started floaty, like I was hovering an inch above the passenger seat of Cyrus's car, which was itself hovering an inch off the road. Then, it was like wind lifting us up, like wind lifting off a leaf, like the wind saying its own name—that uncanny and light.

Jude's house was a tidy ranch home just off the highway. He came to the door before we knocked, wearing, as ever, nothing but his loose tighty-whities, buttery yellow around the crotch and waist, and sagging from his groin as his blotchy pale skin sagged over them. He walked us through his house, where two blond dogs slept cramped over each other in a wire living room kennel, and out to his back-yard. There were wind chimes hanging in front of every window in the house, but on the inside, like low-tech burglar alarms. Some windows had multiple sets of wind chimes, wind chimes even hung from the blades of the ceiling fan in the living room.

"What're the dogs' names?" I asked Jude, trying to make con-versation.

"The big one is Noah. The loud one's Shiloh."

The dogs looked like brothers. At a glance they seemed the same size, and neither one was making a sound. Cyrus shot me a quick smirk.

In the backyard, there was a massive stack of logs, and a cartoon-ishly large axe leaned against a great tree stump.

"I'm having some friends over for a bonfire tonight," Jude said. "I need that chopped into firewood." His pink nipples were nearly invisible, almost as pale as his skin. "Quickly." Without another word, he pulled his lawn chair into the shade of the patio awning, put on a pair of headphones, and began watching us.

The air was thick; I was already sweating from the fentanyl. A light breeze made my clammy arms feel extra cold, the way chewing mint gum makes water taste cool. Cyrus looked at the wood, then at me, and asked, "Have you ever, uh, chopped wood?"

We both laughed.

"What do you think?" I said.

Cyrus shrugged.

"People way dumber than us do it all the time," he said, picking up the axe.

"I don't know that intelligence is the success variable here," I said. Cyrus was tall but the axe was giant. It made him look slight.

"Here, hold this," he said, balancing a triangular log on the stump, holding a finger on its tip like a football.

"Excuse me?" I said. "Hold this here with my finger, my finger on my lovely hand, which is still attached to my lovely arm? Like Lucy from *Peanuts*? While you swing at it with an axe?"

Cyrus paused.

"Damn, maybe we *are* too dumb for this." He laughed.

"Or too high," I added.

Jude was watching us from his chair, unmoving. From somewhere he'd procured a can of Coors Light, which was sweating, unopened, at his feet.

I took the axe from Cyrus and set the log up on the stump. It felt kind of deliciously elemental, like the whole heft of it had just been shot out of a volcano, or pulled from a magical stone. Most of my days were spent tapping food orders into point-of-service computers at work, thinking about playing drums without actually finding time or occasion to play them. The axe had a drumstick's simple sense of purpose. Hold this, hit that. I brought it behind my head and onto the wood. Clumsy, but I did chip away a little corner piece of the log.

"Kindling!" Cyrus shouted, excited. "You made a kindling!" For all his oscillating between self-loathing and self-pity, Cyrus always seemed sincerely joyful at his friends' most banal successes. Even then.

"We're a couple of regular Johnny Appleseeds," he said.

"And there's our big blue ox," I said, nodding over to Jude.

Cyrus furrowed his brow, then nodded:

"You're thinking of Paul Bunyan," he corrected.

"Hm?"

"Paul Bunyan had the giant blue ox." Cyrus was always doing that, correcting people. Even while stoned on fentanyl. Even on the whitest shit imaginable.

"Man, shut up," I said, bringing the axe back down on the wood. The sun was weaving in and out behind the clouds. Jude adjusted his crotch, cracked open the beer.

Slowly, Cyrus and I made messy work of the logs. It felt like we were controlling geometry, bending physics to our will. Occasionally, sparrows would come into the yard around us to peck at the soil.

"Li'l worm gobblers," Cyrus said idly, which made us both laugh way harder than it should have.

After we'd been at it for fifteen, twenty minutes, Jude shifted a bit, called out, "Hey!" He pointed to a rubber tire in a brush pile in the corner of the yard. "You guys can use that if you want," he said.

Cyrus and I looked at the tire, then at each other, then back at Jude, perplexed.

Jude sighed, stood up, walked dramatically over to the tire. With exaggerated effort, he lifted it and placed it down on the stump.

"You put the logs in this," Jude said. "Then you don't have to collect them when they split everywhere."

His voice was weirdly baritone, like hearing a small bird sing like a tuba. He sighed again in extravagant exasperation and went back to his chair. His back was streaked with oily white suntan lotion skids, barely visible against his pale skin.

"Thanks," I called to him, standing a couple logs up within the tire, then stepping back so Cyrus could swing. He brought the axe down on a log, hard, and it fractured neatly inside the tire.

"He was right," Cyrus said in mild surprise. "Cool."

"I still can't figure out if this is fucked up," I said. "Letting him watch us like this. Are we doing an ethical compromise?"

"That's a you question, Zee," said Cyrus.

"What's that thing about money being the externalization of all man's capacity?" I asked. "How do groceries fit into that?"

"Look at me being a capacious man!" Cyrus said, grinning, bringing the axe down hard.

"For canned beets and mushroom soup," I said. "That's . . . better? Than money? I think?"

Cyrus had stopped listening. An arc of sweat had formed around the neck of his green T-shirt, making a little brown parabola beneath his Adam's apple.

"You think we could lick a couple more squares when we get home?" he asked. "Without getting pukey?"

"I don't know. I'm still feeling pretty good."

My brain felt like a flooded orchard. All the flowers—gold, indigo, white, violet—just floating along the water. Cyrus heaved the axe again. Each hard crack of the wood felt momentous, like it was announcing a great person's birth. One of the dogs inside had begun barking at the cracking wood.

"Shut up, Noah!" shouted Jude, annoyed to be broken from his observant trance.

"Wasn't Shiloh supposed to be the loud one?" I whispered to Cyrus. He just smiled, brought the axe down. It thudded dully and bounced out of his hand. I saw it sitting on the grass, but it took a beat to comprehend something was amiss.

"Ah, are you okay?" I asked Cyrus. The axe had struck the rubber of the tire, then sprung free from his grip.

"Shit—" he said. I looked down. The axe was lying on the grass by his left foot, but peering over I saw his blue canvas shoe was torn open, purpling.

"Oh fuck," I said.

Shiloh or Noah was barking uncontrollably now. Jude shot up.

"What happened!" he asked. Running over to us, catching sight of Cyrus's foot, he said, "What . . . what is that?"

"Fuck," said Cyrus.

"It's *blood,* Jude!" I snapped. "Do you have—can we use your bathtub?"

Cyrus had gone pale. He was moving his head to look at his foot from different angles, almost incredulous, studying it like, what's the trick? What's really going on here?

Jude led us quickly back through his house to a bathtub, Cyrus leaning on me and hopping along on his good foot. A wooden wind chime hung in front of the bathroom mirror, doubling itself in the glass. A smaller one dangled from the towel rack.

"It honestly doesn't even hurt," said Cyrus, stunned, staring at his bloody shoe.

"That's not a good thing," I said, shooting him a look to remind him we'd been licking potent pain meds designed for the terminally ill.

"Shit shit shit shit," Jude said, who in his ludicrous underwear looked like a boiled chicken.

Cyrus said, "I should take my shoe off?" asking it like a question.

"It's probably going to look worse than it is," said Jude to himself, more wish than assessment of observable reality.

Cyrus sat down on the toilet lid and held his feet over the bathtub. He looked some combination of stunned and high. So was I, to be honest. The flooded orchard in my head was a roiling ocean now, the flowers all lost under the fuzz of sea foam. Jude was pacing between the bathroom and hallway, staring down at the little carpet trail of blood and muck we'd brought in, shaking his head.

I helped Cyrus take his shoe off, a ratty blue canvas Vans sneaker that was torn open just below the toe, wet with a purple-black throb of blood. I slid it off gingerly. Cyrus winced, and—there's no other way to say it—I poured it out. I was shocked at how much blood there was, how much hadn't been absorbed by Cyrus's sock and the shoe itself. It seemed to violate some physics principle, how the shoe could have held that much blood plus a whole foot. Jude gagged theatrically behind us. Cyrus smiled a little—

"Okay, *that* did hurt," he said, inhaling through his clenched teeth as I pulled off his wet black sock. Somehow he was still grinning.

"Do you need . . . gloves? Gloves? I have some gloves, some-where," Jude said, recovering from his gags, disappearing into the hallway eager to have landed upon an excuse to leave.

A dog was barking. I turned on the bathtub faucet. From the hallway, Jude screamed, "Noah! Shut! The! Fuck! Up!"

"You know, in Islam, Noah's this totally messed-up prophet," Cyrus said, eerily nonplussed. "His neighbors ignore him when he tries to convert them, so Noah *asks* God to drown them." I gently pulled his foot under the stream of water, which turned pink-red as it went down the drain. I could finally see the gash—not much bigger than a quarter, but it seemed deep.

"I think we might need to go to the hospital, Cyrus," I said.

He wasn't paying attention.

"The whole thing is nuts," Cyrus went on. "I think Noah was like, Methuselah's grandson. Just asking God to kill basically all of mankind. And then he lived to be a thousand years old."

"Cyrus—" I said.

Jude emerged in the doorway with a pair of flowery garden gloves, crusted with dirt.

"Are these"—he paused, realizing the answer to his question before he asked it—"anything?"

The hole in Cyrus's foot was weirdly round to have come from an axe. I said so, then added, "I guess I don't know what an axe wound is supposed to look like."

"Do you really think we need to go to the hospital?" Cyrus said. "It looks like the blood is maybe slowing down."

He was right. The hue of the water circling the drain now was more a soft pink, like the frayed edges of a sunset.

"Yeah, I think it is too," I said. Then, to Jude, "Do you have any gauze? Or bandages?" Jude disappeared swiftly again. The wind chimes hanging in front of the bathroom mirror rattled with the wind of his exit.

"Do you want to go to the hospital?" I asked Cyrus. "It's up to you."

"Not unless I'm going to like, die, if I don't," he said, then added, "though it would be hilarious to hear you try to explain our foray into lumberjackery."

I laughed a little. We probably *should* have gone to the hospital—for weeks, maybe months after this, Cyrus walked with a little limp. The wound never really healed, just kind of plummed and flared over into a dull ache that according to Cyrus never fully went away, though he hardly ever mentioned it. In that moment though, sitting in the weirdness of the situation, in ridiculous Jude's ridiculous bathroom, I just laughed and turned the water off. The gash was pink, pink turning slowly to red, but not gushing anymore. My ears were ringing with the sound of a gong not struck for years. Jude emerged with an unopened roll of paper towel under his arm and, in his hand, a circle of gray matte duct tape and a tube of Neosporin.

"Really?" I said at Jude's assortment of first aid. Cyrus giggled. Jude was still wearing nothing but his underwear, hadn't used the excuse of his exit to throw on some basketball shorts or a T-shirt, anything more befitting the urgency of the situation.

"I'm not a fucking nurse," he snarled. "And I need you two to leave. People are coming over in a couple hours and now I need to clean all this mess," he said, gesturing toward the blood-stained carpet. "I don't care if you go home or go to the hospital," he said in a high-pitched whine, "but I need you gone." He handed me the paper towel and I ripped it out of the plastic packaging, used it to pat Cyrus's foot dry.

"Do you have any coconut juice?" Cyrus asked Jude. Then to me, "That's a thing, right? Coconut juice is the same thing as blood? Or blood plasma? When you drink it?"

I shrugged. Jude said, "I'm not a Trader Joe's either. I might have some dried coconut for baking, *maybe*."

"That should work too," I said, based on nothing, mostly wanting Jude to leave us alone, which he did. I filled Cyrus's gash with

Neosporin, then wrapped his foot in the paper towel, gingerly, though he still didn't seem to be in any great pain.

"Now we definitely get to lick more squares when we get home," Cyrus said, grinning.

I squeezed his calf a little and looked up at his face, which was unaccountably calm, if pale. He looked chipper even, probably at having a new excuse to take more fentanyl. Something delicate released in my chest, like a gold ring dropping in a bowl of milk.

Jude emerged with an already-opened bag of sweetened shredded coconut, handed it to Cyrus. Cyrus shrugged and began happily munching pinchfuls of the coconut as I duct-taped paper towel around his foot till half the roll had been used up. The makeshift cast I'd given him was almost cartoonishly thick, the size of a basketball, but what else was I going to do? Jude was still standing in the bathroom doorway, occasionally looking over his shoulder to shoot death stares at his dogs.

"We've probably earned some extra grocery bags this week, no?" Cyrus said to Jude, smiling.

I looked at Cyrus, then, following his lead, said, "Oh yeah, and probably some cash for new shoes. And real bandages and gauze."

Jude stared at Cyrus, then back at me. It was impossible to feel intimidated by him, standing there as he was in his sallow underwear. Still, he was trying with all his might to summon some long-forfeited sense of menace.

"How much to get you guys to leave and never come back?" he whispered, deliberately, trying to make each individual word sound like a threat.

"I think probably a hundred dollars," Cyrus answered quickly.

"At least," I added.

"Yeah," Cyrus went on. "Maybe even like, one fifty. I'm gonna need new shoes for sure."

Jude hissed—I remember that so clearly, he audibly hissed—as he left the bathroom.

"You know," he shouted from down the hallway, "this is going to cost me too. Your carelessness. I'm going to have to buy cleaning stuff for my floors. My dogs are freaking out."

The dogs were silent. I shot Cyrus a stifled giggle, which he returned. Jude came back with a pile of crumpled money, not stacked in any way. It was mostly fives and ones.

"This is one hundred and twenty dollars," Jude said. "Leave."

"I want that wind chime too," said Cyrus.

"What?" asked Jude.

I looked at Cyrus, whose face was suddenly dead serious.

"That one," Cyrus said, pointing at the big chime over the bathroom mirror, a half-dozen wooden tubes cut at different lengths suspended from a carved cardinal the size of an apple.

Jude squinted at Cyrus, staring him down for a beat, two. Cyrus maintained eye contact while slowly squeezing a little pinch of shredded coconut into his mouth, chewing it. Wordlessly, Jude reached up to the mirror and took the wind chimes down from their hook, looking over his shoulder as he did it, as if to avoid seeing his own face. The chimes sounded in his hands, their delicate plunky clinks an odd sonic consequence of Jude's furiously thrusting them toward Cyrus.

"Now *leave*," Jude said.

Cyrus laughed, took them into his hands, and actually said "Incredible" out loud before hobbling up onto one foot.

I grabbed the pile of cash and helped Cyrus hop, one-footed, to the front door. Shiloh and Noah were standing at attention within their kennel, looking like carbon copies of each other. Each time Cyrus hopped forward, the chimes jingled a little, and at each jingle the dogs perked their ears, again and again, as Cyrus bounded, grinning, out the door.

THAT NIGHT WE BOUGHT A BUNCH OF LIQUOR WITH THE CASH AND invited some friends over to our apartment. Each time someone arrived and asked about Cyrus's foot, which he'd left embalmed in my paper-towel-and-duct-tape cast, he proudly retold the story. Each time the story repeated, it got a little creepier. Jude's underwear eventually became a thong. In addition to the wind chimes, he'd had raw bacon taped to his walls. The two kenneled dogs became ferocious mastiffs trying to eat our faces off. I always kind of admired Cyrus's imaginative retellings, like he was trying to workshop in real-time how he'd eventually write the story. I loved his enthusiasms, his haplessness.

"Wait, what was the coconut for again?" asked our friend Zain, cracking up.

"So the dude never even put on a pair of sweats?" asked Eleni.

"You should bring him some coconut juice when you go back next week," snickered Sad James.

Everyone licked the chessboard, laughed, chimed the wind chimes, which I'd hung from a corner of our living room record player. We all drank, passed around bowls of this and that, sang, laughed some more. At some point I made my way back to my bedroom to pass out while the room was singing along to an Of Montreal track, the vocals cheerily pleading, "C'mon chemicals, c'mooon chemicals!"

When I woke up the next morning, I walked out into the living room to find it emptied of everyone save Cyrus, who was passed out, half-snoring, still sitting up on the couch with his bad foot balanced on the coffee table like a trophy. The outer layer of his paper towel cast was dirty now, ashy gray visible through the duct tape. Near the toe, a wet red circle, small as a cherry, was just starting to peek through.

NINE

BOBBY SANDS

1954–1981

· · · ·

there's a Bobby Sands Street in Tehran
one block over from Ferdowsi Avenue,
that's true, Ireland, Iran, interchangeable mythos,
petrostates, and besides, nonviolence

is for the pepper trees—*violence,* that's what the church called
your hunger strike, and Thatcher called you *a convicted criminal
who chose to take his own life,* recoil, corrugated iron,
sixty-six days without mint leaf

or a pinch of bread, and just forty minutes from Belfast,
you could walk it in a day with
day to spare, most concepts spend their lives

searching like that, for a purpose,
you lucky and shaved, naked, mint, skylark:
the bars of men rust

· · · · ·

—*from* BOOKOFMARTYRS.docx by Cyrus Shams

FRIDAY

———— ✳ ————

Cyrus Shams and Orkideh

BROOKLYN MUSEUM, DAY I

"I'VE BEEN THINKING ABOUT DYING," CYRUS SHAMS SAID TO THE artist as he settled into the black chair across from her. The words came out fast, surprising him a little. "Dying soon. Or I guess, killing myself soon, but that sounds so mechanical." He worked a pinch of his beard between his thumb and forefinger. "I've been practicing at it. I have this job . . . dying." It had sounded much neater in his head.

The artist made a quick scratch in a little black notebook sitting on the table between them, set it back down. Then she took a slow, deliberate sip from a white mug of water before placing it back at her feet.

"What are you waiting for?" she asked slowly. Her voice was tissue-thin.

Cyrus paused.

"That's the thing, I don't really know. For it to mean something? I've been working this job and studying all these people who died for what they believed in. Qu Yuan, Joan of Arc, Bobby Sands. Dying. It feels like such a throwaway to just die for no reason. To waste your one good death."

The artist lifted her eyes to Cyrus, curling the edges of her lips into a smile. She watched him remember in one beat, two, that *she* was the one literally dying, terminal cancer, in that moment.

"Er, I don't mean 'to waste,'" he corrected quickly. "Or 'good.' I mean, death is death. It's all a waste and none of it's good. Immortal soul sick with desire and fastened to a dying animal, whatever. But you're not wasting your dying, you know? You're here doing this thing, and so your dying actually means something."

When he said "this," Cyrus lifted an arm to gesture around the dark gallery, waving his hand in the air like a dice player shaking before a big roll. He was speaking too quickly, betraying his anxiety, his anticipation of this moment across the country, across days of logistics. His right knee was bouncing manically.

The artist snorted a little laugh, then coughed, gently.

"Let's slow down," she said, patting the air with her open palms. "I'm Orkideh. What's your name?"

Sitting on a simple black metal folding chair, just a thin black pillow between her and the seat, Orkideh looked a little like a sculpture she herself might have made earlier in her career. The single standing lamp in the corner of the gallery room cast a hard shadow against the wall behind her, where the soft round shape of her hairless skull arced over the narrowing angles of her jaw and neck like a divining crystal dangling from an invisible string.

Behind her, the eggshell wall of the Brooklyn Museum gallery had the words DEATH-SPEAK in massive black Helvetica. There was a description of the exhibition beneath it announcing the artist, known simply as Orkideh, was dying of a terminal cancer, and had two months ago stopped all treatment. She would spend her final days here in the museum, talking to whoever came in about whatever they wanted to talk about. Guests were encouraged to ask about what dying felt like, or simply sit quietly with the artist, who today was dressed in a loose black sweater, accenting a crisp pair of men's slacks, navy with white pinstripes. Orkideh had cuffed the legs up above her ankles, highlighting her blue and skeletal bare feet.

Orkideh had talked about this in the past—some interview long ago—how she saw a private nobility about feet, the way, like the body's most intimate parts, they mostly stayed hidden from the world. But unlike those tucked away bits, she'd said, feet were constantly performing thankless and often demeaning work while mostly the other parts drowsed, swaddled in nylon or cotton or lace. Even wearing something open like sandals or heels, the soles of one's feet were concealed, secretly pressing themselves into and pushing back against the world, as if to halt its ever-encroaching advance.

"Cyrus," he said.

"Cyrus!" said Orkideh, smiling. "Such a princely name!" She said "princely" with a thick Persian accent and an extra syllable, "PREEN-seh-LEE. "What's your last name?" she asked.

He told her. She paused, studying Cyrus's face. He imagined what she must be seeing when she looked at him: his facial hair like makeup poorly applied, dark beard short but not trimmed, and thicker in certain areas—his mustache, his chin—than others. He didn't look old, exactly, but his face seemed to be older than the rest of his body, its gaunt eye sockets and the buggy purses beneath them amplifying the roundness of his eyeballs, giving him an uncanny urgency. He had deep laugh lines that swallowed his face when he smiled, and when he sat quietly, they drew the eye down from his Persian nose—"noble," he often called it, the only part of his face he liked—and into his mess of patchy beard.

"Cyrus Shams," Orkideh said slowly, as if laying the sound like a sheet over his face. She cocked her head to the side. "That's a beautiful name. And how old are you, Koroosh?"

"Twenty-eight. Twenty-nine in a month," he replied, feeling suddenly self-conscious. "And you?"

Orkideh sucked her teeth. She squinted a little, opened her mouth to say something, then closed it. Finally, she answered:

"I'm fifty-four." She studied his face. "And you are Iranian, yes?"

"Yeah. Born in Tehran but came to America when I was a baby."

If Orkideh had been drawing Cyrus, the first thing she'd have noted would have been his large wet eyes. Eyebrows resting in a semi-perpetual furrow, like he was always a little worried. Wrinkly tan T-shirt with a pocket over the left breast. Dark black curls. Thin gray denim pants, well worn. Dirty blue canvas sneakers. He was skinny in a scrawny way, not like a runner but like a mathematician who forgets to eat. She scratched the back of her bald head. Somewhere in the next room a woman sneezed.

"Do you worry," Orkideh began, after another long pause, "about becoming a cliché?"

"How do you mean?"

"Another death-obsessed Iranian man?"

Cyrus deflated, slumping in his chair and letting out a soft sigh.

"See, that's the thing. I didn't even know about all that cult-of-the-martyr stuff until relatively recently. Families picnicking at cemeteries of the war dead, the state hiring poets to read at their graves. That wasn't me."

"But you want to die. And you want for that death to be glorious. Like all Iranian men."

"I mean, yeah, but doesn't everyone want that in the end? For their deaths to matter? Or shouldn't they?"

Orkideh lifted an eyebrow, leaned in.

"So you grew up insulated from death?"

"Well, that's not exactly true either. But it wasn't a Persian thing. I grew up eating Hot Pockets and watching Michael Jordan, not thinking about Hussain or Ashura or the fucking Iran-Iraq War. My dad wouldn't even let me speak Farsi in the house."

"No?"

"He thought it'd slow down my English learning, or confuse me as a kid. He wanted me to be American. He'd actually check out these massive SAT preparation books from the library. He'd teach himself all the vocabulary words in the back, these ridiculous words nobody actually uses. He'd learn them and then start peppering them into his vocabulary when he spoke to me. The apartment wasn't *messy*, it was *squalid*. I didn't *count*, I *enumerated*. I was the kid in first grade who still couldn't tie my own shoes but would say things like 'I'm ambiguous' about whether I wanted peanut butter or cheese crackers."

Orkideh smiled. Behind Cyrus, a chic German tourist couple had come in, weak-jawed men, one wearing dark round sunglasses even in the dark exhibit room. They stood back, whispering and smiling at each other.

"My point," Cyrus continued, "is that I come to it honestly. The martyr stuff."

"Martyrs!" Orkideh said. "My god, now you want to be a *martyr*?"

Cyrus ignored this.

"It's not an Islam thing. It wasn't martyrs in textbooks or dead soldiers on mosque walls or a brass key to heaven around my neck or anything like that. But there's no escaping it. The Iranian cult of the martyr stuff. If I died trying to kill a genocidal dictator tomorrow, the news wouldn't say a leftist American made a measured and principled sacrifice for the good of his species. The news would say an Iranian terrorist attempted a state assassination."

Orkideh chuckled.

"Are you trying to kill a genocidal dictator?"

The German tourists shifted uncomfortably. Cyrus sighed again.

"Of course not. I wish I were that brave. But no. I just want to write an epic. A book. Something about secular, pacifist martyrs. People who gave their lives to something larger than themselves. No swords in their hands."

"Oh my God, so you're a poet too! All the Persian checkboxes."

Both of Cyrus's knees were bouncing now, syncopating each other's fever dance. A thin layer of sweat formed on his brow.

"I didn't say it would be poetry! I don't know what it's going to turn into. So far, I'm just typing. Really, I'm serious. I think it's the book I was born to write."

"And you want to end this book about martyrs with yourself."

Cyrus winced. He had thought of this, reading about Malcolm X, the Tiananmen Tank Man, and Hypatia of Alexandria. He'd stared at picture after picture of Bhagat Singh, the Souliot Women, and Emily Wilding Davison. Cyrus felt ready to join them, to enter the ranks of the honorable dead. He even felt ready to carry himself to that end. Most of the time. He was ready, then he wasn't. Like one of those perpetual motion swinging ball cradles, his desire to die kept striking back equal and opposite against his desire to make his dying dramatic, to make it count. Was it ego? Was it fear of being forgotten?

"I don't know yet. I think elegizing myself in advance would probably void my right to be considered a martyr. Secular or otherwise. Right? But I haven't written the book yet, so I don't really know all the rules."

"The rules! You're talking about people who die for other people. Not dying for glory or an impressable God. Not the promise of a sunny afterlife for themselves. You're talking about earth martyrs."

Cyrus's eyes widened.

"Earth martyrs—that's good."

Somewhere in the next room over a camera flashed. A docent's voice loudly scolded the photographer. The two German men stood motionless.

"Why are you here, Cyrus Shams?"

He was sweating all over now, in his armpits and the circle around his belly button. He hadn't expected to find himself so nervous.

"Well, I'd like to write about you. For the book. You . . ." He hesitated. "You dying here, like this."

Orkideh pulled a handkerchief from her pants pocket and coughed into it. Cyrus looked at her eyes, which had begun to glaze dully, white clouds over brown moons. He had expected either amused tolerance or stormy rebuke, but sensed neither. The artist just sat there staring at him for ten seconds, fifteen, thirty, her expression seemingly larger than what was visible, like it continued somewhere else beyond her face. Finally, after what seemed like an eternity but was likely only a minute, she reached her hand across the table.

"It has been my incredible luck to meet you, Cyrus."

He met her hand, almost weightless, with his own.

"Erm. Thank you. But—"

"Come see me again tomorrow, if we're both still here."

"I'm actually just in town for a couple days and I was hoping—"

Orkideh smiled toward the German couple, tilted her head to gesture for them to come sit. Cyrus stood up, gathering himself. The Germans avoided eye contact with him, the one without sunglasses sliding slowly into the seat. Cyrus began to walk out of the room confused, replaying in his head what had just happened. The Germans were talking about a taxi driver they'd had once in New

York, who told them about a time he'd driven Robert De Niro to the airport. They said the punch line together in unison: *Taxi Driver taxi driver!*

Cyrus quickly made his way through the museum and out its front doors. An old man sat shirtless on the great steps. Yellow and white carts sold hot dogs, halal meats, soft-serve ice cream. Seeing them, Cyrus suddenly felt desperately thirsty and bought a Coke from the woman at the halal meat cart. He stood nearby gulping down the chemical sweet, trying to calm himself. *Earth martyr,* he thought.

This idea for the book, for his own dying—going into the museum he'd had a grasp of its shape, why it mattered. It was a tidy, gallant idea about leaving life for something larger than mere living. Becoming an earth martyr. It made sense, and then suddenly it didn't. It held a shape and then suddenly it didn't. Like boiling water poured into a cup then poured over his head. He felt scorched, confused, suddenly alive.

TEN

I AM SETTING OUT TO WRITE A BOOK OF ELEGIES FOR PEOPLE I'VE never met. Yes, there is an unforgivable hubris in my imagining any part of their living, and presuming to write about it. There is also hubris in writing about anything else.

—*from* BOOKOFMARTYRS.docx by Cyrus Shams

ALI SHAMS

———— ✦ ————

THE CHICKEN FARM WHERE I WORKED IN FORT WAYNE WASN'T A normal farm. We didn't raise chickens for you to eat. We raised the grandparents of the chickens you eat. A breeder farm. And really, it was more laboratory than farm. The goal: to create, through selective breeding, a chicken that would go from egg to harvest in as little time as possible, on as little feed as possible. A chicken was a machine that converted grain into protein. That was the line. Easy enough.

As soon as Cyrus was in first grade, he was getting himself dressed and on the bus to school. I'd leave our apartment in the outskirts of Fort Wayne at five with him still sleeping in our shared bedroom. When I got to work, I'd have to take a shower and change into scrubs. Like a nurse. With our chickens, the first thing to be bred out was their immune systems. A waste of calories in chickens that never left their biosecure barns. Any germ someone brought in could wipe out a whole flock.

Probably you're imagining chickens pecking around in the dirt, splashing themselves in muddy puddles. Our chickens would never survive real dirt. Bacteria, viruses. Industrial chickens, that's what we called our birds. They were like magic. Grew like weeds and you barely had to feed them. Our chickens, you slaughtered at thirty-five days when they were nearly seven pounds. A backyard chicken might not get to that weight in a year.

At home I'd cook big pots of stew and rice on Saturdays, and we'd eat that through the week. Potatoes, cheap organ meat. A few tomatoes. On Friday nights, Cyrus and I would bake a frozen pizza and watch movies together. He looked forward to that all week, going to the library and picking out a VHS, a DVD to borrow. We'd each choose one. He liked everything I liked. Mostly I liked Westerns. John Wayne and Clint Eastwood. They did good and things turned out all right for them. Cyrus liked comedies, silly dumb stuff. Adam Sandler, Eddie Murphy. I liked watching Cyrus laugh. When it was basketball season we'd watch Pacers games. Our favorite player was Reggie Miller. We loved how mean he was, how he'd score and then taunt the player who had tried to guard him. We liked the Muslim players too, on principle—Kareem especially, but also Hakeem Olajuwon, Shareef Abdur-Rahim. Sports was a language everyone at the farm, and in Cyrus's school, spoke. So we learned to speak it too.

I bought gin in bulk, giant half-gallon plastic bottles with British names: Barton's, Bennett's, Gordon's. There were people back in Iran who believed the mullahs were installed by the British to keep Iran backwards. Maybe the British were doing the same to me with their gin. Filthy medicine. But what was the alternative?

At work, I ate like a king. Small joy. Our first break came at ten, then lunch at twelve-thirty. The farm managers filled the work fridge and freezer with snacks for us—biosecurity meant we couldn't bring our own food in. What they gave us was all vegetarian; meat had too many germs. But it was unlimited. I'd eat bean burritos, frozen rice dishes. The other men would talk about sports, talk about women, or just not talk. Most were immigrants like me, so we tried to stay in English so we could all practice. "The plates are dirty." "We have no more coffee." From the guys, I learned a bit of Spanish, French.

My job, first thing, was to walk from barn to barn collecting eggs. Each barn had 1,000–2,000 eggs buried in the shavings. Some hens would make little nests in the shavings, and we learned where each of those were. But there were also hiding places, clusters of eggs in random clumps of debris. The birds would really bury them; we had to dig deep. And of course they'd shit right there. The eggs were always covered with all kinds of bodily fluids.

Our job was to pick the eggs daily while destroying as few as possible, set them onto these monorail trays hanging at eye level. The eggs were slimy, fertilized, sturdier than people imagine. You could drop one from your hands and it'd usually be fine landing on the shavings. Still, I was careful about where and how I stepped. Wherever I moved, the birds would flee.

The other guys rarely talked about home, their old ones or their new ones. A mercy. We did talk about food. A Congolese guy, Jean-Joseph, would talk all the time about cooking. Cassava, fufu, fish. And also French stuff. People were interested in Iranian food and I shared what I could about it, but I was never much of a cook. Pomegranate molasses, walnuts. Eggplants. Rice. Koobideh. We couldn't bring anything in to share, so what we described just had to live in our heads. One time Jean-Joseph came in, excited to tell the Spanish guys he'd tried tamales, how it reminded him of kwanga back home. But of course, none of them, none of us knew what kwanga was. That kind of thing.

Cyrus grew, I worked. What more to say?

For his part, Cyrus was basically an adult from the beginning. I'd tell him about his mother, his uncle, our families when he'd ask. But mostly he didn't ask. He was a good boy.

Once, when I was a boy, our teacher told us the hadith of the starving man. The man was dying in the desert, got on his knees and begged to God, "Please help me, I'm starving, nearly dead, too tired to continue looking for water. I don't want to hurt anymore. Please, almighty Lord, take pity, end my suffering." God, in his infinite wisdom, sent the man a baby. An infant to take care of. And so the man had purpose, a reason to stay alive.

I remember thinking the story didn't make sense. Why not just send him food, water, a bed? God stories always seemed to work that way. Sideways, convoluted. Like one of those elaborate chain-reaction machines built in the most deliberately nonsensical way, using a track and a spring and a candle and a balloon to ring a bell.

But Cyrus was a good boy. Never had problems in his studies. He liked to read, same as his mother. Sometimes it felt like I barely knew him. We'd call his uncle Arash international long distance once a year for Nowruz, around Cyrus's birthday, and I'd be shocked at what I'd learn. He'd tell his uncle he'd taught himself to play chess from a book, had been practicing against himself using a little board he'd drawn and pieces he'd cut from paper. After the call, he showed me the board, tried to teach me. He told his uncle he was working for the school newspaper, writing about movies and music. I didn't even know his school had a newspaper. He spoke English like a professor.

After lunch, on the farm, me and the Guatemalan guy Edgar, it was our job to wash the eggs, one by one. It was a big job. Edgar would complain about football, his kids. He'd tell dirty jokes. Mostly I'd listen, laughing a little, rinsing mucus and shit from the gray eggs. Every day, six days a week, for years, washing thousands of eggs.

Cyrus loved to show me stuff he was learning in his books. I used to call him Doctor Shams. He'd come home from school, or excitedly emerge from our shared bedroom holding a book, eager to tell me that male seahorses were the ones that carried the babies, that the sun was a gigantic nuclear furnace, how to count to ten in Russian. He wanted to write songs for Tina Turner, for Bruce Springsteen. He wanted to learn Mandarin so he could move to China and teach. I never knew what to say. Usually something like "Well, you'd better clean the kitchen first."

Once, he showed me a picture of an ancient clay tablet, Babylonian or Sumerian, something like that, 4,000 years old. I expected it to be something holy, a poem to a fertility goddess, some ancient fable. But it was, Cyrus told me, just a lengthy complaint from a business transaction about receiving the wrong kind of copper. "The copper is substandard. I have been treated rudely. I have not accepted the copper, but I paid money for it." I never forgot that. Cyrus was laughing of course, he thought it was hilarious. "Ancient one-star review!" he said. I'm pretty sure I didn't even say anything.

I used to think slow, slower than language moved. By the time I settled into an idea about anything, the moment for me to say something had passed. Roya used to say I was a good listener. Mostly, though, I was just a bad talker.

For weeks, I kept thinking about that tablet. Walking around the shavings, hens running from my boots, the image of that ancient stone hung in my mind. For all our advances in science—chickens that can go from egg to harvest in a month, planes to cross the world, missiles to shoot them down—we've always held the same obnoxious, rotten souls. Souls that have festered for millennia while science grew. How unfair, this copper delivery. How unfair, this life. My wounds are so much deeper than yours. The arrogance of victim-hood. Self-pity. Suffocating.

Maybe it's because we could pass along science. You wrote a fact in a book and there it sat until someone born five hundred years later improved it. Refined it, implemented it more usefully. Easy. You couldn't do that with soul-learning. We all started from zero. From less than zero, actually. We started whiny, without grace. Obsessed only with our own needing. And the dead couldn't teach us anything about that. No facts or tables or proofs. You just had to live and suf-fer and then teach your kids to do the same. From a distance, habit passing for happiness.

Go to work. Dig through shavings, find the eggs. Eat. Clean the eggs. Put down new shavings. Clear the driplines. Go home. Eat with Cyrus. Put on basketball, put on a movie. Drink. Dreamless sleep. Medicine-deep. Go to work. Find the eggs.

What was there to complain about? A murdered wife? A sore back? The wrong grade copper? Living happened till it didn't. There was no choice in it. To say no to a new day would be unthinkable. So each morning you said yes, then stepped into the consequence.

FRIDAY

✦

Cyrus Shams

BROOKLYN, DAY I

ORKIDEH'S WORDS WERE STILL ORBITING CYRUS'S SKULL LIKE AN invisible halo as he walked away from the Brooklyn Museum into Prospect Park. Earth martyrs, Persian checkboxes. The difference between wanting to not be alive and wanting to die. Cyrus finished his Coke and bent over to tie his shoes. He wore dark blue canvas Vans that required replacing every six months, like clockwork, when the soles wore through. Every six months, he'd order an identical pair from the Vans website, dark blue with gum soles and black laces. He'd walk around in the new ones on wet days to wear them in, phasing out the old holey ones by using them like rich white men used topless convertibles, driving them only on perfectly clear days, only to flaunt their capital.

Cyrus's holey shoes were flaunting something too: his authenticity, his class antipathy, his allegiance to the proletariat—it was all right there at his feet, waving like two ratty flags. Yes, they were ratty flags made by a billion-dollar shoe company, but there was no ethical consumption under late capitalism and sometimes, Cyrus figured, one had to pick one's battles. He tried not to think too much about these contradictions.

For two full years, his roommate Zee had been wearing the same pair of forest-green camouflage Crocs every day, everywhere.

"Fashion is a capitalist weapon," Zee smirked when asked about them, and before long it became impossible to imagine him wearing anything else on his feet. Cyrus's sneakers seemed to him a quieter political cousin to Zee's Crocs, and he liked not having to think about what to put on his feet. *A martyr wears simple footwear,* he thought to himself.

Nearby, a woman was lifting a long blunt to the lips of the copper bust of John F. Kennedy while a friend snapped a picture. Cyrus was trying to be better about noticing these moments, about feeling grateful for the texture and specificity they lent his life.

And you want to end this book about martyrs with yourself, Orkideh had said. Did he? Cyrus wanted to sit on a park bench. He wanted to get something to eat.

Cyrus believed a hyper-focus on occasions for gratitude would make his eventual death more poignant, more valuable. When a sad-sack who hated life killed themselves, what were they really giving up? The life they hated? Far more meaningful, thought Cyrus, to lift yourself out of a life you enjoyed—the tea still warm, the honey still sweet. That was real sacrifice. That meant something.

He considered making this an essential quality in his book, leaving behind a life you cared about. It was one of the things he would have to work hardest on. He had a decent life, didn't need to work too hard to stay where he was. His rent was cheap, he had friends, there were books he was excited to read. But some days, that all felt so abstract as to become totally meaningless. Cyrus often wept for no reason, bit his thumbs till they bled. Some nights he'd lie awake till morning, frightening sleep away with the desperation of his wanting it.

Cyrus also worried that the whole idea of gratitude was possibly classist, or worse. Did a poor Syrian child, whose living and dying had been indelibly shaped by the murderous whims of evil men, qualify for grace only if she possessed a superhuman ability to look beyond her hardship and notice the beauty of a single flower growing through a pile of rubble? And would the gratitude for that flower be contaminated by the awareness, or ignorance, of the bodies turning to soil beneath it?

And then, if the girl herself was rubbled by an errant mortar shell, her eyes full of tears and aimed in their final living moment at that flower, which would weigh more on the cosmic scales: a tear of gratitude at the great beauty of a flower lifting through ash, or a tear of delirious rage?

It's possible, he thought, that the experience of gratitude was itself a luxury, a topless convertible driven through a rainless life. Even the platitudes offered after a tragedy—a divorce, a dead pet—seemed built around the expectation that gratitude was a base level to which you returned after passing through some requisite interval of grief: "In time, you'll remember only the joy." People really said that, people who, like Cyrus, could reasonably expect that sufficient training of the spirit would reveal a near-infinite supply of gratitudes hidden in every leaf and sound and mortarless sky.

Orkideh's words: *Another death-obsessed Iranian man.* The unforgivable vanity of fantasizing about one's own death. As if continuing to live was a given, inertia that needed to be disrupted inorganically.

Cyrus considered for a moment whether it was fucked up to imagine a dead Syrian child as the foil to his relative fortune, as a prop in his psychic play about the ethics of gratitude. He wanted to ask Orkideh what she thought about this, what she thought about gratitude broadly. So much of his psychic bandwidth was taken up with conflicting thoughts about political prepositions. The morality *of* almond milk. The ethics *of* yoga. The politics *of* sonnets. There was nothing in his life that wasn't contaminated by what he mostly mindlessly called "late capitalism." He hated it, like everyone was supposed to. But it was a hate that made nothing happen.

He wanted to be on "the right side of history," whatever that was. But more than that (he admitted this to himself when he was practicing being rigorously honest), he wanted other people to perceive him as someone who cared about being on the right side of history. It's hard to imagine an earth martyr who was also a fervent eugenicist, or one who had supported Mussolini. Being on the right side of history seemed a bedrock feature of the sort of people in whom he was interested.

Cyrus remembered Orkideh had been barefoot when he saw her in the museum. That suddenly seemed significant. He leaned over and untied his sneakers before walking three blocks back to the subway station.

ELEVEN

. . . .

HYPATIA OF ALEXANDRIA

370–415

not unlike the library
you believed yourself dangerous
and you burned,

men pitiless as wire mothers
crushing your astrolabes, your hands,
the meek off inheriting this or that,

sweet heaven already astrew, friend,
it's lonely here in the future
with all our drugs and knowing,

you brigadier,
incautiously declaring
this is a circle and *this is a cone,*

the stone comfort of x and y
amidst the dawning collapse

. . . . .

—*from* BOOKOFMARTYRS.docx by Cyrus Shams

ARASH SHIRAZI

——— ✷ ———

I ENLIST BECAUSE I HAVE TO ENLIST. THE FEW WAYS OUT—CHRONIC illness, being the eldest son of a widowed parent, being rich—aren't available to me. I know men who have tried to convince doctors they have bad backs, bad knees, bad hearts. Sometimes it works, even. The men stay at home with their families and neighbors are not even particularly cruel to them. Most people understand not wanting to die for a country you no longer recognize. Somehow the idiot zealots ended up with all the guns, tanks. Five years after a revolution led by students and idealists, pacifists with hyacinths in their breast pockets. How did this happen? Zealots. Guns, tanks. And now, war.

When I die they'll put my picture in the mosque. Arash Shirazi, shaved head, shaved face. Hairless in a way that makes my skull louder, the angles of my jaw. Not a handsome face, exactly, but ugly in a way that works. Rows of our pictures striping the mosque wall. The martyred. How to make out which bald dead martyr belonged to you. Belongs to you. A scar on a cheek, a mole over an eye.

While I'm getting my vaccinations before training, a young woman in the waiting room seethes at another man even younger than me; he looks like he hasn't even begun shaving.

"You wanted this," she says. "You could have told them about Beeta. You could have gotten out of this and now you have what you deserve."

The man stares at his hands, his long soft fingers. I imagine maybe he's a brilliant pianist, a prodigy. Maybe Beeta is his teacher, his piano trainer, who he is disappointing by enlisting. There is a station on the AM radio that plays classical music every Thursday and Sunday morning and I try to listen to it when I can, often just lying in bed the whole time with my eyes closed and the songs circling around me like planets. I like the loud guys best, Rachmaninoff and Mahler and Vivaldi. But I imagine this man, this boy really, this soft boy, playing Debussy, he looks like he'd love Chopin but especially Debussy, I imagine him swimming through an underwater cathedral, stained glass and tiny fish, with just his fingers, just his soft hands making sunken cathedral sounds. That's what he should be doing. I can't do anything, I have no great talent or even minor ones, I belong here. But not him, this boy, not his cathedral hands.

As the woman—his wife? his sister?—berates him, the shadow of a flinch in his hands. A rage flashing, then expiring like smoke off a match. Maybe Beeta is their daughter, sick with some congenital disease. Maybe they're cousins. Maybe Beeta is his mother, already dead, and he is the one taking care of their younger siblings.

I imagine what might make a boy choose to go to war. Ideology, personal belief, sure. Iraq invaded us. They thought they'd kick down the door and the whole house would collapse, something like that. We were weak after the revolution. They wanted Khuzestan's oil and Saddam wanted us to kiss his hand. To bow, yes. Of course we didn't believe the Ayatollah's nonsense. But we hated the idea of foreign meddling more than we hated him. So we went along. This man sitting in front of me, this boy being berated by his wife or sister, he doesn't have the set jaw, the conviction of an ideologue. His hands are too pretty to belong to a nationalist. Maybe his father pressured him. Maybe his imam.

For my part, I don't feel much one way or another about my service. For me, it is inescapable, a thing like sickness or death. Why kick and flail when the whirlpool is already sucking you in? I've seen the faces of the war dead in the mosque and in the markets. Our ugly-beautiful martyrs staring ahead into the place only they can see.

I wonder what they imagined that place being, before they arrived there. I wonder if they were disappointed, or if there was no place to arrive to at all.

My mother shaved my head ahead of my vaccinations. She thought the buzz of the clippers concealed her almost silent sobs, and I let her believe it did. I am poor, unmarried. I didn't finish high school, just screwed around in the countryside for a few years working where I could, chasing girls. This means I am expendable, a "zero soldier." Zero education, zero special skills, zero responsibilities outside of my country. There is an expression: "If a zero soldier has to use a grenade to escape with their life, they shouldn't waste the grenade."

"Expendable" may seem a bad word to use to describe your own life, except I actually find it liberating. The way it vents away all pressure to become. How it asks only that you be.

I leave home on a bus with a couple dozen other shaved vaccinated young men for a makeshift training camp at the base of the Alborz mountains. My mother gives me a picture of the family from years ago, me a brooding self-serious teen, mustache just starting to come in. My little sister Roya smiling the way she only does in pictures, with her top and bottom teeth all showing. My mother and father standing gravely behind us like stone lions. After the picture was taken my sister and my parents got into a fight. A neighbor had been arrested, some surreptitious meeting of Tudeh Party socialists my parents believed Roya knew about. There was shouting all night, silence for a week.

At the camp all the soldiers are sent to three areas according to their level of education—college graduates, who had begun their training in the summers between semesters, sent to one area for officer training. High school graduates sent to another for their high infantry training. And those with less than a high school education like me—despite our doting mothers and overachieving sisters—we are the zero soldiers. We stay in the area of Alborz where we were all first dropped.

It is cold. I have never been to the mountains before. It's a little hard to believe they're real, they look so much like pictures of themselves. Kind of waxy, even almost flat against the sky. The dirt is hard and the camp itself looks like it was thrown up in a day: all the walls are plastic sheet and tent pole. It's the sort of place we could take down and evacuate in a few minutes. Which I suppose is the point.

A man in fatigues with a thick mustache and sunglasses arranges all us zero soldiers according to height and gives numbers based on where we fall along the line. I'm tall, so my number is 11 out of 208. That becomes my name. 11. یازده. Yahz-dah. Something monolithic about that. Clean.

ONCE, WHEN I WAS STILL JUST A BOY, MY SISTER ROYA AND I WALKED to a frozen pond near our apartment. I was maybe nine so she must have been seven. We were alone together there at the pond save the massive blocks of ice bobbing almost imperceptibly on the water, like cars hovering a centimeter off the road. We would go there sometimes and chase each other around or throw rocks at water flowers. Rarely would we see anyone else.

My sister was afraid of nothing, but even as we circled the pond I could see her trying to stifle her shivering from me. At the time I assumed all little sisters were this way, eager to prove to their older brothers their toughness, and I resented her for it, wanted to deny her the approval she too desperately sought. She would never be what I was, a boy, a burgeoning man, with all the manlinesses, the tolerance for pain that implied. It was better she learned this from me than from the world.

Our pond was in the center of a kind of valley, a few spoonfuls of soup at the bottom of a big bowl. The hills leading into it were speckled with shrubs and winter wheat, all frozen over. At the top of the hill, we broke off stalky reeds and used them to smash other reeds. We hurled rocks down into the floating ice, Roya pouting a little when hers didn't travel as far as mine, trying again and again. There at the top of the hill, the land plateaued into a frozen field, all hard dirt punctuated by the occasional dead brush, a desiccated stalk of something once green. From up there the pond looked like a purple eye, glazed over. Our blind mamabazorg had eyes like that, cataracts thick as bottle glass.

"Hold my hand," Roya said, staring down at the pond. Glad to take her request as an admission of fear, I grabbed it with glee. Her gloves were black and soft, cotton maybe, and mine were bright purple and plastic, still very much a child's gloves. I remember that, remember my surprise when she continued, "Let's race down the hill toward the water. First person to stop running and let go is a coward!"

There was, of course, only one choice for me. To say no would forfeit my position as oldest and bravest. Even if I mustered some protest about her safety, we would both rightly hear it as fear. I snorted a bit and some birds took off nearby at the sound of our conversation, perhaps to ensure my sister and I would be left truly alone. I squeezed her hand, and we took off down the hill.

ONE OF THE OLDER MEN HERE, NUMBER 137, MAYBE A FEW YEARS older than me, tells us over a meal of watery obgoosht about an old family friend who served two different compulsory two-year military services. The neighbor, a man named Alireza, had had a brother who died two years before he was born. Alireza's parents, in order to advance him in school more quickly, had Alireza adopt the name of his dead brother. This was before all the associated paperwork became more standardized, and so Alireza seamlessly became his dead older brother, completed all his education under his dead brother's name. When he finished, of course, he had to serve his brother's two-year conscription, which he did, dutifully and without complaint.

But then, after returning home for just a month or two, his parents got a note saying it was Alireza's time to serve. The government, which had kept no record of the baby named Alireza's education or his hospitalizations, had remembered, to the day, eighteen years later, when it was his time to serve in the military. Naturally.

Alireza's choice then: admit years of his parents' deceit and subject them (and himself) to the consequences of lying to the state, or serve another two years. 137 said that for Alireza, it wasn't even a choice. He reenlisted using his own real name for the first time in years (even his parents had addressed him by the name of his dead brother). Less than a month into his second service, Alireza was killed in a training accident. Alireza, martyred. At least with his own name.

While 137 tells this story, the other men laugh.

"No way that really happened," one says. "Somebody would have figured out their trick years before conscription."

"He should have just told the truth," says another man.

"And now the grief of two dead sons belongs to his parents too," says the first man.

It is a funny story, I think, funny the way crows are funny birds, more knowing than they let on. The story pretends to be about names but it's actually a story about time, how time flattens everything. Family, duty, whatever. Into dirt. There's something comforting about that, something vast and, yes, inescapable. Like bright ink spilling over everyone at once.

SO, ROYA AND I WERE HOLDING HANDS AT THE TOP OF THE HILL, me in sneakers and cotton pants, my casual dress another assertion of my disregard for the cold. My sister was bundled up in a thick plastic hooded coat and puffy denim pants, the bagginess of it all coming to points at her head, hands, feet, making her look like a starfish. We held hands and I counted out loud—three, two, one, now!—and we were off running down the grass toward the frozen pond, instantly unstoppable, or so it felt, like two drops of water beading down the side of a cool glass.

Nothing could stop us from our descending, our legs were

running the sort of running that wasn't even running anymore just desperately trying to keep up with the rushing world, the speed of the ground moving under us and only our clumsy skinny legs, idiot technologies, to keep us from crumbling in a heap, and my sister laughing, I was terrified and shouted like it but Roya was laughing while the pond kept getting bigger and bigger, I was trying to figure out how to get the world to slow down, slow down enough to let my legs catch up to its racing, but my sister the starfish less than a meter tall was laughing, gobbling like a turkey, holding my hand and still running straight ahead, her legs not even a blur anymore but a straight single shape, like the rims of cars in car commercials that stay still even as the car curves down the road, and finally the pond was everything in front of us and somehow I slid, I can't remember exactly how it started but I think I jammed my sneaker into the frozen dirt, locking my legs, kicking up ice, and I slid that way and the earth stopped moving maybe too suddenly, I felt my brain slosh against my skull, that fast, maybe the earth even moved backwards a bit as if to correct itself, and in my sliding I let go of Roya's hand, the world stilling around me I could finally see how fast she was moving, all rush and wild, I remember I shouted Roya no! as she lifted her hand, the hand that had held mine, into the air like a boxer, like a boxer's trophy, or more than a trophy, like a little piece of the sun that she had finally been able to stretch out and grab, that hot and full of power, all the warmth she needed as she laughed triumphantly straight into the icy water.

I HAVE HEARD PEOPLE SAY SMELL IS THE SENSE MOST ATTACHED TO memory, but for me it is always language, if language can be thought of as a sense, which of course it can be. Compared to even the dullest dog humans can smell nothing. But compare us with—what?— a monkey who can say "apple" with her hands?—and we are the gods of language, everything else just chirping and burping. And how fitting, too, that our superpower as a species, the source of our divinity, stems from such a broken invention.

It was invented, of course, language. The first baby didn't come out speaking Farsi or Arabic or English or anything. We invented it, this language where one man is called Iraqi and one man is called Iranian and so they kill each other. Where one man is called an officer so he sends other men, with heads and hearts the size of his own, to split their stomachs open over barbed wire. Because of language, this sound stands for this thing, that sound stands for that thing, all these invented sounds strutting around, certain as roosters. It is no wonder we got it so wrong.

Lying there on my butt, I just watched her disappear. My sister ran into the water completely, ran in so quickly she couldn't anticipate how immediately the water dropped, manmade ponds are like that sometimes, they just scoop straight down. How instantly she was swallowed.

For a moment I lay searching for her, but she vanished almost the second she hit the water, the only sign left of her the giant arcs bobbing the ice chunks out from where she went in, like sound waves searching for an ear. And then, before I could even process what had happened, before I could make a decision to be brave or a coward, before I could arrive at that inflection point that would no doubt shape my idea of myself for the rest of my life, a crashing of water, Roya's ridiculous soggy face popping above the break, heaving, her starfish arms splashing to hold position there, heaving and, I swear to God, laughing, laughing like a maniac between heaves.

"You coward!" she shouted, coughing up water as she paddled her way back to the shore. Massive floating blocks of ice pulled apart as she moved. "You dog!"

I AM NOT A MAN WHO COMES EASILY TO TEARS. I'VE KNOWN SUCH men, men who weep like girls, men in my own platoon who sobbed after lights went out each night, or Rostam, our dimwit neighbor who almost daily wandered out of his house to mumble and cry and laugh, sometimes all at the same time, until one of his exasperated nieces would emerge to bring him back home. There is something pathetic about such men, of course, an unforgivable softness, but I've secretly always envied them a bit too. The clarity of a physical emotional response. Something to do with the sadness, terror. A way to give it away.

All around Iran everything was changing. Streets named after flowers and birds being renamed after clerics, martyrs. Posters advertising watches, cars, movies, ripped down and replaced with the glowering face of the Ayatollah. I didn't know what any of it meant, but I knew it meant intensely. The adults talking to each other in hushed whispers when they thought we were sleeping. Sometimes I heard my mother crying, my father scolding her to stop. But I thought it lucky, the clarity of tears. Instead of the loose riot of confusion and dread webbed up in my chest, in my head, probably wearing lesions into my gut and brain.

I remember in school Agha Pahla holding up a stone suspended in the air by a string, telling us how the stone was full of potential energy—potential energy, the names we give things!—and how when the stone is dropped all that potential energy gets converted into motion, into kinetic energy, action, something like that. And that transformation, potential energy into motion, is what makes stones powerful, terrible, how they can crush people. Sometimes I feel like that, like I'm walking around all stuffed up with potential energy, a stone hanging in the air with no knife sharp enough to cut the rope.

I do wonder sometimes what it would feel like to cry, to beat my chest and wail like an old woman at a funeral, no potential anything being stored for later, all motion, all energy. I think about that and feel stuffed up even in my imagining, like a nose you can't breathe out of, my brain can't even move me into that place, can't even pretend it to be true. One thing happens, then the next. For a long, long time.

Needless to say, when Roya's head popped up from the water, when she began laughing and splashing and calling me names as she paddled back toward shore, I didn't cry. Even then. I think about this now, if I had cried, would it have been out of happiness at my sister's safety or relief for my own? It's hard for me to remember today exactly what I was feeling then, only that when she emerged I got up without thinking and ran to the edge of the water.

She was laughing and calling me a chicken and I shouted, "What the hell are you doing! Get out! Get out!" I was fully possessed by fear, uncertainty bowing to action.

"I'm coming, my dove," she laughed. "I'm coming!"

When she paddled to the edge of the water and reached out her hand to mine, I wanted to smack it away, to say you ran in there yourself, you get yourself out. Or maybe I wanted to make her feel as afraid as I had, as I still was. Something about her laughing, her smile, the way she was acting so invincible filled me with fury, or maybe not fury exactly because there was a baffle to it, dumb fury, a rage so deep you couldn't help but be a little impressed.

I did grab her hand, I pulled her out of the water, her splashing probably more than she needed to, to get me wet as well, to implicate me even more in the soggy mess she'd made. I pulled and she climbed out and lay down on the bentgrass, the mud-dirt, gasping, soaking wet, laughing, panting like an idiot fish, idiot girl.

IN TRAINING CAMP WE WAKE UP EVERY MORNING AT 4:30, HAVE A half hour to prepare ourselves for the day. We make wuzu, morning ablutions, then fajr prayer together as a group. We call each other brother. *Excuse me, brother; brother, pass me the towel.* My parents weren't especially religious growing up and the only times we ever prayed together as a family was when an aunt or our grandparents from Qom were staying with us. Fajr was always my favorite of those prayers because it was so short, only two rakats. The whole experience of the prayer fit tidily into the span of a single dream, a fifteen-minute sleepwalk into surrender, obedience, God, whatever. Smart, I thought, for God to demand prayer from his servants while their minds were still gummy with dream, while the partition between our world and his was thinnest.

This is, of course, all ruined by the army, which calls for physical training between fajr and breakfast, meaning no return to sleep, meaning no mind gummy with dream, meaning once you are up you are up. Fajr takes on a totally different meaning here, the final moments of relative stillness, the last quiet of the day, a time before the omnipresent gaze of our superior officers turns each of us twitchy and strange. There are no mirrors in our shared bathroom, something about preventing ego, idolatry, though the real result is a squad full of sloppy uniforms, missing buttons, and crooked lapels. When I make wuzu and wash my face with the water, I sometimes imagine it to be a kind of solvent, eating away my skin, the muscle beneath it, and the bone beneath that, the water stripping not just the dream from my head but my head itself, until by the end I'm just scrubbing whatever vanity isn't, whatever *to be* is, whatever's beneath my body and all its equipment for keeping me here, that's what I imagine myself washing. I get the sense my *is* is filthier than other people's. Heavier with all that dirt.

WHEN ROYA WAS LYING THERE HEAVING ON HER MUD, THAT POND mud, I wanted to strangle her. Not to hurt her exactly, but to make her feel afraid, afraid the way I felt afraid, or afraid the way I felt I should have felt afraid, the way I felt blocked from feeling. Maybe I just wanted to take away the feeling of invincibility. A girl cannot go through life acting like nobody can hurt her. This world? No. But even that frames my rage—the rage that felt like a hot white pin shot through my eye—as something purposeful or noble, but it wasn't that. There was just something in her okayness that disgusted me, that made me dizzy with anger.

"What were you doing, you goat?" I hissed. "What are we going to do now?"

She was dripping wet, dripping water that might soon freeze into ice against her coat and against her body.

"Why are you so—" she said, before I cut her off:

"Poison of the snake!" I shouted, something I meant like "shut up!" and "bullshit!" both but meaner than either.

I realized that to get Roya home I was going to have to sneak her into our house without our mother noticing. Luckily our father was away at work; he fixed power lines, whenever power went out anywhere in Tehran they called his company, all hours of the day and night even on weekends, and that week he had been working long hours in the heart of the city, near the Masjid-e Ark.

I walked Roya back to our house, her pride giving way to shivers, deep shivering, she was trying to hide it but before long she couldn't, I could hear it even without looking at her, her teeth vibrating, and I did give her my coat eventually, even though I wanted her to suffer, even though I wanted her to feel ashamed and contrite I gave her my jacket. When we got to the house I ran to my mother who was slicing cucumber in the kitchen and started talking with her, telling her about this and that, I don't even remember what, and I think she was so excited I was talking to her, me who was usually such a quiet boy, that she thought nothing of it, and Roya was able to come in a few seconds after me and sneak up to the shower, the shower where she stayed for what must have been twenty minutes. And I don't remember what my mother and I talked about, what she ended up cooking, just that while we talked about nothing, even as she was asking me about my friends or my school or just generally relishing having her only boy present and chatty, I could hear Roya in the shower upstairs, I could hear her stomping around warming up, giggling, laughing, singing.

TWELVE

GILLES DELEUZE CALLED ELEGY *LA GRANDE PLAINTE,* "THE GREAT complaint," a way of saying "what is happening is too much for me." In Iran, Ashura is a day of elegy where people fast and mourn the martyrdom of Imam Hussain, killed in 680 CE on his fifty-fifth birthday in the Battle of Karbala. A day of elegy. "What happened thirteen centuries ago is still too much for us," Iranians say. It is in our blood, la grande plainte. Shekayat bazorg. We remember. Of course we remember.

—*from* BOOKOFMARTYRS.docx by Cyrus Shams

CYRUS SHAMS

——— ✳ ———

IT HAD BEEN STORMING ONE OF THOSE UNIQUELY INDIANA SUMMER storms. Merciless, without beginning or end. To Cyrus, then, the storm and all other meteorological phenomena happened directly to him. Against him. Storms existed expressly to piss Cyrus off, snow to make him late to his job answering phones at the all-night Chinese takeout place on campus. The sun came out to burn Cyrus specifically, to make him wince at its white.

That summer, Cyrus was also trying to expand his horizons by dating a Republican.

He was raised Iranian in the American Midwest, amidst 9/11 and the subsequent jingoism and lawn flags and yellow ribbons and the "aren't you glad to be here" set. Cyrus could see it in their chests when they looked at him. It was like Americans had another organ for it, that hate-fear. It pulsed out of their chests like a second heart.

Once, shortly after 9/11, Cyrus's middle school math teacher, bald save a bright orange ring of unkempt hair around his ears, hung a poster of George Bush by his blackboard. Later that term, he told Cyrus after class, conspiratorially, that he'd heard a new term for people like him. He whispered it though they were alone in the room. Two words, the first was "sand." Cyrus's teacher laughed, as if Cyrus was in on the joke. Cyrus didn't know what to do so he laughed along with him. He hated himself for that.

Another time, Cyrus's social studies teacher, a woman just out of college, referred to him mid-class, pointing out how "our troops" were helping Cyrus's "people over there" to "figure out democracy." Most of the other students in the room nodded approvingly at the idea, if they registered it at all. So Cyrus did too. He didn't mention what *our troops* had done to his mother *over there*. He hated himself for that, too.

At the intersection of Iranian-ness and Midwestern-ness was pathological politeness, an immobilizing compulsivity to avoid causing distress in anyone else. Cyrus thought about this a lot. You cooed at their ugly babies, nodded along with their racist bullshit. In Iran it was called taarof, the elaborate and almost entirely unspoken choreography of etiquette that directs every social interaction. The old joke, that two Iranian men could never get on an elevator because they'll just keep saying "you go," "no you," "no no please," "I insist," as the doors opened and closed.

Midwestern politeness felt that way too, Cyrus learned, like it was burning cigarette holes in your soul. You bit your tongue, then bit it a little harder. You tried to keep your face still enough to tell yourself you hadn't been complicit, that at least you weren't encouraging what was happening around you. To you.

Kathleen was the first Republican he ever dated, the first wealthy person too. She was a business grad student at Keady's famous Morris School of Management. She came from a rich family in Arizona. Not my-mom-is-a-dentist rich—that was the kind of wealth Cyrus had seen, peripherally, growing up in Fort Wayne, and the kind around which he'd built his lifelong distaste for the moneyed.

Kathleen was oil-rich, charm-school-and-family-stables rich, a new kind of rich that made Cyrus's moral compass spin all the way through contempt and back around to curiosity. Once, she told him John McCain had come to her college graduation party.

"An old friend of my dad's," she'd shrugged.

For a couple months, Cyrus successfully suppressed his distaste for her politics in favor of this new novelty: Kathleen would buy books and leave them sitting in the coffee shop, only quarter-read. She'd tip 100 percent on one bar tab, then nothing on the next. Money meant nothing to her. She'd borrow Cyrus's jacket, his hoodie, and never return them, not realizing he had no replacements. She knew the name of the guy who flew her father's helicopter, of her nanny's kid, which she'd bring up frequently as evidence of her magnanimity. She was Christian but American Christian, the kind that believed Jesus had just needed a bigger gun.

Cyrus loved that she was more ambitious, more driven, more beautiful than he was. When they slept together, she would just kind of lie back and smile a little, like, *you're welcome.* That sort of beautiful.

Cyrus also loved, if he was being very rigorously honest, that she picked up every food and bar tab. That she could order delivery twice a day without thinking anything of it. That her groceries came from Whole Foods, not Aldi. The fresh-squeezed grapefruit juice alone was almost worth the cognitive dissonance.

One night, the two drove Kathleen's BMW from her apartment through a summer storm to the Green Nile, the campus hookah bar. That was where Cyrus met Zee for the first time; he was their server. He introduced himself with his full name, Zbigniew, to which Kathleen immediately asked, "Zbigniew? What is that?"

Zee didn't hesitate a moment before grinning, saying, "Sounds like a sneeze, doesn't it? I'm Polish Egyptian, it's from the Polish part. My friends just call me Zee."

Cyrus had chewed some Klonopin before leaving the apartment, the little yellow-orange ones that tasted like citrus when you bit into them—Cyrus believed the pharmaceutical companies did it on purpose as a gift to recreational users—and then snorted a bit of Focalin to level out the high. At the Green Nile, he just nodded lazily along as Kathleen ordered the first of many pitchers of "house sangria," which Zee told Cyrus many months later was just Franzia Chillable Red with chunks of frozen apple in it.

After Kathleen and Cyrus finished their first hookah, Zee offered to make their next one "special." Cyrus found the whole experience of American hookah bars vaguely off-putting and orientalist, the children of soybean farmers and insurance salesmen sitting around eating stale falafel dipped in Costco hummus, smoking "Electric

Raspberry" shisha from hookahs made in Taiwan. But he'd never been one to let his beliefs get in the way of a buzz, and the prospect of free-to-him booze and weed made Cyrus squirm with glee.

"Apologies to Edward Said," Cyrus said under his breath, thinking himself very clever.

"Huh?" Kathleen asked. Cyrus just shook his head. In Cyrus's addict calculus, getting to feel morally and intellectually superior to Kathleen, despite her great wealth and beauty, somehow put them on level ground. Each of them fascinated the other.

When Zee brought out the second hookah, he said, "This is pretty intense stuff, so take it slow."

They did not take it slow. At first Cyrus felt paranoid the smell of weed was overpowering the smell of the shisha—Zee'd recommended "White Gummi Bear" flavor as the one best at masking the scent. Cyrus often got that way on weed, anxious, unable to escape the idea everyone was hyper and negatively focused on the granular details of his person. It was for this reason weed wouldn't have made his list of top ten favorite highs, which didn't stop Cyrus from smoking it practically every day, ubiquitous as it was. He drank more, faster, to mellow out his paranoia. The alcohol calmed him a little, and he came to realize none of the other patrons seemed to notice the weed smell, or at least none of them seemed to care. As the rain outside relaxed to a drizzle, the night accelerated toward its natural conclusion.

Kathleen talked about small grievances with her friends, her classmates. She complained about a professor who never answered his emails, a friend who was cheating on her boyfriend and expected her to support it. Cyrus tried hard to focus on her eyes, which were the kind of blue many blond people's eyes are. So common you forget how pretty they are. Like pigeons. At one point, she exclaimed, "I feel so outnumbered in this place!" She laughed, taking a strong sip of her sangria, their third or fourth pitcher.

Cyrus studied her face. Those blue blue eyes. Straight blond hair down past her shoulders. Her houndstooth blazer was spinning a little, but so was the wallpaper. She was gorgeous in that aggressively

American way, the kind of woman you might see in an ad for cold medicine. She'd taken an acting class in LA with James Franco once, Cyrus remembered her saying. She said he'd tried to sleep with her.

"Outnumbered?" Cyrus asked, trying to get his eyes to focus on hers.

Green Nile's décor was vaguely pan–Middle Eastern: framed Arabic calligraphy, a photograph of a camel, a pyramid, a river, a rug. The checkout counter had a Chinese lucky cat, its arm waving up and down through the fog of hookah smoke.

"C'mon. Look at this place. You and the server and the music and walls. It's like Baghdad, Indiana!"

Cyrus hadn't noticed the music till she pointed it out. That's how nondescript it was—strangely quiet, some sort of poppy sitar affair, maybe Ravi Shankar. Cyrus wondered what about him made Kathleen feel like he'd think "Baghdad, Indiana" was funny. His unaccented English? The sex they had? His perpetually bitten tongue, the way he rarely challenged her regressive political takes? All these things sat outside Kathleen's experience of *them*-ness, so to her Cyrus was an *us*.

Cyrus wondered about how much of his living he owed to other people's assumptions of his us-ness. The middle school teacher who surreptitiously offered him a racial slur, like a juicy orange they might peel together and share. Even his name could pass as white. Cyrus Shams. Weird, probably ethnic, but kind of inscrutably so. Cyrus felt like Blade, the Wesley Snipes hero, half human, half vampire, with all the superpowers of each species, super strong but also capable of walking around in sunlight. Like Blade, Cyrus was a day-walker, American when it suited him and Iranian when it didn't. Bullets bounced off his chest! His teeth could cut through metal! He was really, really stoned.

"Let's get you out of Baghdad," Cyrus said, trying for a moment to figure out a shock-and-awe joke, failing, then feeling grateful to have failed. He was too high to feel disappointed in himself. Kathleen smiled and flagged Zee. She handed him her credit card, dull black metal.

"How are you guys feeling?" Zee asked when he brought it back.

"Pretty. Fucking. Good!" She said each word like a teenager over-reading a poem. "I think we might've made the rain stop." Outside it was still a bit wet, but Kathleen was right, the full fury of the storm had abated.

Zee smiled and said something Cyrus couldn't make out, but it made Kathleen laugh so Cyrus laughed too. Zee shot him a look, a fraction of a fraction of a glance that Cyrus took to mean "You sure about her?" but might have meant "You aren't driving, are you?" Cyrus shrugged in the direction of nobody and carefully stood up out of his seat, trying not to wobble.

The rain had completely stopped when they got to Kathleen's car, leaves around them dropping onto sidewalks and puddles rippling in the wind. Kathleen drove the two of them up Old 233, streetlights breathing heavy the whole way. At her apartment Cyrus tucked Kathleen in and told her he was going for a walk. She was too sleepy to protest.

"Be careful" was all she said, rolling over.

Cyrus poured himself a plastic cup of fancy grapefruit juice and took it with him out into the night.

Walking back in the general direction of campus, he was listening to Sonic Youth's "Sister," on his iPod from its first track. Coming down from wine drunk and weed high, in that gummy interstitial state of psychic congestion and heightened emotional arousal, Cyrus began suddenly crying at Kim and Thurston's harmony singing:

"It feels like a wish coming true, it feels like an angel dreaming of you . . ."

Ugly crying. Bawling, really, as he walked. Cyrus felt in that moment like he was wearing a crown. Sonic Youth, the streetlights, the smell of ozone after rain—it was all for him. His grapefruit juice had transubstantiated into ambrosia. It tasted so good it made him dizzy. Cyrus felt new. Sinless. Invincible.

He would think about this a lot in the years to come. Before addiction felt bad, it felt really, really good. Of course it did. Magic. Like you were close enough to God to bop him with an eyelash.

"You've got a magic wheel in your memory. I'm wasted in time . . ."

If he'd had a block of marble he could've carved the David. If he'd had a sword he could have sliced through a car. If he'd had a mother she'd be delirious with pride, holding him against her chest, wiping away his tears.

AFTER SOME TIME—FIFTEEN MINUTES, AN HOUR—CYRUS FOUND himself across the river, walking toward the Green Nile. Lucky's, his go-to bar, was a block away. He saw a couple of regulars in front of its neon Old Style sign smoking cigarettes. Usually he'd have joined them, bumming a cigarette then going inside to order a $5 pitcher of PBR for himself. But something was calling Cyrus back to the Green Nile. When he walked in, the Indian guys were still at their table, working on a new hookah.

"Whoa, hey," Zee said, on seeing him. "You lost your girlfriend."

Cyrus considered lying, saying he'd forgotten his umbrella. On the one hand, it would sound nobler than "I put my girlfriend to bed so I could come back here and keep drinking." On the other hand, Cyrus knew his desire to return to drink would be laid bare no matter what he said, the phantom umbrella obvious as any other smoking gun.

"She's back home," Cyrus responded. "Finished her tour of duty." He was proud of this joke, even if Zee wasn't in on it. It made him feel like he'd regained a shred of the dignity he'd lost earlier. "Did I miss last call?"

Zee walked back behind the bar. "You just made it. What do you want?"

"What's the cheapest way to drink here?" Cyrus had long grown past feeling shame at asking this question.

Zee pulled two bottles of High Life from a mini fridge:

"You let me buy you one of these."

Zee was compact, had light stubble that blended into his hairline, which he shaved close to the skin every couple of days. His skin was

coppery and his stubble black; his mother's Egyptian genes dominated his Polish father's. His physical compression felt anything but
slight—not intrinsically small like a mouse, but coiled, gathered into
himself, like a cat preparing to leap.

Before long, the Indian guys were closing their tabs and heading
out into the night. Zee said goodnight to each of them by name.
He went to the iPod plugged into the restaurant speakers and
switched it from the sitar raga that had been playing almost inaudibly
to a custom playlist of his own that opened with EPMD's "Strictly
Business." Turning the volume way up, Zee began wiping down
tables as Cyrus sat at the bar.

"Can I help with anything?" he asked. Cyrus liked having something to do with his body.

Zee just laughed and said, "Nah, I'm almost done."

Zee made banter about this or that. He pointed out the samples
used in the song—Eric Clapton, Kool and the Gang. He continued
closing and talked about flying planes, an aeronautics course he was
taking at Keady for fun—"you lose eight ounces of water for every
hour you're in the air, but you can't really drink either because there's
nowhere to pee"—his father's half-hearted conversion to Islam—"we
were as Muslim as a Catholic family that only goes to church on
Christmas and Easter"—and the drums on Erykah Badu's *Mama's
Gun*—"it's this boom tik boom boom thing, instead of boom boom
tik boom." Cyrus didn't follow most of it, but was content to nurse
his High Life, vaguely enthused by Zee's scattershot enthusiasms.
After telling a somewhat confusing narrative about busting his kick
drum at a jazz ensemble gig, Zee started counting tables left:

"Just have one, two, three, four, five more, and then I'm done," he
said. When he counted them, he used his fingers—one on his pointer,
two on his middle finger, three on his ring, four on his pinky, and then
he looped back around to count off five on his pointer again. Cyrus
thought it enchanting and said so—

"You don't count on your thumb?"

Zee looked at him, then back at his hand, as if suddenly remembering it was there.

"Oh," he said, not self-consciously but as if remembering suddenly the two were strangers. "When I was a kid, I was a really late talker. So my mom taught me to count on my fingers like: one, two, three, four, and then my thumb was for 'many.' She'd ask me how many French fries or crayons I wanted, and I'd just hold out my thumb to say 'lots!' It wasn't for counting like the other fingers. I've never really thought about it much."

"Whoa," Cyrus said, then suddenly felt dumb for saying it. He tried to rally by adding something quasi-profound: "Infinity on the thumb of your hand, eternity in an hour . . ." then felt even more ridiculous.

But Zee just laughed, said, "Hah, I guess! I don't really know. What do you do, Cyrus?"

Cyrus felt glad for the opportunity to jet past his nonsense.

"I'm still a student," he said. "A super-senior going on . . . I don't know. I've been here awhile. English major. Most nights I answer phones and take delivery orders at Jade Café."

"I don't mean what do you do for school or money," Zee said. "I'm asking what do you do. What do you love?"

Zee had just finished wiping down a table, and now was sitting down marking up receipts. Over the speakers, Emmylou Harris sang about popping the heads off dandelions.

"I mean, I write. I write poems, but I haven't published anything."

Zee looked up from his receipts, eyes wide: "You're a poet!"

"I wouldn't say that," Cyrus answered, tipping his High Life bottle into his mouth before realizing it was already empty. Zee smiled.

"Well, do you write poems?"

"Yeah."

"Then you get to call yourself a poet." Zee said the final word, "poet," smugly, like a lawyer closing an argument. "I've never cut a record," he said, "but I have no trouble calling myself a drummer."

Cyrus wanted to object, point out something vague and political about the *responsibility* of calling oneself a poet, but Zee's confidence was catching, and besides, Cyrus was feeling a little drunk again. He *did* write a lot. And certainly he read as much poetry as anyone he knew, indiscriminately pulling handfuls of books off the 811.5 section of his library to pore over at home. In fact, that very afternoon he'd skipped a quiz over "Hero and Leander" in his Elizabethan drama class because he'd been so immersed in reading Jean Valentine: "I came to you, Lord, because of the fucking *reticence* of the world."

Zee walked behind the bar, put the receipts inside the register. Looking at Cyrus, he said: "I've got some rum back at my place just up Chauncey. You wanna listen to *Mama's Gun?* My partner is at his parents' in Chicago, so we can turn it way up."

It was still only a little after two in the morning and Cyrus was ideologically opposed to, and constitutionally incapable of, turning down free alcohol.

"Cool, yeah," he said.

They gathered themselves and walked the few blocks to Zee's apartment, a fourth-floor studio overlooking River Road, with two old mountain bikes in front of the kitchen sink. Zee pulled a half-full fifth of Captain Morgan from his freezer and plugged his iPod into a set of cheap computer speakers. They sat on a ratty old couch that looked like it had been upholstered with burlap.

Passing the bottle back and forth, talking a little, Zee would occasionally illuminate an important musical or biographical detail—this is a Stevie Wonder sample, this line is about her breakup with Andre 3000. Halfway into "My Life," Cyrus asked to pause the album so they could go outside and smoke. It was windy, and Zee bent over holding his unlit cigarette between his lips to light it within the shield of his coat. Cyrus thought that was very cool. Mostly though, the two drank and listened in silence. Some point before "Green Eyes," Cyrus passed out; when he woke up again it was morning. The bottle was nearly empty on the couch between him and Zee, and their shoulders were just barely touching.

THIRTEEN

THE IRON LAW OF SOBRIETY, WITH APOLOGIES TO LEO TOLSTOY: the stories of addicts are all alike; but each person gets sober their own way. Addiction is an old country song: you lose the dog, lose the truck, lose the high school sweetheart. In recovery you play the song backward, and that's where things get interesting. Where'd you find the truck? Did the dog remember you? What'd your sweetheart say when they saw you again?

When I got sober it wasn't because I punched a cop or drove my car into a Burger King or anything dramatic like that. I had a dozen bottoms that would have awakened any reasonable person to the severity of the problem, but I was not a reasonable person. The day I finally lurched my way toward help was like any other. I woke up alone on my floor still drunk from the night before. I remember taking a pull or two from the nearly empty bottle of Old Crow bourbon by my mattress, then searching for my glasses and car keys. Finding them, I calmly drove myself to help.

Beautiful terrible, how sobriety disabuses you of the sense of your having been a gloriously misunderstood scumbag prince shuffling between this or that narcotic crown. The superficial details may change—it wasn't a truck, it was a business; it wasn't a sweetheart, it was a family—but the algorithm is inexorable. A drug works till it doesn't. Dependence grows until it eclipses everything else in the addict's life. Rotten sun. Joy withers in the absence of light. Passion, jobs, freedom, family. We all have the snorting-spilled-coke-off-bathroom-tile stories. That stuff is only interesting to those blessed with a rare cosmic remove from knowing actual addicts. Active addiction is an algorithm, a crushing sameness. The story is what comes after.

—*from BOOKOFMARTYRS.docx by Cyrus Shams*

ROYA SHAMS

———— ✦ ————

I NEVER REALLY LOVED BEING ALIVE. IT'S HARD TO GET THERE without some sort of distance. Hard to describe the shape of a cloud from inside the cloud. Like how I would appreciate gravity more if I'd had trouble floating off in my teens. And what I could sneak away for myself felt notable only in contrast to that baseline of self-lessness. A half hour stolen in the morning to quietly sip tea alone or mindlessly doodle only felt like a reprieve because it was what everything else—cooking, cleaning, shopping—wasn't.

That's why I was so annoyed when I met Leila. Our husbands had been friends since their military service. Once a year, they'd drive north to the woods of Rasht, near the Caspian, to smoke cigars and drink and fish and retell the same stories they told each other every year. Gilgamesh, Leila's husband, was a squat man, muscular, balding. Leila was taller than him, not by too much but still notice-ably so. She told me once he asked her not to wear heels, which she said she was happy to oblige. Gilgamesh had worked for the Tehran police since leaving the military. Ali told me that during their trips, he sometimes shot squirrels and doves with his service revolver. I didn't much like that, but my eagerness at having our house to myself for a few days each year dwarfed the distaste I had for whatever Ali was doing or who he was doing it with.

I knew wives then who couldn't use the bathroom without first asking their husband's permission. My marriage with Ali was never one of those, but just being perceived, all the time being perceived, was itself exhausting. Ali's vacations were vacations for me too.

This was around the time I realized I was pregnant with Cyrus. I still hadn't taken a test, not wanting to confirm what I already knew was true. But I was spotting, and my spit tasted like copper wire. My breasts were heavy and sore; it hurt to inhale too deeply. I knew what was happening. Making some blue lines appear on a pregnancy stick would mean I would have to tell Ali, and once I told Ali, I knew nothing would be the same. I just wanted to be vacant a little longer. Free from his devout attention, his pity.

When Gilgamesh showed up at our house to pick up Ali, he'd packed a car full of camping supplies: a tent, little pans, gin, wine. He'd married Leila that summer, a small ceremony I remembered mostly because the bride had so few relatives present—a stern doughy father chain-smoking Russian cigarettes, a few ambivalent cousins. And then there they were in our driveway, Gilgamesh and his new bride. She was maybe twenty-four, twenty-five, stout, eyes constantly moving around with an air of boyish mischief. Gilgamesh asked Ali if she could stay with me during their trip, something about it not being safe to leave Leila alone in their house—I wasn't sure if he meant not safe for her or for him to leave her alone. I begged Ali with my face to say no, wanted desperately to protect my precious few days of total autonomy. But Ali agreed without hesitation and there was nothing to discuss. Gilgamesh barely even looked at me, waddling around inside our house inside his muscles, inside a body grown two sizes too large for his brain. It was like he was at a bank: he deposited his wife, this stranger, and picked up Ali. And then the men were gone, and Leila and I were alone.

IT DIDN'T TAKE LONG FOR LEILA TO EMERGE FROM BEHIND HER veil of meek decorum. It was like the men took her shyness with them. I had made zereshk polo that first night, but I was, am, not a good cook. I get impatient, distracted, could never get the timing right. My rice turned sticky, my kabobs burned. Serving the meal,

Leila didn't even wait for me to plate myself before diving into her food. She was compact, had cut her hair very short, so her head had these coin-sized curls that moved around as she chewed. We talked about little things for two seconds—yes, the mulberries came from the vendor at the market with the shaggy dog; no, Gilgamesh didn't like zereshk polo.

"He doesn't like sweet things," Leila said. "Sometimes he just grabs a pinch of sumac, a pinch of salt, and he'll suck on that. Is that normal?" she asked.

"I have never heard of that," I admitted.

"He's like an alien who pretends to be human. 'Ah, this is food? I shall eat this. Ah, dancing? Let me try that,'" she said, pantomiming her husband in a sort of dance seizure.

I smiled a little, despite myself, which seemed to encourage her.

"Really! He pours cough syrup in his tea! Every morning and every night!"

I didn't know what to do with my face, so I tried to keep it still. I didn't know this woman at all, couldn't figure out why she was telling me these things. Suddenly, she said, "Ah, I don't want to talk about husbands anymore. They're gone after all, alhamdulillah!"

I said nothing but was a little insulted. She was the one who'd brought up Gilgamesh. I'd said nothing about Ali.

"Okay," I tried. "What would you prefer to talk about?"

"Oh god! If you have to ask that, we are already lost, aren't we?" She laughed, but I was feeling frustrated.

"How about we go for a walk," Leila said. "I want to show you something."

It was late already, maybe seven p.m. But I did not want to be rude to this guest, however unwelcome, however rude she was being to me. She got up from the table, leaving her plate where it was, and walked to the coat rack by the door. I made a point of collecting her plate, silverware, and glass slowly, methodically, to the point where she said, "Oh come on, Roya jaan, just leave it! Who are you even cleaning up for?"

Myself? I thought reflexively but did not say.

"I just want to rinse everything quickly so the grime doesn't set," I said, no longer trying to mask my annoyance.

Leila rolled her eyes, stood impatiently by the door like a petulant teenager while I took my time rinsing the forks, the knives. Finally I met her by the entrance with my coat. She was looking at herself in the little gold mirror we had hanging near the entrance. It was something I'd come to love about her, in time. It wasn't narcissism, the way she was always looking at herself. I recognized later there was a kind of wonder in it, running her fingers over her smile lines, the skin of her forehead, as if to say, "Where did you come from? This skin, what a strange envelope!" But there, in the moment, I just saw a silly vain girl.

"Where are we going?" I asked, opening the door.

"To the lake," Leila said. "I want to show you something."

I was trying to be a good host, but my hospitality was wearing thin. The lake would be a twenty-minute drive, and it was already starting to get dark. I resented having to agree to this stranger's whims. I grieved for my lost aloneness.

"Isn't that a bit far," I asked, obvious in my unhappiness.

"Do you have a pressing appointment?" Leila asked impishly.

I frowned but pulled my scarf over my head. Even though it was beginning to get dark outside, Leila pulled out a pair of sunglasses, big ones with thick black frames that covered up half her face, and we headed out.

FOURTEEN

. . . .

QU YUAN

340 BCE–278 BCE

you laureate of tongue and stone,
among the rarer hues
on the spectrum from brightest bright
to darkest dark—

the villagers throwing rice into the river
to lure fish from your corpse,

stutteringly radiant still, the dragon boats racing
in the pink light—

no I won't sign up for old age either,
anacondas
and common pearls:

of the beginning of the beginning
who spoke the tale?

you did, you did

. . . . .

—*from* BOOKOFMARTYRS.docx *by* Cyrus Shams

SATURDAY

————— ✳ —————

Cyrus Shams and Orkideh

CYRUS WOKE UP IN HIS BROOKLYN HOTEL WITH ZEE'S THUMB IN his mouth. They'd split the cost of a single bed single room for a weekend, which made it surprisingly affordable. The hotel they'd found was even one of those hip Brooklyn-y places with loud music and a live DJ in the lobby at night. The mini bar boasted two different kinds of mezcal, and a "feminist icons" tarot deck with a picture of Gloria Steinem as the Queen of Cups on the box's outside.

Cyrus had been a late-in-life thumbsucker. When he was thirteen, his father became determined to fix the problem once and for all. He began making Cyrus soak his thumbnails in hot pepper juice nightly after dinner. For weeks, Cyrus would rise in the middle of the dark, his thumb in his mouth, his lips and tongue on fire. Nothing could shrink the pain. It took ages for his sleeping self to finally reject his thumbs as poison. Later in his life, almost as if out of protest, Cyrus's subconscious began enlisting any bedmate's thumb as proxy for his own, and Zee's was the most common surrogate.

The two had begun rooming together shortly after meeting, and sharing each other's beds not long after that. When they'd sleep together, it mostly wasn't sexual. In one of the very few occasions over the years when they'd spoken about it, Cyrus told Zee it was like that line from *Moby-Dick*.

"The bit about putting up with any half-decent man's blanket?" Zee'd asked.

Cyrus had been thinking about a different line, about it being better to sleep with a sober cannibal than a drunken Christian. He thought of himself as the sober cannibal, and Americans broadly as drunk Christians. But he just laughed and said: "Yeah, that one. You do have very nice blankets."

Cyrus had gotten to know Zee's thumbs well. They were long on Zee's hand, but still considerably shorter than Cyrus's. At six-foot-three, Cyrus was nearly a foot taller than his roommate, but more often than not Zee still ended up as big spoon when they cuddled. Zee's thumbs were like miniatures of Zee himself, compact but muscular, sturdy and strong. They could have belonged to a masseuse or a sculptor, a seamstress or a carpenter.

The two rarely kissed, and if they did it was almost never on the lips. Mostly they held each other, played against each other's skin and backs and fingers. Mostly they slept.

Sometimes Cyrus would turn to face Zee and reach his hand down his shorts, or Zee would reach around Cyrus and softly scratch his fingers through his pubic hair into his crotch, and they'd finish the other off like that, eyes closed and breathing heavy. Or sometimes, facing each other, they would touch themselves, using their off-hands to trace the other's nipples, Adam's apple, lips.

Usually though, they just held each other and slept. It was simple that way. Just two half-decent men sharing a blanket.

When Cyrus or Zee was dating someone, they'd introduce their roommate as their best friend. When they were both partnered, they'd go out on double dates, play loud music in their respective bedrooms to cover the sounds of their sex. Cyrus never told his partners about sleeping with Zee, and Zee never told any of his boyfriends either.

It wasn't out of secrecy or shame—Zee was openly and happily gay, and Cyrus just ended up with people, their gender rarely figuring significantly into his interest. They found it impossible to describe their relationship to others without over- or underselling the kind of intimacy they shared. So they didn't try.

That morning in their too-hip Greenpoint hotel, Cyrus took Zee's thumb out of his mouth and set it gently on the bed, slipping out of the bed and into the shower. Zee turned over in his sleep, grunted a grunt that meant something along the lines of "Goodbye be quiet have a good day shh."

Cyrus emerged from the shower, quickly put on clean clothes, trying hard not to think too hard about his choices, settling on the same pants he'd worn the day before and a clean black T-shirt. Glancing back once, quickly, at Zee, who was still fast asleep, Cyrus stepped out the door.

CYRUS ARRIVED AT THE BROOKLYN MUSEUM AROUND ONE, MUCH later than he'd intended, after taking the train in the wrong direction all the way uptown and then finding himself hopelessly lost. The maps app in his phone was no help. He'd never been to New York—embarrassing to admit as a writer approaching thirty—and he was trying desperately not to look lost. Unfortunately, this just disoriented him more. He'd heard that only tourists look upwards in the city, native New Yorkers stared straight ahead, and he kept catching himself unconsciously gazing up at the hulking steel. It was impossible to imagine that humans like him had erected such alps. This awe made him feel good, still permeable to wonder, but also shamefully provincial. Country mouse.

Finally, after what seemed like an eternity of half-lost wandering and stepping onto and off of trains to confirm he was indeed headed back to Brooklyn, he managed to find the museum again. Dumb luck, that it'd been so effortless the day before. On entering, he bee-lined straight for the *Death-Speak* gallery, which he was surprised to find completely full, a long curling line of people waiting to talk to Orkideh. Cyrus spotted the same docent from the day before—thick septum ring, feather earring—sitting near the doorway of the gallery, looking at his phone.

"What's going on today?" Cyrus asked him.

"Hm?" grunted the docent.

"Why such a long line?"

The docent shrugged:

"Weekend? It always gets like this on Saturdays," then looked back down at his phone.

Cyrus took his place in line behind a father and his young daughter each dressed in athletic sweats. There was a not insignificant part of Cyrus's mind that resented everyone else waiting in the gallery. *Interlopers,* he couldn't help but feel. Vulgar looky-loos here to gawk at the dying woman, the "peanut-crunching crowd" shoving in to see her suffering. That Cyrus was here on a mission—and possibly, or maybe even hopefully, to plan his own death—exempted him from this gross voyeurism, he thought, though even as the idea was forming in his mind he wasn't sure he actually believed it.

At her table, Orkideh was talking with a muscley white guy with a black-and-white U.S. flag on his shirt. The man had a stump for a right arm and was speaking passionately, gesturing wildly, while the artist smiled in what seemed like tolerant bemusement.

Cyrus checked his phone. Several messages from Zee's day: a picture of a Daniel Johnston record with a line drawing of a woman's bust on the cover. A discarded paperback of Dante's *Purgatorio* abandoned fanned open in a sidewalk puddle. A gauzy poster in some nondescript store featuring Mick Jagger and Klaus Kinski in a summery European bell tower, which Zee had sent with the message, "do we need this?" Cyrus texted him back, "We ABSOLUTELY need it." Zee responded with three thumbs-up emojis.

The line moved a little. Cyrus checked his other messages. A text from a woman with whom Cyrus used to work asking if he was around to cat-sit. A link from Sad James to a YouTube video of an old The Locust show. And a text from his sponsor Gabe, the first since their fight. "Still sober?" Gabe had written. "Yep." Cyrus typed flatly, reflexively. Looking at it, Cyrus decided the terminal period made his text look overly harsh. After a few seconds, he added a "You?"

Another notification popped up from his bank app telling him he'd already spent 411 percent more this month than the previous. Cyrus closed it quickly and put his phone away. He focused on taking in the gallery and its attendees. One by one people sat in front of the artist—a bald man with a bushy sailor's beard, a teenager in a skullcap. To Cyrus, Orkideh looked half engaged, or perhaps just exhausted. She was letting her interlocutors do most of the talking. There was a flash of a second when she looked up from the sailor-beard man and caught a glimpse of Cyrus standing in line. He smiled at her, and she smiled across her whole face—she had little dimples above her eyebrows when she smiled this way—nodding happily to Cyrus just slightly before returning her attention to the man in front of her, who checked behind his shoulder, confused.

Finally, after three more people sat in the chair and got up, it was Cyrus's turn. As he was sliding into the chair, before he could even say hello, Orkideh said, "Cyrus Shams! You came back!"

"Of course I did," he said. "I'm here in the city to talk to you!" He said this, then considered it might perhaps feel like a burden to the artist, like he was pressuring her to be sufficiently brilliant as to make his trip worthwhile. He added, "I mean, I'm doing other things too. Walking around, watching, eating and writing. But I just find what you're doing here so incredible."

Orkideh rolled her eyes a bit, waved Cyrus's words away with her left hand. Her fingers were long, skeletal, her fingernails chewed to nibs.

"When I first came to New York City, that's all I did too," Orkideh said, shifting the subject. "Wander, watch, wander, watch. It's so much like Tehran, really. Here and there. Poor people putting out blankets on the street, selling picture frames and movies and wrist-watches. Right by them, in Central Park, on Park-e Shahanshahi, rich people have their servants, their nannies, spread blankets over grass so they can eat fruit with their babies, so they can sleep in the sun."

"I've never been to Iran," said Cyrus, embarrassed. He longed to be able to nod knowingly along with the artist's references.

"No?"

"I mean, not since I was a baby."

"You're not missing much." Orkideh smiled. "People are people, everywhere. Grass is grass, blankets are blankets. Countries are countries."

"You don't miss it?" Cyrus asked.

"Oh, I don't know. I miss places, foods. Fresh noon barbari, real mangoes. That kind of thing."

"You've made so much of your being here."

Orkideh rolled her eyes again.

"Really," Cyrus continued, "I've never heard of anyone doing anything like this. I mean . . . with their final days or whatever. It's so exactly what I've been wanting to write about, how to make a death useful. Who knows how many of these people"—he gestured to the line behind him—"needed to talk to you. How many lives will be changed—it's heroic, literally it's—"

"Okay, Cyrus," Orkideh said firmly. "Now you've said this part, now it can be behind us. Can we just be friends now? And talk like regular people?"

Cyrus paused for a second. He felt a flash of familiar shame—his whole life had been a steady procession of him passionately loving what other people merely liked, and struggling, mostly failing, to translate to anyone else how and why everything mattered so much. He realized he was perhaps doing what Sad James had once called The Thing, the overliking thing, obsessing over something in a way that others felt to be smothering.

As if sensing Cyrus's fluster, Orkideh added, "Cyrus, it is lovely to hear this feels meaningful to you. But I know myself too well to allow anyone to sit across from me and call me heroic. What, because I have cancer and a couple metal chairs in some museum?" She laughed, and Cyrus smiled a little. "Besides," she whispered conspiratorially, "I'm too fucking high on these pain meds. When you're dying they give you the really good stuff."

She laughed and so did Cyrus.

"That's hilarious," he said, suppressing the part of his brain that immediately wanted to ask what pain meds she was on specifically, opiates almost certainly, maybe even fentanyl. How many milligrams, though? A patch? This was such an evergreen wildness, to Cyrus, how strong his addict reflexes remained, in spite of his sobriety. *In the back of your brain, your addiction is doing push-ups, getting stronger, just waiting for you to slip up,* an old-timer once told him.

Cyrus shifted the conversation, saying, "I've been thinking about our conversation, a lot. I don't know how much you remember . . ."

"Hah, Cyrus, I remember it perfectly. Most of these people are not Iranian boys bent on martyrdom." She chuckled. "You're a very strange one. I'm afraid you've added us both to all the CIA lists!"

Cyrus smiled. "I honestly actually do worry about that, no joke. Being a young Iranian man making a book about martyrdom, going around talking to people about becoming a martyr. It's not inert, you know?"

The line behind Cyrus nearly filled the entire room. Already, their conversation had lasted longer than some that had preceded it. Cyrus went on: "W. E. B. Du Bois, the American sociologist, do you know his work?"

"I don't," said Orkideh. "Tell me about it."

"I'm not an expert. I just read a bunch of his stuff in school. He wrote about civil rights, racism. And I remember he had this idea of double-consciousness, how Black people in America always have to be mindful of how racist white people see them. And how that applies to a lot of marginalized people, always having to see themselves through the eyes of the folks who hate them. And being an Iranian vaguely Muslim man in a country that hates those things, each of those things, and then also writing about *martyrdom,* obsessing honestly over what that word might mean for me in my own life or in my own death . . . It's just hard not to think about, like, 'what would a person who hates me think about this.'"

"Why are you worried about what people who hate you think about your art?"

"Well, because the people who hate me also own all the guns and all the prisons." Cyrus laughed.

"Hah. Ah, yes, there is that," Orkideh said.

"Sometimes I just imagine the Fox News headlines, 'Iranian Muslim's Death Cult Manifesto Seized in Indiana' or whatever."

"It is probably not a good practice to start imagining headlines about your art before you even make it, Cyrus jaan."

"But see," Cyrus smiled, "that's a whole part of it too. How much of this whole thing is my ego? How much is it me wanting to matter more than other people? In life or in death?"

"I was thinking last night, your project reminds me of all the great Persian mirror art," Orkideh said. "Do you know much about that?"

"Nothing at all. Can you tell me about *it*?" Cyrus said. He felt he might explode with all the things he wanted to say to her, but he was also desperate for Orkideh to teach him, to sit at her feet and learn. Selfishly, he wanted to stay in the chair all day, all week, not let the line move. He wanted Orkideh all to himself.

"Some centuries ago all these Safavid explorers from Isfahan go to Europe—France, Italy, Belgium—and they see all these gargantuan mirrors all over. Ornate, massive mirrors everywhere in the palaces, in the great halls. Building-sized mirrors. They come back and they tell the shah about them and of course he wants a bunch for himself. So he tells his explorers, his diplomats, to go back to Europe and bring him mirrors, giant mirrors, buy them for any price. And so they do, but of course as they bring these massive mirrors back across the world, they shatter, they fracture into a billion little mirror pieces. Instead of great panes of mirror, the shah's architects in Isfahan had all this massively expensive broken mirror glass to work with. And so they begin making these incredible mosaics, shrines, prayer niches."

"Whoa."

"I think about this a lot, Cyrus. These centuries of Persians trying to copy the European vanity, really their self-reflection. How it arrived to us in shards. How we had to look at ourselves in these broken fragments, and how those mirror tiles found themselves in all these mosques, the tilework, these ornate mosaics. How those spaces made the fractured glimpses of ourselves near sacred." She paused, took a little sip from her white mug of water, then continued:

"It means, in my humble opinion, we got to cubism hundreds of years before Braque or Picasso or any European. That maybe we've been training for a long time in sitting in the complicated multiplicities of ourselves, of our natures. At least for a time. No monolithically good Siegfried hero versus monolithically bad dragon."

Cyrus knew she was talking about the hero and villain of a

Wagner opera, but only because of a joke in an old episode of *The Simpsons*. He nodded, and Orkideh went on:

"And look at what belief in that kind of total good versus total evil did. Hitler listening to Wagner in Nuremberg. That's what I'm getting at, you see? The flatness of me being this hero artist, or you being this martyr NSA threat. None of that is real. You know this. I'm not Siegfried any more than you're a dragon."

Cyrus and Orkideh were leaning over the table to speak to each other now, voices familiar, hushed. Behind them, people in line were starting to shift around passive-aggressively. An older woman in the middle of the line sighed loudly.

"I get that," said Cyrus. "I do. Maybe part of it is just wanting my tiny little life to have something of scale. For the stakes to matter." He paused, then added, "For my having-lived to matter."

Orkideh smiled, placed her hand on Cyrus's. It felt cold, dry, like canvas.

"We won't grow old together, Cyrus. But can't you feel this mattering? Right now?"

When he hesitated, she said, "It matters to me. Know that. It matters deeply." Then, looking up at the line, she sighed, leaned back in her chair. "You'll come see me again tomorrow, won't you?"

"Yeah, yes. Yes, of course, I'll be here. Yes, thank you." Before he knew it he was standing, walking away from the artist and her table and folding chairs, away from her dry hands and drier lips and the winding line of impatient patrons. Walking, suddenly, back outside the museum into the startling February air, Cyrus felt the artist's conversation, her voice and mind and presence, surging like a wildfire through his mind. Safavid glass, stakes. The dimples above her eyebrows. *We won't grow old together, Cyrus. But can't you feel this mattering?* He *could* feel it, he realized. He wished he'd said that.

FIFTEEN

IT FEELS SO AMERICAN TO DISCOUNT DREAMS BECAUSE THEY'RE not built of objects, of things you can hold and catalogue and then put in a safe. Dreams give us voices, visions, ideas, mortal terrors, and departed beloveds. Nothing counts more to an individual, or less to an empire.

—*from* BOOKOFMARTYRS.docx by Cyrus Shams

KAREEM ABDUL-JABBAR
AND BEETHOVEN SHAMS

———— ❄ ————

THE FIRST THING CYRUS SAW WAS THE SETTING, AN EMPTY PARKING lot raised a couple stories off the ground and surrounded by trees. This was almost never the case. Usually the people emerged first and began talking, usually these dreams started that way—not an absence of context but an absence of the need for context. The way a charming speaker blurs the room around them, and two make the room disappear entirely. But in this instance the dream parking lot came into clarity before the dream characters. The trees around the structure were full of ripe blooms, magnolia maybe. It wasn't a forest exactly, since beyond the trees were sprawling plains of yellow grass. But there were lots of trees, and in the center of them, in a neatly cleared square: a parking lot empty of cars, forty or so feet off the ground.

Within the parking lot, eventually, two men walked into clarity, one about a foot taller than the other. They were both wearing basketball clothes, the taller with clear plastic goggles and yellow short shorts, a too-tight #33 jersey. The shorter had long curly hair the color of wet earth, red Nike sweatpants over scuffy blue-and-white Jordans.

"What do you love?" Kareem Abdul-Jabbar asked the shorter man, who Cyrus recognized as the younger brother he used to imagine himself having when he was a kid. Kareem was a regular in these scenes, but Cyrus hadn't seen his imaginary little brother in a while; he wasn't among his usual cast of dream characters. Cyrus was excited to see him now, excited to see how his hair had grown long, down below his shoulders.

"Excuse me?" asked Cyrus's pretend brother, whose name was Beethoven, "Beethoven" after the titular dog in the 1992 family movie *Beethoven*. If Cyrus had it to do over, he'd name his imaginary brother something better, something human and aggressively Iranian, Shabahang or Rostam or Shahryar. But he knew once you named someone, even if you did it when you were a little kid, you didn't get to rename them, so "Beethoven" stuck.

"What do you love?" Kareem repeated.

"Basketball, I guess," Beethoven answered. The two men were circling the parking lot, walking the square brick edges and turning right at sharp angles. The trees nodded along. "Borges. Pecans. Magic tricks. *Twin Peaks* probably."

Both men laughed.

"*Twin Peaks?*" Kareem asked, scrunching up his face. "Wow. So you're one of those dudes. You drink IPAs too? You like to go hiking on the weekends?"

Beethoven smiled:

"I mean. Probably something insufferable like that, right? Maybe I'm really into turning people on to *Infinite Jest*. Or CrossFit. Or Tesla."

They both laughed again. Kareem said: "I don't know, man. You seem like you'd be into DJ-ing or hacking Bitcoin. Or improv classes."

"Damn, I bet I actually am really good at improv. That'd make a lot of sense." Beethoven ran a hand through his hair. His curls fizzed like soda bubbles.

"Tell me a joke," said Kareem.

"I don't think that's really how improv works," said Beethoven.

"I don't care, tell me a joke. Make me laugh."

Beethoven stopped walking for a second. His eyes got big and neon. For a second, they looked like marguerites, that yellow. Then he said, "What's red and invisible?"

Kareem shrugged his shoulders.

Beethoven said, "No tomatoes."

Kareem winced.

"That's a terrible joke, Beethoven."

They both laughed. The sky was shining blue over and over itself, like a mirror spinning on a string. Beethoven looked up at Kareem and asked, "How about you? What do you love?"

"I love basketball too," Kareem said, without hesitation. "Still. And I love movies. And jazz. You know about the fire?"

"Yeah, how your home burned down and all your records got destroyed."

Kareem nodded.

"Thousands of them. Years' and years' worth. Some really rare stuff. Irreplaceable. My dad played jazz and all his old records burned in that fire. So all the Lakers fans started sending me their records, records from their own personal collections."

"That's so strange," said Beethoven.

"Strange?" asked Kareem. The trees were flowering now into little pink and purple crowns.

"I mean," Beethoven began, "I don't want to speak for you. But it seems like it wouldn't be the physical records that mattered to you, but the stories behind them. Where you found them, your dad giving them to you, that sort of stuff. And you probably made more money than ninety-nine percent of the people sending you their records. Probably orders of magnitude more, right?"

"Wow," Kareem looked down at Beethoven. "Is this you talking, or is this Cyrus?"

Beethoven winced. "How would I even know?"

The two walked in silence for a minute. Two yellow birds, goldfinches, flew in from opposite sides of the lot and crashed violently into each other mid-air. A tantrum of feathers fell to the parking lot asphalt. There, they kicked up the sort of angry dust bubble you see in cartoon fights. Claws, beaks, exclamation points.

"First of all," Kareem began, "it was absolutely about the records themselves. It wasn't like now where you could go on YouTube and listen to anything. If I wanted to hear 'Nina at Newport,' I had to put the *Nina at Newport* record on the turntable. Some of the guys my dad played with gave him demos, home recordings. Irreplaceable shit."

Beethoven was starting to sweat. Kareem continued: "Can you imagine just losing access to all the art that you most loved, to all the stuff that gave your living purpose? Purpose and fluency? The stuff that made you feel like a member of the human tribe? That made you want to stay alive?"

"I can't," said Beethoven, honestly. "To stay alive. I can't imagine that."

"Imagine all that stuff disappearing," Kareem continued. "Literally going up in smoke."

Beethoven said nothing. The two kept walking.

"Then imagine," Kareem said, "that a bunch of people who'd never met you, for whom you're just a myth, began sending you the art you loved, or the art they loved, the art they thought you might love too. An old woman sending a bunch of old standards. Or an eight-year-old boy sending you his prized Monkees record. Imagine how that might contribute to your sense of amongness. To your sense of earth maybe actually being the right place for you."

"I never thought about it like that," Beethoven confessed.

"Obviously."

"But," Beethoven continued cautiously, "but these people didn't really know you. You said so yourself, you represented a kind of myth to them. And myths are the stories we tell ourselves to make living tolerable. To make shitty lives seem worth enduring. The gods lived on Olympus, a climbable mountain whose peak was in plain sight."

"Man . . ." Kareem was sweating now too. He wiped his brow with the back of his right forearm like he'd do in the fourth quarter of a close game.

"How much of the people's kindness had to do with their own sense of responsibility, their obsession with their own goodness? Ta-Nehisi Coates talks about 'the politics of personal exoneration . . .'"

Kareem laughed.

"Wait wait wait. I cannot continue this conversation with you if you're going to stand there quoting Ta-Nehisi Coates at me," Kareem said. "Look at yourself. Look at what's happening to you."

Beethoven looked at his hand, which was growing paler and paler by the second. It was like someone in Photoshop was slowly sliding the brightness filter up.

"Damn," said Beethoven, his face going from basketball-leather brown to referee's-uniform white. "Shit. Shit."

Beethoven should have been at least a bit younger than Cyrus but now he looked much older. Older than Kareem, even. His long black hair was wild with curls; it waved along with the tree branches, growing gray. He was beginning to look less like a person and more like a part of the scenery. Almost meteorological.

"Sometimes I forget you've never actually been alive," said Kareem.

"That's super real, yeah," said Beethoven. "I do too."

It began to snow. Kareem and Beethoven both began saying a line by Pablo Medina, "The rich man cannot buy snow," then stopped when they heard the other saying it. They smiled. The rest of the line, the part neither said out loud, was "and the poor man has to wear it on his eyebrows." They both thought of themselves as the rich man.

"Tell me another joke?" Kareem said.

"I really don't think you understand how improv works," said Beethoven.

"Or maybe you're just not very good at it."

Beethoven sucked his teeth.

"Fine. Here's one: Why did the scarecrow get a promotion?"

"Why?"

"Because he was out standing in his field."

Kareem groaned and then laughed, a big laugh that seemed to rattle the floor and the sky itself.

SIXTEEN

From: Rear Admiral William M. Fogarty, USN

To: Commander in Chief, U.S. Central Command

Subj: FORMAL INVESTIGATION INTO THE CIRCUMSTANCES SURROUNDING THE DOWNING OF A COMMERCIAL AIRLINER BY THE USS VINCENNES (CG. 49) ON 3 JULY 1988 (U)

1. **Intelligence Background.**
   a. *The Gulf War*
   (1) The war between Iran and Iraq is the latest iteration of a conflict dating back a thousand years.

ARASH SHIRAZI

———— ✳ ————

KHUZESTAN, IRAN, MAY 1985

ARMAN SAYS THERE'S A MAN LIKE ME IN EVERY PLATOON, ONE
Arash in every five hundred men, a me who keeps his horse away
from the other horses, who tucks a robe in his rucksack. A long black
robe like the hair of a god, robe finer than Moroccan silk, blacker
than the black you're imagining, black like the way your mind goes
black, atomic black spinning around the black like little cartoon birds,
that robe to wear over all my other clothes, my uniform and gun
and scabbard, yes, and even my helmet, a little black hood for that,
it goes over everything. Black robe on a black horse at night. With a
DC flashlight mounted in the neck beneath the hood. I saw Arman
put it on once, he put it on to show me at night how the flashlight
lit up his face, how the face isn't really so much a face in that much
dark, just a ball of light, how they painted the prophets in the old
paintings with a ball of fire for a head, a ball of light riding around
dressed in black, atop a black horse. Arman showed me, he got up
on Badbadak, that's my horse Badbadak, it means "kite" but really
it means "little wind wind," Badbadak like a horse from a picture
book, that dark and mighty, with a little extra fur around his hoofs
that made the bottom halves of his legs look like they too were wearing cloaks, long robes, Arman on Badbadak like a bit of divine light
galloping on a black wind and of course I saw it, the angel of it, of
course that was the point.

One man in every five hundred dresses like an angel, like this,
lit up like this angel of night, of history and death and of light and

relentless fucking war. Everything needs its angel, even war. A man like me in every platoon becomes an angel like this, a man like me who calls his sister once a month and sends money to his parents and eats cold rice and shits once a day like me, a man who dreams of Mira from the market with fluorescent scarves around her breasts, one man like me in every platoon sets out after battle and rides in my robe, rides with my flashlight, gallop around the war dead and the war dying, give them a glimpse of an angel protecting them, being among them. That's the secret, don't you think, the amongness, to be among with an angel means you were right all along, all your wincing and kneeling, your fasting, your scowling, that amongness might send you to Jannah, an angel to send you to Jannah and Riswan with conviction in your heart and not fear of pain, suffering, nothingness, conviction, yes, of seeing an angel in black riding the wind, riding the night, conviction to remain as long as suffering demanded, to not end it, not kill yourself.

Arman has been doing it for ages. He reminds me of the hadith about Muhammad and the soldier, the soldier who lay dying on the battlefield, sword wound opened up his side, all his companions gone or dead, dying soldier just dying there, staring at his own insides, alone, more alone than anyone's been since Hussain, and even Hussain at least had his family with him. And so this soldier dying there, he took his knife, it took some time he had so little strength, but he took his knife and cut his own throat open, it took some time because he was so weak by then, and so lost in agony, the agony that few living will ever know alhamdulillah, and so he died, the soldier died right there half by the enemy's blade and half by his own, and he goes to Jannah, to the gates of Jannah where he sees the Prophet, close enough to the Prophet's holy face peace be upon him to step forward and touch him, to breathe on him. And he was weeping, the holy Prophet's face! The face of God's final messenger peace be upon him was weeping as he turned away from the soldier, as he turned away the soldier yes, the Prophet peace be upon him sent the soldier away from Jannah, the soldier who had spent his life fighting a war he never understood and lived his final hours suffering so painfully on earth was sent to the other Hereafter, the place-name Arman won't even say when he tells me this story, like the name of a djinn, better not to even say it. How saying it calls on language to represent it, this sound is that thing, how some things rebuke sound, rebuke representation, we call the sun the sun as if that means anything, call such-and-such person a hero, such-and-such person a coward. The Prophet sent him away because he put his own knife into his own neck instead of suffering like a man, that's the lesson, that's the thing Arman wants me to remember.

So there are the men like me peppered into every platoon in the Iranian army, men who ride among the dying men to bolster their resolve, the men sent into battle with keys around their necks, keys to heaven they're told, and some of them not even men yet, it must be said, some of them boys with men's names, a child named Nassir, a child named Sohrab, named Houshang named Abbas named Pouyan, children walking around puffed up like men in men's clothes and men's names, as if the names made them men, as if wearing a man's boots could, and I ride around them as they die to keep them from cutting open their throats in their final moments, to remind them to suffer manfully, men like me preserve for them their hereafter. That's how Arman says it, "preserve their hereafter," let them be reunited with their babas and mamabazorgs and yes, their prophets, the prophets in whom I can only muster for myself scattered belief, like a light flicking on and off in a room I can see their shapes sometimes but never with any depth, never with anything like depth, or maybe it's the other way around where I can see their depth but can't quite make out the shape of them, the prophets, the why or how or even the what of the whole thing.

But what I do or don't or can't believe doesn't matter. Arman believes, his forehead often has the mark of his janamaz indented into it from him kneeling there so long, bowed on the rug so long, but I think Arman suspects I'm a little more confused, I think he knows because he always reminds me I ride for the men, for the dying men, not for myself, not for my country even but for the men and their desperate and spoilable souls. Action will be judged according to intention, that's what he always tells me, action will be judged according to intention, that's from the Quran somewhere. And I do, I intend to help these men, if it helps them to see a ball of light riding the wind then that's what I'll be.

And I haven't even mentioned yet the sword, the sword Arman gave me a year ago now, the same sword every Arman gives to every me in every platoon, sword with the end of the blade splitting into two fangs, twin fangs, really they look like demon teeth, this sword of course meant to look like Zulfiqar, sword of Hazrat Ali, an extra little flourish, though it never really totally made sense to me because why would an angel be carrying Hazrat Ali's sword, or am I supposed to be Hazrat Ali and then why am I personally on the battlefield, or maybe this angel is one of Ali's guards? Anyway, it means riding Badbadak mostly one-handed because if I keep the sword in its scabbard it just looks like any old sword, like any old sword handle, it has to be out and drawn for the blade's two fangs to catch the light, which is always moonlight, moonlight bright enough to cast shadows, when there's light at night that's where it comes from.

I wish I could see myself or I wish Mira from the market could see me, without the light without the hood but maybe on the horse, maybe with the sword, maybe she'd love me then and throw a scarf behind my neck to pull me closer to her mouth, her breasts, but she's hundreds of kilometers away from me now, it may as well be thousands, millions, me dressed as an angel traipsing around the mostly dead mostly indistinguishable men who I've been sharing meals, stories, showers, with, sometimes even that morning, now I was their angel, galloping around as an angel, angel with a fanged sword in the moonlight.

When he sees me, one man cries ob, ob, water, water—this happens a lot, Arman told me this would happen, the dying take their thirst with them, maybe the only thing they take, their thirst and their dying, thirst tearing open their chests worse than any sword, like a lion might, and I'm not allowed to give them water, absolutely not is what Arman said when I asked, why would an angel be carrying water he said, which makes sense, but so I just have to hear them cry and beg and die and I sit there on my big horse in my little costume holding my fake sword.

At the market Mira with her scarves had a child's plastic sword hung from her stall, hanging from her stall with scarves draped over it. Hilarious, a child's toy sword with scarves blue green yellow white hanging from it. Imagine a white scarf out here, imagine Mira out here with her breasts, her lips, her plastic sword. One man begged me so violently for water he began vomiting, first bile and then blood, then he was quiet. Another man offered me a gold wristwatch and then, as I rode away, I heard him calling, "Mehrnaz, Mehrnaz, Mehrnaz," and I believed he was calling for his wife, his mother, until I remember Arman telling me some men are disgusting, will offer their own wives, their own sisters or cousins to escape the certainty of death. All these men's faces obscured in the night and mud and dying, their own dying which was like a fog that hung above the fields, death just a cloud lowered over the valley, and a man like me among every five hundred who rides among men who he did not fight with, a man like me too important to fight, that's what Arman calls it, too important even though probably I was only chosen because I fit the cloaks, because I could ride a horse, because I had no real friends in the platoon, and Arman says it's too secret to train multiple men in a single platoon to do what I do, too important and secret, so I ride among my dead, look at that "my dead," how language fails again and again, I ride my horse, my kite, my little-wind-wind among them, the men who fought where I did not fight and died where I did not die.

I try to give them something, faith, resolve, courage, in their final minutes, or final hours for some of them yes, or even final days; a man sees me, his entire right leg is opened and tucked behind him like a strand of hair behind Mira's ear, his leg open and bleeding, I see him see me and he bursts into tears, bursts yes like a lotus bursting into a tantrum of blades, he bursts into tears and crying, slopping he begins gurgling through Ayat al Kursi, I can barely make it out it sounds so wet but he slops through, I think at me, he says *His throne doth extend over the Heavens,* the man gargles and smiles, I think he smiles maybe, maybe I'm imagining but I don't think so, I think there's a break in the tears maybe, or a break in the gargles, certainly I can't see him or his lips, I'm just sitting there on Badbadak the horse with my face lit up by a DC flashlight and it's getting hotter, the bulb burning hot now, it always happens this way, *he feeleth no fatigue in guarding them* the man says and it's never sounded so wet, I swear now I can hear him smiling through the gurgling, through the dying, and it really does make sense for that second, gurgling, the horse and the cloak and the hot flashlight, I know he's smiling and maybe I am too, *for He is the Most High,* it's almost funny how hot it is, funny how wet the man's gurgling, the silly sword in my hand with moonlight curling off its fangs.

SEVENTEEN

. . . .

<u>BHAGAT SINGH</u>

1907–1931

Who am I? swigging from the bad jug,
dying my robe the color of spring—
damn the gallows, stuff me
in a cannon, you wrote that too,

scarlet prophet, quartz rose,
it hurts to speak with you this way
like literature, like private property;
one day I will be only gently and barely dead,

still practically capable of making love,
and you'll still wear your exasperating little
mustache—is it vanity? if it is, then I stand for it,
how time makes everything bigger,

all of us fighting like it still matters,
the blank canvas staying blank

. . . . .

—*from* BOOKOFMARTYRS.docx by Cyrus Shams

SUNDAY

— ❋ —

Cyrus Shams and Orkideh

BROOKLYN, DAY 3

HIS THIRD DAY IN THE CITY, CYRUS GOT TO THE MUSEUM TEN MIN-
utes before it opened. He'd wanted to get there with enough time
to have a substantive conversation with Orkideh before lines formed
and snuffed it out. He'd picked up two coffees along the way, the second as a little offering for Orkideh, a small gift to communicate that
he'd been thinking of her before he saw her. This gesture, this possibility, had always struck Cyrus as particularly moving—an evergreen
wonder that anyone remembered him when he wasn't in the room.
That people found the surplus psychic bandwidth to consider—or
even worry over—anyone else's interior seemed a bit of an unher-
alded miracle. Cyrus read on a website once that there was a word
for this: sonder. "The realization that each random passerby is living
a life as vivid and complex as your own." Incredible, how naming
something took nothing away from its stagger. Language could be
totally impotent like that.

Cyrus was also aware of the possibility that his marvel at this
seemingly mundane phenomenon might be an indictment of his
own self-absorption. He hadn't cured a plague, he'd purchased a two-
dollar cup of coffee. This overblown moment of self-satisfaction at
what was essentially a very, very minor favor.

Upon arriving at the museum—quicker this day and with only a
brief period of confused wandering—and staring through the glass
at staff shuffling around, Cyrus suddenly realized he was going to

have to throw away the extra cup. There was no way the attendants—hip, self-serious to a person, statement glasses and austere all-black dress—would allow him to take in coffee among all the art. He felt stupid. He looked around for a homeless person to whom to give the coffee, a way to assuage his pathological guilt around wasting food or drink. When Cyrus was still a child, his father would force him to sit at the dinner table to finish whatever he'd put on his plate, even if it meant going to the bathroom to throw up and come back. In the Shams apartment, no sin was worse than waste.

In Cyrus's adult life, this training meant he'd eat around the mold on strawberries, ask to box his friends' food at restaurants, finish half-empty cans of flat soda the next day. At busy nights at Lucky's when he was still drinking, the bartenders would consolidate other patrons' abandoned drinks into a single pitcher and bring the murky liquid over to Cyrus. He was grateful for the free booze and for the feeling of conservation this gave him, and the servers were grateful for the tips he left on disgusting drinks they'd otherwise just dump.

He wandered around the museum's outdoor entrance for a few minutes, sipping his own coffee. He saw a young professional woman in heels juggling two carrying trays of iced lattes. A tattooed man dressed in black, perhaps a server on his way to a brunch shift, scowling up at the pigeons flying overhead, willing them to hold their droppings till he passed. Finally, Cyrus spotted a young crust punk sleeping on her dog's ribs, a dirty comforter spread over them both. He walked over to set the coffee down near them, close enough that the dog raised its head to study him, then set it sleepily back down.

But Cyrus considered, at the last moment, that he might be able to smuggle the coffee under his shirt. Maybe he could get it in there to Orkideh after all. Maybe this whole episode would be a conversation starter. He picked the coffee back up from in front of the crust punk. She hadn't stirred from her sleep. The sleeping dog's breath made little gray clouds in the cold.

Cyrus tossed his cup in the bin after chugging the dregs as he walked through the museum doors. He paid three dollars (the suggested donation was ten) and proceeded through to the stair area, where a stern-looking middle-aged woman in a nondescript suit, with long dreads down to her rear, stopped him.

"You can't bring that in here," she said, face pinched forward toward the coffee cup Cyrus was still half hiding behind his back.

"Ah, whoops, I didn't even notice," Cyrus lied, turning around and tossing Orkideh's cup. It pained him to waste the coffee and the money he'd spent on it, especially since he'd not left it for the punk, who may not even have wanted it, who was really a foil for Cyrus to feel good about his own goodness, which shamed him doubly now. He knew that if Zee was with him he'd have left her the coffee. Zee made him want to be better like that. Cyrus's ears flushed with shame.

When he finally got to the third-floor gallery where Orkideh was sitting alone resting her skeletal bald head on her hand, he was already feeling anxious, anxious about his place in the world, his relative goodness or inescapable selfishness. Outside the gallery entrance the same docent, no older than twenty or twenty-one with a long feather earring dangling from his left earlobe and a thick gauged septum piercing, was still scrolling through his phone. He looked up as he saw Cyrus coming in.

"Less crowded today," the docent said, smiling.

Cyrus smiled back, nodded, grateful for the acknowledgment, for the tiny moment of being treated like an insider.

As he stepped into the gallery, Cyrus tried to take in the room as a whole. If art's single job was to be interesting, then the room with Orkideh sitting in it was art of the highest order. The artist's tiny living body swallowed by an inorganic frenzy of clothing, shadow. The eroded surfaces of Orkideh's face were like Martian crags and craters that, like a perfect photograph, caught in astonishing clarity the entire spectrum of visible light from pure light to pure dark. The shadows against the wall played up the gulf between the size of the physical objects—two folding chairs, a mug of water on a small table, a lamp, a notebook and pen—and the scale of their purpose. And today, something new—an oxygen tank, ominous oval looming like a deactivated missile, with its gleaming control knob and thin translucent tube coiling down around the floor and then back up to Orkideh's two nostrils.

One could paint the scene and hang it next to a Vermeer or a Caravaggio for parallel master studies in isolation, in the drama of light and dark playing against basic shapes. There was an almost operatic quality to the simple contours competing with each other for the eye's attention—Orkideh's round skull, her billowing black dress—and bare feet again, Cyrus noticed. The air felt like marble hardening all around him.

At the sound of his footsteps, Orkideh's face rose to meet Cyrus with recognition and a joyful smile, and some third thing he couldn't quite decipher.

"Salaam, Orkideh," said Cyrus, smiling as he settled into the chair. "Chetori?"

Orkideh inhaled deeply, smiling a crooked smile. Every time she breathed out, the tube in her nose fogged.

"Cyrus Shams," she said, "you're back!"

"How are you feeling today?" he asked.

He regretted asking this almost instantly. What an obvious question, what a ridiculous way to greet someone dying of cancer. It was like asking someone just struck by lightning about the weather.

For her part, Orkideh just shrugged and smiled in the direction of the oxygen tank.

"Right. Sorry," said Cyrus.

"It's fine, Cyrus. I'm not scared of it. Please, tell me something! Tell me something good this morning."

Cyrus thought for a moment, but just one.

"I've been working on that book I was telling you about," he said. "I thought I was going to call it *The Book of Martyrs* but now maybe I'm going to call it *Earth Martyrs*." He looked at her and quickly added, "I mean, if that's okay with you. It's your phrase."

Orkideh laughed.

"My gift to you, Cyrus jaan." Her thick accent warmed the room. It felt like a sunrise.

"Thank you," he said sheepishly. "I really am grateful for it." He paused for a second, staring at the artist's face, finding it warm, as if suddenly saturated by his presence.

"Can I ask you something? Something . . . uncomfortable?"

Someone in another gallery sneezed loudly and the docent stuck his head out the doorway, but otherwise, Cyrus and Orkideh were alone.

"That's why I'm here, isn't it?" she said.

"Is it?"

"I don't actually know." She laughed. "I think so, though, probably. To talk about things people are normally afraid to talk about."

"Sure," said Cyrus. All of a sudden, he felt nervous. "That makes sense." The back of his neck was sweating and he noticed he suddenly had to pee. "Why aren't you spending these last days with your family? With the people who love you?"

Orkideh didn't smile at this but didn't look wounded either. She let her mouth hang open for a moment before saying, "Cyrus," snapping the r the Iranian way, drawing out the ooo. "I'm an artist. I give my life to art. That's all there is. People in my life have come and gone and come and gone. Mostly they've gone. I give my life to art because it stays. That's what I am. An artist. I make art." She paused for a moment. "It's what time doesn't ruin."

Cyrus wanted to object. It was the kind of pronouncement that inspired in him immediate skepticism—the grandness of it, the certainty. Sensing his reticence, Orkideh smiled.

"I'm not bereft, azizam. I've had a rich life. I've eaten oysters fresh out of the Caspian! I've been to the Frida Kahlo Museum in Mexico City! I've made love and been in love and fallen out of love. I've made art. I've been so lucky."

Her oxygen machine wheezed. Cyrus's knee was bouncing.

"What's the trick, then?" he asked. "The trick to being at peace at the end?"

Orkideh laughed. "If I knew, do you think I'd tell you?"

"I mean, I kind of guess, yeah, I do. Why wouldn't you?"

They both laughed. Cyrus was beginning to feel more comfortable.

"I brought a coffee for you, but I had to get rid of it before I came in," he said.

"Aw, that's very sweet, Koroosh," said Orkideh. She reached over to him and pretended to grab an invisible coffee cup from his side, then took a pretend sip.

"Beh beh beh," she said. "Delicious!"

An older man with long gray hair and a tweed coat walked into the gallery. Both Cyrus and Orkideh looked up at him, and the man, confused, turned around and walked back out.

"He must have been surprised to see two Iranians whispering conspiratorially in a dark room," Cyrus said, and he and Orkideh laughed again.

"What about you though, Cyrus Shams?" Orkideh asked. "If you become a martyr, won't you be hurting the people who love you?"

Cyrus nodded. "Of course," he said, then after a beat, "but it's hard to figure out if that hurt would be worse than the hurt of my being here."

Orkideh shook her head.

"It will be worse," she said. "I promise. If you let yourself get a little older, you'll understand that."

"Maybe," said Cyrus. "My mother died when I was very young. My father never really got over it. I feel like in a lot of ways he blamed himself. Maybe he even blamed me. I think my being around made it hard for him."

Orkideh winced, studying Cyrus. He was a handsome man, strong jaw. High, thick eyebrows. The Persian word for "eyebrow" literally deconstructs to "cloud-above." Cyrus's made his eyes look pained, stormy, even when he was laughing. Much older and darker than the rest of his face. So many Iranian men she had known had eyes like that. Her breathing tubes were fogging up a little more than before.

"And I have friends, some of them really close. My best friend Zee, he came with me on this trip. He would probably be mad at me forever if I killed myself. But it's not like he'd spontaneously combust or anything. He'd understand, eventually. Probably he already does."

Orkideh inhaled deeply.

"I had a friend too, a novelist," she said. "And one time I asked her about whether she plots out her books in advance and just fills in the details, or if she moves through the story as she writes it. She looked at me and without skipping a second, she answered like an oracle: 'Behind me is silence, and ahead of me is silence.' And that was it. That was her whole answer. Isn't that perfect?"

"Yeah, that's beautiful," said Cyrus, though it confused him.

"What I mean is, I think maybe you'll find your real ending once you stop looking for it," Orkideh said. "I think real endings tend to work their way in from the outside."

Cyrus was struggling to keep up. He had so much to say, so much to clarify and challenge, but he could only find himself nodding, grunting in vague affirmations. He felt self-conscious talking to the artist, like she was going to think him a voyeur, or a morbid child. In the gallery a new guest had walked in, a younger woman, maybe in high school, listening to headphones shaped like cat ears, shuffling awkwardly from foot to foot.

"When my mother died I was a baby," Cyrus finally said. "And so I didn't really know what I'd lost until I was much older. I mean, maybe I still don't. But there was this one day when I was fifteen or sixteen when I decided I was really going to feel it. Like, I didn't get to have a day to grieve my mother properly when it happened. So I made one up. I skipped school and just wandered around downtown Fort Wayne listening to my Walkman, weeping wherever I went, trying to picture her in my head. I kept ducking into these alleys and side streets bawling my eyes out, imagining all the days she'd never seen me. All the days I'd never see her. I got dehydrated from all the crying, I remember feeling super thirsty. I remember stopping into a gas station to buy a Gatorade, and the clerk there asking if I was okay, if I needed any help. That's such a funny detail, I'd forgotten about that till just now. It tasted like trash, so sweet it burned. But I chugged it! I was so thirsty from crying. I felt it I think maybe for the first time then. All that grief consolidated, concentrated into a single hard point. Like a diamond. That one day."

"Wow," said Orkideh. "Wow." Her own eyes had begun to water as Cyrus spoke. She paused, took a sip from her mug. Her oxygen machine rattled. Clearing her throat Orkideh said, "So then what? How did you feel after?"

"That's the thing," Cyrus said. "I got home and ate dinner and watched TV and went to bed. The next day I went to school and nothing had changed. My mother hadn't come back. My father wasn't any less sad and neither was I. I was still the same person."

"Of course," said Orkideh. "It seems very American to expect grief to change something. Like a token you cash in. A formula. Grieve x amount, receive y amount of comfort. Work a day in the grief mines and get paid in tickets to the company store."

They both laughed.

"Yeah," said Cyrus. "This was I think the beginning of my understanding that. And when my father died a few years later, after I went to college, I felt like I was more ready for it. Like he had done his job, delivering me to college. And so he could finally clock out, as if he'd been waiting for that moment of being allowed to rest. I was able to really feel it, and mostly I felt gratitude. Sad too of course, but I remember it mostly being just so grateful that he kept himself around as long as he did, for me."

Cyrus noticed Orkideh's eyes were totally clouded with wet— now flushed, red, gauzy.

"Jesus. I'm so sorry, we don't even know each other. I don't mean to put this all on you," Cyrus said.

"No, no, it's beautiful. It's exactly what I'm here for." Orkideh smiled, dabbing each eye with her black sleeves, then gesturing with the back of her hand toward the gallery title painted on the wall behind her, DEATH-SPEAK.

"Sure, but you're holding so much already, with your own . . . "

"Cyrus, yesterday a woman came in here. Showed me a picture of a gorgeous little girl, said it was her daughter, said now she was in a coma, brain dead from a heroin overdose. Asked me what to do. Whether she should—" Orkideh winced, saying the next words as if trying to force a large rock up her throat, "—*pull the plug.*" She put her hands up on the table between them. "What am I supposed to say to that?"

"What *did* you say?"

"Ah, I don't know. What can you say? Only stupid things. Something about it being a horrible disease, a horrible choice. I think she left disappointed." Orkideh coughed into the crook of her arm. "But my point is, I'm happy to talk with you. It's easy. Lovely. I enjoy it."

Cyrus nodded, then blurted, "I've been sober for a couple years too." He felt suddenly self-conscious. "Or, not 'too.' I mean, I like talking to you too. But yeah, it is a horrible disease, you're right."

Orkideh's eyes widened.

"Wow. Good for you. You've really had a whole life already, Cyrus Shams."

When he looked at the artist, he noticed suddenly how veiny her skull was. How the blood vessels bulged, blue arteries almost phosphorescent in the dim light. On TV when he'd seen people bald from cancer their skulls always seemed so flat, ghostly and powdered. In real life it was so much more vascular, animal. There were tiny wispy strands of hair growing back over it too, he saw now, so thin you could only see them when they caught the light.

"I'm supposed to be talking to you about *your* life, though. For the book."

"Ah yes, the book, the book. Your book of martyrs," she said, drawing out the word "martyrs" like it was a punchline to a bad joke. "And you still think I might feature in this book?" Orkideh said, smiling.

"I do, yeah. I mean, I don't know for sure yet. But I think so. What you're doing here. It's incredible. I flew here to talk to you about it. I don't even really know what to say about what you're doing, but it's remarkable."

"Ahh yes, remarkable." She laughed, gesturing toward her oxygen machine, which wheezed a gassy wheeze as if to punctuate her point.

"It is," Cyrus went on. "And I feel so inadequate. Like, just the writing of it, trying to put it into language. It feels so damned."

"How do you mean?"

Cyrus fidgeted, putting his hands on the table then taking them back off. The table, matte metallic black, held the imprint of his hand for a flicker of a second, a little ghost of Cyrus's heat. There, then gone.

"I guess, I write these sentences where I try to lineate grief or doubt or joy or sex or whatever till it sounds as urgent as it feels. But I know the words will never feel like the thing. The language will never be the thing. So it's damned, right? And I am too, for giving my life to it. Because I know my writing can never make any of these deaths matter the way they're supposed to. It'll never arrest fascism in its tracks or save the planet. It'll never bring my mother back, you know?"

"Or any of the people on that flight," said Orkideh.

"Exactly!" said Cyrus. "Exactly."

The girl in line was still awkwardly shifting from foot to foot listening to her cat ear headphones, and behind her a couple more people had joined the line, another younger person with wireless headphones and the older man with long hair from before, perhaps now emboldened by the presence of a line.

"It has been so very lucky to have these talks with you, Cyrus Shams," said Orkideh. "I really truly enjoy it. Will you come back and see me again tomorrow, if you're still in town?"

"Of course, of course, I'll be back tomorrow," said Cyrus. He had so much more he wanted to say, but he wanted to respect the line, wanted to respect Orkideh's project. He took a sip from his imaginary coffee, and then Orkideh took a sip from hers, smiling across her whole face. Cyrus stood up.

He said, "May I give you a hug?"

Orkideh responded, "Please."

They hugged and Cyrus breathed in her scent, some combination of rosewater and antiseptic lotion, the former perhaps meant to mask the latter.

As he walked out of the museum, his head was spinning. He replayed the conversation over and over. He'd never told anyone about his grief day, not even his father. Not even Zee. He'd almost forgotten about it, forgotten about the Walkman and the Gatorade. He tried to remember who he had been listening to—Elliott Smith maybe, or Billie Holiday. Orkideh had held that conversation so carefully. He'd seen her eyes water.

He wished he'd spoken with her more about martyrdom specifically. Did she consider herself a martyr? An earth martyr? If not, was it okay if he did? What about the mother who'd had to "pull the plug" on her daughter? He'd remember to be more focused tomorrow. He'd half forgotten that he was ostensibly there writing his book. Their conversation had been so good, so true. It wouldn't have felt right to press too inorganically.

Cyrus was practically floating an inch off the ground, lost in gratitude and awe and a sense of overwhelming simpatico, when another part of the conversation entered into his head. "My writing will never bring my mother back," he'd said. And Orkideh replied, "Or any of the people on that flight."

He tried to remember if he'd ever mentioned to Orkideh how his mother had died. He sat on a park bench. He'd told her about Zee, about his father, about his mother dying; but, for the life of him, he couldn't remember ever saying anything about Flight 655.

INTERLUDE

———— ✳ ————

ONCE THERE WAS, AND HOW MUCH THERE WAS. IN THE LAND OF Tus there was a young boy named Ferdowsi. Ferdowsi was an adventurous child, loving to play outside in the wind and green. His favorite place was the howling Tus River, a great surging river continuing forever in both directions, as wide as ten houses. Ferdowsi would spend hours and hours watching wood and whitecaps drift down, listening to the river gurgle and groan. Sometimes he would very carefully dip a foot, a hand into the river till he couldn't feel it anymore, couldn't tell where he ended and the river began. Some days he would write small poems for the river, reading them to nobody but the river itself.

One day he walked to the river to find the water had swallowed the ancient stone bridge connecting the two sides. Families were tearfully shouting across the great divide—brothers to brothers, young women to their parents. They knew their families would now be separated forever. Seeing this, Ferdowsi shouted, "My people, I will build us a new bridge, stronger than the last one! A bridge that will never disappear! No rain, no wind will destroy it."

The rope-maker said, "Ferdowsi, you are a child, not an elder. You don't have the knowledge to build a new bridge."

The jewelry merchant, said, "Ferdowsi, you are a poor boy, not a prince. You don't have the money to build a new bridge."

Finally, the carpenter cried out, "Ferdowsi, you spend all your time daydreaming and writing silly poems. You don't have the discipline to build a new bridge."

But Ferdowsi was determined. He ran away from the river and back to his home and left the rope-maker, the jewelry merchant, the carpenter, and all the other villagers to their wailing. Over the next many years, the villagers seldom saw him. Ferdowsi's mother and father provided food and water for him far past the age he should have been providing food and water for them. He grew into a man this way, hidden away from everyone but his family. Occasionally, some farmer would report they'd seen him wandering around at night, muttering to himself.

AFTER MANY SUCH QUIET YEARS, ONE SPRING AFTERNOON FERdowsi finally went out from his parents' house and into the center of his village.

"I have written a poem for the king!" he announced. "It is the greatest poem Tus has ever produced!"

The few villagers who heard hardly looked up. The sun was high in the air. A little girl chased a chicken.

Undeterred, Ferdowsi prepared for his next step: the long journey to the king's palace. He set off alone and arrived at the palace weeks later, exhausted and barely able to hold his own weight.

"Who are you?" the king's courtier asked when Ferdowsi arrived.

"I am Ferdowsi, the greatest poet in Tus," he replied. "I have written a poem for King Mahmud."

The young man's boldness amused the courtier, so he brought him inside the castle to meet King Mahmud.

"Who are you?" asked the sleepy young king Mahmud from his throne.

"I am Ferdowsi, the greatest poet in Tus," he answered. "I have written you a poem."

"Go ahead then," said King Mahmud, only mildly interested.

But as Ferdowsi read his poem, each of the twenty couplets was flawless, like a string of perfect pearls. The king's great eyes began to twinkle.

"Ferdowsi," said the king when the poem was complete, "that is the most brilliant poem I have ever heard. Truly, you are the greatest poet in Tus."

"Thank you, my king," said Ferdowsi.

"I would like you to write the great poem of our people," continued King Mahmud. "Tell the history of all Persia. You can live here at the castle. I will feed you the richest meats, clothe you in the finest silks."

Ferdowsi said, "You are very generous, my king. But I do not need rich meats or fine silks to write poetry. I just need my family's house in Tus, and our wild river. I would like to write this poem for you. But I will write it in my own home, with my own family."

"Well then, how shall I compensate you for your verse?" asked King Mahmud.

"How about this," Ferdowsi said, smiling, "I will write your poem, and you can pay me one gold coin for every couplet. And you do not need to pay me until I finish the poem."

King Mahmud thought to himself. What little sense poets had! The silks and fine cuisines of his palace were worth far more than a couple dozen gold coins.

"Very well, poet!" said the king, smiling. "You have a deal!"

The courtier drew up a contract and, when it was signed, the king sent Ferdowsi back to Tus in a comfortable caravan.

FOR MONTHS, THEN YEARS, FERDOWSI WROTE AND WROTE. SOME-times, villagers would gather outside his family's house and beg him to come to the window to read to them from his poem. Sometimes, he would, and then the villagers of Tus would gasp, cry out, weep. This is how he met his wife Sara, with whom he had two children, Sohrab and Tahmina. His children would grow and become adults themselves, but every day was the same: their father would write, write, stroll down to the river once each night, and then return to the house and write some more.

Sometimes, King Mahmud, who was getting older and older, would send his courtier to Tus to find Ferdowsi and demand the poem. But Ferdowsi would always just say, simply, "You cannot rush poetry. There was no deadline in the contract."

One day Ferdowsi's son Sohrab drowned in a tragic accident on the river. A storm, a collapse. Though Ferdowsi's grief was unimaginable, his habits did not change. Every day he woke up and wrote, and wrote, and wrote.

FINALLY, AFTER FOUR LONG AND SAD DECADES, FERDOWSI SENT notice to King Mahmud that his poem was finished. They had both been young men when Ferdowsi began the poem; now their faces were cracked and deep with wrinkles. They each had children and grandchildren of their own. Ferdowsi called his poem *Shahnehmeh,* "The Book of Kings." He filled it with ancient histories of Persia's kings and heroes, epic battles and romances, fantastical magic and treacherous deceits. He also put his son, Sohrab, in it. Ferdowsi's love for his lost son colored the whole text, like deep wine spilled across its pages.

When the courtier presented the poem to King Mahmud, the king was furious.

"Forty years?! That is unreasonable. We are old men now. And look at this massive poem! It must be ten thousand couplets!"

It had taken four strong camels to carry the whole poem to the palace.

"Fifty thousand, sir," said the courtier. He'd been up the whole night before counting them.

"What did you say?"

"The poem, sir. It's exactly fifty thousand couplets."

The king was livid.

"Ferdowsi will receive his payment," he said. "Send him his fifty thousand coins. *Copper* coins."

The courtier nodded and had the servants ready the camels.

When the king's servants arrived in Tus two weeks later with a caravan of copper, Ferdowsi could only laugh.

"Friends," he said to the servants, "take this copper and begin your new lives far away from traitorous King Mahmud."

The servants looked at each other and happily took the copper, eager to start fresh far away from the palace.

Ferdowsi's daughter Tahmina looked at him, asked, "Why did you give away all that copper?"

Ferdowsi said, "That much copper cannot pay for a good bridge, but it can buy those men a little land, a few goats."

WHEN THE KING'S SERVANTS DID NOT RETURN TO THE CASTLE, Mahmud was even more furious. He cursed all poets and forbade poetry from being uttered in his presence.

But one year later, a short message arrived at the palace. It was a poem, a curse, from Ferdowsi.

"Yes, read it!" the king demanded to his courtier.

Cautiously, the courtier did. When he got to the final lines,

> *Heaven's vengeance will not forget.*
> *Shrink, tyrant, from my fire,*
> *and tremble,*

King Mahmud was scared. He did not want to show it, but he was. Terrified, even. He went back to Ferdowsi's untouched manuscript from the year before, which was gathering dust in a back room of the palace. As the king read Ferdowsi's lines, he began to weep.

"O! I have made a grievous error," he cried out. Summoning his courtier, he said, "Courtier! O! Ferdowsi has produced the greatest poem in the history of all of Persia. We have been fools. Send him his gold coins at once, and with interest."

The courtier loaded up the camels with gold and set off for Tus, this time traveling himself with the caravan.

AFTER NEARLY TWO WEEKS' JOURNEY, THE COURTIER'S CARAVAN came up upon another great caravan, much longer than his own, a caravan filled with agile dancers, musicians singing ballads.

The courtier addressed the head of the caravan,

"I am courtier for King Mahmud! I am traveling to Tus to find the great poet Ferdowsi, to deliver him his life's payment of gold."

A circle of people began to form around the courtier.

"You will not find Ferdowsi in Tus," said the woman at the head of the caravan.

"Where has he gone?" asked the courtier.

"Ferdowsi is dead," she replied. "This is his funeral caravan."

The courtier saw that all the people circled around him were all in mourning robes.

"O! The greatest poet in Tus has died?! The greatest poet in all of Persia! Curse our pride, and our folly." The courtier collapsed upon his knees.

The woman at the head of the caravan stepped forward:

"I am Tahmina, daughter of Ferdowsi, the greatest poet in Tus. I will take my father's payment and use it for the construction of the finest bridge in all of Persia."

The courtier swiftly nodded.

When the courtier returned to the palace and told the king what happened, the king sent his best royal engineers to Tus. They helped Tahmina and the villagers with the construction of "The Poet's Bridge," a great bridge built so strong it still stands today.

EIGHTEEN

∞

. . . .

ROYA SHAMS / MOM

1963–1988

fuck a falling bird metaphor, respectfully,
simple pity and scolding trills too, the asphyxiating
performance of okayness today
sharpened enough to slice an anvil in two,

neither slumbering nor sleeping,
no second-person-singular here, no plotless
evocation of pain shivering the lavender;

here where men fight about justice
like a drowning boy trying to pull himself
out of a river by his own hair—

ruby dropped in an open grave, my old dealer's
Zulfiqar tattoo—also ugly, time spilling
over, unbearable actually, and pestilent,
a thing remaining this wrong forever

. . . . .

—*from* BOOKOFMARTYRS.docx by Cyrus Shams

ROYA SHAMS

———— ✳ ————

TEHRAN, AUGUST 1987

LEILA WAS SO GOOD AT WEARING SUNGLASSES. I FOUND MYSELF watching them, watching her more than I was actually listening to her. It is ridiculous to say that she was beautiful. A horse is beautiful, a mountain or an ocean is beautiful. Leila, in those sunglasses, was something else. Something beyond language. I get frustrated this way so often. A photograph can say "This is what it was." Language can only say "This is what it was like."

Chattering away in that cab—about astrology, British punk music, jungle cats, Greek gods—this is what she was like: a pinwheel of stars. Lightning under a fingernail. I was watching her, nodding, watching, watching, starting to feel light-headed. Her black slacks hugged her powerful thighs. She was talking fast, fizzing like cold soda. She'd taken her scarf off, revealing her short curls, and as I watched her I noticed the taxi driver kept sneaking glances in his rearview mirror, only ever at her. I watched him watch her, occasionally swerving a little because he couldn't take his eyes off his mirror.

"Careful!" Leila shouted to him.

"Are you someone famous?" he asked at last in a thick Bandari accent.

"Do you think I'd tell you if I was?" she asked, putting her scarf back on, laughing at me. She pulled out her cigarettes, unfiltered, lit one, puffing it once, and handed it to me. Then she lit one for herself.

"Roll down your windows please," the cab driver said, scowling, still staring up into his mirror.

We did, and Leila smoked her cigarette with relish. I took polite pulls of mine, staring out the window as the city flitted past in flashes of light and sound. Beat-up Paykans and Saipa sedans growled along like old farm equipment. Women in khimars and hijabs hurried home along the sidewalks while young men with tight bright T-shirts tucked into their jeans stood in packs smoking and laughing. All around us, handsome new parks and plazas effervesced in the night. Many of these fresh constructions, I knew, were converted cemeteries full of the regime's executed political prisoners. Paving over those unmarked mass graves with turf, with water features, to show the world how happy and pristine Tehran had become. Clean. I'd heard this whispered: If you were taken prisoner, they would ask you, "When you were growing up, did your father pray, fast, and read the Holy Quran?" You were supposed to answer no, though most reflexively said yes. "No" meant your delinquency was not your fault. If you said yes, you'd be tortured or hanged.

Suddenly, out of nothing, Leila turned and asked me, "Who has seen you cry naked? Not your parents when you were little, but as an adult. When was the last time someone saw you cry naked?"

I glanced up at the driver, who was furiously concentrating all his energy into pretending he wasn't listening. Even in the dark, I could see his temple throb.

"Excuse me?" I said.

"I cry all the time," she continued, as if I wasn't even there. "I hate it. It embarrasses me. I am not fragile, but sometimes my body just cries and I can't help it. It's a betrayal. Like someone tickling you, you laugh even when you don't want to, even when it hurts. That's how I cry."

I nodded.

"I do know that feeling."

"Yeah?"

"Yeah," I went on. "Last week I was at our neighbor Nafiz's house, watching her daughter while Nafiz hung clothes outside. Her daughter is this brand-new thing, barely even a human, and as I held her of course she started crying. And there was nothing I could do. I couldn't put her down anywhere, all the couches were covered with clothes, the table covered with dishes. That was what got me. There was nowhere to set this angry crying beast howling in my face. And so I just started crying too. I couldn't get her to stop, and then I couldn't stop myself. Nafiz came in to these two hideous beasts just gasping, huffing. She took her daughter and within a minute the baby stopped crying. Nafiz must have thought I was insane. It was just . . . there was nowhere to put her. That's what it was. No place to set her down."

I looked up—I hadn't meant to tell that whole story, hadn't meant to advance in intimacy so immediately. I half expected Leila to retreat, for her eyes to get big as if to say whoa, that's too much. But what she did was laugh—

"Yeah, that sounds about right. That's my point exactly. Anyone can see you cry. We all act like it's this big deal, but it happens all the time. We're just these idiot animals about it. But to be with someone while they cry naked? That's real intimacy. All the dogshit stripped away. *That's* the top of the mountain."

She exhaled smoke while she said this and I still didn't really understand what she was talking about, and so we were quiet for a while, that charged sort of quiet that feels like sand being poured all around you, up to your throat. The driver wove through Tehran traffic like the old man he was, cursing under his breath at boys showing off and honking their horns, shaking his head when they'd roll down their windows to curse.

Finally the taxi pulled up to a campground parking lot by the lake for picnicking families. An old, well-used space. The lake had been manmade, but not recently, not one of the regime's fresh cover-up affairs. Leila handed the driver a wad of toman for the fare and I said, "Leila, let me help with that," but she just rolled her eyes and slipped out of the cab.

"Follow me," she said, pulling her headscarf back off and lighting another cigarette, flame flickering in her sunglass lenses. She held the pack toward me but I shook my head. That she was walking around—at night!—with her hair free was terrifying to me, so terrifying I didn't even want to mention it, afraid it would invite someone else to notice as well. With her curls, her white workshirt and black slacks and sunglasses, she looked more than a little like Bob Dylan. We walked the pedestrian footpath around the water, worn to hard dirt. Leila paced manfully, puffed up. I couldn't take my eyes off her. To our right was the lake, a giant brown thing filled with fat carp and slimy mud. On the left was a wall all along the path, three meters high, decorative round gray bricks laid over each other with little protruding lips.

It was dark and getting darker, and cold, and as we passed people walking in the dim light Leila would dip her head and say "salaam" in a gravelly man's voice, and the men passing by would salaam right back without missing a beat, as if greeting any other man. Leila would look back at me with a big smile, her short curls free in the air. What began in me as fear was being eclipsed by utter fascination. Her energy was infectious, a child's glee at discovering the hole in a fence big enough to sneak through.

After twenty, twenty-five minutes of walking and playing Leila's game—one man even responded "Good night, brother"—Leila stopped and leaned against the wall.

"This is my favorite spot on the whole lake," she said.

I looked around. It was pretty enough for a manufactured thing. Fish would occasionally break the water to catch mosquitoes, rippling the light that shone against the surface. But the spot we were at looked the same as anywhere else we had been—water, path, brick wall.

"Why?" I asked.

"You have to get a better look to really appreciate it," Leila responded. "Here, help me climb up." She gestured toward the wall, taller than her by more than a meter. I looked around, saw nobody coming, looked back at Leila.

"Shouldn't we, maybe, start heading back?" I said. I didn't even want to, necessarily, but wanted someone to have said it, in case. In case what? That haunting question, now in my head: *Did your father pray, fast, and read the Holy Quran . . .*

"Oh come on now," Leila said. "You won't believe the view."

I sighed performatively, then stepped toward the wall and helped boost her up, catching a glimpse of her still-firm stomach as she climbed the brick ledges. At the top she stood facing away from the lake, then turned back to me, crouching to reach a hand down. It was hard to get foothold on the lips of the bricks, harder than Leila had made it look. My breasts ached when I reached up, abruptly reminding me of what was growing inside me, and how until that moment I hadn't thought of it all evening. With a little more clumsy struggling—and more pain than I let on—I was able to climb high enough for Leila to pull me upwards the rest of the way.

At the top, breathing heavy, I stared. In the sparse grove of trees on the other side of the fence were three massive giraffes, real live giraffes, close enough to us that we could have whispered to them. I nearly fell off the wall.

"Shhhhhh," Leila said, seeing my face.

"How?!" I stammered.

"It's the backside of the zoo, Roya jaan," she said. "This is the fence. Just watch."

Two giraffes were chewing lazily. Totally uninterested in us. The largest of the three was on the ground sleeping with its giant neck looped around to its backside. It looked like a colossal purse. Each giraffe had the long eyelashes of horses, and those same sad eyes, like they knew they weren't made for this world. Or worse, like they knew they were.

"How did you discover this?" I whispered to Leila, sitting down with my back to the lake, kicking my feet out to hang into the giraffes' enclosure. Leila shrugged mysteriously, smiling at my side. We sat there in silence for five minutes, ten, watching the giraffes do basically nothing, just stand there and chew sadly, I never thought about how sad something could look chewing.

Suddenly, a bright light on our backs. We turned and looked down. It was some sort of park security guard shining his flashlight on us.

"What are you two doing?" he shouted. His face looked like crumpled paper. Leila shouted down in her deep pretend man's voice:

"We're just sitting, baba! Leave us alone!"

"Come down from there, you two! The park is closing. You shouldn't be up there!" I could see the sweat forming on his forehead. He could probably see the sweat on mine.

"Baba, I am a soldier!" Leila shouted. "I am just here with my girl! Don't you love your soldiers?"

I stared at Leila. I couldn't believe what was happening. If the security guard realized who he was speaking to, that she was a young woman with no scarf trespassing out at night, pretending to be a man . . . It's unthinkable. What he might have done.

"Get! Down! Right! Now!" he said, furious.

"Why don't you climb up and make me, baba!" Leila snapped, laughing. All the dread in my body hardened into a stone organ in my gut.

The old guard scowled hard at Leila, then at me. For fifteen seconds, maybe a minute he stayed there staring at me, as if the sheer force of his contempt would topple the wall itself.

"Leila," I finally managed to whisper without moving my lips. The moon was bright in the sky now, nearly full. It felt like it was pulling all my blood to the surface of my skin, like it wanted to rip my eyes and ears out through my face.

Then, with a snarl, the guard said, "If you're still here when I come back, I'm calling the police."

Leila gave him a sarcastic double thumbs-up as he scuttled off, cursing under his breath. We turned around. The giraffes were unmoved.

"What are you doing?" I hissed in a mix of terror and awe.

"I want to sit with our friends for another couple minutes," she said, pointing to the giraffes. "And with you." Saying that, she scooted closer to me and rested her head on my shoulder. I was too flustered, too suddenly dizzy to say anything back, so I just let her head rest there. The giraffe that had been lying there still was, lazily blinking his eyes open and closed. Its great neck curled like some alien punctuation.

NINETEEN

SUNDAY

———— ✳ ————

Cyrus Shams and Zee Novak

BROOKLYN, DAY 3

CYRUS WALKED TO MEET ZEE AT A CAFÉ CALLED DAYLIGHT ON THE opposite side of Prospect Park, settling into a small outdoor two-top. It was way too cold for outdoor seating, but he knew Zee would want to smoke, and he didn't mind the chill. His head was still spinning from his conversation with Orkideh. How did she know what she knew? Strangely, there were other people seated outside too, despite the temperature. A high-cheeked woman in a thick coat and leather gloves was smoking elegantly and cooing into a smartphone. Across the patio, two bearded white guys laughed and ignored their mimosas. Car doors slammed. A waiter with a tray of espressos was looking around, confused.

Cyrus had texted Zee asking if he was around for coffee and a quick chat. In their private idiom, asking for a "quick chat" meant there was something fairly urgent to be discussed, and Zee replied with "no problem," and then the address of this coffee shop. Cyrus knew talking to Zee might break the cycle of circular thinking in his head, the cycle that went something like *I met Orkideh, I told her my mother was dead, Orkideh referenced a plane crash, I never told her about the plane crash, I met Orkideh . . .*

Cyrus felt his phone vibrate, a text from his sponsor, Gabe: "You STILL still sober?" Cyrus typed, "STILL still, yep. u?" Gabe replied, "Indeed I am. You still mad?" Cyrus paused. "i dont know. not really," he typed. A beat. Then, three dots appeared to indicate his sponsor was typing: "There you go," Gabe wrote, finally.

Cyrus smiled, despite himself. He remembered reading about how children who had lost a parent would often act out against the one left, an unconscious way of testing whether that parent could be trusted to remain, unconditionally. Cyrus had never really done this to his actual father; but then, he had no memory of his mother. Her loss was totally abstract. It was excruciating, now, for Cyrus to think of himself as the unwitting subject of the same predictable psychic tempests as every other human on the planet. Painful, too, for Cyrus to accept how naturally he'd drafted this grizzled midwestern John Wayne as de facto father. But he knew Gabe could be trusted to remain. That much was clear.

Clicking away from his texts, still waiting for Zee and idly scrolling the news app on his phone, Cyrus saw a picture of President Invective shaking hands with a group of foreign businessmen. "President Invective" was what Cyrus and Zee privately called the sitting president, both of them feeling that to say his name was a concession to power, like the man got some sick eldritch shiver of pleasure whenever his real name was uttered by anyone anywhere in the world. President Invective gave the camera a grimacing smirk. Cyrus clicked the button on the side of his phone to shut off the screen and sat there thinking about Orkideh, thinking about Zee, thinking about President Invective.

Cyrus wondered sometimes how much ideas of leadership in the West (a term he was also dubious of—west of what? The earth is a sphere where every spot is west of every other—calling America "the west" and Iran "the Middle East" placed the center squarely in Europe) had to do with notions of an infallible Christian God. How the best leaders in America professed to be moving toward "godliness," that's what they always said, that was the horizon leaders were always trying to approach, "godliness," with all its intractable convictions. Cyrus thought about President Invective, a cartoon ghoul of a man for whom Dantean ideas of Hell seemed specifically conceived. The sort of man whose unwavering assertions of his own genius competence had, to the American public, apparently overwhelmed all observable evidence to the contrary.

Only in a culture that privileged infallibility above all else could a man like President Invective rise to power—a man insulated since birth from any sense of accountability, raised in a pristine cocoon of inherited wealth to emerge pristine, dewy, wholly unsullied by those irksome mortal foibles, grief and doubt.

Even Jesus doubted, his moment of "eloi eloi lama sabachthani" on the cross, incredulous with grief and doubt at his own suffering, calling up Psalm 22 to try to self-soothe, to assuage his own agony. Or Muhammad who, being told to transcribe God's word by a literal archangel, protested to Gabriel again and again that he *could not write.* He doubted hard enough to say it to the face of a fucking angel. Imagine! Never mind the prophets, the saints—to lead in the new world meant all the infallibility, none of the doubt. Nothing like a light bulb flickering in an Indiana apartment that may or may not have been the voice of God.

Sitting there at the café table, trying to refresh the same sites he'd just looked at a minute ago on his phone, Cyrus thought about what an aggressively human leader on earth might look like. One who, instead of defending decades-old obviously wrong positions, said, "Well, of course I changed my mind, I was presented with new information, that's the definition of critical thinking." That it seemed impossible to conceive of a political leader making such a statement made Cyrus mad, then sad.

Of course, Cyrus himself wasn't impervious to this way of thinking. That was the whole martyr book. He wanted to live perfectly enough to die without creating a ripple of pain behind him, like an Olympic diver knifing splashlessly into the pool. The marvel would be how little the water moved, how the deep seemed to gulp him whole without even opening its mouth.

Cyrus looked around the patio. A whiff of bread in the air, and coffee. Supernaturally beautiful people walking around busily, tapping into cell phones. Still no sign of Zee.

Cyrus's father told him once about his mother's learning, how whenever he asked her something she didn't know the answer to, she'd write it down on a little notebook she carried everywhere and then, as soon as she could, she'd take it to the library to look up the answers. Why do fireflies glow? A chemical reaction a hundred times more efficient than light bulbs. Why does the sea have salt? Rainwater washing minerals away from rocks. She'd copy diagrams from the books she read into her notebook. Photocytes, erosion.

Even Cyrus's father, who had been a quiet man, tended to avoid claiming knowledge not his own, though of course he didn't have his wife's driven curiosity. He preferred to ignore such questions, or change the subject. Cyrus prided himself in descending from people comfortable sitting in uncertainty. He himself knew little about anything and tried to remember that. He read once about a Sufi prayer that went "Lord, increase my bewilderment." That was the prayer in its entirety.

Cyrus thought of the other people standing in line to speak with the dying artist, how desperate they now seemed in his recollection, and how Orkideh still welcomed them, grinning, probably a little stoned. The performance of certainty seemed to be at the root of so much grief. Everyone in America seemed to be afraid and hurting and angry, starving for a fight they could win. And more than that even, they seemed certain their natural state was to be happy, contented, and rich. The genesis of everyone's pain had to be external, such was their certainty. And so legislators legislated, building border walls, barring citizens of *there* from entering *here*. "The pain we feel comes from them, not ourselves," said the banners, and people cheered, certain of all the certainty. But the next day they'd wake up and find that what had hurt in them still hurt.

Cyrus was on his first refill of coffee, absorbed in the frenzy of his own mind, when Zee emerged through the throng of pedestrians. He was wearing a white T-shirt with red letters that said LIGHGHT along with loose black slacks and his signature camouflage Crocs. He was carrying a brown paper bag with finds he'd acquired over the course of a morning scrounging Brooklyn's vinyl stores—he'd hardly packed any clothes so he'd have room in his carry-on to bring records back home. Zee smiled when he saw Cyrus waving him over.

"Ah, Brooklyn town!" grinned Zee. "An agreeable sight for an old knickerbocker such as myself!"

Cyrus couldn't help but smile.

"What'd you find?" he asked as Zee settled into his chair.

Zee eagerly opened up his haul—a hippie acoustic-era Tyrannosaurus Rex record (once in their first apartment Zee had ordered a bunch of old *Tiger Beats* off eBay and cut out enough gauzy pictures of Marc Bolan to paper a whole wall of their apartment), and a beat-up live Dinah Washington record (Zee had this monologue he'd give sometimes about how the sound of a jazz singer's voice cracking on a record was the sound of an emotional event too urgent for the medium assigned to record it; Cyrus knew he'd read that in a Brian Eno book but it didn't make it any less true).

Cyrus tried to muster what enthusiasm he could, knowing how much Zee loved this stuff, but it was obvious to both parties he was distracted. As their server, dressed in a puffy black coat, came over and took Zee's order for hot tea, Cyrus began recounting that morning's conversation with Orkideh, about the coffee and his mom-grief-day and then about the artist's uncanny mentioning of the flight, the flight Cyrus had never brought up.

"You're sure you didn't just accidentally mention it yesterday?" Zee asked, stirring a second half-and-half into his tea.

"Yeah, like ninety-nine percent sure. I'm basically positive. I know I said she died, but I can't imagine why or when I would've explained how."

"Could she have Googled something?"

"I can't think of what she could have possibly Googled that would have had my name on it in relation to that flight."

He'd written about the flight, of course. He was an orphan now; he'd written a lot about both of his parents over the years. But the handful of poems he'd ever shared with the world were in tiny fold-and-staple journals, not online as far as he knew. And even those were written after he got sober, when poetry simply became a place to put his physical body, something he could do for a few hours without worrying about accidentally killing himself. That was poetry then, a two-by-four floating in the ocean. When Cyrus wrapped himself around it, he could just barely keep his head above waves.

Those poems were understandably obsessed with his recovery, which at the time was so touch-and-go, so monolithic and all-encompassing, it didn't let much other light in. Certainly the deaths of both his parents inflected everything he wrote, but in what Cyrus had given to the world, in what he shared at the open mic, their deaths never manifested directly in any obvious or explicitly legible way.

Cyrus hesitated, working up the courage to ask something that had been on his mind since leaving the museum. Something nearly inconceivable, but nevertheless a possibility that needed to be crossed off. He looked at Zee squarely and asked, "You didn't go to see her without me, did you?"

Zee's eyes widened.

"Excuse me?"

"Like after I went yesterday, you didn't go in and talk to Orkideh about me?"

Zee smiled.

"Oh yeah, she and I have actually been texting each other this whole time, waiting for you to catch on. She's gonna swing by the hotel later to watch the new Avengers movie with us."

Cyrus smiled too, rolling his eyes.

"Seriously, Cyrus, what the fuck? Do you know who I am? Sometimes I feel like you don't see me at all," Zee said. He was still smiling, but less convincingly now.

"I just don't understand why she would have said that about the flight."

Zee sighed, asked: "Do you think she might have known your dad somehow? Back in Iran? I can't think of how else."

Cyrus considered this. He thought it unlikely. From the old life in Iran his father really only talked to Arash, his mother's brother, and even him only once a year on Nowruz. Cyrus's grandparents were long gone. And given how unwell Arash was, how he never left his house, it didn't seem likely Orkideh would know him.

"I don't think so. I guess it's not impossible," Cyrus said. "I honestly don't know a ton about Orkideh's story. If she knew my dad, wouldn't she have said something about it?"

"I mean, I would think so. Have you looked her up?" Zee asked, flagging the server for more hot water. The records were still fanned out on their table, and inside the restaurant was getting busy. The server looked flustered and a little annoyed that they weren't ordering food.

"Just quickly with Sad James before we left Indiana. Not in depth, no. I'll check again."

With this, he pulled out his phone and opened the web browser, typed in "orkideh artist." When he had looked her up prior to leaving for New York he'd just scanned Google images to get a sense of her projects. He'd seen some professionally shot photographs of her, most in dramatic black-and-white lighting and with Orkideh wearing stern expressions. And then a handful of her pieces too: many pictures seemed to be of one large entire exhibit space filled with frayed FedEx and UPS boxes, various international shipping containers, all shredded and filling the room all the way up to viewers' knees—they walked through almost like a ball pit made of ripped-up cardboard. Another involved an empty room with some sort of mechanical device activated with a button push that dispensed ice cream into a small bowl in the center of the room, which ran over onto the floor in sloppy pools. There were some paintings, many abstract, that Cyrus had scrolled through idly in search of something more figurative to give him a sense of who the artist was. And of course, he'd found a good deal of promotional material about her final installation, *Death-Speak*.

Clicking back, he navigated to her Wikipedia page and was struck by how scant it was. For someone with a major show at the Brooklyn Museum next to pieces by Judy Chicago and Mark Rothko, Cyrus had expected a Wikipedia page with sections—Personal Life, Career,

Awards, Controversies, Further Reading. But this was all it said for "Orkideh (Artist)":

"Orkideh (ارکیده) is the stage name of an Iranian visual and performance artist. She is best known for her 1997 exhibit 'SHIPPING AND HANDLING,' which was featured at the Venice Biennial. Though she is famously reclusive and avoids interviews, she has revealed that she fled Iran sometime after the Iranian Revolution (hyperlink). Her work often deals with themes of loneliness, exile, war, and identity. In 2005, she divorced her wife and gallerist Sang N. Linh. In 2017, The Linh Gallery announced Orkideh was dying of terminal breast cancer and would be spending her final weeks living in the Brooklyn Museum for an exhibit called *Death-Speak*."

The page had a handful of links and citations—a 2009 write-up in *Artforum* was the source of the "fled Iran" moment. And a link to the Sang Linh gallery site, which Cyrus clicked. It loaded quickly on Cyrus's phone; there was a home page collage of several different artists represented by Linh—a Colombian husband-and-wife sculptor team who made hip bronze reimaginings of Mesoamerican deities, an Atlanta artist who crafted massive mobiles out of still frames from French New Wave films. Orkideh's picture, younger, with a full head of long wavy black hair, was near the bottom of the page—still there, Cyrus noted—the divorce apparently hadn't severed Orkideh and Sang's business relationship. Cyrus tapped his thumb on her picture.

On the top of Orkideh's page there was a flyer for the *Death-Speak* exhibit in Brooklyn with the same gallery copy Cyrus had seen in Indiana. Beneath were names and pictures of previous exhibits: *Jigaram, Minus Forty, Comprehension Density*. But as Cyrus kept scrolling, one piece caught his eye.

A large rectangular image, a painting, showing a battlefield strewn with dead soldiers, many mustached, many wounded, many lying in puddles of blood. And in the middle of the battlefield: a giant black horse with the black silhouette of a rider in long black robes. The rider was haloed in yellow light, and there was a big silver line— a zipper—running up the front of the robe. The artist had created with the halo a sort of X-ray effect that allowed the viewer to see through the rider's black robes where, illuminated inside, the body of a scared naked little boy curled tight, holding desperately on to the horse. An expression of pure agony lurched across his face, almost like a kabuki mask but it was no mask, it was the rider's face, the man-boy naked under the black robes riding a horse through this field of dead.

Cyrus's breath caught in his throat like a fist. He handed his phone over to Zee and told him about his uncle Arash, how he had been the one to wear the black robe and ride among the dead in the Iran-Iraq War.

"That's fucking *wild*," Zee said when Cyrus had finished. "That really happened?"

"Yeah."

"It's nuts that people did that. It's nuts your uncle did that." Looking closer at the painting, Zee said, "'Dudusch'? The title of the painting—what's that mean?"

"Brother," Cyrus said. "It's Farsi for 'brother.'"

TWENTY

WHAT MIGHT COMPEL A MARTYR TO MARTYRDOM:

- · god
- · beauty
- · family
- · land
- · love
- · history
- · justice
- · desire
- · sex

Martyr. I want to scream it in an airport. I want to die killing the president. Ours and everyone's. I want them all to have been right to fear me. Right to have killed my mother, to have ruined my father. I want to be worthy of the great terror my existence inspires.

—*from* BOOKOFMARTYRS.docx by Cyrus Shams

SUNDAY

——— ✳ ———

Cyrus Shams and Zee Novak

BROOKLYN, DAY 3

THAT NIGHT CYRUS AND ZEE ORDERED PIZZA AND STAYED IN TO watch the hotel's basic cable, HGTV and *Office* reruns. Zee talked about how luxurious it felt to do nothing in New York City, a place where you could do anything. He kept saying "opportunity cost," that the opportunity cost of doing nothing in the city was so immense that it felt opulent.

Cyrus had planned to walk around the streets, people-watch, maybe post up at a bar somewhere to nurse a Coke, but Zee made his absurd but charming case and Cyrus assented. The pizza was half pineapple, and Cyrus said something reflexive about fruit on pizza being bad, the sort of uncharacteristic inherited nothing people said just to say something, and to which Zee replied by stating "fruit" was a botanical term, "vegetable" a culinary term, and that such distinctions were meaningless. Cyrus smiled and picked a stray pineapple off his cheese piece and flicked it at Zee. They ate happily in their bed, pizza box sitting on a towel laid out between them, eyes fixed on the flat-screen TV showing a rerun of *The Office*.

"They'd never be able to make this today," Zee said about the episode in which a character claimed to have invented a gaydar after a member of the office was outed.

"You don't think so?"

"No way. You think they could?"

Cyrus thought for a second:

"I guess not. But that's the point, I think."

"What do you mean?" Zee asked.

"Like you couldn't make *The Honeymooners* or *Cheers* today either."

"Was *Cheers* the one with Archie Bunker?" Zee asked.

"Nah, that was *All in the Family.* But that was fucked up too. That kind of comedy always exists on the edge of what you're allowed to say at the moment. And that edge keeps moving. With the moment. The Everton window or whatever."

"Overton," Zee said.

"Huh?"

"Overton window, not Everton."

"Oh, whatever," Cyrus said, sucking his teeth. "But it's everywhere. I'm constantly afraid to read the books I loved as a kid because I know there's going to be some awful shit in there."

On the TV, there was a commercial for some drug—a white-haired woman in pastels was jumping on a trampoline with two little boys.

"I reread the *The Bell Jar* a year ago, and yikes," Zee said. "There were pages I just had to flip past."

Cyrus laughed.

"That's right. I haven't read that since high school and I remember it heebying my jeebies even then. That scene where she kicks the guy for serving two different kinds of beans?" He took a bite of pizza. "But that's still how I still feel about pretty much every John Hughes thing."

"Yes!" Zee exclaimed. *"Pretty in Pink* is so fucked up."

"Right? And there's that one with Long Duk Dong or whoever, which I remember seeming messed-up even when I watched it as a kid."

"Yes yes, your ethical hygiene has always been immaculate, dear," Zee teased. "I did forget about that, though, Long Duk Dong. How did that happen, even then?"

"That's what I'm saying! This stuff is in pretty much everything. It's not even old white dudes either. Adrienne Rich was a TERF. Sontag announced she was 'turning her back on' Gwendolyn Brooks."

"See, this is why everyone should just do what I do," Zee said. "Be right about everything, and shut up about it."

Cyrus laughed and touched his arm. On the TV, a commercial for Adidas featuring a soccer player neither Cyrus nor Zee recognized.

"I'm gonna take a shower," Cyrus said. "Do you need anything?"

"Do I need anything . . . from the shower?"

"Hah. Do you need anything broadly?"

"Can you arrest the world's encroaching entropy? Fix irreversible ecological collapse?"

"I cannot," said Cyrus, smiling.

"The rising specter of global fascism?"

"Nope."

"New Vistalite drum kit?"

"Sorry."

"Okay, then I'm good," Zee said, grinning.

Cyrus got into the shower. Afterwards, when he emerged still wet, wearing just a towel, his roommate patted the bed and turned off the TV. Zee looked firm, saturated with life, like crisp wood. Cyrus dropped his towel and crept under the covers.

AFTERWARDS, ZEE WANTED A CIGARETTE AND CYRUS FOLLOWED him out to the front of the hotel. Inside the lobby, chic thirty-somethings sipped thirteen-dollar cocktails and tried to talk over too-loud Dutch techno.

"So what's tomorrow?" Zee said.

"You mean at the museum?" Cyrus asked.

"Yeah, what's your plan?" Zee rolled his cigarette autonomically, tobacco from Bugler pouch into paper, filter into paper, like he could have done it all one-handed walking into a breeze.

Cyrus considered.

"Well, I guess I'll ask Orkideh how she knew what she knew."

"And what are you expecting her to say?" Zee put the cigarette between his lips.

"I haven't really thought past that first step," Cyrus said honestly.

"I just don't want you to be blindsided," Zee said. "Er, some non-ableist synonym for 'blindsided.'"

"Hurt?"

"Yeah, but also with surprise. Hurt-surprised."

"I appreciate that. I mean, what can she really say? My parents are dead. I have no siblings, no partner. I got sober two years ago, meaning I've lived two years of useful life more than I was supposed to."

"Says who?"

"Huh?"

"Who judges 'supposed to'?"

Cyrus shrugged.

"I just mean, I passed over that moment, the moment I could've died but didn't, and I didn't even know it. I didn't even know it happened. And everything since has been bonus, you know? Whatever Orkideh says, she knew my uncle or she did some weird Google deep dive, I'll put it in this book I'm working on and then I'll die and life will move on."

Zee said nothing, pulled hard from his cigarette. Cyrus went on:

"What's that bit of Auden about the 'expensive delicate ship' that saw a boy falling out of the sky, but had somewhere to be so it sailed calmly on? That's what I'm talking about. Like I'm the boy, and the rest of the world is the ship. Or I'm the water, maybe. I don't know."

Zee took another long pull.

"You know how fucked up this is, right?" he asked, exhaling smoke between syllables. Beautiful underdressed lobby patrons came out to shiver, to wait for Lyfts.

"This whole wanting to die bullshit," Zee went on. "It's so fucked up."

"How do you mean?" Cyrus asked.

"I mean what I said. This 'poor little orphan boy with nothing tethering him to this world' shit." Zee looked sharply at Cyrus. "You know I have your cum on my chest, right? Like, right now this second? While you opine about how nobody will care if you kill yourself?"

An older South Asian woman huddled in furs looked furtively over at Zee and made a face.

"Zee," Cyrus said.

"You have no idea how selfish you can be," Zee continued.

Two Latina mothers in colorful dresses and parkas pushed strollers down the sidewalk, laughing. Across the street a skinny white kid in a MAKE NOISE NOT LOVE T-shirt was doing some sort of calisthenics near his bike.

"You act like you live in this vacuum. Like there's already this frame hanging around your life. But you can't use history to rationalize everything. You realize that's what countries do, right? What America does? And what Iran does, specifically?"

Cyrus winced. Zee was referring, maybe, to the way the Iranian regime posted images of its war dead everywhere. Cyrus had told him about the Iranian government putting an image of the plane crash that had killed Cyrus's mother on a state postage stamp to stoke anti-American sentiment. How one nation flattened history into a statistical anomaly, collateral damage, and the other minted it into propaganda.

"That's not fair," Cyrus whispered.

"No, it isn't," Zee agreed.

"I'm just tired," Cyrus continued. "You know that."

But Zee wasn't hearing it. He put his cigarette out and wormed his way through the doors back into the hotel. Cyrus followed him wordlessly back up the stairs to their room. Zee turned around and stared at him. Cyrus shut the door and said, "Okay, you really want to get into it? It's true. Nothing here makes me feel compelled to stay. Not my dad, not drugs or booze, not recovery or Gabe or fucking poetry. Nothing."

"That's not normal, Cyrus. You know that's not normal?"

"I know! And I don't want to be normal. Maybe you're okay waiting tables and playing drums occasionally for the rest of your life, but I actually want to make a difference. I want my having-been-alive to *matter.*"

At that final beat, *matter*, Zee squinted at Cyrus, cocking his head. He tried to reconcile the words he'd just heard with the image of the man he quietly loved, the gentle writer with whom he'd spent years swinging from joy to joy, despair to despair. His mouth hung open for just a second, a flicker. Then, quickly, he gathered himself and began going around the hotel room to wordlessly collect his things.

"Ah, Zee, I didn't mean it like that," Cyrus said. Shame flooded him immediately, like seawater filling a lung.

Zee pulled his head back, his cheek muscles pulled tight. He said nothing. Cyrus stared at his friend's face, which had grown hard, jaw set firmly. If Zee had looked soft, quivering, like he was about to cry, Cyrus might've instinctively held him, rubbed his back, apologized. But Zee's hardness, his armor, immobilized Cyrus. His eyes looked like black thorns.

"I'm sorry," said Cyrus. "I'm sorry."

Finally, Zee snapped.

"Cyrus, for months, every song I've listened to has been directly about me. About my life. And my stupid fucking life with you. Every flower has been blooming straight into my fucking face. Do you know what that is? It's like being insane. Like the fucking pigeons are speaking to me. Have you ever felt that? Do you have any idea what I'm even talking about?"

When Cyrus didn't answer, Zee shook his head and bent down to his backpack. Clipping his wallet into the bag's front pocket, Zee walked over to the hotel door and opened it; hallway light poured into their darkened room as if to illuminate the cruelty of what had been spoken. Without another word, without even looking back up, Zee was gone.

TWENTY-ONE

. . . .

ALI SHAMS

b. 1961–2007

With all due respect, you staying alive for me
was a lousy reason to live. I kept only a bit:
the rubber fish, a few chicken feathers,
your lips hardly moving when you spoke.

Victims die, that's their main verb.

Also: how to love a man. I kept that too.

Bright silhouette, you were lovely
as the landscape curved past our
understanding—it was there to crack us
open, across. A curve: any straight line
broken at every point. Doomable

dad, hour of the world! I understand now
why you stayed and why you left.
But I did love you here, hour of the world.

. . . . .

—*from* BOOKOFMARTYRS.docx by Cyrus Shams

SUNDAY

———— ❋ ————

Cyrus Shams

BROOKLYN, DAY 3

CYRUS TRIED CALLING ZEE. HE WASN'T SURE WHAT HE'D SAY IF ZEE picked up—sorry, probably, though he still wasn't exactly sure for what—speaking cruelly, yes, but there was more. And anyway, Zee didn't answer, and Cyrus didn't leave a voicemail. It was 8:30, too early to sleep. Cyrus didn't feel like going back outside. His hands, he noticed, were quivering involuntarily, erratically, as if they were trying to shake themselves out of a dream.

When his father was buried, a couple people from his farm showed up. Ali's boss and his boss's wife, who were closer to Cyrus's age than Ali's. Cyrus's favorite high school English teacher, Mr. Orenn, came. Shireen, Cyrus's then girlfriend, came. His roommates at the time, Zeke and Chang. Bilal, Cyrus's then friend, future lover, future ex. Cyrus hadn't asked anyone to say anything so everyone mostly stood around somberly. Mr. Orenn said something secular and sweet, Cyrus couldn't really remember much about it other than how he felt grateful that someone was doing something. Mostly he remembered the smell of wet soil, sickly sweet, that earthy sweet he could still sometimes smell in the air after rain.

His uncle Arash wouldn't have been able to fly over from Iran even if Cyrus had remembered to call to invite him, but Cyrus hadn't, and when he eventually called to deliver the news, his uncle was furious. He'd screamed and cursed at Cyrus over the phone for the first and only time ever.

Cyrus got up from the bed and cracked open the hotel window, which looked out at some sort of brick structural organ of the hotel's anatomy. The cold came in and for a moment, two, Cyrus was able to just think of that, the feeling-cold. It stilled his higher brain a bit, one of the few minor highs still left in Cyrus's ever-dwindling arsenal. After a minute, he pulled his phone back out and dialed his uncle Arash's number in WhatsApp.

Even though it was the middle of the night in Alborz, Arash picked up on the second ring, remaining silent, waiting for the caller to introduce themself first. Cyrus had grown accustomed to this in their infrequent phone calls over the years, and said, in his heavily accented Farsi, "Dahyi Arash, this is Cyrus. Did I wake you?"

Arash's voice filled the line brightly: "Cyrus jaan! My heart!"

Cyrus was always a little surprised at the high pitch of his uncle's voice; a tonsillectomy decades ago had gone slightly awry, leaving Arash with a permanent falsetto one might think was mocking, if one knew no better.

"How are you, my boy?" Arash asked eagerly.

Cyrus realized it had been years since the last time they'd spoken. He generally avoided it, preferring the guilt of not calling to the guilt of calling, hearing his uncle's endless conspiracies, digressions into his medical histories, of having to apprehend fully the weight of his only living relative's unwellness. Still, to his credit, Arash never shamed him for this.

"I'm good, uncle. I'm content. How are you?"

"Ah, the same story. I am alive, which pisses everyone off." Arash laughed. "There's not much more to say about it than that. My new helper here is nice, a little Lebanese girl. She's teaching me some French. Je m'appelle Arash. Do you know French?"

Cyrus had cheated his way through a couple undergrad classes, expecting to both be able to skip all his classes and also emerge fluent enough to offer the definitive English translations of Dumas and Rimbaud. Mostly he remembered foods, pain au fromage, that sort of thing.

"No, not really."

"What I just said was 'My name is Arash.'"

"Ahh," said Cyrus, smiling.

"It's a lot like Farsi, actually. A lot of the same words. Conquerors, colonial vampires."

"Iran was colonized by the French?" Cyrus asked.

"'Merci amperyalist! Merci burokrasi!' Where do you think these come from? A coincidence?"

"I guess I never really thought about it."

"You know what she taught me the other day?" Arash asked. In the background of his end was a loud whirring sound.

"Are you grinding coffee, dahyi?"

"Impressive ear!"

"What time is it there?"

"A little after four," Arash told him. "But I was already up, don't worry. Why should I lie? Between death and I, it's like this." Cyrus knew his uncle was holding up four fingers close together to indicate the width between himself and death, a strange gesture his father sometimes made too. As an idiom it always seemed out of character for his father. When Cyrus asked him about it once, he just laughed.

"From an old TV show. I'd actually forgotten where it came from."

Now, Cyrus could hear the gas stovetop clicking on, likely under his uncle's Moka coffee pot.

"Now, can you guess what Ghashmira taught me the other day?" Arash asked.

"Ghashmira?"

"My Lebanese assistant! Do you listen at all, nephew?"

"Ah, sorry."

Cyrus knew part of his uncle's soldier's state pension was the government providing him with assistants to do his shopping, to make sure his bills were paid.

"Tenez fermement à la corde de dieu," Arash said in an exaggerated French accent. "Do you know what that means?"

"Something about God? And firmament?"

Arash laughed. "Exactly, some mullah nonsense. You know I hate that shit."

Cyrus said nothing. His uncle talking that way over the phone made him anxious. Even for a "war hero," such talking in Iran was needlessly reckless.

"So why are you calling, Koroosh baba? Are you safe?"

"Yes, uncle, I'm safe. Everything is fine." Cyrus hesitated. "I saw a painting and it made me think of you."

Silence from his uncle's end. Then—

"A painting?"

"Yeah, it's by an Iranian artist, and I think it was one of the soldiers, the kind you were, in the war."

"The kind I was?"

"Like, with a robe and a horse and a flashlight."

Arash laughed:

"You saw a painting of a soldier with a flashlight and it made you think of me! Made you call your dear sick uncle! Praise the propaganda empire! Some good comes from it at last!"

Cyrus chuckled weakly.

"It's just—it seemed exactly like your stories, or the stories my dad told me about what you did. Like . . ." Cyrus paused. "Riding around all those bodies, a guy on a horse with a sword and a flashlight, riding around the—." He paused.

"Riding around the dead?" his uncle said.

"Yeah."

"I'm not a child, Cyrus. I'm crazy, they say, but you can talk to me like a real person."

"I know, dahyi. I am."

"A couple years before your dad died, I sold my little white four-door Paykan sedan. I had it since around when you guys left. I used to take it on these long drives, trips through the countryside. And that Paykan had this broken tape player. I couldn't get it to spit the cassette back out, it was just permanently stuck in there. Do you know what the tape was?"

"What was it?"

"Allegri's Miserere." Arash waited a beat for Cyrus's recognition. When it didn't happen, he asked, "Are you familiar?"

"I don't think so, no. Maybe if I heard a bit of it—"

"If you'd ever heard it before, you wouldn't forget about it. Anyway, it's a very famous piece of music. Very particular." He took a sip of coffee. "The story goes it was only ever taught orally, in the Vatican, only to be sung for popes on holy days. Total psycho Catholic bullshit. But then three hundred years ago, little fourteen-year-old Mozart comes in and gets to hear it, he's the pope's special guest. And then that little teenager goes home and transcribes it from memory. The whole composition, start to finish. There are five distinct choral parts, and Mozart transcribes the whole thing off that one listen. He goes back the next year to check his work and fine-tunes his transcription and then he took the song, this perfect protected angelic thing, and gave it to the people."

"Wow," Cyrus said, in English.

"Right? This music the church thought was too beautiful for common people, pearls before swine, isn't that what they say? Though pigs are smarter than dogs, and pearls are just rocks. But Mozart got it so right, so perfect off hearing it just twice, that the church didn't even punish him. They said Mozart brought thousands of new converts into the church."

"Wow," Cyrus said again, in English, immediately regretting it.

"Anyway, I had this Miserere tape stuck in my car for years, and I couldn't get it out. So I just listened to it again and again and again, the whole tape was only twenty minutes long, less than that even, and then the tape player would automatically rewind itself and start over, which was a very advanced feature for a tape player back then, by the way. I must have listened to it one thousand times, maybe more. Why should I lie? Between death and me, it's like . . . Certainly the mullahs would say the tape was an apostasy. But I just kept listening to it over and over. And do you know what happened? What changed?"

"What?"

"Nothing. It felt like a miracle every time. It didn't matter if I came in just for the last minute, the last ninety seconds of the tape. There were five voices and I heard something new every time. The idea that someone, a child, could hear it once or twice and remember everything, and I could hear it a thousand times like I'd never heard it once before? What does that tell you?"

Cyrus was confused. He'd felt confused all night.

"I have no idea. I'm sorry. I don't understand."

Arash laughed.

"Of course you don't. You've never heard the song."

"I'll listen tonight. I can even play it for you right now on my laptop if you—"

"No!" said Arash, sharply. "No." Cyrus was on his heels.

"You wouldn't understand even if you heard it, nephew. Get it? I listen to it and see God in it because I've *been* God. I've spoken to those same angels, right? But you see a picture of an angel and a sword and think only of your crazy uncle. The most human thing in the world. Because that's as close as you've ever been. Or you *believe* it's as close as you've ever been."

Cyrus sighed, then blurted:

"It was called 'Dudusch.' "

"Excuse me?"

"The painting. It was called 'Brother.' "

A pause.

"A lot of people have brothers, Cyrus. There were many men who did what I did. One in every company."

"Right."

"What are you trying to say, Cyrus?"

"I don't know, uncle. It just made me think of you, and my mom."

Another pause, longer.

"Are you doing okay?" Arash asked. "Do you have enough money? How are your poems?"

"I'm fine. Really, aziz. I have money. I'm working on a new writing project and it's good to feel busy."

"Good to be busy indeed." Cyrus heard his uncle take a gulp of coffee. "The next time you call, I'll be fluent in French, if this woman has her way." His tone had shifted.

Cyrus smiled, then laughed a little so his uncle could hear it.

"I'll call again soon. I promise."

"You're a young man, Cyrus. Full of life. I understand."

Cyrus winced.

"You know what happened to that Paykan?" Arash asked. "When I was in the hospital they said I saw things that weren't there, that I couldn't drive anymore. Even though a blindfolded man would still be the safest driver in Tehran! But they took my driving license and so I had to sell my Paykan. I loved that car. But I couldn't sell it with contraband in it. So I took a screwdriver and shoved it in the tape slot. And I shoved it in again and again until I heard the cassette crack. And I swear to you, when it cracked, I heard giggling. Giggling! It wasn't mine."

"Giggling?"

"The devil, Cyrus. It's not supernatural. It's not make-believe. They play chess with us. That's what we are. I destroyed that tape and it was like the devil killing a queen on a chess board. Checkmate."

Cyrus had so many questions. Who was "they"? Why "killing" instead of "captured"? Cyrus felt like he was two beats behind his uncle this whole conversation.

"You'll call again soon Cyrus, right?"

"I will, dahyi. I promise."

They hung up. Cyrus imagined his uncle across the world setting down his telephone receiver and walking back to the window, pulling the curtain back just an inch to stare out into the vast black outside. Stars, even on a morning like that. It would be all dark in his house, and the darkness outside the window would reflect his own face back from the glass. His uncle would shut the curtain quickly, wait a couple seconds, and then flash it open again, just to be sure. To be sure of what? Arash wouldn't know. But he'd pull a chair over to the window, sip his coffee, and concentrate.

Cyrus went to grab his headphones, turned off all the lights in the room and lay down on the bed. He queued up a recording of the Miserere on his phone and, as the voices began, Cyrus closed his eyes.

TWENTY-TWO

ORKIDEH AND
PRESIDENT INVECTIVE

———— ✴ ————

TWO FIGURES WALKING THROUGH A MALL, A FANCY MALL, THE kind that has a Crate and Barrel and an Apple store. Cyrus recognized the woman immediately as Orkideh, who appeared in this dream bald and warm as she did in the Brooklyn Museum, though here in the dream she also had big bushy eyebrows that sat on her forehead like storm clouds. Beneath those, a pair of large-framed fashionable sunglasses that seemed almost out of place on her head, like a child trying out random pieces of her mother's clothes. Walking a step behind Orkideh, breathing heavily inside his strangely large body, was President Invective, wearing one of his signature blue blocky ill-fitting suits.

Cyrus didn't typically cast characters who so repelled him in these dreams, but sometimes it just happened, unbidden. For a time in his teens he dreamed almost obsessively, unwillingly, of the bully who tortured him. Once, he dreamt he was eavesdropping at a dinner table between Hannibal Lecter and Jeffrey Dahmer. Another time he was on a plane with Dick Cheney. Here in this dream, President Invective was panting through the mall as if lugging a heavy load, though he carried nothing, and Orkideh's face glinted mischievously, seemingly relishing her companion's struggle.

"Keep up," she urged, waving toward herself.

The mall was neither crowded nor empty. The density of fluorescent lighting and mercenary corporate energy in such spaces usually felt suffocating to Cyrus, but Orkideh looked totally at ease, amused even. It was President Invective who seemed to be struggling.

"Why are we here?" he said, looking embarrassed to be asking a question. It was not something he did often.

"Here in this mall, or here in this dream?" Orkideh asked, playfully. Her face looked old and young at once, like an antique doll. It was nice to see her moving around without an oxygen tank. Despite her bald head she looked healthy, spry even, and familiar in a warm way, more like the pictures Cyrus had seen of her face in his internet searches.

President Invective didn't answer Orkideh's question, as if out of protest. They walked forward past fancy clothing and jewelry stores. As they passed a tea store, he popped in for a quick sample in a little Dixie Cup, which he shot like cheap tequila, then grimaced.

"In Farsi," Orkideh said, "the word for tea is 'chai,' which I'm sure you know."

"Of course," President Invective lied, making his face pulse with a low green light. Orkideh smiled.

"But the word for cardamom, which we add to our tea, is 'hell.' When I first came to America, I spent all my time in this cheap little diner on the Lower East Side. There was a Persian waitress there, a young girl, maybe nineteen, twenty, who spoke almost as little English as I did. Every day I would sit at the table in the morning before going to look for work and she would come over and say 'hell chai' and we would giggle. I knew enough English to know 'hell' was a bad word, we giggled there with the naughty zeal of a child saying 'the beaver's damn dam,' something like this. It was my first English joke, my first American friend."

President Invective snorted, unimpressed. He was staring at his reflection in a children's toy store glass window. He'd only been half listening, popping back into the conversation when he heard "American." Secretly he was confused. He hadn't realized Orkideh had ever lived in New York. But it was his habit to ignore such dissonances. Usually they resolved themselves without him needing to expend energy. Studying his reflection, it looked like his face was beginning to sprout tiny black worms.

Orkideh and President Invective pressed on, past stores hawking kitchenware, basketball cards, fossils, comics, plague masks, electron microscopes, until they arrived at a store that seemed to be selling original works of classic art. In the store window was the *Mona Lisa*, and President Invective lit up.

"I've seen this one! I know this one," he said. "Fantastic painting. Beautiful painting, beautiful woman." He had a coffee mug with the *Mona Lisa* on it, an old Father's Day gift from one of his children, he couldn't remember which.

"You know why it's so famous?" asked Orkideh.

"Because it's perfect! Look at her. Look at that smile! The best painting. The very best."

Orkideh ignored him.

"It's famous because it hung in Napoleon's bedroom. It is not so remarkable a portrait. It's not even on canvas, it's painted on a poplar plank. Scrap wood. Da Vinci would have been horrified to know that five hundred years later it would become his most famous piece."

"Napoleon's bedroom?" President Invective was enthralled. His jowls were flapping open and shut like happy gills. He had to have it.

They walked into the store, past the Venus of Willendorf, past tile from the Blue Mosque and lions from Persepolis, past Hokusai's *Great Wave* and Géricault's *Raft of Medusa*. Right before the counter, where a goth cashier was texting into her phone, was another massive original painting, a seaside landscape bustling with life.

"Do you know this one?" Orkideh asked President Invective, pointing to the canvas.

"Sure," he lied, "but I don't want it. Come on, I need to pay for the Lisa before someone else does." He felt particularly suave calling it that, "the Lisa," like he and the painting were already intimates.

Orkideh continued as if she hadn't heard him.

"Bruegel's *Landscape with the Fall of Icarus*," she said. "Icarus flew too close to the sun and his wings melted. Other artists painted it by focusing on his father Daedalus's grief, or Icarus's joyful hubris in the moments before his descent. 'His waxen wings did mount above his reach, and melting, heavens conspired his overthrow.' You know?"

President Invective shuffled from foot to foot. He didn't like this talk of "overthrow." But he did like the painting well enough. Good people working hard. Lovely water, sturdy ships, a horizon. Mostly he wanted her to stop talking so he could pay for his da Vinci.

"But Bruegel paints Icarus way out in the margin of the painting. Just pair of legs drowning in the water. Everyone else is going about their work. The mule plows, the sheep graze. 'White legs disappearing into the green water, and the expensive delicate ship that must have seen something amazing, a boy falling out of the sky, had somewhere to get to and sailed calmly on.'"

President Invective hated this. Bruegel had ruined his perfectly lovely landscape with that pair of legs. He hated being condescended to, hated people who thought they could teach him. He hated Orkideh and Bruegel both. Ignoring them, he walked up to the counter. The cashier looked up from her phone.

"Can I help you?"

"I want to buy the *Mona Lisa*. How much?"

"Hm, let me check." The girl shuffled through a notebook.

Orkideh walked up to the counter too, said: "I'd like to know the price on the Bruegel, the Icarus, too, if you don't mind."

"Okay, hold on." The girl flipped through her notebook, a big binder full of tiny print, though there were only a dozen or so pieces of art in the store.

"The *Mona Lisa* is four segments. That's a sale, it had been six all month. The Bruegel is two."

President Invective had been fishing through his wallet, counting his bills.

"Segments?" he asked.

"That's a great price on the Bruegel," Orkideh said to the girl. "I'll take it."

"Cool," said the cashier. "Any preference which hand?"

"Surprise me," said Orkideh, setting both hands down on the counter and looking away. Her hands were missing several fingers, some cut off at the top knuckle, others cut all the way down to the palm. The cashier squeezed her left middle finger, still full, at the base, and then pulled a great cleaver from behind her back. Orkideh breathed a deep breath and the cashier dropped the cleaver down in one massive stroke, cutting the finger at the middle knuckle.

Orkideh sucked in air through her clenched teeth, said, "Fuck! Fuck."

"Do you want me to wrap the painting up for you?" asked the cashier as she cut the loose finger into two segments at the top joint.

"No, I'll carry it out as is." Orkideh pulled a white handkerchief from her pocket and wrapped it around the bloody stump of her finger, the red growing through the white like a flag, like weather.

"You people are crazy!" President Invective screamed. "You people are absolutely batshit crazy!" He ran out of the store as fast as he could, leaving a trail of low green light behind him.

Orkideh smiled a little at the cashier, shrugged her shoulders, then walked out of the store with Bruegel's *Landscape with the Fall of Icarus* under her arm.

TWENTY-THREE

ROYA SHAMS

———— ✳ ————

TEHRAN, AUGUST 1987

THAT REST OF HER VISIT DURING OUR HUSBANDS' CAMPING TRIP, Leila was an eager horse charging out ahead of me, dragging me through the grass. I was trying desperately to hang on to the reins. The second day, there was a moment when we were walking through the bazaar. It was unseasonably cold; Leila wore a heavy coat and a long scarf. All along Bazaar-e Tajrish corridor, the street webbed off into side paths and alleyways, many with vendors selling cut flowers, kabobs, powdery cookies, perfumes, beads, carpets, underwear. Men called out to each other unintelligibly. An old woman tasted soup from a great cast-iron pot. Beside her, a younger woman—clearly her daughter—sold steamed sweet beets and fava beans to passersby.

As we walked between people, Leila suddenly pulled me into a bare alley that bent into another alley. The path was thin, dirty, ending in brick apartments and garbage cans. Above us, clothes drying on balconies. A blue-gray sky. Without any explanation, Leila got on her knees and bent her ear down to the asphalt.

"You can hear it!" she said, smiling up at me, ear still pressed against the earth. "The angels playing their drums deep down in the earth!"

I had no idea what she was talking about and looked around nervously.

"Roya jaan, you can hear them too! You know very well that the earth is filled with angels and djinn partying like teenagers, spinning around like waterwheels. Come listen."

People walking through the alley that turned into ours passed by, ignoring us. At least I hoped they were ignoring us. Hesitantly I got on my knees and put my ear to the ground, near Leila's. The path was cold. A thin ribbon of sky loomed over our heads like a chaperone.

"I don't hear anything," I said. I don't know what I'd expected but I was disappointed. The earth sounded like nothing, like earth. I felt a little embarrassed, like I wasn't in on the joke.

"You have to listen, really listen. Not like with all this bleating," she said, gesturing back toward the bazaar, "but to the sounds beneath the sounds beneath the sounds. You know what I mean?"

I didn't. Her ear was still pressed against the asphalt and she began tapping out a rhythm with her hand, pum PO-POP pum, pum POP-POP pum.

"Under the soil, under all of us and all our dead ancient skeletons with arrowheads broken off in their ribs," Leila said, "the angels are drumming!" She kept tapping her hand. "For us, I imagine."

I had no idea what she was talking about.

"Are you making fun of me?" I asked, pulling my head off the ground.

Leila sat up too, scooted closer to me, still on her knees. She grabbed the middle finger of my right hand and, shutting her left eye, held my finger gently but firmly on top of her closed eyelid.

"Do you feel this?" she said, moving her open eye up, down, up, down. Beneath the eyelid beneath my finger, her other eye was matching the movements of its sibling. "You feel how even the closed eye is still searching for your face?"

I nodded. Her hand tapped, pum PO-POP pum, pum POP-POP pum.

"That," Leila said, "is how I have been searching for you."

And then she leaned forward and kissed me. Right there in the alley path off the bazaar. It wasn't an insubstantial kiss. It wasn't familial. It was on the lips, my eyes still open and all surprise. I must have looked like a fish. And though I should have been afraid of being seen, of bystanders peeking in off the main bazaar strip, I held it, Leila's kiss, and I kissed her back. Her hand was on my cheek then. My finger had moved itself from her eyelid to her earlobe.

The kiss lasted three seconds, maybe four, but it set everything else in motion. My life was a painting I'd been staring at upside-down up until that moment, that moment when Leila wandered in and flipped it right-side up for me. Just like that. Everything clicked into place, the picture came into clarity. Even Leila, in all her poise, looked surprised and, after those few infinite seconds, pulled away.

"I'm sorry," she said, studying my face.

"No—" I said, pausing. My ears were ringing, I could feel the blood rushing through my skull.

"No?" she said, blinking once, then twice, waiting for me to respond.

"No, don't be sorry," I said. "The eye, the angel's drums." I paused. "I think I understand."

She smiled. A few curls peeked out from under her headscarf. We were on our knees in the alley staring at each other like children. Like chickens. I felt dizzy again from aliveness. Flush with baffle and excitement, like the first person to taste snow. And then, natural as air, we stood up and walked back into the bazaar, where men were arguing about nonsense, where women swept dirt from dirt.

After that first kiss, I wouldn't have questioned anything. Possibility, freedom. If a great winged angel had come up from the earth and burst apart, I would have gathered its feathers.

TWENTY-FOUR

. . . .

ORKIDEH

b. 1963?

When one is dead it's for a very long time,
sure, but you found the loophole,
suspended yourself in dying,
wearing dying like a child wears a white sheet

to seem a ghost, but why would any ghost
look like that and who are you trying to convince?
Art? What is beautiful is not always beautiful
in company: Prussian blue, men like me—

of course there's weather under the seeds,
the doomsday clock blinking in 8's which look like
mountains in Farsi, no euphemism for that hateful light
or the crushing sameness of our species—

each person throbs like an idiot moon:
death is their job, dying is yours.

. . . . .

—*from* BOOKOFMARTYRS.docx by Cyrus Shams

MONDAY

———— ✴ ————

Cyrus Shams

BROOKLYN, DAY 4

CYRUS WOKE UP THE NEXT MORNING COLD, HEAVY. WET TOO, HE
soon realized, though it took a moment, with *cold* and *heavy* being so
much of *wet*. He looked around the dark hotel room, remembered
he was alone. Zee hadn't returned in the night. Cyrus got out of bed,
spent too many seconds trying to figure out how to turn on a light,
and then discovered the genesis of the cold and heavy and wet: he'd
pissed the bed.

During the deepest stages of his drinking this had been a regular occurrence; in the night he'd sleepwalk to get more beer, more
booze, but his lizard brain cared more about the alcohol's acquisi-
tion than its orderly discharge. That was just life then, waking into
the familiar braid of self-loathing and duty that governed his living—matting up what he could of the wet, spraying it with Febreze,
peeling off his clothes and getting into the shower. If Cyrus woke
somewhere besides his own bed, he had to navigate the cost-benefit
of explaining himself or just wordlessly slipping away. These rituals
had, blissfully, ended when he got sober.

But even though Cyrus hadn't pissed himself like this in ages, not
since he was still drinking, all the old feelings immediately swarmed
back in, like lakewater flooding into a sinking car. First, the still-
reflexive swell of exoneration, the how-do-I-avoid-getting-in-trouble-
for-this. Then the thought of the hotel, the poor maid who'd have to
discover his mess and clean it up. This brought in the self-loathing,
the exasperation with living. Cyrus knew his pragmatic brain would

click into fix-it mode soon, but he first allowed himself a few sump-
tuous instants of self-pity. He wanted, acutely in that moment, to be
not-alive. Not to be dead, not to kill himself, but to have the burden
of living lifted from his shoulders.

When they were still in the warm dawn of their friendship, Cyrus
and Zee used to spend so much time happily blacking out together—
whole years that had become cavities in their memory but for flashes
of late-night sidewalks and unfamiliar faces deliriously shouting lyrics over living room record players, nights of key bumps and swigs
from plastic liquor bottles and pouring crushed pills into cigarettes
unsure if smoking them would even do anything besides taste bad.
Nights of weeping in the moonlight because it was so beautiful to
love and feel the world as deeply as they did, so unexpected and rare.

They'd have laughed at Cyrus's pissing the bed. If there were
other people around, Zee would have flashed his smile that folded
his whole face into his lips, the one that made everyone else in the
room unconsciously smile along, and it'd be a joke for a minute
before everyone moved on to something else. One night at Keady,
Cyrus drunkenly drew two big crowns at the top of Zee's bathroom
mirror in permanent marker. Below them he wrote, *We can wear these
crowns forever.* When Zee asked about it the next morning, Cyrus had
no recollection of it, but the crowns, and the maxim, stayed on the
mirror till the two moved out.

There was a part of the Big Book of Alcoholics Anonymous Cyrus
had read over and over when he first got sober where it talked about
self-pity and resentments being the "dubious luxuries" of normal
people, but for alcoholics, they were poison. Instead of "self-pity"
and "resentment," Cyrus remembered it called them "the grouch
and the brainstorm," which he'd always thought was quaintly of its
time. But that phrase, "dubious luxury," that was tremendous. "For
us, these things are poison." His best friend was gone. He was in a
cold war with his sponsor, with recovery in general. His book—if
it could even be called that—was going nowhere. His life was too
fucked at present for his death to even count toward anything. A
meaningless life meant a meaningless death. He wasn't even sure if

he believed that, but his current state had increased his tolerance for despondent generalizing. In that moment, it felt like the only true thing.

When Cyrus got sad like this, most people treated him lightly, hastily, like he wasn't worth the trouble. Only Zee took it seriously, never shaming Cyrus for canceling plans, sometimes actually sitting with him in silence for whole afternoons or evenings saying nothing, occasionally putting on a record only to let it go still for twenty minutes or an hour before flipping it again.

Cyrus balled up the sheets and the comforter, which had absorbed most of the piss. He took his sweatpants off and threw them in the garbage, then stepped into the shower. If he'd been drunk, if he'd relapsed at the hotel bar, this would have all made sense. The fight with Zee, the piss. But Cyrus was doing everything he was supposed to do. Sobriety, writing. What was the point if every road led back to the same shame?

Sometimes when he closed his eyes in the shower in the morning, he could catch sparks of whatever dream he'd forgotten about from the night before: a girl kneeling in the middle of a country road with a black coin in her palm, a pink lamb pulling a rusted plow. But today, when he closed his eyes in the shower, which took him a full minute to figure out how to turn on (Zee had joked that a hotel's fanciness was directly proportional to how long it took you to figure out how to turn on the showerhead)—when Cyrus closed his eyes, all he saw was the backs of his eyes. He felt desiccated. He tried to put it into language, tried to salvage some kernel of the feeling to write down later. But all he could think was "inside my heart is a little man with a broken heart."

When he got out of the shower, he put on clothes and ran down to the lobby ATM, got forty dollars cash to leave for the maid (the ATM only dispensed in multiples of twenty, and Cyrus spent more than a few seconds deliberating between forty and sixty) along with a note that said "Sorry!" He winced at the gesture but didn't know what else to do. He made coffee with the room's Keurig and drank it scalding. Gathering his phone cord and socks and toothpaste, he proceeded to check out. The man at the lobby desk was wearing a nametag that said "Hua"—instead of saying "How was your stay" Hua asked, "Did you make anything cool while you were here?" which caught Cyrus off guard. It was the sort of stock query this genre of corporately hip Brooklyn businesses traded in. Not a bad question, even, but damned by its context. Cyrus looked down at his hands, which were still shaking. Where was Zee? Why had they come to New York? Why was Cyrus doing any of this? Writing, talking, living? He wanted to run into traffic, into the sea. He wanted to disappear. Cyrus just shook his head at the lobby attendant and, without looking back, set off for the museum.

It was a beautiful day, though cold, the kind that might look in a picture like it was the middle of summer, if not for all the people in boots and heavy coats. Cyrus checked his phone, but still there was nothing from Zee. He typed a quick text: "Hey, I'm sorry. Really. Where are you?"

He checked his phone twice more in the next minute to see if Zee'd respond right away like he usually did, but he didn't. Cyrus put on his headphones and played the Miserere, a 1980 recording off YouTube, and found it to be a hauntingly good score to the city. Everything around him was syncopating, or illustrating, or complicating, the song's rhythms, deepening its haunted voices. Pigeons tucked themselves into the soft-edged letters of a Duane Reade sign, the cradles in the *D*'s and *E*'s and *R* full of sticks and leaves and hair. Two boys walked side by side with plastic bags over their feet, protecting their sneakers from the city's omnipresent slime.

Cyrus decided he'd ask Orkideh about the Miserere. He made sure his headphones were clean so she could listen through them if she wanted. He hoped she'd want to. He hoped she hadn't heard it before either. He'd tell her about his uncle, how he was a soldier, the kind in her painting with the flashlight and the horse. He'd ask her how she knew what she knew about the plane crash, delicately, not trying to imply anything.

It wasn't a big deal if she'd Googled him, followed some trail of digital breadcrumbs that led her from him to the plane crash. After all, Cyrus had Googled the artist too. He wasn't sure exactly what cyber pathway existed between him and his mother, but it wasn't impossible that one was out there. Of course, there was the other explanation too, the one Cyrus couldn't even articulate. The impossible one.

When Cyrus had still been drinking, whenever people asked him how his poems were going, he'd answer that he was just "living the poems he wasn't writing." He'd say that with a straight face. It made him wince to even think about. But now, this journey into the city felt like what he'd meant then—looking at all the shattered fundament of his living and thinking "this will be useful, I'll use all this later"—as a writer there was always that. It always gave him a faint shudder of guilt to think this way, but it wasn't something he could turn off.

So many of Cyrus's heroes rebuked abstinence, with its abstract promises of spiritual reward in exchange for corporeal restraint, preferring instead the booming immediacy of physical pleasure. "Paradise is mine today, as cash in hand," Hafez had written. "Why should I count upon the puritan's pledge of tomorrow?" Cyrus wasn't sure how many tomorrows he had left and considered briefly that Zee might have been right, that he might not be fully inhabiting his todays.

It felt like the only time Cyrus ever really felt now-ness was when he was using. When *now* was physiologically, chemically discernible from *before*. Otherwise he felt completely awash in time: stuck between birth and death, an interval where he'd never quite gotten his footing. But he was also awash in the world and its checkboxes—neither Iranian nor American, neither Muslim nor not-Muslim, neither drunk nor in meaningful recovery, neither gay nor straight. Each camp thought he was too much the other thing. That there were camps at all made his head swim.

He wanted to talk with Orkideh about it. Surely her vantage point in thinking about place, time, belonging, would be illuminating, alit as she was within a mortal immediacy Cyrus could not fathom. He sniffed at himself, worried he still smelled vaguely of piss.

When Cyrus got to the museum, he recognized the two black-clad employees taking admissions. He paid five dollars and climbed the stairs to the third floor, passing the docent with the thick septum ring who gave him a slight downward nod. At the third floor, Cyrus turned past Judy Chicago's *Dinner Party,* where a man was walking hand in hand with his daughter, both listening to headphones, and a nerdy-looking teenager was dutifully reading placards. Walking toward Orkideh and *Death-Speak,* Cyrus found the lights to the gallery totally dimmed, a velvet rope spread across the doorway. On it, a laminated note with a black-and-white picture of a young Orkideh wearing some sort of mesh veil, dark eyes cast upward in equal parts mischief and provocation. The note read:

The *Death-Speak* exhibit is now closed. The Brooklyn Museum thanks Orkideh for trusting us with her final installation. Donations in her memory may be made in the lobby gift shop.
"Art is where what we survive survives."

—Orkideh, 1963–2017

All the blood left Cyrus's head. He felt like puking, then he felt like shitting. He leaned against the wall. To live eternally or die. Those were the options, and there wasn't much evidence to point to the viability of the former. Cyrus knew the artist was dying, of course. But this little sheet of paper, Orkideh's face glowering up from it, testified to the way what was inevitable could still be, what? Immobilizing. Eviscerating. And yes, surprising.

She had been fine the day before. They'd laughed. Hugged. Cyrus stumbled back to the stairs, nearly tripping over his feet. When he saw the docent with the feather earring and septum ring, he stammered, "Did . . . *Death-Speak* is closed."

He meant to ask it as a question but instead delivered it flat, a statement of fact. The docent nodded.

"Yeah. The artist passed away last night. You know she was living in the museum?"

Cyrus didn't move.

"I guess they found her this morning in her room." He looked around, then said, in a low voice, "I heard maybe she took a handful of her pain pills, something like that. She was totally fine yesterday. You were here, weren't you?"

Cyrus couldn't say anything. The docent raised his eyebrows, then offered:

"I'm not sure when the next exhibit will open, I think it's a French photographer. I forget her name. But it won't be for a bit still."

Cyrus was trying desperately to keep himself upright. He scoured his mind to find the vital information around how to stand like a person, how to inhabit a body, but there was only shadow, shadows of half-remembered shadows. He felt like a windmill stilled in a field. He shook his head. A whole field of stilled windmills. The docent asked him something. Asked him something else. All Cyrus could hear was ringing in his brain, some ear cell's final song, a frequency never to be heard again. He collapsed.

TWENTY-FIVE

IF THE MORTAL SIN OF THE SUICIDE IS GREED, TO HOARD STILLNESS and calm for yourself while dispersing your riotous internal pain among all those who survive you, then the mortal sin of the martyr must be pride, the vanity, the hubris to believe not only that your death could mean more than your living, but that your death could mean more than death itself—which, because it is inevitable, means nothing.

—*from* BOOKOFMARTYRS.docx by Cyrus Shams

ALI SHAMS AND RUMI

———— ✦ ————

TWO FIGURES. ONE TALL, GAUNT, SOLEMN, DRESSED IN FARM COV-
eralls and high boots, Cyrus recognized immediately as his father.
It was rare for Ali to appear in Cyrus's dreams, almost as if out of
respect for the rest he'd finally found after a relentless life—wartime
service (Ali had a desk job managing supply-line logistics, which,
though comparatively safe, was still surprisingly high-stakes and
left him with no small amount of survivor's guilt), a wife's sudden
and meaningless death, immigration to a hostile nation, nearly two
decades of six-days-a-week manual labor. Ali had earned the right to
rest, even in Cyrus's dreams.

Still, it made Cyrus glad to see him outside on the steps of what
looked to be a small music venue, smoking a cigarette. Like pretty
much everyone else he knew, Ali had smoked heavily in Tehran, but
as a cost-saving measure he'd quit on arriving in America. It was
one of those billion little sacrifices a parent makes that a child never
considers. The kind, Ali thought, only the worst, most loathsome
parents ever mentioned. On the steps though, Ali seemed at such
ease with the cigarette, so natural. It was like his hand had regained
a digit.

Next to Cyrus's father was a gorgeous man in orange and purple
silk robes taking a deep drag of a blunt. The man had high, super-
model cheekbones and a long black beard the color of deep night
with little braids woven into it, a few decorated with tiny shells and

beads. On the step to his side was a red plastic cup filled with dark wine.

"You're Ali Shams!" the beautiful man said, exhaling a thick swirl of smoke. "Wow wow wow, I've been dying to meet you!"

Ali, sitting next to him on the steps of the venue, smiled unevenly. From the club behind them loud bass and drums throbbed from a hardcore show. Young people with geometric tattoos and tight black clothes milled about, walking to and from their cars.

"I am, yes," said Ali. "And you're really you?"

The second man laughed, taking a sip from his Solo cup.

"Haha, Ali Shams, I am. My name is Jalal al-Din Muḥammad. You might know me as—"

"Mevlana. *Rumi.* Wow. My son Cyrus wants to be a poet. Koroosh. He loves you. He would love to meet you," Ali said, then paused. "Do you know about Cyrus?"

Rumi smiled.

"Of course! How do you think I got here?"

"Ahhh," said Ali. "I'm still figuring out how all this works."

"It took me a bit too."

From inside the club a singer screamed "crowquill," screamed "threnody." As smoke lifted from Ali's cigarette and Rumi's blunt, it appeared to reveal more stars in the night, like the smoke was clarifying the air instead of fogging it. It was bringing the stars closer. At such near distance, they almost looked edible.

"Shit, where are my manners—you want some of this?" Rumi asked Ali, holding the blunt out toward him. It smelled like fresh bread, like noon barbari. Ali shook his head and Rumi shrugged, taking another long drag.

"Yeah, it took me a while to get the hang of things here." When he said "here," Rumi pointed not to the parking lot or the sky around them, but to his own head. "What I've noticed," he continued, "is that here, it's the little details that matter the most. In life we were yoked to all these big details—bodies and tribes, who is family, who is enemy, where and what to eat. All that shit drowned out the subtler shades of experience. Here, it's about this Swisher, this cheap wine, this crystal." When he said "crystal" he reached absentmindedly toward the sky and plucked a small star, which burned heatlessly— like a firefly—in his palm.

"I think I'm starting to understand that," said Ali. He reached up to pluck his own star, but when he opened his palm it wasn't a glowing firefly star but a tiny chicken egg. Rumi laughed. From inside the venue the crowd was chanting "O time! Thyyy pyr-a-mids!" over and over and over.

"Should we go inside?" asked Ali, tugging at the edges of his farm boots.

"I think we've got a bit more time," answered Rumi. "And I wanna finish this," he said, pulling from his blunt, which seemed to be getting even longer as he smoked it. Ali frowned. He didn't like people smoking marijuana, but he figured if anyone could, it was Rumi.

"Tell me something real about yourself," Rumi said.

"What do you mean?"

"I mean, I don't want whatever bullshit tactical non-secret secret that passed for intimacy down there. I want you to tell me something real."

"I don't even know you," Ali said.

"That's not true," Rumi said, placing a hand on Ali's back, glowing a little. Ali dragged from his own cigarette.

After a long pause he said, "I think my wife was cheating on me before she died."

"Whoa. No shit?" said Rumi.

"Hm?" asked Ali.

"It means like, 'for real'? You really think that? Why?"

"Ah, I don't know. Little things. She never looked at me like she desired me as a man. I don't think she ever really wanted me that way. From when we very first met. I think she always looked at me different, like the way you'd look at a baby bird you found and tried to nurse back to health. Some combination of affection and pity. The pity, though. That was such a big part of it."

"Yeesh. I'm sorry, man. But that doesn't mean she was cheating on you?"

"Yeah. When Roya was pregnant with Cyrus she got weird, especially toward the end. Maybe somehow she sensed what was going to happen. Something in her knew about the plane, about the end coming. That's what I thought for a long time. But more than once in those last months I heard her on the phone, and she'd go silent when she realized I was near. Sometimes she'd hang up mid-sentence. After Cyrus was born she seemed so happy, but not necessarily around Cyrus. Happy like she'd freed herself of something. Or was about to? I don't know. I was working a lot then, trying to save money . . ."

"Christ. I'm sorry, man." Rumi looked down at his own shoes, and Ali used the nub of his cigarette to light another. "That's super real."

"I thought this all would be different," Ali said, gesturing toward the parking lot. The full moon overhead was spinning in a slow clockwise circle. "Rivers of honey, eternal sunshine, all that."

"Hah, yeah. That's how they get you," Rumi said. "That stuff is around. You can have it if you want. It's fun for maybe three days. But honestly, it's kind of played out. Have you ever tried eating more than like, two spoonfuls of honey?"

Ali laughed a strange creaking laugh, like a heavy door opening for the first time in years.

"It's gross, man!" Rumi said, pulling from his blunt. "It's super fucking gross. It makes you sick."

The band inside was in a long instrumental riff now, orchestral almost. Amidst the heavy drums and bass was the sound of flutes, a harp, maybe even birdsong.

"That makes sense," said Ali. "You're still so beloved on earth anyway, it makes sense you'd want to stay near it. Cyrus told me once you were the best-selling poet in America. A dead Persian poet! I thought that was crazy."

"Well, I don't know how Persian the me they read in America really is."

Ali nodded, though he had no idea what Rumi meant. He noticed suddenly that Rumi's arms were covered with colorful tattoos depicting negargari, little illuminated Byzantine miniatures, and the figures, some on horseback, some firing bows, were moving all around, playing out their little lives across Rumi's skin. Ali hated tattoos, thought they were the stamp of low people, but as with the marijuana, for some reason it didn't offend him so much on Rumi. The poet's robes were flowing now too, fluorescent rivers of deep oranges, yellow-blues emptying into each other. Behind the two men, a twenty-something in a tight T-shirt that said JANE DOE came out of the club doors.

"You ready?" she asked Rumi.

"Yup yup," he said.

She nodded and went back inside.

"You're going on?" asked Ali.

"Yeah, sounds like it's about time."

"How is Cyrus doing? With . . ." He paused. "With all the Orkideh stuff?"

Rumi tipped the last dregs of his Solo cup into his mouth, snubbed out the remainder of his blunt, which sparked out in tiny little strawberries. The venue behind the two men had grown silent, and the stars above them were glistening Technicolor: garnets and emeralds and sapphires, fat jewels set in the night's crown.

"Man, it's a trip, isn't it? Hard not to think it was fated."

"You don't think he'll do it, do you? You don't think he'll . . ." Ali paused. "Kill himself?"

"You know what I think?" asked Rumi. The bright colors from his robes were passing freely now from his arm tattoos through his beard and back into his robes. "I think Cyrus is going to be able to write a hell of a book. I really do. I hope I get to read it." He paused. "Martyrs, man. We just can't escape it, can we?"

Ali wanted to ask him what he meant by "we"—men? Persians? Something else? But Rumi had gotten up, was pulling him through the venue. It was pitch-black, and nearly silent save deep, undulating throbs coming from the house speakers as the two men worked through the crowd. As they got up to the stage, only barely visible through the legions of anonymous bodies, Rumi drew near Ali's ear.

"Watch this," he said. When he leapt up onto the stage the entire hall went silent—completely silent, even the throbs from the house speakers muted now.

Ali watched from just beneath the stage as Rumi smiled a great smile, a smile that seemed to start in his chest, eight hundred years of smile lines working their way across his entire person. The hall was somewhat illuminated now and Ali looked around to see hordes of hardcore kids, hundreds of them dressed in black, pierced, tattooed, all of them looking at the stage as the brilliant colors swirling around and through Rumi moved from his hair to his skin to his robes and back.

Onstage, Rumi began humming a tiny melody, no microphone, maybe just four distinct notes, but the sound repeated loudly and echoed throughout the hall, and the throngs of young people began swaying along to it, like skinny trees in a great wind.

A short man next to Ali, whom he recognized as his son's friend Zee, put his arm around his shoulders and together they swayed as Rumi began to speak in a bottomless baritone:

"An atash-e sadeh ke to ra khord-o-bekest . . ."

Zee looked up at Ali and mindlessly, reflexively, Ali translated for him: "The simple fire that ate you . . ."

Rumi was repeating it, and as he did the audience began chanting in unison, "An atash-e sadeh ke to ra khord-o-bekest, an atash-e sadeh ke to ra khord-o-bekest."

And then Zee and Ali were chanting it together too, arm in arm, louder and louder with everyone, and as they did Rumi's head began to glow more and more until suddenly it was white hot, on fire, his whole head like the burning faces of the prophets in old paintings, just one great flame. The audience and Zee and Ali kept chanting as the ceiling of the venue peeled back like a tin of salty fish, and the smoke from the fire that had now consumed Rumi rose up into the night. All at once, ash coated every glowing gem in the sky.

MONDAY

———— ✳ ————

Cyrus Shams

BROOKLYN, DAY 4

STARS. THE DOCENT SAYING SOMETHING INTO A WALKIE-TALKIE. A white thigh floating in water, leeches fattening around it. Their writhing glee. Cyrus's eyelids, fluttering. Zee's face smiling, sticking his tongue out. Orkideh's wide eyes. Her mouth opening, revealing the black void where a tongue had once been. Trees erupting with snow. Stars. A windmill. The docent's voice. A leech. Stars. Stars.

TWENTY-SIX

In the balancing act between prudence and resolution that presidents are constantly asked to perform, Mr. Reagan decided to be tough.

"In these tight situations, things sometimes go wrong," a long-time Presidential adviser said yesterday. "You have sophisticated machines and young soldiers and sailors operating under hard conditions. So you take what you consider reasonable chances on behalf of important goals, and you hope for the best."

"The Downing of Flight 655,"
The New York Times, July 5, 1988

ROYA SHAMS

———— ✴ ————

THAT FIRST KISS BETWEEN LEILA AND ME WAS A STRANGE AND foreign word, one someone might clumsily translate as "sky" but that actually meant something closer to "heaven."

Ali and Gilgamesh called the house the next night from the campsite pay phone. They were silly, drunkenly checking in on their wives. They must have imagined us bored out of our minds. Ali shouted, laughing:

"Gilgi nearly shot off his foot this morning!"

"Don't believe him, he's lying!" shouted Gilgamesh. "Full of shit! He's a cow! Chert-o-pert!"

While I held the phone, quietly telling Ali to be careful, that it was no time to get caught drinking, I watched Leila look through Ali's old rock records. They were contraband I could never bring myself to let him throw away. Leila made little faces at certain records, smiling at Aretha Franklin, laughing at the Monkees. Gilgamesh asked to talk to Leila and she accepted the phone from me, tucking it between her shoulder and ear and rolling her eyes. As she listened to her husband, she surreptitiously held up the pointer finger of one hand and used the other to make a fist around it, then pantomimed snapping the finger off. She smiled knowingly at me, though I didn't recognize the gesture.

When Leila hung up the phone, her eyes flashed with trouble. Or maybe more like inspiration, or purpose. She knelt back down to the records and put one on our turntable, a little puke-green plastic RCA player left over from my teens, speakers popping as she moved the needle around the vinyl looking for a specific track. As the first notes began to play, she stood up and held out her hand.

That's when everything became supersaturated. One of those memories you can squeeze like a rag and watch details drip and pool. Minor chords on a twelve-string guitar twinging out of the little speakers. Leila, a full head taller than me, pulling me in close to dance. Her smell of sweat and jasmine-cedar. Mick Jagger's voice, "I want you back, again. I want you back, again." The dry copper taste of my tongue.

"I wish it wasn't so hard to be good," I whispered, surprising myself, not even sure Leila could hear me. "I'm trying. I really am. I'm just exhausted."

"I know," she said. "I can see it, azizam. I know."

She squeezed me tighter, rocking from foot to foot to the music. The sad song turned jaunty, though the lyrics didn't. Jagger pleaded, "Tell me you're coming back to me, you gotta tell me you're coming back to me." How it felt like the perfect song then, even though we were together, the bud of us just starting to open. Something in the song's plaintive yearning, that's what it was, bone-deep yearning. We held the song's preemptive nostalgia between us like a candle, swaying as its flame smocked the wick, our faces illuminated and flickering in it, that flame, yearning, idiot yearning, yearning so strong it bends you, buckles you, like waves or miracles.

Then the song was over and Leila bent back over to the record player and started it again, staying crouched down there as the song began, staying down there and then kissing my ankles through the guitar, my shins, my ankles again as Keith Richards howled and whooped his harmonies, and then the song was over again and she started it again, put the needle into the groove of the vinyl, kissing my knees, my hands, my wrists, and as the song faded out a third time Leila didn't start it back over again, she let it finish and turn into silence. It was silence louder than the music had been, silence made big by the loudness preceding it—the silence after a scream, the silence after a gunshot. And then? And then we were touching everywhere. Then there was no separation between us, Leila and me, between our bodies. No separation anymore: not music or country or clothes. Not fear. Not even history.

MONDAY

———— ✷ ————

Cyrus Shams

BROOKLYN, DAY 4

WHEN CYRUS CAME TO, HE WAS ON THE LANDING IN THE STAIRS. A group of museum employees, all clad in black, were huddled over him. The familiar docent with the thick septum piercing was standing behind them.

"Hey, are you okay? Can you hear me?"

Cyrus blinked. Three heads bent over his, more hovering behind them. Cyrus struggled to nod but the synapses weren't connecting. He thought about Orkideh's body, frail and weightless, someone having to find it. To "discover the body." Unbearable. One of the hovering heads procured a bottle of water, and Cyrus's hands somehow found it, drew it to his lips. Someone somewhere would bury Orkideh's tiny body and then the green world would swallow her up. *Everything green just farms us,* Cyrus thought. *Feeding us oxygen and eating our corpses.*

"Prateek said you fainted," one of the heads said. Cyrus focused on it. A balding older white man with a bushy gray goatee. "Do you want us to call an ambulance?" Prateek, that was the septum docent's name.

"I'm fine," Cyrus managed to stammer, sitting himself up slowly, then leaning back on his fists.

"Do you have a history of fainting? Medical conditions?"

"I'm fine," Cyrus said again. "I just—" He tried hard to think of something to defuse the situation. "I didn't eat breakfast today." That was the sort of thing these kinds of people seemed like they'd believe. Slowly he lifted himself up. Prateek reached over to help him up—

"Hey, take it easy," he said, a hand placed behind Cyrus's upper back.

Cyrus smiled weakly. Another person manifested with a banana and a Snickers bar, handed them to Cyrus.

"I'm fine. Thank you, guys. I'm sorry, I'm really embarrassed."

"You sure you don't want us to call somebody?" the bushy goatee man asked.

"Really, it's not a big deal."

The docents looked at each other, furrowed their brows. They helped Cyrus down the stairs, guided him to a bench.

"Why don't you just rest here, and we'll see how you're doing in ten minutes?"

"Sure, that's fine," Cyrus said, thanking them. The banana-and-Snickers docent left the banana and Snickers. The water-bottle docent left the water bottle. They wandered off, looking back over their shoulders to ensure Cyrus was still conscious and upright. Only Prateek stayed.

"Did you know Orkideh?" he asked Cyrus, like a secret. "Is that what's going on?"

"Oh, no, not really," Cyrus said, honestly. "Just a fan, I guess." Cyrus realized only after saying it that it was the truth.

Prateek nodded.

"Yeah, I'd never heard of her before the *Death-Speak* thing. But she was kind of incredible, wasn't she?"

He sat down on the bench next to Cyrus. He had short cropped black hair, gelled to a point. His soft cheeks and deceptively smooth face made him look younger than he probably was. If not for the gauged septum ring, he might have looked outright wholesome.

"I didn't know much about her either until *Death-Speak*," Cyrus said. He ripped open the Snickers bar, offered a bit to Prateek, who smiled and waved it away. Taking a bite himself, Cyrus managed—

"I'm okay, really. You can go."

"I know," said Prateek. "I think my boss wants to make sure you don't die—er, you know. Everyone's already pretty on edge around here today."

"Sure," Cyrus said.

"I had an aunt who died of breast cancer," Prateek continued. "Stage Four, just like Orkideh. She was always in rooms filled with all these tubes and metal frames, handrails and tubing, that's what I remember most about visiting her, all these different kinds of tubes, rubber ones but also like, vacuum cleaner tubes, those and handrails on everything. Like, handrails on the handrails. And all these tubes woven through them!"

Cyrus looked up at him. Quickly, he tried to remember the sorts of things the doctors-in-training at his job said to console grieving family members, but all he could summon were the office posters: anatomy of the inner ear, stroke warning signs, understanding cholesterol.

"I—I'm sorry," Cyrus mustered.

"Oh, it was forever ago," Prateek said. "I'm good. Just to say, it was a mess. She forgot who we all were at the end, stuff just leaking out of every orifice. It was so dark, cruel even. Like, fucked up that that is even an option, that that is a thing that can happen to a person. But Orkideh was Orkideh right up until the end. Still herself. That's luckier than people realize."

Cyrus nodded a little. His eyes felt hot, like he was going to cry, but no tears came out. His vision was still coming in and out of focus; the scar on his foot throbbed.

"I talked with her about it," Prateek went on. "With Orkideh. I told her about my aunt, how she was an artist too, how she'd draw these little cartoons for my cousins and me. Even when we were way too old, she'd still draw these goofy cartoons, dinosaurs on skateboards, that kind of thing, and she'd mail them to me and my sisters. And do you know what Orkideh told me?"

"What?" asked Cyrus. His heart was in his throat, his throat was in his hands.

"She said, 'Isn't it good to be able to speak to each other this way?'

She just said that and reached out and held my hand for a second and smiled really big at me. She said, 'Thank you for sharing her with me. It is so good to be able to speak this way.' And that was that. The next person in line came and sat."

"Wow," Cyrus said. He shook his head; his vision seemed to have mostly cleared up. He said, "Thank you, Prateek. Really."

Prateek smiled, patted him on the shoulder.

"Okay. I'm trusting you're gonna be okay." He looked like he might be getting ready to add something else, but elected against it, standing up and walking toward the stairs. Cyrus felt his body still vibrating. His whole life was a conspiracy of other people helping him, other people teaching him this or that. He felt like Hamlet, just moping around waiting for the world to assuage his grief, petulantly soliloquizing and fainting while everyone else fed him bananas and candy bars. Hamlet died at the end, of course. "The rest is silence," Hamlet declared, though he also demanded his best friend tell everyone else his story. Cyrus felt that full of shit.

He wanted to apologize to Prateek. To Gabe. He wanted to take a long shower, to hug Zee, to spend hours curling into him, kissing the same spot on the back of his neck over and over and over. Cyrus wafted to the front doors of the museum and then found himself back out in the cold, shivering. Vendors all selling the same hot dogs, waters, biryanis. A street performer was dancing acrobatically around an old-fashioned boombox as a crowd of tourists was assembled around her.

Nobody was observing the perimeter of austerity he felt wrapped like a velvet rope around the museum. Wrapped, vibrating around his chest. "If we meet each other in Hell, it's not Hell." Who had said that? Faintly, Cyrus became aware the vibrating was real, external, was coming from his coat pocket. He pulled out his phone, saw he had missed two calls from a number he didn't recognize. There was a voicemail. Cyrus pressed the phone to his ear, and a woman's voice said, in a thick accent:

"Hello, uhm, this is, uh, this message is for Cyrus Shams. My name is Sang Linh, I represent the artist Orkideh. I got your number from, ah, online—I, she asked me to, ehm, there are some things I'd like to discuss with you. If you could please call me back at this number I'd—yes, call please as soon as you're able, this is my cell phone number, please call me back as soon as possible."

TWENTY-SEVEN

WHEN ASKED ABOUT THE DIFFICULTIES OF SCULPTURE, MICHELAN-gelo said, "It is easy. You just chip away all the stone that isn't David."

It's simple to cut things out of a life. You break up with a shitty partner, quit eating bread, delete the Twitter app. You cut it out, and the shape of what's actually killing you clarifies a little. The whole Abrahamic world invests itself in this promise: Don't lie, don't cheat, don't fuck or steal or kill, and you'll be a good person. Eight of the ten commandments are about what thou shalt not. But you can live a whole life not doing any of that stuff and still avoid doing any good. That's the whole crisis. The rot at the root of everything. The belief that goodness is built on a constructed absence, not-doing. That belief corrupts everything, has everyone with any power sitting on their hands. A rich man goes a whole day without killing a single homeless person and so goes to sleep content in his goodness. In another world, he's buying crates of socks and Clif bars and tents, distributing them in city centers. But for him, abstinence reigns.

I want to be the chisel, not the David. What can I make of being here? And what can I make of not?

Normal people think of recovery as a kind of abstinence: they imagine us sitting around white-knuckled, sweating as we count our hours trying desperately to distract ourselves enough to not relapse. This is because for normal people, drinking is an activity, like brushing their teeth or watching TV. They can reasonably imagine excising drinking, like any other activity, without collapsing their entire person.

For a drunk, there's nothing but drink. There was nothing in my life that wasn't predicated on getting drunk—either getting fucked up itself or getting money to get fucked up by working or slinging this drug for that drug or that drug for cash.

Getting sober means having to figure out how to spend twenty-four hours a day. It means building an entirely new personality, learning how to move your face, your fingers. It meant learning how to eat, how to speak among people and walk and fuck and worse than any of that, learning how to just sit still. You're moving into a house the last tenants trashed. You spend all your time ripping up the piss-carpet, filling in the holes in the wall, *and* you also somehow have to remember to feed yourself and make rent and not punch every person who talks to you in the face. There's no abstinence in it. There's no self-will. It's a chisel. It's surrender to the chisel. Of course you don't hope to come out a David. It's miracle enough to emerge still standing on two feet.

—*from* BOOKOFMARTYRS.docx by Cyrus Shams

SITTING ON A PROSPECT PARK BENCH JUST ACROSS FLATBUSH FROM the museum, Cyrus pulled out his phone, listened again to the voicemail message from Orkideh's gallerist, Sang. She'd been married to the artist. They'd been in each other's lives for decades. Why was she calling Cyrus on the day of her ex-wife's death? How could she? Cyrus, who had known Orkideh for days, not decades, felt gutted. It was hard for him to do anything but tremble. How was Sang making phone calls, speaking in sentences?

Seneca said grief should last no longer than seven years. Anything more was indulgent. Nazim Hikmet said twentieth-century grief lasted at most a year. It dwindled like that. Maybe twenty-first-century grief had gotten down to a fraction of that fraction, just a few hours before it was supplanted by necessity. A death announcement you scrolled past on your phone, situated between ads for toilet tissue and cell phones. Everywhere around Cyrus, people walked with infuriating ease. The trees sprouted wet black scabs from their bark, and still the clouds hung above them, dutifully. He pressed the white rectangle with Sang's number on his phone and she picked up on the fourth ring.

"Hello?" Her voice sounded weaker than it had on the voicemail. Lighter.

"Uh, hi. Is this Sang Linh?"

"Speaking?"

"Uhm. This is Cyrus Shams. I had a missed call—"

"Ahhh, Cyrus. Yes. I've been waiting to hear from you."

He said nothing.

"Orkideh passed away, Cyrus. She . . . It was herself. She did it herself, her own terms."

A dog leading a man on roller skates whooshed by. Cyrus's throat felt cold. His father had always made him wear scarves, some old-world belief about sickness coming in through the neck.

"Can you hear me?" Sang asked. "Orkideh was, uh, the artist you've—"

"I know. Right. Yes, sorry. I mean, I'm sorry. I know. I was just at the museum."

"Oh Cyrus. I'm sorry." A pause on the line. Sang's voice was airy, all downbreath. It was the voice of someone not often overcome by sentiment. She continued:

"She mentioned you'd been coming to see her? That you were working on a book?"

"Why?" asked Cyrus, more sharply than he'd intended.

"Pardon?"

"Why did she tell you about me?"

A pause.

"Those conversations meant a lot to her," said Sang, finally. "I am—was. Er, I *am* her gallerist, but we were married for years."

"I know, yeah. I'm sorry."

Cyrus held the phone with one hand and used the other to rub his neck, trying to warm it.

"Oh? She told you about me?"

"Well, no," Cyrus said, quietly. "But I've read about you and her online."

Sang laughed. "Haha, that makes more sense," she chuckled. "She wasn't much for talking about her personal life. Or for looking back."

"I'm sorry for your loss," said Cyrus, because it was what one said.

"I'm sorry too," Sang responded. They were both quiet for a moment. Then Sang said, "She lived for something. And she knew when she was done living. That's not nothing."

"I—" Cyrus began. His ears felt hot. It was a cold day, but the earth beneath his feet felt on fire. "Why are you calling me?" He quickly added: "I mean, why me specifically?"

"Ah, I don't mean to be so mysterious. It's hard, you know? I'm very mad at her."

There was something pressing cold at Cyrus's throat, something that made him feel dense and terrible, like a moon capsizing boat after boat. The unspeakable thing, an impossible thing. Cyrus wished to be swept away before he had to ask, before the desperate embarrassment of the question rising in his mind could find words. He wanted to be extinguished, a candle dropped in the snow. Cyrus closed his eyes for a moment, two. Opening them, finding himself still inside his self, he blurted—

"Was Orkideh my mother?" It came out of his mouth like a bullet shredding through porcelain, shattering the partition between him and a great unacceptable.

A beat. Another beat. Bundled-up people scuttled by, frozen trees throbbed. Then—

"How long have you known?" asked Sang.

"I didn't," said Cyrus.

Silence.

"She wanted to tell you, Cyrus. She wanted you to know. I think—I think she thought she had more time? Well, no, that's not it. She knew it was coming. I—I'm sorry. I don't know. I'm sorry."

Cyrus said nothing. In the grass, a white woman rubbed an older white man's shoulders. They both wore leather gloves. Black scabs roiling on the trees.

"I didn't know," Cyrus repeated.

"Roya told me she knew before you even told her your name," Sang said. "She recognized you immediately, standing in line at the museum, all these years later. She hadn't even known you were in America."

"Roya," said Cyrus. "Roya was my mother."

"Where are you right now? Are you still in the city?"

Cyrus clicked around on his phone, away from the call and into his web browser. In his web browser, he called up pictures of Orkideh.

The image search was mostly of her artwork but scattered through-out were pictures of the artist herself. Cyrus clicked one open with his thumb—an older picture, Orkideh looked maybe forty. She was wearing dark makeup around her eyes and the photograph had been taken from slightly above, drawing her eyes up to the lens, her lips pursing slightly, somewhere between interest and violence. He stud-ied her eyes. They were deep black but flashed with a brightness, like they held tiny fish that turned to catch the light on their scales. An incitement. Cyrus looked for the Roya of his father's wedding photo in her face. Then he looked for himself.

"Cyrus?" asked Sang, a barely audible voice, the phone pulled away from his ear. He put it back up to his head.

"Sorry, yeah. I'm still here. I'm right across from the museum. Prospect Park."

Within a few minutes, Sang was driving to him.

TWENTY-EIGHT

I believe that the actions of Iran were the proximate cause of this accident and would argue that Iran must bear the principal responsibility for the tragedy.

William J. Crow Jr., Chairman, Joint Chiefs of Staff,
5 August 1988

The United States is responsible for the consequences of its barbaric massacre of innocent passengers.

Iran Foreign Minister Ali Akbar Velayati, 4 July 1988

barbaric (*adjective*) /bɑːˈbærɪk/—the term originates from the Greek: βάρβαρος (*barbaros* pl. βάρβαροι) to refer to for-eigners from "lands beyond moral influence," especially those from rival nations like the Persians, Berbers, and Turks, whose languages Greek soldiers mocked by saying "bar bar bar."

ORKIDEH

————— ❋ —————

WHAT DISTINGUISHES GRACE FROM EVERYTHING ELSE? GRACE IS unearned. If you've moved through the world in such a way as to feel you've earned cosmic compensation, then what you've earned is something more like justice, like propriety. Not grace. Propriety is correct. Justice is just. There's an inescapable transactional quality: perform *x* good, receive *y* reward. Grace doesn't work that way. It begins with the reward. Goodness never enters the equation.

Many have done worse than me and been punished less. But most have done less and been punished more.

My name is Roya Shams. I died in a plane crash on July 23rd, 1988, when the USS *Vincennes* shot down my plane over the Strait of Hormuz. The U.S. Naval warship mistook my plane for a fighter jet and fired two RIM-66 Standard MR missiles at my plane. One of them hit the left wing, tore the plane apart. The plane and all of us on board were eviscerated almost immediately. Two hundred ninety of us, there, then not-there.

Except I'm still here. Wherever I go, there I am. Not there on the flight. The flight I was never on. Leila and I traded papers so she could escape Iran, escape Gilgamesh and his gray watery eyes. He'd found out about us. I was going to meet back up with her later, out of the country. In Dubai. Leila had my passport, I had hers. The passport photos were so high contrast, everyone basically looked the same, a wash of flash-white, two eyes and a mouth. Solemn black chador. Her precious face. It was a perfect plan.

Except Leila was plucked from living, like a tomato off a vine. There's no meeting someone once they've been plucked from living. You just live with their absence, whispering "jaya shomah khallee" to a chair in which they might sit, a second unused pillow on the bed. Your place is empty. Except? Your place is empty.

Wherever I go, I carry the grace of having lived after I died. What did I do to deserve that? Nothing. That's what makes it grace. It was my name on the flight log. My body that never washed up bloated on some poor fisherman's beach. Grace to live at all—none of us did anything to deserve it. Being born. We spend our lives trying to figure out how to pay back the debt of being. And to whom we might pay it.

But that's a misunderstanding of grace, which doesn't ask to be paid back. Even when you've been given the gift twice, emerged from your own death to run away from your husband. Leaving him to grieve you, to raise your child by himself.

I read an interview with a famous romance columnist where she said the question she gets asked most often was some version of: I love my partner but the relationship isn't going anywhere and our lives are so intertwined at this point, I find myself fantasizing about him dying. It would solve everything without me having to become a villain. I could mourn him and then move on with my life. Is this normal? Am I a monster?

Grace: that I had enough money to get to Turkey. That I dressed in layers for cold. That long train ride alternating between crying so hard it was hard to tell if I was crying or laughing, and then feeling totally numb, a numb that terrified me with its stillness. Like a dead bird with all its guts scooped out.

Grace: that the man—the boy, really—at the border accepted my bribe, didn't run Leila's papers, which were all I had with me. Had he run them, whatever alert Gilgamesh put out on Leila would have been triggered. I would've been sent back to my life and punished. Or worse.

Grace: that the boy-man at the border accepted my bribe and was too young to demand more. That he didn't know, or pretended not to anyway, that I would have done anything he asked. I'd pulled my blouse low to talk to him.

Grace: that he had eyes to see.

Grace: being able to use Leila's passport in Ankara to buy a one-way plane ticket to New York City. Grace the ticket agent only glanced once at the photograph of dead Leila and thought she was me, also dead, though standing before him. Grace for the terrible quality of the photo. Grace that perhaps we all look the same.

God will never forgive me. Why should I?

Grace: to land in a city that is always on, lit up. To be able to wander twenty-two hours a day, learn the city, think, weep, watch, weep, wander, listen, wander, learn, listen, weep, wander, then pass out on a bench, on some grass, without being bothered.

Grace to own nothing worth stealing.

All around me, people had less. Men with plastic bags over bare feet mumbling gibberish to themselves under their breath, drinking from plastic bottles of clear liquor. Women hunched on stoops who could barely keep their eyes open to beg. I still had a good mind. I had words—enough to say "please" and "sorry" and "thank you"—all you need in any language, really, unless you're a philosopher.

I stole a lot. Dressed as I was, I looked like a businesswoman. I tried to keep my clothes clean. Nice blouse, sharp pants. People didn't watch me like they should have. I stole potato chips, water. I stole sleeping pills, socks. Pens, apples, maxi pads. In a bookshop I stole a Persian-English dictionary. In another, a *Time* magazine with a missile shooting off a warship. I had to look up the big white words: "Gulf Tragedy." فاجعة. "Catastrophe." Like a natural disaster. Not "massacre." Not even "murder." The imprecision of American justice was a given, even to Americans.

I read that dictionary as much as I could. I ate with it, slept on it, sometimes. It was soft enough, a paperback three inches thick. It was a place to put myself.

When I was outside the dictionary, I was hungry, desperately sad. Tired, afraid. I missed Leila. I missed her so frantically that saying "I missed her" isn't enough. I could feel it in my body, the tips of my fingers and the soft skin of my ankles, in my eyelids. It all throbbed for her. I missed Cyrus too, but that was different. I missed Leila in my body. I missed Cyrus in time. I had all this time, wandering the city, no mouth to feed, no tiny body to rock to sleep. Too-open time made me think of Cyrus. I felt guilty for hardly thinking about Ali. So I wandered, I stole, and I studied the dictionary.

Grace, that dictionary. A place where every thing was attached to a meaning.

IN AMERICA, THAT DICTIONARY TAUGHT ME ALL I NEEDED. HOW TO ask for a "bathroom," how to read "uptown" on the subway signs. When I learned how to say "cigarette," I walked around saying it to myself like a prayer, like an incantation. see-GARR-ett. It was my favorite word. If I walked up to someone and said it, one time in every five they'd hand me one. Language could make a meal like that.

But the dictionary didn't prepare me for how much junk there was inside the language. How I could say "water"? or "Please, can you give me a glass of water?" and they'd be, for all intents and purposes, the same. Or just so subtly different that I could never hope to be able to learn the difference. Articles, formalities: ligature. Connective tissue filling the air. Filling time. It's the difference between language and communication, yes. But then, communication was what I was after. I think it still is.

Even the letters themselves carry this junk. If I write "wri†ing" or "wr¹t¹ng" any fluent English reader will still understand what I've written. I could even replace all my *i*'s with *l*'s, "wrltlng," and it's still basically legible. Clearly some of the compositional parts of the language itself are junk while others are essential. There is no dictionary to tell you which is which.

I read that our genetic code works this way, that most of the sequences are evolutionary fossils, replicated endlessly and meaninglessly, trillions of cells copying the same nothing for millennia.

If so much of my language is junk, both the language of my

speech and the language of my body, it seems like a not insignificant portion of my living must be doomed to junk. There's nothing in my life that isn't bound to my language, or my DNA.

What comes the closest, I think, is sex. Not entirely without language of course, and certainly not without the body. But in terms of earnest, mellifluous human communication involving the least junk, sex reigns. It's where the comprehension density is the greatest. A discerning lover can read an *Odyssey* in a gasp, a *Shahnehmeh* in a sigh.

I do not like to be penetrated. When I have been with men, I have had to explain this at great length. And then repeatedly defend the position against their "but what about's" and "well you haven't tried mine's." As if changing the label on a jar of poison would make it more appetizing.

Most of my female partners over my life have not needed to be told. More fluent, perhaps, at the semiotics of passion, though not all exchanges were passionate.

Leila was, though. Passionate. She discerned everything from a wince, a sigh. When Leila's fingers first crept down and met an unconscious stiffening of my stomach, she read as robust an autobiography as I'll ever write. And then she added her own movement, her own chapters to it. She changed the text of my living.

Others, of course, ignored these inferences when they perceived them, moving forward manfully. But these lovers didn't lack the ability to perceive my desires. They lacked faith in my conviction. Quickly, though, they too would be convinced.

One of my first major installations, at the Detroit Institute of the Arts, was a piece called *Comprehension Density*. Two great slabs of copper, monolithic, each nearly four meters tall, facing each other. The copper was matte, but still reflected a bit of light from the bright of the room, some of that light bouncing back and forth between the slabs, like they were looking into mirrors of each other. But they weren't mirrors of each other, one bent slightly into the other, slouching. They were all potential, great heavy wedges inside of which the soldier, the horse, the Venus, might be patiently waiting to be carved. And between the two monoliths, the little gap at their nearly squared bases, was a small television, a little box of a thing, with a streaming video of me reading the *Shahnehmeh*, in its entirety, fifty-six hours of video recorded in a single take. The video is pulled up to frame just my face—no need for everyone to see my water glass, my bathroom setup. I wore no makeup. My eyes were rheumy, the hard edges of my face contrasted usefully with the blunt copper monoliths. And as I read Ferdowsi's text, I kept switching between English and Farsi, I'd switch back and forth and back and forth:

"Sohrab was astounded that the able warrior who had been fighting him was indeed a woman . . ."

Later,

بر ایرانیان زار و گریان شدم
ز ساسانیان نیز بریان شدم
دریغ این سر و تاج و این داد و تخت
دریغ این بزرگی و این فر و بخت

The glow from the television reflected between the slabs, multiplying itself, warping and diminishing itself in each repetition.

I'm proud of *Comprehension Density*. I think it holds up.

Of course, everything works this way in my head now, where I am. The when of now—dying my final, true death. It bungles everything. Time braids and frays.

My second year in America I had my first dream of Leila where she spoke to me in English. So many little dyings in this country, but that one was the most vicious.

In the dream, a man had cut down our fifty-year-old pistachio tree, Leila's and my tree. In the dream, we had a pistachio tree. Fifty years old. That alone.

And so we were deciding what to do with this man, what his just punishment should be. I said something stupid about him owing us a year's pistachio harvest, the cost of the tree. And then Leila said, in English:

"I do not care about the pistachios, Roya jaan. I do not care about the tree. He owes us the fifty years of sun, fifty years of water inside that tree. Fifty years of sun and water. That is the price."

She said it in English. I woke screaming. English, fifty years of sun. I wept for a week. Separation from what you love best, that is hell. To be twice separated, first by a nation and then by its language: that is pain deeper than pain. Deeper than hell. That is abyss.

I had started working in a dumpy Greek nostalgia diner that served watery coffee and played the same loop of Jerry Lewis and Bobby Darin songs over and over and over every day. There, I'd scrape fries congealed in ketchup off our red plastic serving trays, chop onions and tomatoes for hours. I'd suck hard knots of white bread while I chopped onions to keep the tears back. When it was slow, I'd draw. I've drawn my whole life—when I was in school, when I was bored, when I was nursing Cyrus—but at the diner, where everything was automatic, autonomic, where I was selling my body's labor but not my mind's, I found my sketches became so much more interesting, free. Unencumbered by higher brain, which clocked out when I clocked in, my whole person was functionally unconscious, bussing from table to table and then stealing away a minute or three drawing at my notepad in the dishroom.

I had a little apartment in the meatpacking district. Lower Manhattan then was full of burnt-out buildings, useless streets. Pork plants made everything smell like blood. Construction sites constantly whistled—a short one to announce a blast, a long one to say all clear. The mayor had closed down all the bathhouses (I didn't know what these were until I lived by one), so there was all this empty space, restless energy. Prostitutes walked in pairs up and down Washington Street.

Really my apartment was just a mattress and a window, a toilet. But that was all I needed. I began papering its walls with my sketches. Water, rays of light breaking against water. Men, soldiers, bodies laid out like calligraphy. Lines and shapes fracturing, too vital to be contained within themselves.

I started using my diner money to buy oil paints, canvas, experimenting in my studio. Light washes of big colors, bold shapes. Then details. Playing with value, hue. Fat dark blues, arthritic grays.

It was a place to put myself. The less time I spent in my higher brain, in the abyss, the safer I was. In New York, my papers said my name was Leila. Everyone called me my dead love's name. The love I had killed when I died. Except I was still here, living inside her name. I was here, Ali and Cyrus were *there,* and Leila? Leila was nowhere. Here, there, nowhere. When I painted, I could be nowhere too.

IT HAPPENED LIKE IT DOES FOR ANYONE, FAME. BULLSHIT LUCK disguised as a lifetime of hard work. But also vice versa. Years I spent chopping onions, buying paints. My apartment was so small I had to stack my canvases; in summer the paint from one sometimes stuck to the back of another. A few of those early canvases still have these paint spots on the back.

The handful of hours a week I wasn't painting or working at the diner, I'd visit galleries. Obsessively. Always the little tiny ones in Chelsea, in the East Village. I wanted to see what everyone, absolutely everyone, was doing. Right then at that moment. Not the Met or the Frick. I knew well enough what the masters had made of things. I wanted to understand the visual vocabulary of the current moment, learn how to use all of it: textile art, neon sculpture, photography. Each felt like vital phrases within this new language that might allow me to communicate through—with?—the abyss. It was a way to stay on earth.

Over time some of the gallerists began recognizing me. Most were aloof, vaguely contemptuous at seeing me come in for the third time in a week, not buying anything. Others would be overly familiar, optimistically hoping I might be a casually wealthy connoisseur there to buy out the show's centerpiece. I didn't pay them much attention either way.

One Sunday I had just finished a breakfast shift at the diner. I smelled like hash brown grease and burnt onions, had a big pink blister on a knuckle from cleaning the grill. I walked straight from my shift to the art supply store to buy canvas and a quart of turpentine for my brushes. On my way home I passed the Linh Gallery in Chelsea, a small bright space for global contemporary painting. I'd met the gallerist a handful of times before. She was a puffy matriarch with short cropped black hair and a strangely geometric—nearly triangular—brown mole above her left eye. I stepped into her gallery on my way home. Featured was the work of a young Algerian painter, loose squares of color and texture inscribed within each other, with shadowy line drawings of people, animals, farm technology laid out around them.

After nodding in my direction as I walked past her, the gallerist noticed my bag from the art supply store.

"You are an artist!"

I was surprised to hear her. I looked around to see who she was speaking to, realized we were the only two people in the gallery.

"Ahh no, no. I work in a restaurant," I said, pinching the collar of my work shirt as if to prove it was true.

The woman laughed.

"Every man who walks in here calls himself a painter, tells me about some Guernica he painted in high school art class. But you, with paint on your neck and a bottle of turpentine, say 'I work in a restaurant.'"

Reflexively I felt for my neck, ran my fingers around it till I found a big scab of paint I'd missed under my jaw.

"I like to paint," I stammered. "But I, I work in a diner."

"I worked in a button factory for twenty years," she said. "Not even making the buttons. Clearing the trash, cleaning the toilets of the people who made buttons. But even then I knew I was an artist, not a toilet cleaner." She pulled a strand of hair behind her ear, set her jaw defiantly. "They were lousy buttons too! Warped in the heat, cracked in the cold."

I laughed.

She came out from behind her desk and we talked that way for some time, her on the clock, me reeking of grease. She told me her name was Sang; "Linh" was for her last name. She told me about her escape to the United States after the America-Vietnam War. She worked in the button factory in the Bronx and raised a family there, three boys. Over time she put together her savings to open this little gallery for her own work. She told me about the vast public indifference to her paintings.

"I'm sure they were amazing," I said. I meant it but it sounded idiotic coming out of my mouth, condescending and false.

"They were fine," Sang said with the comport of someone not seeking compliment, someone who long ago moved on. "Nothing special. But I found what I was really, really good at was looking at other people's work. Seeing what they couldn't see in their own pieces. For better and worse." As she spoke, she would squint her eyes, then relax them almost unconsciously. It looked like she was solving little mental math problems in her head while the rest of her face talked to you.

Sang said she began inviting other artists to feature work in her gallery. It turned out buyers were much more interested in their work than Sang's own. Soon the rent became a little easier to secure each month, and then in time artists and their agents were fighting over her attention.

"Fucking creeps!" She laughed. "Like snakes in a chamomile field."

I smiled, though the phrase made no sense to me. Sang would do that all the time, say these bizarre idioms that I couldn't find in any book. "He's wearing two hats!" she'd shout about some politician, or "he's got stones for eyes" about an artist she didn't like.

"Do you still paint?" I asked.

"This is my painting now," she said, gesturing to the art on the walls, to the gallery as a whole. "All the art of the world, I mix it together, create new composition. You know curating is its own art, of course."

I nodded, not really sure whether I believed it. For my part, I said little about myself. I had come to the U.S. from Iran after the revolution. I had no family here. I did not go to school for art, nor did I want to. I didn't know this person or that person. I bought my supplies from the cheap chain store a few blocks away.

Sang said, "Okay, Miss Mysterious. Bring something in tomorrow then. One of your paintings."

I was mystified. I'd never shown my work to anyone. Sometimes I'd make a little cartoon on a note to Leila, a little goose or a kite, or I'd doodle in the margins of something I was meant to be writing. But my painting, the painting that had become the bedrock upon which I'd built my new life, was mine alone. Other people never really entered the equation of my making. Why would you want to show your lifeboat to strangers? I mustered only "I . . . I work all day tomorrow."

"Fine, Tuesday," replied Sang, undeterred. "I will be here."

"I actually work every day this week. I mean, all day. I don't get off till late."

Sang rolled her eyes.

"Bring it in when you can, then. I'm not going anywhere."

She smiled when she said this, not warmly exactly but proudly, like she'd gotten me cornered. Two of her teeth had silver crowns that flashed when she smiled. I said, "You're very kind. I'll see what I can do," and walked quickly toward the door.

"Wait!" Sang said. "You didn't even tell me your name."

I paused. I hadn't been Roya in years. I'd been Leila. But even then, in that moment of dense unknowing and self-consciousness, even deep in the abyss as I was, I recognized my art could not be Leila's, I could not put dead nowhere Leila's name on something I made here with my own oniony blistered hands.

"Orkideh," I said, surprising myself. It's what Ali and I had called Cyrus when we thought he was going to be a girl, after the first ultrasound got it wrong. "It said you were going to be a girl," Ali cooed down to Cyrus the day we brought him home, "but you were just a shy boy. Mashallah! Modest!"

Sang raised her eyebrows for a flash of a moment, then said, "I look forward to seeing your painting, Orkideh."

. . .

I DELIBERATED ALL WEEK ABOUT WHAT I SHOULD BRING IN. I didn't have a cohesive subject. I didn't even have a cohesive style. I knew I was a fraud, knew the gallerist would soon tell me as much.

Eventually what I picked was one of my newest pieces, something I'd been working on for weeks. Since then I've realized this was inevitable. Every time I finish something, still, I am certain it's the best thing I've ever made, that everything else was the useful but disposable compost preparing my living for the masterpiece I've just wrought. Painting saved me, but I can't say I loved painting. I painted because I needed to. What I really loved, what I love, is having-painted. That was the high. Making something that would never have existed in the entirety of humanity had I not been there at that specific moment to make it. I resented work for this reason more than any other. The countless paintings that would never exist because I had to be working for money instead of painting. I resented my body for the same reasons, its ravenous gobbling up of time, its constant calibrations, needing to eat, shit, smoke.

The painting I brought to Sang was a fairly large one, four by six feet. A night scene, a battlefield. Boy soldiers with Byzantine features, mustached faces on pudgy child bodies, strewn across bloody soil like noodles. Armor, swords, guns. A great cloud of smoke, lots of deep grays on blacks, light blacks on darker blacks. Reds. And in the center of the piece, the field of boys, was a frightened child on horseback. He was holding a flashlight under his head. Naked, chubby baby thighs. And my brother's face, Arash's face. All under a great black cloak. Little child Arash pretending to be an angel in that cloak, in that war. Sweet Arash, who was then probably somewhere in Alborz nailing his windows shut, waving his military sword at ghosts.

I've told the rest of the "discovery" story elsewhere. The impossible luck of it all. Sang loved the painting and, after visiting my apartment and seeing the troves of work I had stacked, gave me my first solo show. A *Times* art critic who happened to miss her train was walking home one night and, on a lark, popped into the Linh Gallery to hobnob anonymously with us casuals. Except she too ended up falling for my work, writing a short but fawning article that mentioned the Arash piece, *Dudusch,* calling it "arresting" and "radically human."

The show sold out. I quit the diner. Sang said she should have asked more for the pieces, but it wouldn't have made a difference to me if they'd each sold for twenty times as much. I was officially working as an artist. Impossible. Sang rented me a tiny art studio, and I began getting my first invitations, commissions.

Yes, the sheer dumb luck, as many have said, as I've said myself. To get such a chance from a gallery, even a small one, is one in a million. To catch the attention of a *Times* critic as a nobody, with no connections, no experience. Impossible.

Except when Sang asked me to show her a painting, I had one. When she'd asked to see the paintings in my apartment, I had dozens. I'd worked my whole life to acquire the technical, the emotional skills to make those paintings. I'd chopped tomatoes and peeled half-eaten onion rings off plastic trays for thousands of hours. I'd painted in grief, weeping and painting, painting and weeping. There were probably weeks, whole months when I did not smile even once. I lived in a studio so small I could smell my neighbor's farts. I spent every penny I had on canvas, brushes, paints. I killed myself. I killed my love. I forced myself to forget my husband, my brother. My country. My son.

It's easy for people who have sacrificed nothing to rationalize their own ordinariness by calling me lucky. But I sacrificed my entire life; I sold it to the abyss. And the abyss gave me art.

NO MUSEUM WANTED TO TOUCH *DEATH-SPEAK*. EVERY CURATOR thought it was fascinating, but every legal department said hell no. When we finally worked something out with the Brooklyn Museum I had to sign a giant binder's worth of paperwork. My death would be in no way the museum's fault. I had to sign a paper saying that if a patron accidentally got me sick, the museum would hold no liability.

I had to sign a paper saying that if a patron got me sick on purpose, the museum would have no liability. I had to sign a DNR, then a DNR for my DNR. My oncologist had to estimate, to the day, when she expected me to die, then sign papers saying that if it happened before that day, the museum would not be responsible.

Finally, though, the lawyers were pacified and the gallery was set up. Big white walls, simple dim lighting. Little black chairs, a little black table. I had a small private room of my own in the back of the gallery space with a bed, a fridge, a bathroom. Mostly I didn't use it if I didn't have to. I wanted to be out in front with the people. All of us were dying, I'd remind them. I was just dying faster.

TWENTY-NINE

ORKIDEH

———— ✳ ————

WHAT I WANT TO SAY IS THAT I WAS HAPPY. NOT ALWAYS, NOT EVEN mostly. But I did know real, deep joy. Maybe everyone gets a certain amount to use up over a lifetime, and I just used my lifetime's allotment especially quickly, with Leila. But I don't think it was a tragedy, my life. Tragedies are relentless. Nobody could ask for more than what I've had.

THIRTY

MONDAY

———— ◦ ————

Cyrus Shams and Sang Linh

BROOKLYN, DAY 4

CYRUS THOUGHT ABOUT WHAT SANG WOULD SEE: A SHAGGY YOUNG man, underdressed in a hoodie and jeans, sitting alone on a park bench. Not looking at his phone or reading a book, just hunched over picking at his fingernails. Maybe the pits of his eyes would remind Sang of Orkideh's. Maybe, for a moment, it would catch her breath.

"Cyrus?" a woman asked.

He looked up. His eyes were red and dry.

"Are you Sang?" he asked, though he recognized immediately that she was. She looked older than she had online, but there was no mistaking her. She was a stout woman, short, thin-lipped, hair the color of Pepsi, which she kept pulled away from her face in a loose ponytail. She wore an open thin black coat down to her knees and beneath it, a dark gray button-up dress shirt. Her large eyes and deep nose-to-mouth lines gave her face an expression of perpetual concern, halfway to a wince. There was nothing ostentatious about her appearance, nothing to suggest she was a major player in the city's art scene.

Sang nodded—

"Can I sit?" she asked.

"Of course," he replied, scooting over.

They sat there for a few seconds, then a full minute, each quietly measuring the texture of the silence, the history between them. A dog-walker passed by, being pulled along by a blue heeler and two border collies. A nanny pushed a double stroller. Sang pulled out a

colorful pack of cigarettes, bright Nat Shermans, and offered one to
Cyrus. At first he shook his head, then he reconsidered and reached
for one. Sang lit it for him and they sat there. The cigarette smoke felt
to Cyrus like a beloved ghost returning after a long absence, filling
him with warmth, making his fingertips tingle. Even the ground felt
hot beneath his feet, though the day was uncommonly cold. Was it
vibrating slightly, or humming?

"Do you hear that?" Cyrus asked about it, finally.

"The city?" Sang asked.

Cyrus listened again for the humming, the vibration, but he
couldn't find it.

"Ah, never mind," he said. His neck was throbbing with cold.

"It's different here, the cold," Cyrus said. "It smells different
than it does in the Midwest. The sky looks different too. It's wetter?
Heavier?"

"Where do you live?" Sang said, exhaling a thick plume into
the air.

"Indiana. Kinda by Chicago. Not really."

Sang nodded. They smoked quietly for another minute. The silence was a mercy for which each felt grateful as their hearts cali-
brated to the moment, to the day's wild and vertiginous revelations.

"You know," Sang said, eventually, "when Orkideh started losing
the weight, the cancer weight, we became obsessed with trying to
feed her. My wife would cut her these fruit bowls filled with kiwi,
pear, starfruit, peach slices so soft your breath could bruise them. My
middle son, Truong, he's a chef. Has his own little spot in Jackson
Heights. And he'd make her these incredible spreads—bone broths,
dumplings, steamed spring rolls. He used to do these coconut rice
cakes that she loved. Everyone just wanted to feed her and feed her.
And here you are all skinny and hunched over in the cold and immediately all I want to do is take you to Truong and feed you too, just
stuff your mouth full of French fries and noodles."

Cyrus smiled a little. Sang continued:

"Orkideh—Roya—used to say there were only two kinds of people in any relationship, the feeder and the eater: the person who

wanted to give care and the person who wanted to be taken care of. Maybe she said it more crudely, mommy and baby, something horrible like that." Sang smiled and shook her head. "She resented ever needing anything from anyone. The whole thing was an elaborate self-loathing, I think."

"That sounds exhausting," Cyrus said.

"She was a complicated woman," Sang added simply, the sort of nothing meant to vent—something—but it just kind of hung there.

I wouldn't know, Cyrus thought, bitterly, but did not say. So much of what he was feeling was rage, it occurred to him. Swallowing it as best as he could, he feebly offered, "I appreciate you coming to see me. I just don't know what to say."

Sang nodded, then looked at her phone, which was vibrating.

"Shit, I do have to answer this one," she said, standing up from the bench. "Two minutes," she mouthed to Cyrus, holding up two fingers, before walking a little distance away.

Cyrus watched her pace off, conducting what seemed to be a stern business call. He looked up at the sky, which had begun to clot into blotchy purple clouds. Why hadn't Orkideh told him who she was? His own mother? Why hadn't she tried to find him? Or her husband? And what about the flight? None of it made sense. Cyrus pulled another cigarette from the colorful pack Sang left sitting on the bench, but realizing he had no lighter and Sang hadn't left hers, he gave an exasperated sigh and put it back in the pack. A tide of self-pity swallowed him. He was alone and cold in a strange city he had no business being in. Friendless, sponsorless, possibly smelling faintly of piss, he was now also somehow even more motherless than he had been when he woke up that day. *If this is a sign, it's a fucking dumb one,* he thought to—at?—god. His foot pulsed with its familiar dull ache. The wind plucked at the park air like an unattended harp.

Finishing her phone call, Sang paced swiftly back over to Cyrus, sitting back down beside him. She smelled good, sturdy, like tarragon and tobacco.

"Sorry, dear. I'm still her manager," Sang said.

"It's no problem," Cyrus said. "I'm surprised you have time to talk to me at all," he added, aware it sounded a little pathetic.

Sang rolled her eyes, then said, "Orkideh told me you're in recovery?"

Cyrus looked up at her, nodded.

"I've been sober for nearly thirty years," said Sang. "In the rooms."

"Wow," he said. "That's an eternity."

Sang smiled, said, "I mention it because, when I first started going to my Tribeca meetings, I was a mess. Noon meetings, just these big clouds of smoke. And afterwards my sponsor—or, she would eventually become my sponsor, Janet—she would take me to the Possum Diner next door for coffee and egg sandwiches. She was this old biker lady, leather jacket, the whole deal. We did that daily for months and months. My kids at school, and me sneaking off at noon to hang out with all these drunks and eat drippy egg sandwiches with this crazy old white lady.

"One day, I was maybe three months, four months sober, and my kids were nuts, the oldest kept getting into fights at school and I could barely keep my head attached to my neck. We have the meeting and I am so eager to go to the diner with Janet because I have all these grievances to list, all this stuff I wanted to talk with her about. But as soon as the meeting's over she invites this raggedy newcomer lady to come eat with us. She was clearly straight off the street, probably just at the meeting to drink free coffee and bum smokes. And of course we get to the diner and this lady won't shut up, talking about how her boyfriend fucked her over and how now he's looking for her, something like that. I remember just sitting there, seething at this trespasser, hating the way she chewed, the way she guzzled her water and coffee. She was swallowing up the whole conversation, not letting me get a word in. And then at some point she gets up to use the bathroom and it's just me and Janet left in the booth and before I can say anything, Janet leans across the table and says, very very slowly and clearly,

"'Sang. Listen to me. You are not the patient today.'

"And that was that. I think about it every day. *You're not the patient today, Sang.* It's lucky to get to be on the other side. It's a good day when you're not the patient."

Cyrus smiled up at Sang. There was a softness to her speech that felt incongruous with the crags in her face, her severe posture. He could see why important people trusted her.

"That's a great story," Cyrus said, earnestly. "Do you and Janet still work together?"

"No, she died a few years after I got sober. Went back out and it only took her a couple months to OD."

"Jesus Christ. I'm sorry."

"It's fine!" Sang said. "She was sober for a decade, lived ten years longer than she was supposed to. She helped many women get sober, and who knows how many people we've all helped ourselves, who everyone we've helped has helped. You know? She did good. God loves Janet."

Cyrus smiled weakly. He felt dizzy, still. He said, "I say that about myself all the time, 'Lived years longer than I was supposed to.' My liver was pre-cirrhotic when I quit. I was only in my twenties. A baby. And I'm still here when all these other people just like me aren't. So who decides 'supposed to'? Who chooses?"

Around them, it had started to snow. Or maybe it had been for some time. The flakes hung in the air, big globs, neither rising nor falling, just suspended there, like sounds.

"You don't have to do this gracefully," Sang said, after a pause.

Cyrus nodded slowly.

"I always . . . I always thought my mom was on that flight, you know? What that meant to me, how that related to this big idea of martyrdom."

"Not wanting her to have died for nothing," Sang offered.

"Right. Exactly. And then my friend told me about Orkideh and her installation and I thought I could write a book about it. Martyrdom. The gulf between my mother making nothing from her death and this artist in Brooklyn making something. These two opposite Iranian women . . . except it was the same person." Cyrus turned and looked at Sang, hard. "How was it the same person? How was my mother not on that flight?"

Sang sighed:

"She gave her ticket to her lover. Leila. They switched passports. They were going to run away separately, meet up, and start life over again. Together. Somewhere else."

Sang's words—not even the words, their sounds—crushed whatever feeble sense of bearing Cyrus had built up. He reflexively shook his head, baffled, trying to apprehend what Sang just said. Leila. Lover. Start over. Without him? Had Sang said "without you"? He couldn't remember, though she'd just spoken. "Without you" was everywhere apparent, even if Sang hadn't said it out loud. His mother had not been shot out of the sky at all. Some random other woman—Leila, was it?—had been. Cyrus's mother was another one of those just-stepping-out-for-a-pack-of-cigs family abandoners. He'd been a tiny baby. It felt so pulverizingly mundane. Roya Shams, the deadbeat mom. Or at least, she'd planned to be a deadbeat, before her lover—her lover!—Leila!!—was shot out of the sky. Cyrus felt annihilated. Furious. He felt angry for his sweet sick dead father. He felt angry for himself. Then at himself, for feeling angry instead of something more enlightened: acceptance, or perhaps compassion. That's where he quickly settled, the vector of his rage, his hurt, pointed directly back at himself. Every cell of his body wanted to drink, to jettison out of the moment, out of consciousness entirely.

After what felt like an eternity, Cyrus heard himself ask, "Did my father know?"

Sang looked at Cyrus, then took a final drag from her cigarette.

"Not much, I don't think. Maybe about Leila. Leila's husband found out, so probably he did tell your father something, at some point. But Leila's husband finding out, that was why—" She paused, looking at Cyrus.

"Why they had to leave?" he finished for her.

Sang nodded. A sinewy woman walked by, struggling to pull a complicated caravan of roller bags. Snow caught in her hair and didn't melt, like cotton in the wind.

"I hate this," said Cyrus.

Sang looked at him. The chain of her modest gold necklace had popped from under her shirt, was sitting on the collar of one side of her blouse. Given how put together Sang was, it looked doubly strange.

"Gay people dying for love," Cyrus stammered. His mind was racing too far ahead of his language. "It's bullshit" was what he said, was all he could manage.

"It happened. And it still happens," Sang said. "You Americans act like this stuff is over. Like George Bush standing on that ship in front of the Mission Accomplished banner. It's not over at all. It's not in the past. You and I are sitting here right now because of it."

Cyrus winced at "you Americans," though Sang wasn't wrong.

"I can't stand that I'm so mad," he said, desperately.

"You think there's some nobility in being above anger?" Sang asked. "Anger is a kind of fear. And fear saved you. When the world was all kneecaps and corners of coffee tables, fear kept you safe."

Cyrus said nothing.

"When we were still in Vietnam, my husband was a drunk," Sang continued. "He'd drink all our money, gamble anything left over. I drank too, but not like him. There was no money for anything. I was scared all the time of going hungry, of losing our home. The universe—you can call it God if you want, it doesn't bother me— gave me my first son. And then I was scared for *us*, instead of just myself. My boy gave me a reason to stick around. I stopped drinking. I started making my own paintbrushes out of clothespins and bits of old sponge, making paint from flour and food color. I made these tacky landscapes and sold them to tourists, hid the money. Fear made me work hard, get better. It's a dirty fuel, but it works. And anger? Anger helped me to leave him. To get my boys away from him as soon as I could. To come thrive in this country that didn't even believe we were people. To prove it wrong. You can put a saddle on anger, Cyrus."

Cyrus looked at her. He was suddenly embarrassed, hopelessly embarrassed to have made this grieving widow-of-sorts have to come console him, today of all days. He wanted to say sorry, to say, somehow convincingly, that he was fine, that she didn't need to speak to him this way. But before he could put any of that into language, Sang continued:

"I'm mad at her too, you know. For a lot of things. But especially for making me be the one to have to have this conversation with you."

"Yeah," Cyrus said. "I can imagine." Though he couldn't.

The wind stirred up a flurry of snowflakes, lifting them off the dead grass like sparks rising off a beach fire. Cyrus felt light-years away from the world.

"'Whoever climbs over our fence, we shall climb over his roof,'" Cyrus mumbled.

"What?"

"Saddam said that, at the beginning of the Iran-Iraq War. That kind of anger, retributive. That half-your-face-for-an-eye shit. There's nothing uglier."

"Ahh."

"I just think about that a lot. The ugliness of anger. I don't disagree that it can be harnessed. But it's so irredeemably ugly."

"You're a human being, Cyrus," Sang said, gently. "So was your mother. So am I. Not cartoon characters. There's no pressure for us to be ethically pure, noble. Or, God forbid, aspirational. We're people. We get mad, we get cowardly. Ugly. We self-obsess."

Cyrus blinked. Sang was right—whatever storm of confusion, anger, betrayal he was feeling in that moment began and ended with himself. Globs of snow were falling from the clouds that had begun, almost imperceptibly, growing lighter, like someone was emptying out them out with a teaspoon.

"I'm so sorry, Sang," Cyrus said.

"For what?"

"All this. Taking up your day. I can't imagine all you have to be doing right now. And Jesus, I haven't even asked: How are you? How are you handling all this?"

"I'm okay, Cyrus," she said. "Mad, like I said. But not surprised.

Not really. It wasn't a surprise. And"—she took a deep breath—"and honestly, it's thrilling to meet you. I never imagined I'd be able to. Plus," she added, "every minute you keep me from my inbox, from the art-world death vultures, is a kindness."

Cyrus smiled.

"It's exciting to meet you too, Sang."

They sat quietly like that for a time, snow dusting them like sugar. Then Cyrus said:

"There's this story I read one time, some old-school Muslim fairy tale, maybe it was a discarded hadith I guess, but it was all about the first time Satan sees Adam. Satan circles around him, inspecting him like a used car or something, this new creation—God's favorite, apparently. Satan's unimpressed, doesn't get it. And then Satan steps into Adam's mouth, disappears completely inside him and passes through all his guts and intestines and finally emerges out his anus. And when he gets out, Satan's laughing and laughing. Rolling around. He passes all the way through the first man and he's rolling around laughing, in tears, and he says to God, 'This is what you've made? He's all empty! All hollow!' He can't believe his luck. How easy his job is going to be. Humans are just a long emptiness waiting to be filled."

Sang smiled.

"Sounds like some men I've known for sure," she said.

Cyrus laughed too. "Right?" He went on, "I think the moral is supposed to be that you fill the hollow with God. And that everything else is a distraction."

"Hmph. Is your hollow filled with God, then?" she asked.

"Oh, no," Cyrus said quickly. "Or mostly never. Maybe a couple times in my life. I think I've tried to fill it with booze, with drugs. Maybe with writing. But obviously, none have really worked out very well."

"Never love? That seems like the big one."

Cyrus thought. The ground burning under his feet. He felt a pang, thought about Zee.

"Not as much. Not as much as I probably should."

"Oh, I don't know about 'should.' But mostly, it's a cleaner fuel than getting high. Cleaner than art too, mostly."

"Is that yours then?" Cyrus asked. "How you filled your hollow?"

"What, love?" Sang thought for a moment. "Probably these days, yeah. I mean, I could also say your mother. Her self, her history, her art. Holding all of that. But then, also, my boys. And their families. Their wives, my grandkids. I hope you'll meet them one day, Cyrus. But I don't know what fills me!" She laughed. "I don't have one piece of my brain for romantic love and one for narcotic love and one for family and one for art. It all washes together. Tintoretto makes me think of my youngest boy. O'Keeffe makes me think of my oldest. Right now Roya makes me think of lavender. Of Sarah Vaughan's 'Solitude.' And also this song from my childhood, 'Hạ Trắng.' Which also makes me think of my wife! Which is fucked up," she laughed. Cyrus laughed too.

"I think I get that," he said, "the mess of it."

"I think you do too," Sang replied.

They sat there quietly for a time, watching. Cyrus's foot pounded. He felt angry, confused, sick—but also a little excited. Which confused him. A pretty couple walked by eating kimchi sandwiches, a gray old man was studying a chessboard he had balanced on his knees. Cyrus once read an anthropologist who wrote about how the first artifact of civilization wasn't a hammer or arrowhead, but a human femur—discovered in Madagascar—that showed signs of having healed from a bad fracture. In the animal world, a broken leg meant you starved, so a healed femur meant that some human had supported another's long recovery, fed them, cleaned the wound. And thus, the author argued, began civilization. Augured not by an instrument of murder, but by a fracture bound, a bit of food brought back for another. It was an attractive idea.

The sun, Cyrus noticed, was cracking back through the sky in waves.

THIRTY-ONE

There are no "flawless" operations in combat—even when there is a successful outcome. But to say that there were mistakes made, says very little by itself. Some of the information given to Captain Rogers during the engagement proved not to be accurate. Unfortunately the investigation was not able in every case to reconcile the inaccuracies.

William J. Crow Jr., Chairman, United States
Joint Chiefs of Staff, 5 August 1988

ORKIDEH

———— ✦ ————

THE FIRST TIME I DIED, I WASN'T EVEN THERE. THE WHOLE PAYOFF, the answer to the question of what happens afterward—I didn't get any of that. Maybe Leila did. Maybe she got something like clarity, or peace, when that plane blew up. But I was left with all the loss, none of the reward. Stuck here lurching through my living, lurching from grief to grief. Just inertia, just tumbling forward. No carrot at the end of the stick. This time I wanted to at least be present for it. My death. My final installation, *Death-Speak,* is a way of being in the room, literally being in the room as it happens.

There's a moment of Farrokhzad where she says,

> *I won't see spring,*
> *these lines are all that will remain.*
> *As heaven spins, I fall into bedlam.*
> *I am gone, my heart is filled with sorrow—*
> *O Muslims, I am sad tonight.*

I think about that often. I don't even really feel particularly Muslim, I don't suspect Farrokhzad did either. But this bit, I wanted to pin it to my shirt when I first read it. The simpleness of it, the clarity. It's like she's reaching out from beyond the grave to say no, no, this isn't decoration, this isn't artifice, this is desperate, this is urgent. Let's skip the bullshit, she's saying. We can't afford all that anymore, not here in the abyss.

For our species, the idea of art as ornament is a relatively new one. Our ape brains got too big, too big for our heads, too big for our mothers to birth them. So we started keeping all our extra knowing in language, in art, in stories and books and songs. Art was a way of storing our brains in each other's. It wasn't until fairly recently in human history, when rich landowners wanted something pretty to look at in winter, that the idea of art-as-mere-ornament came around. A painting of a blooming rose to hang on the mantel when the flowers outside the window had gone to ice. And still in the twenty-first century, it's hard for folks to move past that. This idea that beauty is the horizon toward which all great art must march. I've never been interested in that.

"As heaven spins, I fall into bedlam."

That purity, that simplicity, that's it for me. I'm dying. Here I am. It's ugly. There are all these tubes, all this gunk oozing out of me. Sometimes the bigness of the thing is too much for language, for paint, for art. You just have to say it plain: "O Muslims, I am sad tonight." That's what *Death-Speak* is. Being present. Saying it plain.

Of course, Sang hated it. Our romance had ended years before; she got comfortable, I got restless. I had found someone else for a time, but of course I did. A symptom, not the disease. Story old as time. Sang and I were better as friends, as colleagues. I still got dinner sometimes with her and her new wife, their grown-up kids. But while one part of our story ended, she was still my gallerist. And she was a good one, one whose opinion I'd learned to trust over the years. So when I pitched my final installation to her, the one where I died, it was also my way of telling her I was dying. She paused for only a fraction of a fraction of a second, and then snorted dismissively—

"*The artist is present,* AND she's dying?" she said, rolling her eyes. "C'mon."

It was cruel dismissal, barbed with anger at my having withheld my diagnosis from her. Which, yes, was wrong of me. Sang was the only family I had left. She had deserved to know, and I don't know why I didn't tell her sooner. All I could bring myself to say was—

"I'm doing this, Sang. I'd like you to be a part, but I don't need you to be. I'll do it at the Met or in a folding chair at Union Station. It doesn't matter to me."

She studied my face and I studied hers. She had really been in love with me once, and I had really loved watching her love me. Which sounds terrible, but it's not. It's easy to resent those who love you. Those who are over eager with their affection. Too performative. But I loved how Sang loved me, easily, like it was its own soul in her chest, pumping that love through her, animating her as naturally as blood. Even if I didn't have that for her. We both knew it all along, all those years. Me pathologically waiting for her to fall asleep before coming to bed. Sang hoping something would shift, knowing it wouldn't. We were both mostly fine with it, happy enough. Happy winding between museums, her kids' graduations, art openings, fancy dinners. Happy enough, until we weren't.

When I told her about my final installation, we argued some more, but I knew she'd give in. Finally, Sang said, "If you do this, you should call it *Death-Speak*."

"I love that," I said, and meant it. She paused.

"You know not everything is connected, don't you?" she said. "Everything doesn't have to stand in for everything else?"

"I know," I said.

"You don't have to do this," she said.

"I know," I said.

"It's—" she said. "I just—"

"I know," I said.

THIRTY-TWO

I FEEL DANGEROUS. I DON'T KNOW HOW MUCH MORE BALDLY I CAN say it. But how can an Iranian be dangerous without becoming "a dangerous Iranian"? Without becoming dangerous to every other Iranian in the world or contributing to the myth of the pathologically angry Iranian? Coming out of the womb with a burning flag in his teeth?

Any volcano that has erupted since the Holocene, ancient history, is considered active. I haven't. Does that make me inert? Or overdue?

—*from* BOOKOFMARTYRS.docx by Cyrus Shams

MONDAY

———— ✳ ————

Cyrus Shams

BROOKLYN, DAY 4

AFTER SANG LEFT—MAKING CYRUS PROMISE TO CALL HER, MAKING him promise he'd let her know when he got home to Indiana safely—Cyrus wandered around the park. The cold was invigorating, an anchor. When he pulled out his phone to see if Zee'd reached out, he found he only had a single missed notification, a text from Sad James. Clicking into it, Cyrus read:

"Did you see this?"

And below that, a little link. The preview that popped up said: "NYT Obituary: Orkideh, In Her Own Words." Cyrus clicked it and a page popped up with a giant hero photo of Orkideh, the same one the museum had used on their sign, eyes full of coal and mischief, her cheeks still glowing, bright even in the black and white. Cyrus took a moment, a realization that this was an image, a text he would likely visit again and again for however much longer he'd remain alive—he still wasn't sure how long that'd be—and tried to slow himself down. Studying the picture, he looked for his own face in Orkideh's, in her brow or her chin or her smile lines, but mostly she looked like herself, a one of one, like an angel who had adopted a human's face as a concession to convention. Mythologizing this way was dangerous, Cyrus knew. And yet. He scrolled down.

"Orkideh (1963–2017)" said the header. Then: "IN HER OWN WORDS." In italics, an editor's note:

Since January 5th, the Iranian American visual artist Orkideh has been in residence at the Brooklyn Museum performing her final installation, "Death-Speak." Diagnosed months ago with terminal breast cancer that had metastasized across her body, the artist elected to spend her final weeks in an Abramovic-esque performance wherein museum guests could sit with her for a few minutes at a time and discuss death frankly, openly. Orkideh, whose public work spanned three decades and a variety of mediums, was once dubbed "a painful and poignant emotional revolutionary" by Nora N. Barskova, this publication's chief art critic. Below is Orkideh's obituary, in her own words.

Cyrus took a deep breath, then read on to Orkideh's—his mother's—text:

Here's what's important: I was Iranian, then I was Iranian in America. I made lots of art. Some of it was quite good, I think. Plenty wasn't. But I was alive for a long time, long enough to make a lot of art. Creativity didn't live in my brain any more than walking lived in my legs. It lived in every painting I ever saw, every book I ever read, every conversation I ever had. The world was full enough that I didn't need to store anything inside myself.

I wore gold jewelry that warmed in sunlight. I made my friends smile. I did not linger to see what my enemies did.

Even when I was subject to the murderous whims of patently evil nations, men, I knew the badness for how different it was from the goodness. I was not often "a person to whom things happened." And when I was, I had the sanctuary of imagination, of art.

When I say "nations," I mean "armed marketplaces." Always. That understanding made the world a little bit easier to comprehend, if not tolerate. To the extent I was a fraud, I was no less than anyone else. I was grafted onto my living from a part of the universe that remains nameless, like smoke rising from a great fire.

I demand to be forgiven.

I demand the same leniencies, rationalizations, granted to mediocre men for centuries.

I died, if you're reading this, in a museum, of a disgusting and unbeautifiable disease. I reject the reduction of my life to this most grotesque artifact. I used to walk with a sprig of lavender in my pocket—smelling it I could go to almost any other point in my life, which I believe was as close to time travel as anyone's come. I'd like credit for that.

I am flatterable, and obnoxiously disarmed by praise.

Forugh Farrokhzad: "This isn't about terrified whispers in the dark. This is about light and cool breeze through the open window."

When the world was flat, people leapt off all the time. There is nothing remarkable about dying this way, but I hope I've made something interesting of my living. An alphabet, like a life, is a finite set of shapes. With it, one can produce almost anything.

Orkideh, 2017

FINISHING THE ARTICLE, CYRUS FOUND HIMSELF PRAYING, SUDdenly, without even realizing it. Sitting back down on a bench he was forming a prayer not exactly in language, not out loud at all. The most basic form of prayer, he'd heard once, was something like "help me help me help me, please please please, thank you thank you thank you"; and Cyrus's prayer in the park was not much more advanced than that. But it was a prayer all the same, recognizable—like an Archimedian scale—by the heft of what it displaced.

What formed in Cyrus's mind was a blunt and inarticulable plea to be *done*, for a reprieve from navigating what had become to him an unnavigable world, to not have to spend the next decade or decades unraveling what it all meant, had meant, would mean. The anger he felt at his mother. The vanished. The abandoner. But, also, the pride he felt for her, now. The great artist. It was too much. He prayed for an end to the tyranny of *all* symbols, beginning with language. He understood, with a clarity that had until that moment in his life eluded him, that he was not at all made for the world in which he lived, that art and writing had gotten him only trivially closer to compensating for that fundamental defectiveness, the way standing on a roof gets one only trivially closer to grabbing the moon than standing in the dirt.

Let me be done, he thought, this time in words, his mother's letter still glowing on the screen in his hands. He closed his eyes, said it again out loud: "Let me be done."

When he opened his eyes, he was still alone on the park bench. Planted there, the city's motion around him felt like a broken video clip, like the same fifteen seconds were just playing over and over on loop, yellow taxicabs and bits of snow moving along the horizon, then hard-resetting to their original position. The wind smelled faintly of almonds. In his pocket, his phone was vibrating. He pulled it out, saw "ZEE NOVAK" was calling him. Quickly, he answered:

"Hey!"

"Cyrus," Zee said, "I just got to the museum and saw—" He paused, realizing Cyrus might not yet know. "Have you been here yet?"

"Yeah, I was there this morning," Cyrus said.

"I'm sorry, man." Cyrus could hear plainly in Zee's voice the pain that had inspired his exodus from their hotel, but also that the pain was, in that moment, eclipsed by an acute concern for Cyrus, for the possibility Cyrus might do something rash in the wake of the artist's death. The clearness of it, of his friend's love and distress, suddenly felt pulverizingly obvious. How negligent Cyrus had been with Zee's loyalty. With Zee's devotion. Cruel, even. Sobriety meant Cyrus couldn't help but see himself, eventually. And it hurt. He was repulsed by what he saw.

"I'm so, so sorry too, Zee. Not just for last night. All of it. Truly."

A beat—an hour, a second—passed.

"Where are you?" Zee asked. There was a faint shuffling from his end, the phone being passed from one ear to another.

"I'm actually still right across from the museum, in Prospect Park."

"Oh—is it okay if I come over there with you?"

"Of course, please, please, yes," Cyrus said, excited at the opportunity to apologize to Zee in person, to hold him, catch him up on all that had transpired. "I'll drop a pin. I really am sorry, Zee."

Cyrus waited, and in his waiting became increasingly aware of how hot the ground had gotten under his feet. He could hear the humming, the vibrating, like the earth was very thin paper wrapped around a hornet's nest. By the time he saw Zee approaching in the distance, the ground felt like a great kiln firing something massive and delicate, sand into glass. At the sight of Zee, Cyrus's heart caught in his chest, with—he realized almost all at once— what must have been clarity. Clarity like he'd never known: sweet and unequivocal. The smell of walnut and woodsmoke on the wind. The air felt thick. Somewhere in the distance, someone was singing.

"Zee!" Cyrus shouted, waving him over.

Zee smiled and made a show of jogging over to Cyrus, though he moved slowly to not slip on the ice in his ridiculous Crocs. Cyrus gleamed, Zee's woven backpack flopping up and down on his back in time with the bouncing of his curls. Cyrus loved him so much.

"I love you so much," Cyrus said, immediately falling into a deep embrace as Zee got to him. He used his thumbs to part the curls crossing over Zee's forehead and kissed him there. "I'm so, so sorry." He meant it. Zee's goodness filled him like a drug.

"Hey!" Zee said, smiling, pulling his head back from Cyrus's. "I love you too, you idiot." They kissed on the lips, a quick and firm kiss that seemed at once tiny and unbreakable, like a pebble. It wasn't right, how Cyrus had treated Zee. His barb the night before, yes, but also their entire relationship. Like he was entitled to his friend's adoration. How had he been so oblivious? Love was a room that appeared when you stepped into it. Cyrus understood that now, and stepped.

Around them, something like seafoam blew across the park. The tree branches had lowered themselves down to meet the new grass rising through the snow.

Cyrus and Zee sat. Zee admitted he'd spent the whole night wandering Brooklyn, alternating between feeling angry at himself and at Cyrus, finally passing out sitting up for a couple hours on a train station bench. Zee said he'd planned to talk to Orkideh that day, to go ask her—"well, I don't know what," he'd said. He just wanted to see her with his own eyes. He believed that would make a difference, that the words would come. But when he got to the museum, she was gone.

Cyrus winced at every detail. He kept saying he was sorry. And he was. Zee said, "I know," again and again, but only once Cyrus truly believed him did he tell Zee the story of *his* day: going to see Orkideh that morning, fainting on the staircase, Prateek and his aunt, Sang's voicemail, then meeting her, what Sang told him about his mother, his mother and the plane crash and Leila and Orkideh's final letter in the paper, all of it, all of it whooshing out of him like steam.

"Holy shit," Zee kept saying. "Holy shit."

As Cyrus finished catching Zee up, he felt immeasurably lighter. Whatever was merciful in the universe lived in Zee, Cyrus suddenly realized. The way Zee held, understood, knew, him. Grace. How when he saw a bird or a tree or a bug, Zee really saw *that* bird or tree or bug, not the idea of it. How he really saw Cyrus, really heard him, beneath all his beneaths. Cyrus loved that Zee moved through life unencumbered by the flinching anxiety that governed, corroded his own soul. Cyrus was dizzy with it, this love, its abrupt and total overwhelm.

All around them, the city's skyline of desiccated towers blinked absently, some of them crumbling around their edges. The trees of Prospect Park had at some point shaken off the snow and erupted into bloom. Lavender buds, blue and yellow and crimson flowers Cyrus didn't recognize.

"Are you seeing this?" asked Zee, gesturing to the wilding world around them.

"I am." Cyrus nodded. "I think it's maybe because of us." His words weren't moving quite in sync with his lips.

"Of course you do!" Zee laughed. "You're not wrong, though." His hands were cupped in front of him on his lap. "You're not wrong."

The scent of feathers and copper filled the air. If there had been other people around before—Cyrus couldn't remember—they were gone now. It was just Cyrus and Zee and whoever was making this music that was all around them. Trumpets, saxophone. Further away, voices. The humming had turned into a kind of flat scraping, like a tooth sliding across a wooden floor. Cyrus felt light-headed—his foot pulsed hard.

"It reminds me of this one Milosz poem," Cyrus said. "'Those expecting archangels' trumpets and locusts and horsemen will be disappointed,' something like that. I'm probably bungling it." He slipped his hand into Zee's and squeezed it tightly. Zee kissed him on the cheek.

"All those severe poets talking big about the wages of sin all the time," Zee added, "but nobody ever brought up the wages of virtue. The toll of trying really really hard to be good in a game that's totally rigged against goodness."

Glassy moans barely audible over the horizon. Dark clouds against a bright sky, like blackberries in a bowl of milk.

"You're so good, Zee. I see it."

Snow falling faster than what should have been possible.

"That's not what I mean," said Zee in an unexpectedly high, strange voice. "It's just. Where does all our effort go? It's hard not to envy the monsters when you see how good they have it. And how unbothered they are at being monsters."

"That's why heaven and hell, right? Why people talk about that stuff?"

"Nah, fuck hell," Zee said, shaking his head. "Hell is a prison. All we do is build those on earth. No need to imagine more."

Cyrus smiled.

"And fuck heaven too!" Zee continued. "Like goodness is a place you can arrive at, a destination. Where you're either standing in it or you're not. It fucks you up. Royal you and also you-you, Cyrus-you. All of these symbols being so literal."

The topography of the Brooklyn skyline—and somehow, also Manhattan's, and several unfamiliar skylines too—was blistering all around them. Towering cracks now running up the sides of skyscrapers, molten liquids roiling, smoking, pooling against the marble and steel and glass. Lava hardened into new land.

"Somebody's feeling frisky," Cyrus teased. Zee pulled his head back, raised his eyebrows.

"See, *that's* how you know all this is real," Zee said, fanning his hand out to the city wilding around them.

"What do you mean?"

"I mean, that's like, *the* difference between real life and dreaming. Nobody's ironic in a dream. Nobody goes around winking and smirking."

Songbirds were darting almost imperceptibly across the sky, wailing broken half ballads back and forth to their mates. Two pigeons crashed into each other, then flew off in the same easterly direction. A hawk was flying straight upward with a tiny starling in her claws.

"Nobody smirks in your dreams?" Cyrus asked.

"Of course not," Zee said, definitively. "Dreams are the great preserve of the earnest. People smirk in your dreams?"

Cyrus thought for a second:

"I can't remember now. I don't think so. Maybe you're right."

The ground was breathing, revealing tiny little golden fissures in the earth as it swelled. The trees dropped their flowers, then their branches, to the ground—slowly, almost delicately, like new lovers undressing in front of each other for the first time. The sky had gone from white to gray to bright orange, a great cigarette sucked back to life. There was thunder but no rain. Or maybe not thunder, but great cracking sounds all around.

"It won't be long now," said Zee.

Cyrus squeezed his hand again, took a deep breath.

"Why don't I feel startled by any of this?" he asked. "Shouldn't I be more scared?"

"Underneath being-startled is the expectation of calm," Zee said, then paused. "I mean, a person gasps because the ease they were expecting was interrupted. I think probably your life hasn't taught you to expect ease."

"Jesus," Cyrus said. "Yeah."

"A lot of people mistake neglect for calm. Cosmic neglect, or otherwise. But nobody's neglected you, Cyrus. You see that now, don't you?"

"I think I am starting to, yeah," Cyrus answered. Then, "Where is all this coming from?"

Little spirals of snow on the horizon, still, despite the heat coming up from the ground. The smell of deep forest, rotten and damp. Tarragon, pomegranate molasses, vetiver. The sound of brass again, trumpets, saxophone, horns. And now, drums too. A whistling on the air, nearly jaunty.

"I've had a lot of time to think about it," Zee answered, laughing. "A long long time."

"I see," Cyrus said, laughing a little too, though he was still confused.

The two sat there, watching as a herd of wild horses galloped by them in the park, nostrils flared, hulking muscles steaming in the cold. Behind them, a great black stallion, twice the size of the rest, with an illuminated rider gripping the reins dressed in a long black cloak.

"Really?" said Cyrus.

Zee smiled, shrugged.

"You'll forgive the universe its moment of high drama."

They sat for another moment watching the sky curl, churn, like cream in coffee—they held hands, watching, thinking about blissfully little. Then Zee asked, "You feel ready?"

"I think so," said Cyrus. His foot was burning, a heat so hot it looped through so-hot-it-feels-cold and felt hot again, scorching.

Cyrus looked down at his shoe, the foot that had been throbbing, and saw a swirling void, a cosmos of deep gravity and pale bones. He saw his family, both of his parents, his book, his own face. Futureless, like a shattered crystal ball.

Together, Cyrus and Zee stood up. The golden light cracking through the ground had gathered into a vast and deep pool, warm and gurgling absently like an unattended infant. Cyrus knelt over the swirl and gasped a little. He was, somewhere in the back of his mind, aware he was crying, that Zee was there kneeling beside him, wiping the tears from his cheeks, kissing them. It was almost unbearable, how good and warm it felt to be there—together—in the pond's golden light. The feeling of prayer—not prayer itself, but the stillness it leaves—lifted from the earth, smelling of grass and woodsmoke. Cyrus reached his hand into the pool and closed his eyes. He felt another hand—was it his own, or Zee's?—grab it.

Around them, birds and bright blossoms dropped like fists of snow from the sky.

CODA

SANG LINH

———— ✳ ————

NEW YORK, 1997

TAKING DOWN WHY WE PUT MIRRORS IN BIRDCAGES *WITH ROYA AND Duy, I remember thinking that was it, the top of the mountain. My younger two boys were home with the babysitter—Mytoan, an acquaintance's teen-age daughter. This was before we could afford Marguerite, the kids' favorite nanny—but only just before. Birdcages was Orkideh's third exhibition in my gallery and her third sellout. I couldn't raise prices enough.*

I was stubbornly still working as my own courier, installing and unin-stalling my shows with the help of my oldest son, Duy, who I paid fifty dollars a day to help. Fifty dollars a day felt to both of us like an outrageous fee—and his brothers complained bitterly—but I needed the help, and I liked having him around. Roya also insisted on helping set up and break down, more obsessiveness than kindness. Once she moved her paintings out of her old apartment in the meatpacking district and into her first studio, she never really trusted anyone, even me, to handle the work carefully enough.

She and I were listening to pop radio as we sanded down spackle to repaint a section of the wall for the next exhibition when Duy came over with one of the show's larger paintings, Odi et Amo, wrapped in a cocoon of paper and bubble padding.

"Where does this one go?" he asked.

The painting he carried—a crucified hand curling to clutch the nail driven through its palm—was one of Roya's favorites, though not one of mine. The hand gripped the nail almost tenderly, as one might hold a child's finger while crossing the street. There was, in the meat of the palm, almost the insinuation of a face, a child face. The watery colors felt loose, searching.

Sometimes at night my mother used to dump the leftover tea from her teapot into my bathwater, and the colors of Odi et Amo reminded me of that, the browns into grays. The correspondence was so uncanny that the first time I saw the painting, I got a whiff of pandan leaves. That shock of recall. It wasn't entirely pleasant, and I was glad the painting was going somewhere where I'd be unlikely to see it again.

I pointed to the pallet of work going to David J. T. Swartzwelder, a health-care tycoon who'd purchased a third of the show himself. Roya eyed Duy suspiciously as he walked the painting over to the others. I could see her trying to restrain herself, but ultimately she couldn't resist, shouting, "Careful with the corners! Please!"

Duy rolled his eyes theatrically. I touched Roya's hand. She looked over at me, and, meeting her eyes, I felt overcome suddenly with an eclipsing gratitude. Like a panic attack, but flipped over the badness midline. This brilliant curious woman loved me and we were doing what we always dreamed. My boys were happy and safe. We had made a good life. Of course, for Roya and me, there would be higher planes of professional success, financial success, creative success. Money, prizes, travel. I knew that even then. But for us, our marriage, the us of us, it felt, even in the moment, like a kind of climax.

Often in my life, in the throes of despair, of my husband's abuse, I have held the certainty of the damned, that sense of "everything is going to be just this, this misery forever, till I die." An irrepressible inescapable horror stretching out infinitely in every direction. Tragic, that only terror feels that way. That even in Roya's and my impossibly good moments, I instinctively knew to hold them, to store them inside myself like pockets of fat for the lean seasons ahead.

"He knows what he's doing," I assured, nodding to Duy, and I saw Roya soften a little.

Roya set down her sheet of sandpaper. The boombox was playing a sexy ballad I hadn't heard before. The lyrics went "If I could wear your clothes, I'd pretend I was you, And lose controoooool." As if on cue, Roya stepped over behind me, put her arms around my waist, and kissed my neck.

"You know what I'm going to buy first?" she asked.

"Hm?"

"With the money from the show," she clarified.

"Ah," I replied. "Some deodorant, perhaps?"

She slapped my arm playfully, then said: "It's your fault I've had to be in here these past two days. If you weren't so good at your job, we wouldn't have to ship all these."

I rolled my eyes. "These would have sold anywhere."

She shrugged it off.

"Ask me what I'm going to buy!" she insisted, a little too loud, in my ear.

Duy called out from the pallets: "Was that the last painting for this guy?"

I shook my head and pointed to a small one in the hallway: A Murmur, it was called. The shadow of the shadow of a dove. White on white.

"That one too."

Duy sighed. I added, "Thank you, dear!"

Turning back to Roya, I asked, "What will you buy, great puppy bear?"

"Wow, I'm so glad you asked!" she said, joking at being shocked. "I am going to buy the biggest Cadillac car door I can find."

She was still behind me, her hands around my waist, and pulled me in a little closer, resting her chin on my shoulder. I craned my neck back to study her face. She was smiling her self-satisfied smile, which I loved, despite myself.

"Just the car door?" I asked.

"Yep."

I sighed, playing along.

"Why would you just get the Cadillac door, love?"

She squeezed me hard, then whispered into my ear: "Because when the world ends and it's just us left to fend for ourselves, I can roll down the window when it gets hot!"

At this she started laughing, booming thunderous laughter that I thought for a single irrational second might knock paintings off the wall, louder than I'd ever heard her do anything. I didn't entirely understand the joke, didn't understand who exactly was included in her "us" either. But it was so ridiculous, her laughing so hard at her own terrible joke, that soon I was laughing, laughing just as hard at her laughing just as hard as she was laughing. Duy looked over at us, shook his head, laughed a little too. He was a good boy, took care of his brothers, helped them get dressed when they were little and do their homework when they got older. He taught Truong how to use the stove.

Once when he was younger, Duy and I watched a homeless man trip in the street, spilling his two big garbage bags of cans everywhere. Duy laughed at the sight, at the sound, and when I scolded him for laughing, he said, in English, "Mom, I can't help laughing!"

And I didn't understand the idiom, it was new to me, so I yelled, "Laughing doesn't need your help!"

Which made him laugh even harder. And for whatever reason I thought of that phrase laughing with Roya there in the gallery, laughing at her stupid joke, roll down the car door window when it gets hot, meaningless, delicious, I couldn't help laughing. I couldn't help laughing, but laughing didn't need my help. It already was, holding us there, good and full, where nothing could splinter us into shards, nothing could smear us off the map. The three of us stayed there all night in my gallery working, singing along to radio songs we knew, dancing to the ones we didn't, laughing at everything, all of it, the whole absurd production suddenly blossoming straight into our faces, on purpose.

My God, I just remembered that we die.
But—but me too?! Don't forget that for now,
it's strawberry season.

—*Clarice Lispector*

ACKNOWLEDGMENTS

———— ✻ ————

Thank you, Tommy Orange: bandmate, maestro. This novel would not exist without your example on and off the page. Thank you, Lauren Groff, for seeing the thing I was trying to write beyond the thing I'd written, and for saying so. For vital support across various drafts, thank you, Dan Barden, Marie-Helene Bertino, Ingrid Rojas Contreras, Paige Lewis, Anne Meadows, Angel Nafis, Ben Purkert, Arman Salem, and Clint Smith—the book and I are immeasurably better made for having been loved by you.

Thank you to my editor, Jordan Pavlin, for always recognizing what I am trying to do even when I don't, for modeling exuberant and passionate competence, for letting me call a book *Martyr!*. Thank you to my agent, Jacqueline Ko, for your trust and patience and steady stewardship. Tabia Yapp, thank you for taking care of me all these years. Thank you to my mentors, students, friends, and family, for making such distinctions meaningless.

Paige Lewis, thank you for letting me follow you around watching you watch the world. It has been my life's education and privilege.

Reader, your attention—a measure of time, your most non-replenishable resource—is a profound gift, one I have done my best to honor. Thank you, thank you.

Kaveh Akbar's poems appear in *The New Yorker, The New York Times, Paris Review, Best American Poetry,* and elsewhere. He is the author of two poetry collections, *Pilgrim Bell* and *Calling a Wolf a Wolf,* in addition to a chapbook, *Portrait of the Alcoholic.* He is also the editor of *The Penguin Book of Spiritual Verse: 110 Poets on the Divine.* He lives in Iowa City.

A NOTE ON THE TYPE

This book was set in Monotype Dante, a typeface designed by Giovanni Mardersteig (1892–1977). Its first use was in an edition of Boccaccio's *Trattatello in laude di Dante* that appeared in 1954. The Monotype Corporation's version of Dante followed in 1957.

Composed by North Market Street Graphics,
Lancaster, Pennsylvania

Printed and bound by Berryville Graphics,
Berryville, Virginia

Designed by Betty Lew